CLARA CALLAN

ALSO BY RICHARD B. WRIGHT

The Weekend Man
In the Middle of a Life
Farthing's Fortunes
Final Things
The Teacher's Daughter
Tourists
Sunset Manor
The Age of Longing

RICHARD B.
WRIGHT

CLARA CALLAN

A NOVEL

HarperCollins*Publishers*

 For information, address HarperCollins Publishers Inc., 10 East 53rd Street, New York, NY 10022

HarperCollins books may be purchased for educational, business, or sales promotional use. For information, please write: Special Markets Department, HarperCollins Publishers Inc., 10 East 53rd Street, New York, NY 10022

Originally published in Canada in 2001 by HarperCollins Publishers.

FIRST EDITION

Printed on acid-free paper

Library of Congress Cataloging-in-Publication Data

Wright, Richard Bruce.
Clara Callan : a novel / Richard B. Wright.
p. cm.
ISBN 0-06-050606-7
1. Women teachers—Fiction. 2. New York (N.Y.)—Fiction. 3. Young women—Fiction. 4. Actresses—Fiction. 5. Ontario—Fiction. 6. Sisters—Fiction. I. Title.

PR9199.3.W7 C56 2002
813'.54—dc21

2002068538

02 03 04 05 06 WB/RRD 10 9 8 7 6 5 4 3 2 1

For P again,
With love and gratitude

And if the worldly forget you,
say to the silent earth: I flow.
To the swift water say: I am.

—Rainer Maria Rilke
The Sonnets to Orpheus

1934

Saturday, November 3 (8:10 p.m.)

Nora left for New York City today. I think she is taking a terrible chance going all the way down there but, of course, she wouldn't listen. You can't tell Nora anything. You never could. Then came the last-minute jitters. Tears in that huge station among strangers and loudspeaker announcements.

"I'm going to miss you, Clara."

"Yes. Well, and I'll miss you too, Nora. Do be careful down there!"

"You think I'm making a mistake, don't you? I can see it in your face."

"We've talked about this many times, Nora. You know how I feel about all this."

"You must promise to write."

"Well, of course, I'll write."

The handkerchief, smelling faintly of violets, pressed to an eye. Father used to say that Nora's entire life was a performance. Perhaps she will make something of herself down there in the radio business, but it's just as likely she'll return after Christmas. And then what will she do? I'm sure they won't take her back at the store. It's a foolish time to be taking chances like this. A final wave and a gallant little smile. But she did look pretty and someone on the train will listen. Someone is probably listening at this very moment.

Prayed for solitude on my train home but it was not to be. Through the window I could see the trainman helping Mrs. Webb and Marion up the steps. Then came the sidelong glances of the whole and hale as Marion came down the aisle, holding on to the backs of the seats, swinging her bad foot outward and forward and then, by endeavor and the habit of years, dropping the heavy black boot to the floor. Settled finally into the seat opposite, followed by Mother Webb and her parcels. Routine prying from Mrs. W.

"Well now, Clara, and what brings you to the city? Aren't the stores crowded and Christmas still weeks off? I like to get my buying out of the way. Have you started the practices for the concert? Ida Atkins and I were talking about you the other day. Wouldn't it be nice, we said, if Clara Callan came out to our meetings. You should think about it, Clara. Get you out of the house for an evening. Marion enjoys it, don't you, dear?"

Plenty more of this all the way to Uxbridge station when she finally dozed off, the large head drooping beneath the hat, the arms folded across the enormous chest. Marion said hello, but stayed behind her magazine (movie starlet on the cover). We quarreled over something a week ago. I can't exactly remember what, but Marion has since refused to speak to me at any length and that is just as well.

On the train my gaze drifting across the bare gray fields in the rain. Thinking of Nora peering out another train window. And then I found myself looking down at Marion's orthopedic boot, remembering how I once stared at a miniature version of it in the schoolyard. Twenty-one Septembers ago! I was ten years old and going into Junior Third. Marion had been away all summer in Toronto and returned with the cumbersome shoe. In Mrs. Webb's imagination, Marion and I are conjoined by birth dates and therefore mystically united on this earth. We were born on the same day in the same year, only hours apart. Mrs. W. has never tired of telling how Dr. Grant hurried from our house in the early-morning hours to assist her delivery with the news that Mrs. Callan had just given birth to a fine daughter. And then came Marion, but her tiny foot "was not as God intended." And on that long-ago September morning in the schoolyard, Mrs. Webb brought Marion over to me and said, "Clara will look after you, dear. She will be your best friend. Why you were born on the same day!"

Marion looked bewildered. I remember that. And how she clung to my side! I could have screamed and, in fact, may have done. At the end of the day we fought over something and she had a crying spell under a tree on our front lawn. How she wailed and stamped that boot, which drew my eye as surely as the bulging goiter in old Miss Fowley's throat. Father saw some of this and afterward scolded me. I think I went to bed without supper and I probably sulked for days. What an awful child I was! Yet Marion forgave me; she always forgives me. From time to time, this afternoon, I noticed her smiling at me over her magazine. Mr. Webb was at the station with his car, but I told him I preferred to walk. It had stopped raining by then. No offense was taken.

They are used to my ways. And so I walked home on this damp gray evening. Wet leaves underfoot and darkness seeping into the sky through the bare branches of the trees. Winter will soon be upon us. My neighbors already at their suppers behind lighted kitchen windows. Felt a little melancholy remembering other Saturday evenings when I would have our supper on the stove, waiting for the sound of Father's car in the driveway, bringing Nora up from the station. Certainly Nora would never have walked. Waiting in the kitchen for her breathless entrance. Another tale of some adventure in acting class or the charms of a new beau. Father already frowning at this commotion as he hung up his coat in the hallway. It's nearly seven months now, and I thought I was getting used to Father being gone, yet tonight as I walked along Church Street, I felt again the terrible finality of his absence.

Then I was very nearly knocked over by Clayton Tunney, who came charging out of the darkness at the corner of Broad Street. It was startling, to say the least, and I was cross with him.

"Clayton," I said. "For goodness' sake, watch where you're going!"

"Sorry, Miss Callan. I was over at the Martins', listening to their radio with Donny, and now I'm late for supper and Ma's going to skin me alive."

And off he went again, that small nervous figure racing along Church Street. Poor Clayton! Always in a hurry and always late. Without fail, the last one into class after recess.

Tatham House
138 East 38th Street
New York
November 10, 1934

Dear Clara,

Well, I made it, and I am now at the above address. Tatham House is an apartment hotel for self-supporting women (I hope to become one soon). It's very clean, well maintained and reasonably priced. It's also quite convenient. I stayed with Jack and Doris Halpern for a few days and then I found this place. The Halperns live "uptown" dozens of blocks away, but the subway can get you around the city so fast that you hardly notice distances. New York is not that hard to navigate once you get the hang of it. All the streets run east and west while the avenues go north and south and they are all numbered with a few exceptions like Park and Madison and Lexington. But brother, is it noisy! The taxi drivers are always honking their horns, and you really have to be careful crossing the street. Everyone seems to be in such a blasted hurry (I thought Toronto was bad). There are so many people out on the streets at all hours and I have to say, Clara, that I've never seen so many handsome men, though so many of them are swarthy. I guess they must be Italian or Greek or maybe Jewish. Awfully good-looking though. You also see a lot of colored people down here.

Now about work! On Thursday, Jack took me to Benjamin, Hecker and Freed (an advertising agency) and introduced me to some people, including this writer Evelyn Dowling. How can I describe Evelyn? She reminds me of that song we used to sing when we were kids.

I'm a little teapot
Short and stout
Here is my handle
Here is my spout!

Remember that? She's only about five feet tall and nearly as wide and she has this big head of reddish hair. Wears beautifully cut tailored suits and expensive-looking shoes. She's not going to win any beauty contests, but she's very funny and obviously very successful. Smokes like the dickens. Just one Camel after another and her fingers are yellow with nicotine. Anyway, I did a voice test (several actually), and they liked what they heard, or at least that's what they told me. They haven't promised anything yet, but Jack thinks I am exactly what they are looking for with this new show that Evelyn is writing. Meantime, as I told Jack, I am in this big city and I have to pay bills for fairly important items like food and rent, but he said that he will find me some commercial work within the next week or so and I should be all right. Good Lord, I hope so! I have enough money to last about six weeks and after that I'll have to go on the dole or, what's more likely, they'll probably kick me out of their fair country. To tell you the truth though, I am pretty hopeful about all this. I had a very good feeling last Thursday when I was reading for these people. I just sensed that they liked what they heard, particularly Miss D. So we shall see! Jack and Doris are picking me up in about an hour and we are going out to dinner. They've been just wonderful to me. So, all in all, I would say it's been a good first week and I'm not homesick yet, but *please* write.

Love, Nora

P.S. There's a hallway telephone on my floor and I can be reached at University 5-0040 in case of an emergency. I wish you would get a phone, but we've been through all that, haven't we? So I suppose you can use the Brydens' if you have to, but I wish you'd think about it again, Clara. Wouldn't it be nice if we could "talk" to one another once or twice a week? But what did Father used to say about saving your breath to cool your porridge?

Friday, November 16

This morning I awakened feeling put upon. Over the past few days the winds have blown the first storm of the winter through the village. In other years I welcomed the first snow because it covered November's grayness. Now the snow is just a nuisance that has to be shoveled away and I have been at it off and on since Wednesday morning. Then too I have been worrying about the last hundred dollars Wilkins owes me for Father's car. It was due on the first of the month, and all week I had made up my mind that he was going to take advantage and I would have to hire a lawyer and go through all that business to get the money. I am far too hasty in my judgment of others and probably too pessimistic about human nature. So now, look how benign a place this old world seems! An afternoon of brilliant sunlight (for November), and just as I got home from school, Mr. Wilkins came by with the hundred dollars, apologizing for the delay. God bless him! Now I must get Nora's share off to her; she sounds as though she could use it.

Whitfield, Ontario
Saturday, November 17, 1934

Dear Nora,

I'm glad that you have found a decent place to stay that isn't too dear. I hope you will be careful in that city. I know it would drive me to distraction just walking out the door into such crowds. How on earth do people earn their livings, and where, I wonder, does the food come from to feed so many mouths? There must be thousands out of work down there. We are surviving in the village, though over in Linden they are really up against it. The furniture factory has laid off nearly all the men and things are very flat with many families now on relief.

School is fine though Milton and I now have to do the work of three. Because we got on so well in the spring, I think the board just assumes that the school can be run by two people. They claim they haven't the money this year for another teacher, and that may be so, but I'm inclined to think that they are just being close about it. However there's nothing we can do. Milton is a pleasant fellow to work for, but he dithers a good deal and he lacks Father's authority as a principal. I suppose one can't be too hard on him, but I find he's not strict enough with some of the rougher children who could benefit from a good hiding now and then. I'm thinking in particular of the Kray brothers who are the bane of my existence these days.

Mr. Wilkins finally gave me the last payment for Father's car yesterday and the enclosed money order for fifty dollars is your share. I am sure you can put it to good use. To tell you the truth, I now regret selling the car. It has occurred to me more than once over the last little while that I might have kept it and learned how to drive. I just didn't think that way at the time of Father's death and maybe I was just in too much of a hurry to get everything settled. Speaking of getting settled, I have also dealt with the man from Linden Monuments who finally got around to seeing me the week before last. These people certainly take their time to conduct business; I've been after him since the summer. He wanted to sell me some folderol for the family headstone and showed me a catalog which very nearly struck me dumb with amazement and horror: hundreds of dreadful little verses which attempt to reassure the living that the dead are not so badly off. Perhaps they aren't, but in any case I told him that plain words would have to do the job. And so alongside Mother's and Thomas's names and years will be Edward J. Callan, 1869–1934. I hope that's all right with you.

I think I have now mastered the furnace. It has been worrying me all fall, but Mr. Bryden has given me several lessons on how to start it and keep it going. There is a trick to all this. You have to be careful about allowing enough flame through the coals to burn off the gas, but you can't smother the flame or, of course, the darn thing will go out. I now appreciate the hours Father used to spend watching "this monster in the cellar." And in a way it is a "monster" that will have to be attended to and appeased every day of the blessed week from now until April. These days I am hurrying home at lunch to make sure that "he" is still breathing and satisfied, but I am also learning how to put enough coal in after breakfast ("building the fire," according to Mr. Bryden) so that it will last until I get home from school. I really had no idea what a chore it is just to keep warm. At the same time, there is an undeniable satisfaction in knowing how to do all this.

I was amused by your colorful description of Miss Dowling with her tobacco-stained fingers and tailored suits. You are certainly meeting some exotic creatures down there, aren't you?

I have noted the telephone number you gave me and passed it on to Mrs. Bryden who says hello and good luck. She will get in touch with you if I fall down the cellar stairs and brain myself some evening. And no, I am not going to rent a telephone. As you say, we've been through all that and I still maintain that, in my case, it's a waste of money. I doubt whether I would phone three people in a month and I see no reason why we can't keep in touch by letter. Do take care of yourself in that city, Nora.

Clara

P.S. Had our first winter storm this week but I am finally dug out!

Tatham House
138 East 38th Street
New York
November 25, 1934

Dear Clara,

Thanks for your letter, but please don't talk about falling down the cellar stairs. It gives me the willies when you say things like that. I know you are facing your first winter alone in that big house, but try not to be morbid, okay? Well, I've survived nearly a month down here and, to be honest, I'm really glad I made this move. New York is such a fascinating city and I've just been too busy to be homesick. People have been terrific to me. Americans are much more open in their ways than us. It sure doesn't take them long to get acquainted with you.

If you had been listening to the radio last Tuesday night to a program called "The Incredible Adventures of Mr. Wang" (if you get it up there), you would have heard my voice, though you might not have recognized me. I played a gangster's moll who is trapped in a warehouse surrounded by police and the inscrutable Mr. Wang, and my line was: "Let's get out of here. NOW!" That was supposed to be delivered in a "hard-boiled egg" kind of way according to the director. Mr. Wang is a detective along the lines of Charlie Chan or Fu Manchu. Do any of these names mean anything to you? Probably not. Anyway, it was fun to do, even if I only had that one immortal line. I know it's not *Uncle Vanya*, but it's a start.

I've also been doing some commercial work (thanks to Jack) for Italian Balm. The work is a little boring, but it pays well and, as Jack says, I'm getting all this experience. They seem to like my voice at the agency. Next week we start rehearsals for a show about a surgeon who performs all these lifesaving operations. "Calling Dr. Donaldson." I am going to play the doctor's nurse, June Wilson, and I actually announce the show by saying through this microphone filter, "Calling Dr. Donaldson, Calling Dr. Donaldson." As if it were in a hospital ward. That will be an afternoon show. Evelyn is writing another serial about—get this—two sisters who live in a small town somewhere "in the heartland of America." The younger sister Effie is always getting into trouble (usually men) and the older sister Alice is the wise one who dispenses advice and gets her sister and others out of jams. Now guess which part they are grooming your kid sister for? Wrong! I am going to play the *older* sister, so there! It will be called "The House on Chestnut Street." According to Evelyn (and she should know), the big market in radio in the next few years is going to be in afternoon serial dramas for housewives. It makes sense when you think about it. Women are home all day washing and ironing and cleaning, and while they're doing all that, they can listen to programs about people who lead more interesting lives. It's the perfect escape when you're ironing your husband's shirt to listen to a woman falling in love with a handsome doctor or rich lawyer. There are a lot of food and cosmetic companies interested in this market so there should be plenty of sponsors out there.

The other thing that's happened is this. Jack and Doris took me to a party down in Greenwich Village the other night and I met this couple, Marty and Ida Hirsch. He's a playwright and he and Ida are producing this play. It's not Broadway or anything. In fact, I think it's fairly small potatoes, but they asked me if I would be interested in reading for a part. I had told them about my experience, limited though it was, with the Elliot Hall Players and my radio work up in Toronto. So they asked me and I said sure and next Wednesday I'm going to try out. I figure I have to get all the experience I can and this seems like a good opportunity. Marty asked me all about Canada and what the politics were like up there. He had this strange idea that we were still ruled by the King of England. I've discovered that Americans don't know a lot about some things. But Marty is a nice guy if a little opinionated, and I'm looking forward to joining this group. He told me I had a lot of moxie coming down here on my own from Canada. I've never heard that word before, have you?

Speaking of words, have you written any poems lately? It seems to me you were writing some in the spring just after Father passed away. How did they turn out?

Remember how you used to fill those scribblers with poems and then some Sunday morning, right out of the blue, start tearing the pages and burning them in the kitchen stove? The pipes would get so hot that Father would start grumbling about a chimney fire on the way. But he would never say a word to you about it, would he? Brother, if I'd done something like that, I would never have heard the end of it. I hope to goodness that if you're still feeding the stove with your poems, you're careful. Thanks a heap for the money and write again soon.

Love, Nora

Wednesday, November 28

Commotion in the classroom today. Started by the Krays. During the arithmetic lesson they began pushing and shoving and then they were on the floor at the back of the room punching and choking one another. I tried to separate them, but they wouldn't stop and I had to call Milton. I like to think I can manage these things, but the Krays incite a rage that I find so difficult to check it frightens me. At ten o'clock this morning, I could easily have smashed the yardstick across Manley Kray's face. Even looking at them provokes me: those brutal bullet-shaped heads, the grimy necks, the ringworm and smelly feet.

At recess I sat listening to the measured strokes from Milton's office. He told me that he learned how to apply "the leather" from Father. "It was one of the first things he taught me, Clara. 'Even strokes, Milton,' he used to say. And you never apply them in anger. They have to see the justice in the exercise. You're just doing your job, not venting your frustration."

It's odd that Father never talked to me about strapping. Perhaps he didn't think I needed talking to. How wrong he was! I always have to be careful about my temper. Afterward I stood by the window and watched the Krays walk out into the schoolyard. They were surrounded at once by the other boys who dislike the brothers but admire their defiance.

Mr. and Mrs. Cameron came by this evening with Willard Macfarlane. They were collecting winter clothes for the needy. Last Sunday I told them I had some things of Father's, including the new overcoat he bought on sale in Toronto last January and then refused to wear. He brought it home and, standing in it in front of the hallway mirror, decided that it was too grand. "I can't walk around in a coat like this when so many people are hard up," he said.

I told this story to Willard and the Camerons and they enjoyed it. "That sounds like Ed," said Willard holding up the coat. "But gosh Almighty, this is some coat. It's a dandy!" Since Father had bought it on sale, he couldn't return it and so the coat with its velvet collar hung all last winter in the hall closet. The Camerons told me that they are leaving at the end of the year. I shall miss them.

Saturday, December 1

I was out for a walk along the township roads this afternoon. A raw, windy end-of-the-year kind of day with the sky carrying snow somewhere. Approaching the village at nightfall (5:45), I passed Henry Hill who was too drunk to notice me although I wished him a good evening. Henry was singing a mischievous song about love and trying out a kind of jig in the middle of the road. And all this in Father's new overcoat! I am glad, however, that Henry will have a fine coat for the winter ahead. When I got home, I started this poem, the first in months.

In my father's overcoat
The drunken man performs a jig.
With arms flung wide
And overcoat unbuttoned to the wind
He dances in the street.
That somber banker's coat
Now the glad rags
Of a foolish man.

It will perhaps go something like that.

Whitfield, Ontario
Sunday, December 2, 1934

Dear Nora,
According to the dictionary, *moxie* is American slang for courage, though a more precise synonym might be the old-fashioned word *pluck*. With the car business over now, the only thing I had left to do was clear out Father's dressers and closet. I should have done this ages ago, but I kept putting it off. Then last Sunday Mr. Cameron asked for donations of winter clothes for the needy, so I got busy and packed Father's things into boxes. On Wednesday evening the Camerons came by with Willard Macfarlane and took everything to the church hall. I thought that was the end of it, but then a strange thing happened. Well, strange to me at least. Late yesterday afternoon, just as I was coming home from a walk in the countryside, I saw a man in a long coat and he seemed to be shuffling about in the middle of the road, performing some kind of dance. As I drew nearer, I could see

that it was Henry Hill. Drunk, of course. Then I noticed that he was wearing Father's new overcoat. Do you remember last January when he went down to Toronto and bought it? Saw it in a haberdasher's window on Yonge Street. It was a beautiful coat with a velvet collar, expensive as the dickens but marked down and Father thought it was a bargain. When he brought it home, however, he fussed about it. Said it was far too grand to wear around the village. "I look like a Toronto banker in it," he said. "People will think I'm putting on airs. It's a poor time to go about in a coat like this." He wanted to take it back, but it had been on sale. I told him it looked good on him and he shouldn't worry about what people might think, but of course he did, and I don't believe he wore that coat a half a dozen times all winter. And there it was on poor old Henry last night in the middle of Church Street! But then why not? Winter is coming on and Henry needs a coat like everyone else. Yet it was unsettling to see the old man lurching about in Father's new coat. Well, you've seen him in such a state! Watching him, I wondered if perhaps there was a poem somewhere in all that, though I'm beginning to doubt whether I have the talent or the discipline to write poetry. Still these doubts (hobgoblins who perch on my bedstead at night) don't keep me from trying. I experience this peculiar happiness while puzzling over the selection and arrangement of words on a page even if, in ordinary daylight, their luster has mysteriously vanished and they seem only pale and worn. And, by the way, you were right. I did attempt some verses about Father's death, but they didn't work and they proved to be more useful in the stove, giving off, you might say, more heat than light.

On Friday evening I went with "the ladies of the village" to a performance of *The Merry Widow* at the Royal Alexandra. I don't know why I went; I don't really care for Lehár's pretty tunes and I felt a little misplaced traveling with a dozen older women and their husbands. Three carloads of us! Ida Atkins is after me to join the Missionary Society. "Dear Clara, it would be so good for you to get out. All alone in that big house now. And we do need some young blood." That's true, I suppose. Except for poor Marion, the "ladies" are all in their forties, fifties and onward. Am I now at thirty-one perceived as a member of this group? I expect I am, though I can't help thinking that I'll grow old before my time if I join the M.S. The thought of setting aside Tuesday evening for the next thirty years is dispiriting, to say the least.

I shall miss you coming home on Saturday evenings this winter. I always listened for the sound of the train whistle and so did Father. I know that you used to get on one another's nerves, but he really did look forward to your coming home. The fact that you were often at one another's throats within fifteen minutes is not as important as the fact that he cared about you. After one of your arguments when you'd stay away for weeks, he would say, "I wonder how Nora is getting on." Of course he could never have admitted such feelings to you. It was not his way. I can well imagine how he would worry if he were still alive and with you now in New York City.

I'm very happy to learn that you are making your way in the radio business, Nora. Do be careful crossing the streets.

Clara

Tatham House
138 East 38th Street
New York
December 9, 1934

Dear Clara,

Thanks for your letter. Honestly, I can't see you with all those old ladies like Mrs. Atkins. I can picture Marion Webb, but she seemed "old" to me in high school and she's lame, poor thing. It's just too bad there aren't more people your age around the village, but I guess they're all married by now, aren't they? And here we are, both still on the shelf! Sometimes I'm glad to be on my own like this. I've always enjoyed going out to work and having my own money, but there are times when I think it would be nice to have a home and kids. The other day I saw this family. They were looking at Macy's windows which are all decorated for Christmas. The woman was about my age and pretty enough, but her husband!!! Was he a doll! He could easily have been in the movies. And they had these two cute youngsters, a boy and a girl. I have to admit I envied that woman. Oh well! Maybe Prince Charming is out there somewhere among these millions.

Do you remember me telling you about Marty and Ida Hirsch who run a theater group? They asked me to read for a part in a play they've written, and a week ago I went down to this place on Houston Street. It's just a big hall on the third floor of this old factory, but they've made it into a kind of auditorium with a stage and a lot of chairs. There were about thirty people there and they call themselves the New World Players. They are planning to put on a series of one-act plays this winter on what they call social realism. They are nice enough people but very serious about politics. Before we started reading for the parts, there was a meeting and this guy gave a talk on how things are done in Russia. I didn't catch his name but he writes for a newspaper called *The Daily Worker*. He talked about capitalism and Communism and how there is no unemployment in Russia because the people there are looked after by the government.

Do you follow these things? History and civics were never my strong points in school. Anyway, I read for the part and I got it. I play this rich man's daughter-in-law. He owns a big factory where the workers are so poorly paid that they go on strike. His son has an argument with him because he thinks his father is being unfair and so he joins the strikers on the picket line and he's killed by a gang of thugs hired by the father to break the strike. I have a big speech over his dead body about exploiting the workers and so on. To me, the play is awfully preachy, but everyone else seems to think it's wonderful.

I'm keeping busy with the doctor show and more commercial work. The Wintergreen Toothpowder people really like me when I say, "Wintergreen makes your teeth shine, shine, shine!" There's a cute little tune that goes with that. You would HATE it!! Evelyn is worried that my voice might become a little too familiar on the air so she's after me to be choosy about what I do. "Fair enough, Evelyn," I tell her, "but I have to eat and pay the rent." Evelyn lives in this swanky apartment overlooking Central Park (Jessica Dragonette lives in the same building, for goodness' sake), so E. tends to forget that poor working girls like me have got to earn a living. Jack and Doris have been terrific about inviting me to dinner, but I don't want to wear out my welcome. I don't think I could have survived without the Halperns.

What a fuss they made down here last week over that little French-Canadian doctor who delivered the quints! His mug was in all the papers and last Sunday night he gave a talk in Carnegie Hall. Carnegie Hall!!! They put him up at the Ritz-Carlton and practically gave him the keys to the city. Of course, when you tell people you're a Canadian, they think you lived in a cabin like Madame Dionne. Personally I think that having five kids at a time is too much like a dog having a litter of pups, but people down here just think it's the cutest thing and Doc Dafoe came across as a kindly old gent full of folksy wisdom. I'm beginning to sound like Evelyn. You should hear her go on about Shirley Temple.

I think I'll buy a radio with the money you sent, a nice little table model. It's funny. Here I am working in radio and I don't even own one. So I'll say goodbye for now and take care of yourself.

Love, Nora

P.S. Why would you write a poem about that dirty old Henry Hill and Father's overcoat? Aren't there nicer things to write about?

Whitfield, Ontario
Sunday, December 16, 1934

Dear Nora,

Just back from church and thought I'd drop you a line. Mr. Cameron introduced our new minister this morning and he delivered the sermon. All fire and brimstone! He sounds more like a Baptist preacher than a United Church man. His name is Jackson and he preached here for two or three Sundays in July. I didn't like him then and I don't like him now. Zealots just get my back up; I suppose I just don't like being reminded of my many spiritual imperfections every Sunday morning. Jackson would certainly not have been my choice, but many appear to like his old-fashioned evangelical style. His wife is a shy, pretty little woman and was sitting with the Atkins. I can see her being bullied by the likes of Ida Atkins and Cora Macfarlane.

After a mild spell, it's cold again up here and thank goodness I have mastered the art of keeping "the monster in the cellar" happy. I know now just how much to feed him and when to leave him alone to grumble away and digest his coals and keep me warm. That is our bargain: my labor for his heat. As I go about all this, I can't help thinking of those who are unable to afford a ton of good coal and who will have to make do this winter with green wood or lumberyard scraps. Many families are really up against it and I see it more and more every day now that the weather has turned around. This week a number of the children came to school wearing only light dresses and without coats or leggings. The Kray brothers are always half-dressed, though I suppose they would be in the best of times. Others are evidently without the means to clothe themselves. On Friday Clayton Tunney arrived, late as usual, in a pelting rain, wearing only a sweater and short pants. His hands were so chapped he could barely turn the pages of his reader. It's all very worrying and yesterday's *Herald* had a story about a man over in Linden who hanged himself in a railway shed last Sunday morning, leaving a wife and six children. Apparently he'd been laid off by the railway and couldn't bear the thought of going on relief. According to the paper, there was thirty-five cents in the house on the day he died. I keep wondering what was going through the poor fellow's mind as he fastened the rope around his neck and kicked away the bench. Or however he did it. They are taking up a collection for the family and I'm going to send a couple of dollars. I imagine there must be many such stories in that city of yours. I sometimes wonder if the politicians will ever sort out this problem of getting men back to work.

At least the Christmas concert can take people's minds off things, though I'm glad it's over for another year. On Saturday night as I played "Away in a Manger" for perhaps the hundredth time, I wondered if I would still be doing this in twenty years. In my mind's eye I could see a spare, dry woman of fifty-one in a black dress playing the piano while she watched the children of these children in bathrobes gathering by the doll in the crib. Behind the curtain on the stepladder, a spry sixty-year-old Alice Campbell was still throwing handfuls of confetti onto the sacred scene. I have always wondered about that "snow" in Palestine. It's startling, however, to realize that I've been playing for these concerts since I was sixteen. Do you remember when I took over from Mrs. Hamilton? You were in your entrance year and played one of the ghosts in a scene from *A Christmas Carol.* George Martin played Scrooge and forgot practically all his lines. This year his little boy Donald was one of the shepherds. Who says time isn't fleeting?

Last week I sent a little Christmas package, which I hope will reach you before the holiday. Please don't bother with anything for me. I'm sure that you are busy these days and of course money can't be all that plentiful. So nothing, please. I mean that, Nora.

All the best, Clara

P.S. Henry Hill and Father's overcoat are perfectly good subjects for a poem. The "niceness" of something, whatever that means, has nothing to do with it.

Monday, December 17 (1:30 a.m.)

Notes for a poem entitled *To a Thirty-Eight-Year-Old Father of Six Who Hanged Himself One Sunday Morning in a Railway Shed.*

It happened a week ago perhaps as I was walking to church, enjoying the freakishly mild weather. Your final Sunday felt almost like a late-September morning with its pale sunlit sky. There are things I would like to know. Were the children still sleeping when you closed the kitchen door a final time? Had you looked in on them before you left or is that just sentimental invention? When you think of it, who could bear to? Much better to walk away without a backward glance. But then perhaps you had not yet decided. When are such decisions made anyway? Are they thought through the night before or seized upon in some despairing moment? Your mind was unsettled after a sleepless night. You felt tired, a little dazed. There had been only minutes when you slept (or so it seemed). Between the hours of staring at the darkened shapes (the ceiling, the dresser, the chair, your wife's sleeping body), you lay half-listening to her troubled dream-words, the sighs and whispers born of worry and exhaustion. Perhaps before she slept you talked and the house with its tar-paper sides and cold hallways listened to the murmur of your long-married voices in a back bedroom.

"What are we going to do now, Bert?"

"I don't know."

"You'll have to go down Monday morning and see the relief people."

You are about to say something but the baby stirs and whimpers, and your wife must get up and attend to the child. It's her job and you watch her bend across the crib or perhaps you don't. After all, you've seen her do it so many times over the years. Then bedsprings creak again as she settles in beside you.

"Did you hear what I said, Bert? You'll have to go down and talk to the relief people on Monday."

"I can't do that."

The words imprisoned in your head all day are now set free. The mere thought of dealing with those people can inflame your nerves.

"Well, you'll just have to, that's all. You know as well as I do, we're up against it."

But perhaps there were no words in bed the night before you died. Perhaps they had been said so many times before that your wife turned on her side and quickly fell asleep.

Now it is your last Sunday morning and she stands by the stove stirring the oatmeal. You watch her back and her bare feet in the mules. Your two oldest children are still sleeping but the other four are now at the table, tugging and pushing one another as children do awaiting breakfast. In his high chair the baby is excited and raps his spoon against the table. You see the corn syrup and the teapot and the milk bottle. When you opened the door, did your wife ask where you were going? Or were they used to you by now, accustomed to the ways of a quiet man who liked to be alone? "Daddy's going for his walk."

And so you went out into the Sunday morning streets, passing the churchgoers and the idlers leaning against the bank, leaving behind at last the houses and stores to cross the tracks behind the station. For a railway man, it wasn't hard to break the lock on that shed door. And what did you see in that place you chose for death? Pale sunlight through a cobwebbed window. Your entrance must have stirred the dust motes which settled finally on the shovels and the mattocks, on the iron wheel in the corner, and the overalls on the pegs against the wall, on the length of greasy rope and the girlie calendar. What were you thinking of as you looped the rope across the beam and made your knot? Hanging is a man's choice for death. A woman swallows Paris green, or steps in front of a freight train's yellow eye. What finally did you see, father of six? Were you looking at the floor or at the window with its patch of sky and cobweb? Or did you close your eyes before you kicked away that bench?

Tatham House
138 East 38th Street
New York
December 23, 1934

Dear Clara,

Your package arrived and, of course, I opened it. You know me! I could never wait until Christmas. The sweater is lovely and a perfect fit. Thanks so much. I've had so many compliments on it from the girls here. I've sent off a little something for you too, so there's no point in getting mad at me. I can buy my sister a Christmas present if I want to. But I certainly didn't get it in any swanky shop, believe me. It was just something I saw in the window of a store on Thirty-fourth Street, and as soon as I saw it, I thought, That's Clara! So Merry Christmas. I know it will be New Year's by the time you get it, but better late than never.

I went to Evelyn's last night for dinner. I felt kind of bad because earlier I'd arranged to go to the movies with a couple of girls here, but I wanted to see what kind of place Evelyn has. And you should see it! She lives in the San Remo Apartments on Central Park West. That's just about the ritziest part of town. Did I mention before that the radio singer Jessica Dragonette is in the same building? Evelyn has a Negro maid who served us drinks and dinner. Lamb chops and these wonderful little roasted potatoes and wine. Her apartment is filled with books and paintings and she has this enormous radio and phonograph machine. We listed to Gershwin and Porter show tunes and talked about "The House on Chestnut Street." Evelyn wanted to know all about Whitfield and what it was like growing up there. She was an only child and went to a fancy boarding school, so she was keen to find out what life was like in a small town. She wanted to know all about you and so naturally I told her that you are a schoolteacher who likes to write poetry and are obviously the brains in the family. I told her that we were raised by our father because

Mother died when we were little kids. And I told her how I never really got along very well with Father, but that you seemed to know how to manage him. All kinds of family stuff. Evelyn would love to meet you and I think you'd like her. You're similar in many ways. Very critical of things in general. Oh, you'd have to learn how to tolerate her smoking and drinking, but I bet you'd find her terrifically interesting.

Well, this will be our first Christmas without Father and it feels kind of strange, doesn't it? I hope you don't find it too lonesome being there by yourself. The Halperns invited me to their place for dinner, which I thought was very considerate because being Jewish they don't celebrate Christmas. A few of the girls here who aren't going home for the holidays are having a little get-together on Christmas night and so maybe I'll look in on that too. The girls here are mostly my age or maybe a little younger. Most of them are secretaries and a few have pretty good jobs in some of the big department stores. One woman is a buyer for Gimbels and another woman named Frances is a nurse at Bellevue. That's a big psychiatric hospital and some of the stories she tells would make your hair stand on end.

When I look back at what I've written about my dinner with Evelyn in her swanky place, I can imagine you thinking, Well, there's Nora down in New York, living the life of Riley while thousands of people haven't got any jobs or money. I remember your story about that poor man in Linden. But I don't want you to think that I'm unfeeling. I see a lot of people on the streets down here who don't look too well off, but I don't know what I can do about it. I think Mr. Roosevelt is on the right track and things are picking up. I believe we have to look on the bright side if we want to get anywhere. I'll be thinking of you on Christmas Day, Clara. Hope you like your present.

Love, Nora

Letter from Nora who seems to be thriving in the great metropolis. Where does she get her ambition and enthusiasm? These characteristics are surely passed along through the blood. How did Yeats put it? "The fury and the mire of human veins." She can't have inherited any of this from Father who seemed content enough to spend his days in this village. Yet *seemed* is perhaps the correct verb, for how do I know how he really felt? Father was so closed-in about everything. As for Mother, I can't remember her doing anything but reading books and taking long walks.

Retirement party for the Camerons yesterday evening in the church hall. Ida Atkins in charge of the proceedings. It has not taken her long to boss around the new minister's wife. Helen Jackson is such a meek little thing. Confessed that she likes to read. Enjoys the novels of Lloyd C. Douglas and A. J. Cronin. Well, yes, I can see that but she also admits to an admiration for Emily Dickinson, which is a fine surprise. Husband standing apart with hands behind his back, rocking on his heels. Above all this female chatter. Ida Atkins's tiresome recruiting. "Now, Helen, you must help us to persuade Clara to get out of the house this winter. She has so much to offer our church. Her father passed away last spring. A wonderful man," etc., etc. Can she not detect my hostility, or am I simply too hypocritical and cowardly? I think I am a little.

A title for a poem came to me this afternoon. *Onset of Evening in Winter, 1934*. A painting in words. At dusk a woman is at the piano playing Mendelssohn's *Songs Without Words*. The oncoming night will be cold and so before she sat down to play she moved the bowl of African violets from the window ledge to the mantel. Now she looks out at the falling snow as she plays. What is she thinking of? The elusive nature of happiness. How it arrives unbidden, a brief thrilling moment, summoned perhaps by a smell, a line of verse, a melody. In the senses may be found our source of joy. How it alights upon the heart like a colorful and mysterious bird upon a winter branch. Now what on earth did I mean by all that? It was only a glimpse of what I was trying to get at, but it was all nonsense anyway. A woman at the piano looking out at falling snow! I blame Mendelssohn's lovely little tunes for turning me into such a wistful Sally. Decided it was time to throw some coal into the maw of the monster. That at least is honest labor, duly rewarded.

1935

Whitfield, Ontario
Sunday, January 6, 1935

Dear Nora,

Thank you for the brooch. I told you not to bother, but when did you ever listen to anybody? Well never mind, it is handsome and I shall wear it proudly. Winter now has us firmly in its grip and my palms are growing calloused from the handle of the coal shovel. All right, that is an exaggeration, but I seem to be down in the cellar half the night. I'm deathly afraid of the fire going out and the pipes freezing; that would present a nice mess. I also have a mild grippe but then so does half the village. People are hacking and coughing at you wherever you go. Well, enough complaining. I am reading *War and Peace* these days. I thought a good long novel would see me through January and February and maybe it will. I cannot deny Tolstoy's power, but he does go on. So many digressions.

How are you getting on down there? Have those Reds in your drama group converted you yet? I don't know much about Communism, but I do know they have caused a good deal of trouble in this province, particularly in the relief camps up north. I do think something has to be done about our present troubles, but I'm not sure that the Reds have the answer. Sorry for the dull letter. What is transpiring these days in that metropolitan life of yours?

Clara

Tatham House
138 East 38th Street
New York
January 13, 1935

Dear Clara,

Sorry to hear about the grippe and the calloused hands!!! I can't help wondering if that house isn't too much for you, especially in winter. Could you not close it up next year and board for the winter months? Does Mrs. Murchison still take in boarders? You would be a lot more comfortable and it would save you all that fuss and bother. Why don't you think about it?

You should also get a radio, Clara. My goodness, you just refuse to enter the century. No telephone, no radio. It's a wonder you tolerate running water. But I can tell you this, a radio is a great companion on a long winter night, especially in a village like Whitfield where exactly zero must be happening. You have already expressed your lack of enthusiasm for things like the Missionary Society. So buy a radio. You can't read all the time. I just bought a little RCA table model and it sits right next to my bed. There is some wonderful entertainment on the air these days. You can have your Mr. Tolstoy. I'll take Eddie Cantor if I'm feeling blue and want a few laughs.

I'm getting work on the hospital show and "The Incredible Adventures of Mr. Wang," and my Wintergreen stuff also brings in some money, so I'm getting by. Our serial drama will get under way in the late spring or early summer and then I should see more money, and it will be steady. No, I'm not being converted by the Communists, but we did put on our play last week. It only ran for three nights. It turned out a little better than I thought it would, but it was a flop at the box office. We only got thirty or forty people on each of the three nights and many of them left halfway through. It was funny in a way, but hard to concentrate. I guess they tried to be quiet, but it was so dark in "the warehouse" that they kept knocking over chairs as they left. There I was standing over the dead body of my fiancée (killed by his father's hired thugs on the picket line), trying to deliver my little speech about how he died for the good of the workers, and all these darn chairs were getting knocked over. On Friday night (the last night) I nearly broke out laughing. Poor Marty would never have forgiven me. He has another script he wants me to look at, but I don't know. It's a lot of work for nothing, or so it seems.

It's damn cold here too, but thank goodness they keep this place comfortable. When I leave in the morning, I can hear the janitor rattling the grates of the furnace and I think of you doing all that by yourself. It can't be much fun and I think you should do something about it for next year. I hope you're over your grippe by now.

Love, Nora

Tuesday, January 22

"*I am the rose of Sharon and the lily of the valleys.*" How often as a child on a winter night like this did I read these words! I would speak the line aloud and feel its warmth and color in my mouth like some exotic fruit from Palestine, a pomegranate, for instance. I didn't understand what any of it meant; I just liked the sound and texture of the words and sometimes I imagined that they did make me feel warmer. So on this, the coldest night of the year, I read some chapters from Song of Solomon. Also read again these yellow fragments of our family's history which fell from the leaves of the Bible.

A very pretty wedding took place at Whitfield Methodist Church on Saturday, June 20, at eleven o'clock when Edward J. Callan, principal of Whitfield School, and Miss Ethel Louise Smith of Toronto were united in marriage by the pastor of the church, Reverend John Shields.

The bride was attired in white Swiss muslin and wore a white hat and carried a beautiful bouquet of roses. The bridesmaid, Miss E. Moffat of Whitfield, wore pale blue organdie and also carried a bouquet. John Dawson of Linden acted as best man. To the bride the groom presented a beautiful gold neck chain and to the bridesmaid he gave a handsome gold brooch. After a reception at the groom's home on Church Street, Mr. and Mrs. Callan left on a week's trip to Toronto and Niagara Falls.

Linden Herald
July 7, 1900

Born

CALLAN—at 110 Church Street, Whitfield. On Monday, May 20, to Mr. and Mrs. Edward Callan, a son, Thomas Edward.

Linden Herald
May 25, 1901

Born

CALLAN—at 110 Church Street, Whitfield. On Saturday, June 27, to Mr. and Mrs. Edward Callan, a daughter, Clara Ann.

Linden Herald
July 4, 1903

Died

CALLAN—at 110 Church Street, Whitfield. On Wednesday evening, March 16, Thomas Edward, aged two years, ten months. Beloved son of Mr. and Mrs. Edward Callan.

Linden Herald
March 19, 1904

Born

CALLAN—at 110 Church Street, Whitfield. On Saturday, March 4, to Mr. and Mrs. Edward Callan, a daughter, Nora Louise.

Linden Herald
March 11, 1905

TRAGIC ACCIDENT CLAIMS WOMAN'S LIFE

A tragic accident claimed the life of a popular resident of this community on Tuesday, July 19, when Mrs. Edward Callan of Whitfield was struck by a freight train. Mrs. Callan had left home on Sunday afternoon to pick raspberries and presumably became lost in the vicinity of the Wildwood Swamp. It is conjectured that the unfortunate woman became confused and wandered into the path of the freight train in the pre-dawn hours. Her body was discovered shortly after twelve o'clock noon on Tuesday about two miles from the village station.

Mrs. Callan will be sorely missed by many in the village. She was active in the Methodist church, and as an accomplished pianist, accompanied many local singers in musical evenings. A wide circle of friends will extend much sympathy to Mr. Edward Callan, principal of Whitfield School, and to his young daughters, Clara and Nora. The funeral on Thursday, July 21, took place from Whitfield Methodist Church under the guidance of the pastor Reverend J. Shields. Interment was at Old Road Cemetery.

Linden Herald
July 23, 1910

I was seven and I remember the two men coming to this house. It was a hot day and I was lying in the hammock on the veranda. The house was filled with women who had brought food. The dining-room and kitchen tables were covered with casseroles and fruit pies and fresh bread. There were platters of sandwiches and biscuits and all of it was under tea towels to keep the flies away. I was in the hammock and no one was paying any attention to me. Nora was surrounded by little girls. Mabel Nicholson, Verna Fallis, Muriel Thornton, Irene McNally, Marion Webb. They all stood in a circle under a tree on the front lawn and took turns holding Nora's hand and giving her candy. It was a special occasion and it was her mother and not theirs who was missing, so they were being especially nice to her. Their mouths were black with licorice. I remember that distinctly, those solemn little girls with their dark mouths. And I was alone in the hammock though I don't think I felt particularly put out by it. Or even frightened or saddened by Mother's absence. She had wandered off before, usually to the cemetery to visit Thomas's grave. But she had never been gone for two days. She was obviously lost, but did I have any sense of that? I suppose lying there in the hammock I expected that sooner or later I would see her coming down Church Street with her honey pail filled with berries. That is probably how I saw things on that summer afternoon. Meantime, there was this quiet bustle in the air: women coming and going and carrying pots of tea and pitchers of lemonade, whispering to one another. In their own way, they were like the circle of solemn little girls around Nora on the front lawn. But poor Father! All this must have worn him out. He probably hadn't slept at all during the two days she was gone. He seemed to be on the go all the time, scouring the countryside with other men.

He must have been upstairs trying to sleep on that afternoon when the two men came to the door. They got out of an open car and came up the front walk and climbed the veranda steps. One man had a bald head. He had taken off his straw hat, and I could see where the hat had left a reddish mark across his brow. It's odd the things we remember. The two men talked through the screen on the front door, and they must have told the women inside that they'd found Mother down by the railway tracks. I couldn't hear what they were saying, but a few minutes later Father came out the door in his shirtsleeves and hurried down the steps with the men. He had been sleeping or trying to because the hair was sticking up at the back of his head and I found that peculiar; Father was always so careful about how he looked in public. I sensed that even as a young child. As principal of the school, he considered appearances important. Before that day I had never seen Father out of a suit coat on the streets of Whitfield. But there he was, off with the two men, half-dressed with his hair mussed. It must have been then that I had an inkling that something serious was taking place in my life and things would never be the same again.

Thursday, January 24

There was a fire in the village last night and the Mullens have lost their home. They had so little and now they have nothing. At one point in the night I thought I heard shouting, but wondered at the time if it were only the fragment of a dream, so I returned to sleep. It was a bitter night and this morning the bedroom windows were covered from top to bottom with frost. Then as I set out for school, I could smell the sour fire smoke. Milton told me about it; the family escaped with only the nightclothes on their backs and are now being put up at the church hall until the relief people can find a house for them. After school I walked over to North Street and stood gawking with others at the ruins. What a pitiful sight is fire's aftermath! The iron bedstead, the blackened chamber pot, the smoking pile of rags. One's humble belongings horribly reduced. Walking back I wondered what I would do were fire to engulf my home. Lay awake half the night worrying about this.

Sunday, February 10 (4:00 p.m.)

I cannot for the life of me remember the last time I missed morning service, but today I did not go to church and this is why. I was sitting at the kitchen table after breakfast looking out the window at the snow on the bare trees and the blue sky through the branches. I was thinking of how the light is returning and of how different the morning sky now seems from only two weeks ago. And then it came to me as I sat there at the kitchen table looking out at the trees and the snow and the sky—I no longer believe in God. I have been feeling such intimations for some time now, but today, at twenty minutes past seven, it came to me clarified and whole. God does not exist. The proposition that He does exist obviously cannot be proven, and so we must rely on what we *believe* to be true. Or *feel* to be true. Or *want* to be true. As they say, we must take it on faith. But for some time now, my faith has been like the branch of a tree that over the years has been weakened by wind and weather. And today it was as if that part of me, that branch, finally gave way and fell to the ground. It is a dreadful barren feeling, but I am powerless to repel it. This I now believe. We are alone on this earth and must make our way unguided by any unseen hand. Perhaps a man called Jesus did live in Palestine two thousand years ago. Perhaps he was an inspired orator, a kind of faith healer; he may even have been a little mad. He attracted followers but also made powerful enemies who killed him. His body was placed in a tomb, but his followers carried it away in order to create a mystery and a myth surrounding him. He once walked this earth but he was not immortal. He rotted into dust as shall we all; as did Mother and Thomas; as is Father rotting now beneath the snow; as shall I one day.

(8:00 p.m.)

Marion has just left. She came by after supper, wondering why I had not been in church this morning. I could not bring myself to tell her the reason. It all seemed too vast and complicated and also I feel mildly ashamed for my unbelief. I don't know why, but I do. So I told her that I had been feeling "under the weather," our euphemism for the onset of our periods. There was much sympathetic clucking over this, and I learned more of Marion's monthly trials than I really cared to hear.

Tatham House
138 East 38 Street
New York
February 24, 1935

Dear Clara,

Haven't heard from you in ages. How are you getting on? For the past week or so, I have been mooning about my thirtieth, only a week away now. Did it bother you to turn thirty? I don't remember you talking about it and maybe I'm making too much of all this, but it seems like a kind of important birthday to me. You know, a turning point in life. Most women are married and have kids by the time they are thirty, and it makes you wonder (well, it makes me wonder) if that will ever happen to me. New York is full of good-looking fellows, but they all seem to have wives. Oh well!

I'm working very hard these days, and if you lived in this part of the world, you would hear your sister's voice on commercial announcements for Mother Parker's tea and coffee and Royal Cola. "The House on Chestnut Street" goes on the air in June as a summer replacement. If it gets the listeners we think it will, we'll carry on through the fall. I have been reading Evelyn's outline and it sounds like a wonderful show. Alice and Effie are two sisters (in their thirties!!!), orphaned since childhood and still living with Aunt Mary and Uncle Jim in the town of Meadowvale, which sounds an awful lot like Whitfield, only a little bigger. Alice (me) is the sensible, older one (oh stop laughing!) and Effie is the one who takes chances and gets into trouble (usually with men). Vivian Rhodes, a fine actress who has been on several network shows, will be playing Effie and we will have two real veterans of radio, Margaret Hollingsworth and Graydon Lott as Aunt Mary and Uncle Jim. They seem like really nice folks to work with, so as you can imagine I'm looking forward to all this. I finally gave up on the New World Players. It was just too much work with not much reward, so now I have a little more free time. Anyway, that's what's been happening down here. How are things in dear old Whitfield? I'll just bet you're sick and tired of trying to keep warm in that old house. You should think about some other arrangement for next winter.

Love, Nora

P.S. Have you finished *War and Peace*? I was thinking of you the other day when Evelyn and I were in Scribner's bookstore. I saw all these classic novels lined up on a shelf and there was *W and P*. Yikes, there must have been a thousand pages! I told E. you were reading it this winter. She said she read it years ago.

Whitfield, Ontario
Sunday, March 3, 1935

Dear Nora,
Thanks for your letter. I'm sorry that this won't reach you in time for your thirtieth birthday, but I tend not to make much of a fuss over birthdays. I can't remember feeling especially troubled about reaching the age of thirty. It's true, of course, that most women by then have settled into marriage with husbands and children. But the ones I see don't appear particularly overjoyed by this state of affairs. The young mothers in the village, girls we went to school with like Merle Logan and Dottie Cockburn, look, if anything, a little more careworn than either you or I. Maybe that's just my imagination.

I am sure there are many advantages to life in the married state (a man to keep the furnace going, for one), but then you have to put up with someone else in the house, don't you? I see a husband and children as always being underfoot. I wouldn't know where to go to be by myself when I need to be. Perhaps if I found a man like Father! When he was alive we shared the house, of course, but we never seemed to get in one another's way. I suppose we were similar in temperament and inclination, comforted by each other's presence in the house, but seldom feeling any great need to spend time together. He went his way and I went mine. There were days when we probably didn't exchange ten words and that was fine; it wasn't a matter of ill temper or sullenness, it was just how we felt comfortable with each other. The way I live now, of course, is not for everyone, probably not for most. So maybe I am the wrong person to ask about being thirty.

I should tell you that I have become a topic of conversation on the church porch these days. Or so I am told. This is the fourth consecutive Sunday that I have missed church and apparently the new minister has been asking questions about my spiritual health. Well, I am not going to church these days because I don't feel like it. I seem to have lost interest in what goes on there and they can make of that what they will. Do you go to church down there, or have you pretty much given up on that too?

Yes, I finally finished *War and Peace*. It is an excellent book though I grew a little weary of it in places. A fellow called Pierre is for me the most attractive figure in the entire novel, but I particularly liked Tolstoy's description of the Russian landscape, especially in winter. It reminded me of Ontario in many ways. This long winter will soon be over, and yes, I am fed up with the damn furnace and its daily demands. On the other hand, I am also tired of the voice in my head that is always complaining about things. I am also beginning to believe that somehow I must learn to recapture the pleasure I took in winter when I was a child. I'm sure I tired of it then too, but I must have taken more joy in it as well. It does no good to wish away the days of the fourth season as I seem to have been doing since Christmas. As someone put it, I must teach myself to cherish not only the rainbow but also the winter branch. I am going to work on that next year. Belated Happy Birthday, Nora, and don't worry so about growing old. Think of the alternative!

Clara

Wednesday, March 6

A visit this evening from Mr. Jackson who wanted to know why I have not been attending church. I had been expecting him for weeks and wondered why he had taken so long to get around to me; he is supposed to be such a zealot and saver of lost souls. He sat in the front room with the table lamp catching the light in his stiff coppery hair; long legs crossed and looking at me all the while as if I were not entirely right in the head, a woman mildly unbalanced perhaps by keeping to herself. And I said too much. I was far too anxious to convince him of my sincerity. I shouldn't have gone on the way I did; it is a failing of those who live alone that when we do have visitors, we say too much. Henry Jackson merely smiled at the things I said and from time to time shook his head as if conversing with some harmless madwoman. He began by saying how disappointed many of the congregation were by my absence these past few weeks. "Your friends, Miss Callan, are worried about you," he said. "They think perhaps since your father's death last year you may have become a little too withdrawn. I understand too that your sister is now down in the States and can't get up to visit as often as she might like. Would this not be a good time then to attend your church and see your friends? Worship God?"

I should have told him that he made me sound like an invalid. Instead I said, "I no longer believe."

"No longer believe what?" he asked. He seemed infuriatingly self-assured. Hardly moved in the chair, but lowered his head a little to study me.

"I no longer believe in God," I said.

He smiled at that. "And what do you believe in then, Miss Callan?"

I told him then that I believed in nothing. But I went on about it far too long. Told him that my belief in God had vanished utterly one Sunday morning in February while I sat at the kitchen table. Belief in God now seemed to me only a childish fantasy. There is nothing there and there never has been. There is no Heaven, no Hell, no resurrection of the dead. Why did I go on like that? All that detail about Sunday morning at the kitchen table? What foolishness!

He seemed only amused by me. Then he said, "You seem very sure of yourself, Miss Callan. Do you have any proof that God does not exist?"

"Of course, I haven't," I said. "It's not really a matter of proof, is it? It's a matter of faith and I no longer have that faith. I'm not happy about the way I feel, Mr. Jackson, but I can't help it."

Then he wanted me to pray with him. Get down on my knees with him there in the front room and ask God for guidance. I told him the idea was preposterous and he got a bit huffy about that. In the hallway, as he was putting on his coat and hat, he said he would pray for me, though I somehow doubt it. I sense I made an enemy of him.

Tatham House
138 East 38th Street
New York
March 17, 1935

Dear Clara,

Yes, I am getting used to the idea of being thirty and let me tell you my thirtieth birthday was some night. I don't think I'll ever forget it. Some of the people at the advertising agency took me up to a club in Harlem where we listened to jazz until three o'clock in the morning. Then we had "breakfast" in an all-night diner on Seventh Avenue. It was past four o'clock when I got back here and I was locked out. I had completely forgotten that they lock the doors at one o'clock. So I had to spend the night (well, what was left of it) at Evelyn's. Fortunately she has plenty of room. But what a swell evening it was! Besides Evelyn and another couple of gals, there was a copywriter named Joe (have forgotten his last name) and a fellow named Les Cunningham. He is an announcer and is he handsome!!! Brother, he looks just like Don Ameche. We are talking tall, dark, handsome and very suave.

And guess what? I think he's kind of sweet on me. He sure paid attention to me that night. But here's something that bothers me a little. I get the feeling that Evelyn likes me too. And I mean in another way. I've had this feeling all along that Evy likes women (if you get my meaning). Not that she has tried anything funny. Even the night I stayed over at her place she gave me the other bedroom, but I just get this feeling about her. The way she looks at me sometimes. The thing is, I like her so much as a "friend." She has been really nice to me and I don't want to hurt her feelings in any way, shape or form, but I've tried to hint as strongly as I can that I am not that way inclined. Oh and by the way, as you may have already guessed, the tall, dark and handsome announcer has a wife and two kids. In fact, he had to leave early that night. I might have known that the idea of him being available was just too good to be true. Anyway, enough about my lack of a love life.

Why did you stop going to church? I don't get it. I would think going to church is something you would want to do up there. I'm not saying you should join those old ladies in the Missionary Society, but wouldn't getting out on Sunday morning and seeing other people (even familiar ones) be a good idea? I try to go when I can. If I haven't been out too late on a Saturday, I will go up to Fifth Avenue Presbyterian. It's a little snooty, but I like the minister. He's such a good preacher. I still say my prayers too, by the way. Remember how you used to make me kneel beside you with our elbows on the bed while you made up the prayer? You were such a bossy kid, Clara, but never mind, I loved you anyway. I don't exactly get down on my knees anymore, but I do say my prayers before I go to sleep. Well, most nights anyway.

Is it ever mild down here these days! Just like spring. Oh, Clara, I'm so happy I came down here. I just feel it was the right move for me and things are going to work out. I can't wait for our program to get on the air. They were going to schedule it as a summer replacement show, but the agency likes Evy's scripts so much that they are now looking to May or early June. It's really exciting. Do take care of yourself and write soon!

Love, Nora

Monday, March 25

Showers and the smell of earth as I walked to school this morning. The children were restless today, anxious to be outside even in the rain. There is an eagerness for spring in their blood: farewell to woolen underwear, to overshoes and scratchy leggings. I understand and remember feeling the same way at this time of year. For me, it is now goodbye, at least for a few months, to shoveling coal into that damn furnace.

A letter from Nora today, which I began to answer before supper, but then Marion came by to ask me to go down to Toronto with her next Saturday and see a movie or something. Now that I no longer have the furnace to worry about, I can get away and so I said I would.

After supper the sky cleared and it was such a fine evening that I walked out along the township roads and didn't get home until after dark. I will drop Nora a note in a few days.

Whitfield, Ontario
Sunday, March 31, 1935

Dear Nora,

Well, you are leading quite the busy life down there, aren't you? And yes, I do get your meaning with reference to Miss Dowling. I may live in an Ontario backwater, Nora, but I do understand lesbianism. As a matter of fact, I had my own experience with it when I was in Normal School. A girl there "took an interest" in me. She was always seeking me out after classes, touching me on the arm or shoulder as we spoke, asking me to come home with her for the weekend. I think her parents lived in Belleville. Many of the other girls had boyfriends who would meet them after classes, and perhaps this girl assumed that because I had no beau I was like her. She was a nice young woman too, but it took a bit of doing to persuade her that I was not interested in that kind of friendship. She didn't finish her year, but went into nursing. Used to send me Christmas cards for a few years. These situations can be difficult! I liked that girl very much as a person, just as you like your Miss Dowling. You just have to use tact and judgment and hope the other person understands. I was a little too impatient with that girl, I think. Let Miss D. down gently if you can. As for the tall, dark, handsome (and married) announcer, better leave well enough alone, Nora. A good-looking man like that out on the town without his wife? I can well imagine his intentions, and so can you.

I am glad to learn that you are still going to church, but I'm afraid it has become a thing of the past for me. Yes, it's a morning out of the house once a week, and I am sure that's how many people see it, but if I go to church, it has to be for a reason. I have to go to worship God, and, to put it as plainly as I can, I have lost my faith. It happened this winter. Perhaps it's been happening for some time in small ways, but one Sunday in February, it came with a kind of finality. I just stopped believing. My faith was like a clock winding down until that particular Sunday when it just stopped. So now I can no longer go to church and just sit there pretending to believe. I just can't do that. To tell you the truth, I feel a little sick about it all. I have to learn to live in a world without God, without the thought of ever seeing Mother and Father again—without any of that. And it's difficult.

I was down to the city yesterday. I can finally get away now that I don't have to worry about the furnace. So Marion and I went down on the train for the day. Splurged on lunch at Simpson's and went to an awful moving picture starring Rudy Vallee. Marion is besotted with the man; otherwise she is a reasonable sane thirty-one-year-old woman. She has been asked to sing at Mildred Craig's wedding next month and asked me if I would play for her. I suppose I will, though I am tormenting her a little (for taking me to that awful movie) by telling her I'll think about it. Yes, it's mild up here too and about time. So hurrah for spring! Take care of yourself, Nora.

Clara

Tatham House
138 East 38th Street
New York
April 6, 1935

Dear Clara,

Got your letter yesterday and thought I'd better drop you a note today because I won't have time tomorrow. I'm going to spend most of the day with Evelyn and Vivian Rhodes, going over the first scripts of our show.

I found your letter upsetting, to say the least. You say you no longer believe in God? How could that happen? You were always so religious, or at least I thought you were. You and Father never missed church on Sunday mornings, and when I was home on weekends and slept in, you and Father would give me such dagger looks when you got home from church. What on earth happened? You read the Bible almost right through one summer! Remember? You must have been only eleven or twelve, but you spent nearly every day that summer reading through those long chapters of the Old Testament. I thought for a while you were going to be a missionary or something. I'm worried about you, Clara. I just don't understand how you could lose your faith like that. I wish you would talk to someone about all this. I know you don't think much of this new minister, but maybe if you told him sincerely how you feel, he might be able to help. I mean, isn't that what he's trained to do? It just strikes me as odd. You of all people! What would poor Father think?

I'm afraid I have to run because a girl down the hall (she's a nurse) has asked me to go to the movies with her this afternoon. She's from some place in Minnesota, a small town like Whitfield, and last night she said she was feeling a little blue and homesick. Well, it's been awfully wet and gloomy down here and I'm feeling a bit that way myself, so what better place to be when you're feeling blue than at the movies. Ruth will be at the door any minute, so I'll say goodbye for now and get this in the mail. Please write and let me know if you have talked to anyone about all this.

Love, Nora

P.S. It occurs to me that all this may have something to do with Father's passing. It will soon be a year, and you are probably dwelling on that. You have to put things behind you, Clara.

Saturday, April 13

A letter from Nora advising me to talk to Jackson about my apostasy. Well, she can forget about that. Jackson is the last person on earth I would approach. Have gone instead to the poets. Reading Vaughan and Dickinson at two o'clock this morning.

I saw eternity the other night
Like a great ring of pure and endless light,
All calm, as it was bright;

And Emily D.

I shall know why, when time is over
And I have ceased to wonder why;
Christ will explain each separate anguish
In the fair schoolroom of the sky.

He will tell me what Peter promised,
And I, for wonder at his woe,
I shall forget the drop of anguish
That scalds me now, that scalds me now.

But they lived in other centuries when it must have been easier to believe.

Monday, April 15

Father died a year ago today. A windy cool Sunday with dampness in the air. After dinner he looked out the window and told me he thought he might spade the flower beds by the side of the house, but it looked too much like rain. Said he wasn't feeling well and took some bicarbonate of soda. I told him he always ate too quickly and he said it was a habit picked up from years of eating in boardinghouses before he married. He said he would lie down until the indigestion passed, and so he climbed the stairs to his bedroom. His final words came from the head of the stairs. "Why don't you play something?" I told him I would, but then after I finished the dishes, I sat down to read the rest of the *Herald* and forgot.

At three o'clock I went upstairs; I can't remember why. I could see his stocking feet through the open doorway of his bedroom. He had slept, I thought, too long and would have trouble in the night, so I approached him. He was lying on his back, and when I entered the room, I knew at once that he was dead. I just knew, and I was startled a little at my own certainty. It was the grayness of the flesh around his eyes, I think. Or the perfect stillness of his body. I didn't touch him, but I knew he was dead.

Went over to the Brydens' and Mrs. Bryden met me at the door. She must have seen something in my face, but I was not in tears. Why? Already his death was a fact. Unalterable. I said this to her. I remember the words. "I think Father must have had a heart attack in his sleep. He's gone."

Mrs. Bryden's puzzled, kind little face. "Gone, Clara? Do you mean he's passed away? Oh, my dear child!"

Hurrying across the yard with me, the rainy wind in our faces. Mrs. Bryden surprised me by her quickness. She is Father's age exactly, but nimble and quick, a little sparrow of a woman. In the bedroom she bent over him and pulled the sheet across his face. "Yes, yes, you're right. He's gone, poor Ed. We must phone the doctor."

Friday, April 19

Marion came by this evening with Mildred Craig and her mother to decide on the music for the wedding. Mrs. C. favored "The Holy City," but her daughter wanted "Because." Marion suggested "I Love You Truly." When asked for my opinion, I said that any or all would wring dry the hearts of the wedding guests and therefore would be suitable. Wry little looks of bafflement from the Craigs and Marion's usual benign acknowledgment of my strangeness. "Oh, shoot, Clara. You never take anything seriously." Wrong, wrong, wrong, I felt like saying, but didn't, of course. In the end I played and Marion sang all three ditties. The pretty little bride and Mum were won over by "I Love You Truly," which Marion shrewdly sang last.

Whitfield, Ontario
Sunday, April 21, 1935

Dear Nora,
Sorry to have upset you with my last letter. Perhaps I shouldn't have gone on like that about God and faith. You mustn't worry, Nora. I have no intention of laying the sharp edge of the paring knife against my wrists. It's spring, for goodness' sake. I am reconciled to my state; of course, I have to rethink the notion of time. If I no longer believe in

immortality (Heaven, if you like), then it follows that my time is finite. It will therefore end one day and so the question becomes, How may I best use what time is left to me? That's what I must work on. I have to confess that when I last wrote to you, I was a little edgy and distraught. Perhaps I still am, but not as much. It's just that I must learn how to live another way.

Are you still appearing in those detective shows and hospital dramas? When will Miss Dowling's saga of small-town life appear? Has your handsome announcer made his pass yet? Should I buy a radio or continue to play the piano? Answers to these questions will bring immense peace of mind.

Clara

Saturday, May 4

The Accompanist at the Wedding. I was thinking of those five words as the title of a poem this afternoon. It was three o'clock and Marion was singing "I Love You Truly." The lovely afternoon light was coloring Jesus and the Apostles on the church windows. I was thinking of a woman like myself who plays the piano for other women's celebrations. There she is in her blue dress and white shoes at the piano. And will she be playing for Millie Craig's daughter in twenty years? Will she be there again in say, 1955? A woman of fifty-two with thickened waist and ankles? With gray in her hair? I wonder.

Monday, May 6

The silver jubilee of King George and Queen Mary and all over the province there have been celebrations. Today we marched the children to the cenotaph and stood listening to the local MPP, a well-fed lawyer from Linden, talking about the greatness of the Royal Family and how privileged we all are to be a part of the British Empire, the "greatest family of countries the world has ever known." The children holding their little Union Jacks listening respectfully to this windbag. No mention at all of the men without work who have no means to feed their families. Who each week have to endure the humiliation of Relief. The man's sanctimonious blather made my blood boil. Cheered up, however, by a letter from Nora who seems to be enjoying life in the Great Republic.

Tatham House
138 East 38th Street
New York
April 29, 1935

Dear Clara,
I'm glad you're feeling better about life in general, but I wish you wouldn't be so descriptive. That bit about laying a paring knife against your wrists! I don't particularly enjoy reading that kind of thing from my sister, even if you were just kidding. I still think you should talk to someone about religion, or maybe read some books on the subject. Going to church and believing in God have been an important part of your life, Clara. You can't just cast things like that aside. We all need to believe in something. It's only human nature.

As for your sarcastic questions! Yes, I'm still doing some freelance work on shows. I'm still calling for Dr. Donaldson to do his rounds at the hospital. I've also been a patient of his (I was shot by a gangster boyfriend). It's funny. For some reason producers hear my voice and see me not only as the helpful sister, but also as the tough dame who hangs around hoodlums. No, Les Cunningham has made no passes at me. In fact, I haven't seen Les for a while, though he's been chosen to announce our show and so I guess we'll be working together. We go on the air in two weeks, by the way, so wish me luck. I've lost about six pounds over the last month and I've had my hair cut really short. I'll bet you wouldn't recognize me. But I'm saving the best news for last. I think I can now afford my own place and so I am moving next Saturday into a little apartment five streets from here. My new address will be 135 East Thirty-third Street. My very own place, Clara! No more sharing the bathroom with nine other girls!!! Hope all is well up in dear old Whitfield.

Love, Nora

Sunday, May 19

Walked out to the cemetery this morning. Past the church where I could hear the voices of the congregation.

Unto the hills around do I lift up
My longing eyes,
O whence for me shall my salvation come,
From whence arise?
From God the Lord doth come my certain aid,
From God the Lord who heaven and earth hath made.

One of Father's favorites, and how many times did I stand beside him singing that hymn? Felt a little strange walking there on the empty street in my old brown coat, carrying the garden shears and trowel in a cloth bag. Saw myself as others might; as a woman in an old brown coat turning a bit odd in her middle years. I was glad to get beyond the village and out into the country with the sunlight on my face and the smell of the plowed fields around me.

Spent an hour or so tidying up the grave. I should really have planted something, geraniums perhaps. Yet the plain clipped grass seemed to suit Father best. His name and years are like fresh wounds in the gray stone. Stood listening to some crows across the fields near a woodlot. They were chasing a marauding hawk that was swooping and climbing to avoid them. All those dark birds against a blue sky

Friday, May 24

Victoria Day with flags and bunting on storefronts and verandas. Warm and sunny and two busloads off to Linden for the parade. What a fuss people make over an old dead queen! At noon two tramps came to the kitchen door and asked if I wanted my summer wood split and piled. One fellow was about thirty, tall and thin in overalls with an old suit coat and cap. He had a wide comical mouth and was talkative and eager to please. The other was sixteen or so, a homely boy and simple-minded from the look of him. He had a short thick body and a wall-eye. I had misgivings, but I set them to work, watching from the kitchen window. To their credit they worked steadily all afternoon, the man splitting and the boy piling the wood in neat rows against the side of the shed. They finished about five o'clock and I took out some food to them: cold pork and mustard sandwiches, some tea and half an apple pie. They sat on the back stoop to eat. When they finished their meal, I gave them a package of sandwiches with the rest of the pie and a dollar. I was certainly pleased with the job they did. They had even raked up all the chips into a pile. Just as they were leaving, the Brydens pulled into their driveway. They had spent the day opening their summer cabin at Sparrow Lake. I think they were amused by the pride I took in my woodpile. I can't help it. It was deeply satisfying to show them the neatly stacked cord of wood against the shed. We had supper together and later sat on their veranda listening to the fire-crackers from the fairgrounds. Then some children came running along the street, laughing and holding sparklers. Tiny showers of light in the darkness.

Saturday, May 25 (11:45 p.m.)

A terrible thing has happened to me. This afternoon I was set upon by the two men who came by the house yesterday. They hurt me, or one of them did. I have filled the bathtub twice with hot water. But the kitchen stove has gone out and there is no more, and I am too tired to bother with it until morning. Yet I cannot sleep and must record what happened to me.

This afternoon I went for a walk along the railway tracks. I have done it countless times and usually I go no farther than Henry Hill's. I am afraid of his dog and seldom go past the place. Today, however, the old man and the dog were gone and so I walked as far as Trestle Bridge. I sat on the bridge for perhaps twenty minutes watching the fields turn dark and light under the passing clouds and then I started home. I hurried a bit because I was thinking again of the collie which is bad-tempered. I wanted to get past Henry's before he and the dog returned, and I felt better when I did. Then as I came around the bend in the tracks, I saw two figures ahead. They were dark against the blue of the sky. One had his arms spread wide like a child walking on the top of a fence. From time to time the figure stumbled and fell between the tracks. Then I could see that it was the man and the boy who had split and piled my wood yesterday. As they came toward me, the man ignored the boy's antics, walking quickly and looking down as though he were angry or harried. Each time the boy fell, he would run to catch up and try again to balance himself on the tracks.

I don't believe I felt any fear at the sight of them. I used to watch Father talking to such men through the screen door of the kitchen. Giving them a ten-cent piece or a bag of apples and sending them on their way. Such men nearly always defer to authority. They are used to being told what to do, and so I was not afraid at their approach. When I got within perhaps fifty yards, the man looked up and saw me and stopped. The boy stopped too and stood on the rail with his hand on the man's shoulder. I walked steadily on. I could see now that the man was grinning with his wide comical mouth and he called out to me. "Hello there, Missus. How are you today? Do you remember Donny and me? We chopped that cord of wood for you yesterday, didn't we, Donny?"

The boy said nothing, just looked at me. There was only his vacant face with its terrible white eye. I wished them a good day, and then the man did an annoying thing. As I passed, he turned and began walking alongside me. As I quickened my pace, he did likewise, and all this time he was chattering. "Out for a stroll, are you, Missus? A little nature walk? Sure is a nice day for it. That's what Donny and me are doing. Taking a stroll and listening to the birdies." And on and on with this foolishness. The youth followed. The sole on one of his shoes had come loose and was flapping in the cinders between the tracks. I remember that flapping sound behind me. The tramp's presumption was both irritating and bedeviling. That is how I felt at that point, irritated but not yet fearful, as the man walked along beside me with his chattering, grinning mouth, and the boy followed in his broken shoes.

I kept thinking that it was all quite ridiculous, and finally I halted and told the man to stop his nonsense and get away from me. Then I may have made a mistake. I told him there were men working on the tracks by Trestle Bridge, and they would be along soon, and then he would find himself in serious trouble. The tramp could see I was lying and he may have sensed the beginning of my fear. Then he said something like this.

"Now, Missus, you're telling us a fib and nice ladies like you shouldn't tell fibs. There are no men working on that bridge this afternoon. Section men don't work on Saturday afternoons. Everybody gets a little holiday on Saturday afternoons, even section men. We know that, don't we, Donny? Me and Donny live on the tracks, Missus. We been on railway tracks all over this country and in the United States of America too."

I had started forward again, but suddenly he sprang ahead of me and blocked my way. He was one of those loose-jointed men who are perhaps remembered in country towns for nothing more than step-dancing. I must have said something like, "What do you think you're doing?" and then he said this. I remember these words.

"You live alone, don't you, Missus? No man around? Nobody to chop your wood or warm your little feet in bed. Oh my, what a shame!"

His words unsettled me, and I'm sure it was then that I knew these men intended to harm me. Then the tramp said, "You're a good-looking woman and I'll bet you could use a good ____ing." At that word I screamed, and I remember that at the edge of the pine woods, several small black-and-yellow birds rushed forth from the grass and rose into the air. The tramp seized my wrists. "Come along now, Missus. I just want to give you a little kiss. I haven't had a kiss in donkey's years." *Donkey's years!* Yes, he used that expression. And so began my struggle. He was all sharp and flinty, all bones and edges or so it seemed. I remember the sour tobacco stink from his mouth and the unwashed smell of his overalls. A reeking skeleton of a man with a wide mouth.

We swayed in the grass by the side of the tracks. "Now, Missus, now, Missus, you'll like it, you'll see." A kind of mad, skipping song over and over. So we shuffled around in the grass, and the tramp began to laugh and holding me at arm's length he twisted me around. He was singing a foolish song. "Have you ever been into an Irishman's shanty? Where money is scarce, but whiskey's a-plenty." It was all this mad circling and through the turns I could see the boy sitting on the tracks, watching us. The tramp's face had reddened with his exertions and he had somehow managed to remove his coat and fling it into the grass.

Then I fell and he covered me with himself. There was something sharp against my cheek from one of his pockets. A pencil maybe or the stem of a pipe. The terrible stink of him and his hand was beneath my dress, tearing at my underclothes. Ripping them away from me. I was dizzy from all that turning and sick with the notion of what was happening. I said to the tramp, "You mustn't do this to me. You mustn't harm me like this." But he was only desperate and obscene. "Oh yes, Missus. Yes, Missus. I want to ____ you so bad. I do. You'll like it, Missus. You'll like it." His words were something like that. Then I thought this. A terrible thing is going to happen and I can do nothing about it. It will be an ordeal but I do not think they will kill me. They are not murdering men. They will run away as soon as this is over. My eyes were closed and I shuddered with the pain of his entrance into my body.

Then the frantic thrusting inside me. I counted nine, ten, perhaps a dozen before he spent himself. And all the while I was thinking this. I was thinking how suddenly a life can become misshapen, divided brutally into before and after a dire event. So it must be with all who endure calamity: those who must remember the day of the motorcar accident, the afternoon the child fell through the ice, the winter night's blaze that awakened the dreamers.

The tramp was now quiet. I could feel his racing heartbeat. He had shifted his weight and so my cheek no longer hurt. But my insides were burning and I wondered if I now had some unspeakable disease swimming within me. Or perhaps I had become impregnated. It is indeed something to worry about, for I believe I am about in the middle of my month. When I opened my eyes, he was standing over me, buttoning himself. He looked out of sorts now. Ill-tempered. He called to the youth. "Come over here and have some too. You'll never have a better chance than this." I watched him buckling the straps of his overalls and looking for the coat he had flung aside in the grass. How I longed to set that grass on fire! Consume all three of us in a sudden flaring burst of flame. A field of fiery grass that would scour everything and leave the earth blackened and cleansed.

The tramp now seemed hurried and vexed with the boy. "Come on now, hurry it up! Get that thing out of your pants and give it to her. She's never going to see anything like that again."

The boy had come across from the tracks and was looking down at me. Fumbling with his buttons. His member was grotesque. A huge red thing and I said to myself he will tear me apart with it. Then the boy fell to his knees between my legs and I closed my eyes, for I could not bear to look at that vacant, ruined face. Almost at once I felt him spilling himself across my legs. I could feel it pouring over me as he worked it out of himself with his own hands. And so I was spared that. The tramp was now laughing. Calling the boy a damn fool.

They left then. The man scolding the boy as they went away. I heard his voice fading, and when I turned on my side, I could see his long legs moving through the grass and the boy's too climbing to the railway tracks. I knelt and watched them walking along the tracks toward Trestle Bridge. The boy was hurrying and at one point the man stopped to cuff him across the back of the head. Then he hurried on, the boy endeavoring to keep up, and then they disappeared around the bend in the tracks. I lay down again, for I felt sick to my stomach and I was bleeding. After a few minutes I cleaned myself again with my torn bloomers, and I wondered how I would get home. What I wanted to do was sit in a hot bath and clean myself properly. Yet that seemed like such an undertaking, such an impossibly complicated and far-off task, that I began to weep and beat the ground with the palms of my hands. I also kicked my feet. I had a little spell there lying in the grass. A tantrum such as an hysterical child might have. It left me panting and exhausted in the sunlight. From time to time I had to clean myself again and then I would wonder what to do if my insides were swimming in disease or if I were pregnant with the tramp's child. I could not bear the idea of facing a doctor over in Linden. I would have to go down to Toronto and find someone to help me. But where would I look and what would I say to him? I could not bring myself to tell anyone about this. I got myself into another state thinking about all that, and then I thought how grateful I would be if only I could turn back time and now be walking home with a copy of the *Herald*, looking forward to my supper, dealing as we all do with the fuss and worries of everyday life. Grumbling about them. When what we should do, if we could only be reminded, is to be grateful for the small routine difficulties of our days and nights.

I thought about all that as the sun moved through the pine woods and the air and ground cooled. I would have to wait until dark before making my way home. I imagined myself looking wild-eyed and distraught (perhaps I didn't look that way at all), but I was afraid I might burst into tears or say something outrageous at a simple greeting on the street. And the aftermath of such a display?

"What is it, Miss Callan? What's the trouble?"

There would be talk and talk and more talk.

"She started crying right there on the street? Who? Clara Callan? I don't believe it. That's not like her. Why would she do that? She could be having some kind of breakdown. All alone in that house. Ever since her father passed away."

I would stay where I was until dark. I made up my mind about that.

I thought then of how the tramp had hurt me for no reason other than his lust, and he would go unpunished. A year ago I might have taken comfort believing God had seen this man do what he did to me and He would punish him. But now I believe there is often no retribution in human affairs. People rob and murder and rape one another and often go to their graves without ever being brought to justice. And this notion bothered me almost as much as anything.

Around seven o'clock I heard the whistle of the evening train from Toronto and soon the tracks began to creak under the weight of its approach. Listening to this gathering onrush of iron noise, headlong and terrifying, I wondered again if Mother had deliberately stepped in front of such fury. The train passed by me twenty feet away. I caught a glimpse of the locomotive's wheels and raising myself I saw the coaches passing and a woman's head in profile. Someone reading a newspaper at the end of her ordinary day. How I envied her!

The sky through the pine woods blazed in afterglow and then darkened. Twilight seemed long. A new moon appeared, resting on its back. Farmers say such a moon is holding water so the weather will stay dry. I wondered about the truth of such sayings. Oh, I may not have been in my right mind, for all this time I was walking back and forth, stopping now and then to clean myself. I had thrown away the disgraceful bloomers and had to use my stockings. From time to time I sat down on the track. Just about where the youth had sat watching us. I pictured the boy and the man now crossing a field, chewing on green apples or spring onions pulled from a garden, the man chattering on or perhaps now quietly sullen. I saw this boy crossing the field staring out at the world with his one good eye. Then I started back along the tracks toward Whitfield, thinking how peculiar I would have seemed to anyone who came upon me. Near the station at the edge of the village I crouched in the grass. At the side of the stationmaster's house, some men were leaning against an automobile and talking. Their voices and laughter traveled across the dark fields to me. His children were still playing, running around the house and shouting until their mother came to the back door and called them in. The men continued to talk for the longest time until finally they drifted away to their homes. I waited for perhaps another hour. The dogs stopped barking and then I walked to the railway station and up Church Street and home. It was nearly ten-thirty when I started a fire in the kitchen stove and began to heat the water for my baths.

Sunday, May 26 (4:00 p.m.)

As I read it over, I thought my account of what happened yesterday afternoon was too feverish, but now I don't think so. That is what occurred as truthfully as I can set it down. I finally fell asleep, just as the birds were starting. Awakened to the church bell and thought of how a year ago I would have been walking out the door with others at this hour. Drifted back to sleep for half an hour and then got up to heat more water.

An hour ago Mrs. Bryden came to the door. She had seen no lights until late last night and wondered if I were ill. Was there anything she could do? I told her I'd had a touch of something and had gone to bed early and then awakened later and read myself back to sleep. As I talked to her, I wondered if she believed me or if I looked different to her. There is still a small mark on my cheek from whatever was in the tramp's pocket. And perhaps what happened has transformed me in the eyes of others. Perhaps they can see the violation in my face. I thought I sounded convincing, but Mrs. Bryden gave me an odd look. Perhaps it's only my imagination. After she left, I made some toast and tea. I couldn't face the prospect of a letter to Nora asking for news "of dear old Whitfield."

"Oh yes, and by the way, Nora, here is some news. I was raped yesterday afternoon." Surely such a statement would require at least three of her exclamation marks. Then I thought of how sour and sarcastic and unworthy that was. I can be such a hateful person, and I can seem to do nothing about it.

Monday, May 27

Glad to be back in the classroom and grateful for routine that woe makes way for: a roomful of children allows no time for reflection. When they trooped out to the schoolyard for recess, however, I thought of how it must be like this when you have a fatal disease. A flurry of activity distracts you, but once alone, the predicament returns to poison your day. At the window I watched Milton in his shirtsleeves playing softball with the children. I wondered what he would think if I told him what had happened to me on Saturday. But I cannot imagine myself doing such a thing. It's just too outlandish.

A letter from Nora. The new program appears to be catching on and she has received a fan letter. Well, good for her, but I can't yet summon either the energy or the goodwill to reply.

135 East 33rd Street
New York
May 19, 1935

Dear Clara,
How are things anyway? As for me, I am very happy, believe me. Everyone here is excited about the show and the agency people think that we'll be picked up by one of the networks in the fall. If that

happens, there's a good chance you'll be able to hear me up there. And guess what? I got my first fan letter the other day. A young woman in Queens (that's another borough of New York) wrote me this wonderful letter telling me all about herself. She's confined to a wheelchair (automobile accident) and lives with her mother. She's only twenty-one and says if it wasn't for the radio, she doesn't know how she would get through the day. It's just like I've always said to you, Clara, radio is so important to so many people. Anyway, she just loves "The House on Chestnut Street." It's her favorite program and I'm her favorite character. How about that? She says she admires the way I'm always helping Effie out of jams and she wishes she could be just like me. She says she's rooting for me all the time. It's really something to get a letter like that and realize how important your character becomes in the lives of listeners.

When I showed the letter to Evelyn, she just said, "Get used to it, kid, because once we get on the network, you'll be reaching out to the great spongy heart of America. You're going to be wringing the old sponge dry, and you'll be getting bushels of letters." It was something like that anyway. But that's Evelyn for you. She never takes anything seriously, but I can tell you she's very pleased with how the show is doing.

Anyway, that's my story, but what about you? Do you have any plans for the summer? I wish you'd consider coming down here for a couple of weeks. I'm told by everyone that it just gets boiling hot in New York in the summer, but that shouldn't stop you. I am going to buy some fans. I'd love for you to see my little apartment and you could come over to the studio and watch me at work. You could see how they put a program like ours on the air with the sound effects and everything. People from all over the country visit Radio City and go on tours to see how their favorite shows are produced. I wish you'd think about it, Clara. You'd find New York a fascinating place and if it gets too hot, we can always go to the movies. All the big movie houses are now air-cooled. So please think about. And how about a letter!!!

Love, Nora

Friday, May 31 (5:10 a.m.)

A wakeful and depressing night. At ten past two I was wrenched from an ugly dream in which the tramp had seized my wrists and was dancing with me in the field, twirling me around just as he did last Saturday. This time, however, we were both naked and attached to him was the boy's member, a raw red club. The evening train from Toronto was passing and people were looking at us. Milton's face was pressed against the coach window. And beside him were Ida Atkins and Mrs. Bryden and Cora Macfarlane. Could not get back to sleep and so I read. Chose the Bible. Even though I no longer believe, the words somehow still comfort me.

> Unto thee will I cry, O Lord
> my rock; be not silent to me:
> lest, if that be silent to me,
> I become like them that go
> down into the pit.

Whitfield, Ontario
Sunday, June 2, 1935

Dear Nora,

I'm sorry not to have written before this. I can only plead sheer laziness. I'm happy to learn that your program is doing well and that you are receiving letters from admiring listeners, though perhaps the young woman in the wheelchair would be well advised to read a good book now and then. Depending on afternoon programs to get her through the day strikes me as rather pathetic, if you don't mind my saying so. It's all very well to escape into daydreams, we all do that from time to time, but the young woman sounds . . . Oh never mind, forget all that. It's not important really. If I had the energy, I'd tear this up and start over again, but I haven't. Please forget what I said about the young woman in the wheelchair. She will survive as will we all.

The school year is winding down and I am looking forward to the holiday months. I don't know about New York. It's a long way to go and travel is so dear. I'll have to think about it, Nora. Meantime, I hope everything continues well for you. I shall write when I have more news. I am sorry about this awful letter.

Clara

Saturday, June 8

Two weeks now and I await signs that I am all right. Any day now, and if all is well, I will try never to complain again about trivial vicissitudes. I suppose that is a mere vain hope, for it is in our natures to grumble over trifling setbacks. But I will try. I do promise to try.

Monday, June 10

After school I washed and waxed all the downstairs floors. Grueling labor, but it keeps my mind off things. Tomorrow evening I will tackle the upstairs.

Thursday, June 14

The annual field day and Milton in high spirits, refereeing events and measuring out the long jump. At the end of it all, he said, "Well, Clara. We're nearly there. Another couple of weeks. I think we've both done a fine job. I hope you've been happy working with me. I can't pretend that I've filled your father's shoes, but I've certainly tried."

"Yes, Milton," I said. "It's been a good year. We've both worked hard."

135 East 33rd Street
New York
June 16, 1935

Dear Clara,

I hope you're feeling better than the last time you wrote. Did you get up on the wrong side of the bed that day? I also think you were pretty hard on the young woman who wrote to me. Not everybody enjoys reading, Clara, and that's where radio can help. There are a lot of folks out there (and I'm getting more and more letters from them) who just don't have a lot to look forward to and shows like ours can help them out. They can sit in front of their radios and imagine a whole other world where people have worse problems than they have and sooner or later they see how these problems are solved. It gives them hope, I think.

Just the other day I read this piece in *Radio News* about how listening to "Amos and Andy" actually saved a poor fellow's life. Apparently he was all set to jump off the roof of this apartment building in Brooklyn, but a neighbor talked him out of it. "Amos and Andy" was on at the time and the neighbor said, "Before you jump, you should listen to these guys. They are so funny and every night you can listen to them for nothing. No matter how frightening and imperfect the world may be, every day you can look forward to hearing these comical people in the evening and it's something at least."

I know it was in a radio magazine and maybe it didn't happen exactly like that, but when you think about it, it's true. And it saved the guy's life. People have to have something to look forward to, even if it's only a radio show.

I'm sorry you're so lukewarm to the idea of coming down here for a holiday this summer. I don't understand why. You have all that time on your hands. Wouldn't a change be a good thing? Personally I think it would do you the world of good to get out of Whitfield. We could have a wonderful time together. So think about it some more, okay? And take care of yourself.

Love, Nora

P.S. Happy thirty-second on the twenty-seventh!!!

Friday, June 28

I am sure it's happened and it is nonsense to pretend otherwise. Sick to my stomach this morning. Is that not a clear sign? In my breasts a kind of tingling. In small ways my body feels different and strange. The damnable bad luck of it all. This was the last day of the school year and the entrance form were off at the town hall finishing their examinations. Milton was supervising and so I had the rest of the school to look after. Nothing much one can do with the last day except word games and races. We ate our lunch out under the trees. There was lemonade and cake and the Junior Third girls presented me with an embroidered apron and a box of chocolates. After a year's scolding I wasn't expecting that. Looking back I think I was rather hard on some of them. The boys played in the dusty sunlight or wandered off and I was surrounded by a cluster of little girls. Their chatter and their bright excited faces made me happy for half an hour. I think I must have forgotten my "unfortunate condition." But then, sitting back against a tree and watching them, I decided I must go down to Toronto and find a doctor.

Wednesday, July 3

Train to Toronto and my condition confirmed. I am pregnant. It was not as difficult to find a doctor as I had imagined. Nothing is ever as difficult as I imagine it will be and I should probably take heart from that truth, but I know I won't. I found Dr. Allan in a large house on

Sherbourne Street near Wellesley Hospital and passed myself off as Mrs. Donaldson, newly arrived from Winnipeg. I wore Mother's wedding ring. She had a much smaller hand, and I had an awful time getting the ring off when I got home. Dr. Allan was a cheerful and talkative young man (younger than I am) who is just starting a practice. Told me his wife was going to have a baby too, and they are very excited about the prospect of starting a family. We had a pleasant little conversation, Dr. Allan and I, and my lies were all believed.

"How do you like Toronto after Winnipeg, Mrs. Donaldson?"

"Oh fine."

"And what does your husband do?"

"Tom works for the Canadian Pacific Railway. In their offices. He has just been transferred. We've been trying to have a child for the longest time."

"Well, you're a little old for a first child, but you seem healthy enough."

He told me to expect the baby in February and to come back to see him in a month. I paid the nurse and left.

On the train home, I decided that I must tell Nora, but I am far too nervous about all this to talk to her. I will write.

Whitfield, Ontario
July 4, 1935

Dear Nora,

What you are about to read will no doubt be startling and so you should brace yourself. I hope you are in a chair and not standing by the stove waiting for an egg to boil. Or sitting on the edge of the bed as you used to, trimming your toenails. And leaving the trimmings in a little pile on the dresser as I recall. Be firmly seated then, away from stoves and scissors. I have something important to tell you and it is not easy. It looks as if I am pregnant (a doctor in Toronto has confirmed this, and so I don't know why I say "as if" because I am). And *please* do not ask for details of how this unfortunate situation has come to pass. It has happened and I must deal with it. I simply don't want to go into the whole story at the moment. The father cannot marry me. That is out of the question, and so I am left wondering what to do about it. *What would* you *do if you were in my situation?* I know how excitable you can get, so please try to be composed in your response. I am trying to stay calm in the face of this "event," and so I don't need any "weeping and wailing and gnashing of teeth." It obviously has to be dealt with, and so what would you do? I'm sorry to have to write this kind of letter to you, Nora. I know you're occupied with your radio business down there, but I'm not quite sure where to turn at the moment.

Clara

P.S. Please don't phone the Brydens and ask for me. I can't risk it. Try to understand my situation.

135 East 33rd Street
New York
July 10, 1935

Dear Clara,
Damn it, I wish you would join the twentieth century and get a telephone!!! We are wasting so much time because you insist on living in the last century. God Almighty!!! Well, that's the way you are, I suppose, and so now that I've had my little rant, I will do what I can for you, Clara.

You will see that I have enclosed a ticket with the number on the Pullman car for the New York train for Friday, July 19. I'm sending this letter first class and it should reach you by next Tuesday and that will give you a couple of days to get ready. Can you get over to Linden and phone me from a public booth and let me know that you got this letter and that you're coming a week from Friday. I don't leave for the studio until about ten, so you could take that morning train over to

Linden, or get a ride with someone. You can surely understand how not having a telephone makes everything so damn awkward. As you can see from the ticket, the N.Y. train leaves Toronto at nine o'clock. Show the conductor your sleeping-car ticket and you will get a berth for the night. The train gets into Penn Station around nine-thirty and I'll be there. Just follow the other passengers into the grand concourse. It is a very busy place, so follow the other passengers.

I promise to ask no questions. What's done is done and nobody is sitting in judgment on you. These things happen. I've had a scare or two myself, believe me. You don't say how far along you are. I hope it's not more than two months. After that (so I understand) it can be tricky. Of course, I'm assuming that you'll want to have something done about all this, in which case I can help you. Or I should say, we can help you. I've already talked to Evelyn and she knows some reliable people. There will be no backroom butchers or anything like that, so you mustn't worry. I have complete faith in Evelyn's judgment on this. Things will work out, Clara, if you will just come down here and let me look after you. Don't, for heaven's sake, try to do anything yourself. None of those old wives' tales or home remedies work and they can be dangerous. You need people who know what they are doing.

Please do me this favor. As soon as you get this letter, get over to Linden or some place, find a public telephone and give me a call. Try not to worry, Clara. We'll work this thing out, and *no questions will be asked*.

Love, Nora

P.S. It's hot as blazes down here, so make sure you pack three or four sundresses and plan to stay at least a month. You'll need plenty of rest after all this is over. Thank heaven you're on your summer holidays.

P.P.S. At the train station, I'll be wearing a yellow dress and I'll be looking for you.

Wednesday, July 17

Just back from Linden where I spent the day shopping for New York. I'm sure by the standards of the great city I will look quite dowdy. Phoned Nora from a booth near the public library. Listened to her breathless, worried voice. "Clara! Heavens, it's good to hear from you. How are you feeling?"

"I'm sick every morning just as the book says I'm supposed to be."

"You said you saw a doctor. Where was that? Toronto?"

"Yes. I visited him as Mrs. Donaldson. I got the name from that doctor show of yours."

A bark of laughter. "Mrs. Donaldson? You didn't."

"I did."

"Oh, Clara, you are something. And is everything okay?"

"Everything seems normal according to Dr. Allan of Sherbourne Street."

"How far along are you anyway?"

"It will be eight weeks on Saturday."

"Ouch. You left it long enough."

"I know I was foolish. Worried. Didn't know what to do. I dithered."

"Well, it'll work out. You'll see."

"You didn't have to get me a berth, Nora. That's such an expense. I'll pay you back for this."

"Don't worry about that. Just get on that train Friday night."

"I will, Nora. Thank you."

Told Mrs. Bryden I was going to New York on Friday to spend some time with Nora, and she said she would keep an eye on things for me. So now I feel better. Somehow this must all work out.

Friday, July 19 (4:00 p.m.)

I have brought along a book of Chekhov's stories and on the train down to Toronto this morning read these words.

> A week had passed since they had struck up an acquaintance. It was a holiday. It was close indoors, while in the street the wind whirled the dust about and blew people's hats off. One was thirsty all day, and Gurov often went into the restaurant and offered Anna Sergeyevna a soft drink or ice cream. One did not know what to do with oneself.

How perfectly the writer captures the lassitude in the air of that idle summer day by the Black Sea! The reader understands at once that all that heated air and boredom will draw the man and woman together, and their lives will never be the same again.

Then an unpleasant experience at Union Station. I had bought some magazines and was sitting on a bench wondering how to fill the rest of the day. I was looking through one of the magazines when I noticed a man staring at me. Or rather smiling. He was across from me with his newspaper, which he had set aside. He was middle-aged and respectable-looking, but I was unnerved by his smile. I fancied he was looking at my legs and it made me very uncomfortable. After a few minutes of this, I had to leave. I gathered up my magazines and purse (I had checked my valise) and walked out of the station onto the street. I walked hurriedly, glancing back several times to see if the man was following me. Of course, he wasn't and I can see now how foolish I was. Nevertheless, my fear was real at the time and I walked as far as the cathedral on King Street.

Sat in the cool empty church for nearly an hour. I say empty, but that is not entirely accurate. Now and then a person would enter to pray or sit alone and think, just as I was doing. It was restful and it calmed my nerves. At one point a young woman (she could not have been twenty) entered. She was plain and wearing a simple housedress with a kerchief on her head. I thought she could be a maid or a factory girl. She chose a pew nearby and knelt to pray as the Catholics do with their hands in front of them. She was troubled; that was easy to see and I wondered what burdens weighed upon her. Was there illness in the family? Had she lost someone? Was she also pregnant and alone? And now she was asking God to help her. She didn't stay long and as she left I caught a glimpse of a pale and anxious face.

When I returned to the station, I chose another part of the waiting room and, of course, there was no sign of the smiling man. Then I cashed in the Pullman ticket. I can sit up all night on a train. I would rather do that, in fact, than climb into a berth surrounded by half-naked strangers.

(9:45 p.m.)

Passing hundreds of orchards with figures standing around bonfires. The smell of smoke in the coach. Children are chasing one another among the trees and men are loading crates onto trucks in the darkness. A man holds a lantern to help them see. The fruit pickers must live like gypsies.

At Buffalo a guard walked through the coach and asked us questions about our birthplace and our citizenship. When the train started up again, I stared at my reflection in the lighted window. Saw a serious, haggard face. I thought about the secrets in my life and the awful mystery of a world without God. I thought too of the young woman praying in the cathedral, and the man who had frightened me, and the dark lives of people in detective magazines. I thought of Chekhov writing in a room over thirty years ago, dipping his pen into the inkwell and pausing to imagine what would happen next to Gurov and Anna. After a while they turned out the lights and people began to settle into sleep. Or like me, stare out at the night.

Saturday, July 20 (9:20 a.m.)

I suppose I slept an hour or two, but I awakened at first light. Everyone else sleeping as we passed through green wooded hills and valleys, past farms and small towns. The clanging of bells at roadway crossings and the colorful American flag in front of post offices. The morning brightened and a highway ran alongside the tracks. I saw families in sedans and trucks and beyond the highway a broad river lay glittering in the sunlight. As we drew closer to the great city, we passed freight yards and apartment buildings that were so close to the tracks you could look in on people's lives. In one apartment an enormous Negro woman, her fat bare arms on the sill, leaned out a window to watch us pass. Behind her was a man in an undershirt and suspenders. He was seated at a table, wearing a hat and eating his breakfast. The train had slowed down and we moved slowly past these people. But now we are just pulling into Pennsylvania Station, and I must put this away and find Nora among all these people.

Sunday, July 21 (10:30 a.m.)

Nora has left for church. She attends a Presbyterian church a few blocks away and was a little put out that I didn't go along with her. But I said I was still too tired. In spite of her kindness and goodwill, Nora is in a state and from time to time I catch her looking at me in a peculiarly guarded way. It's as if she is trying to understand how she could have been so wrong. In her eyes, I am not now what I had seemed to be, and for anyone that can be unsettling. Of course, she must think that I have a lover and she is waiting for me to talk about him. I'm not sure I can bring myself to tell her the truth.

It is good to be alone for a while. Everything about this visit is charged with a peculiar and understandable anxiety, but at the best of times, Nora gets on my nerves and leaves me longing for escape. She met me at the railroad station yesterday morning in her yellow dress and white shoes. How confidently she carries herself among all these strangers! Joking with the taxi driver as she gave him her address. Bare legs flashing. I watched a man looking at her legs as she climbed into the taxi. Her blond hair is much shorter now. She looks younger and prettier than she did when she left Toronto.

After the hugs and sticky kisses she said, "We'll have to get you some lighter things, Clara. My God, you'll cook to death in that suit. It's going to be ninety today." It was already hot as we hurtled along in that taxi through the shadowy streets. At intersections there were bursts of sunlight and a glimpse of the sky.

Nora's apartment is tiny but comfortable. She has three small fans going all the time in this heat. They hum away, a background noise along with sounds from the street. I suppose one gets used to all this. We talked until nearly midnight, but I was too tired even to be civil at times. Nora knew better than to press me for details surrounding my predicament. Our talk was mostly harmless reminiscences, recalling other nights when we lay awake as girls and worried over things I have long forgotten. Nora is growing increasingly sentimental about her childhood and the imaginary simplicities and virtues of village life. Another time I might have been impatient with this fondness for nostalgia, but last night I was too tired. Nora's little bed, by the way, is a novelty. It's called a Murphy bed and folds up into the wall of a closet. It is quite the contraption. At breakfast Nora told me that we are going to Evelyn Dowling's for dinner tonight. Apparently we will then learn what arrangements have been made by her friend.

Monday, July 22 (1:30 p.m.)

Nora left for the studio around ten, and I again have the apartment to myself. I have been feeling a little off in the mornings, and so I enjoy sitting by the window and watching the people pass on the street below. So many different lives with all their attendant joys and woes! Nora's street is mostly small apartment houses (brownstones, she calls them) with cement steps leading up to the front doors. They are only three stories high. Her street is busy enough but much quieter than the next one (Thirty-fourth Street) which is a shopping area.

Last evening we went to Evelyn Dowling's for dinner. She lives in what Nora would call "a swanky part of town." Her place overlooks the big park in the center of the city. It's a spacious apartment with paintings on the walls and hundreds of books. Physically Evelyn is oddly put together: she is short and heavyset but not fat. She looks solid enough to batter down a door. She has a large handsome head and intelligent lively dark eyes. Her hair is short as a man's and she appraises you instantly with a shrewd look. She was wearing an expensive-looking linen suit.

"So you are the sister I've heard so much about! You're taller than I imagined and dark-haired. Not at all like our little blond friend here. Nora tells me you write poetry and you like to read. What are you reading these days?"

I told her that on the train I was reading a story by Chekhov, but also *Startling Detective*. Nora looked askance, but Evelyn Dowling just laughed.

"*Startling Detective!* Good for you. Something sordid once in a while can be bracing. I can't get your sister to read anything but *Photoplay* magazine. But a rattling good account of a farmhouse murder in Kansas is better for you than some syrup about how Myrna Loy can't get through a day without her little dogs."

So direct and unbuttoned. Of course, she had been drinking cocktails before we arrived and I wondered if this aggressive familiarity was really her or just the drink. Nora looked nervous at first. Perhaps she was afraid that Evelyn Dowling and I would not get along; in fact, I found myself liking her very much. She drinks cocktails like water and is always smoking her Camel cigarettes. What a name for a cigarette, I thought as I examined the package! Why Camels? Why not Elephants or Buffalo?

Evelyn has a maid, but she was given the night off because, as Evelyn said later, "One has to be careful about who hears what when one is talking about these arrangements." Nora also enjoys a drink now and so the two of them swigged their gin while they talked about the radio show. In another few weeks Effie is going to be accused of passing a bad check. It will all be a misunderstanding, but the police will become involved and Uncle Jim will suffer a heart attack from all the worry and confusion. Overhearing all this, a stranger might have supposed that they were talking about real people.

During dinner (cold cuts prepared beforehand by the maid) the conversation came around finally to what is in store for me next week.

"You will be in good hands," said Evelyn. "From what I hear, he is one of the best in New York."

He, it turns out, is a doctor, or was. He lost his license because of an addiction to a drug called cocaine. I had never heard of it. "What does such a drug do?" I asked. I had a picture in my mind of an old man smoking opium in a long pipe. I have no idea where such an image came from. Evelyn's reply to my question: "It makes you happier than you have any right to be on this earth."

Sitting there last night in Evelyn Dowling's apartment, watching the sky darken into night and the lights coming on in the buildings across the park, I thought of how naive I am. How little I know of the world at my age! Without Nora or Evelyn, I could not navigate the streets of this enormous, glittering city; without them I would be helpless in the face of this dilemma. I am like a child whose hand must be taken and whose way must be guided and I feel so stupid about it all. I am frightened too, not so much at the thought of this so-called doctor bungling things (I have this childish faith in Evelyn's judgment), but more at the notion that both Nora and I could get into serious trouble. At one point Evelyn said this: "Not to put too fine a point on it, ladies, but we are breaking the laws of the state of New York, and if we are found out, we could all go to jail, so you must be very careful next Friday night."

Then I asked how much all this would cost, but Evelyn only wagged a finger at me. "You are not to worry about that, my dear. You have enough on your mind."

What an ungodly mess I have got myself into!

Thursday, July 25 (11:30 p.m.)

Another hot night and the sound of whirring fans. Cars passing on the street below. Nora is sleeping, splayed across the pullout bed, snoring slightly. She used to sleep like that when we were children. She would push against me, throw a leg across mine. I would kick her and she would whimper in her sleep. The week has been so hot and I have stayed in the apartment reading and listening to the radio. In the evenings we go to the movies. Tonight we saw something called *Shanghai*, Evelyn snorting in disdain throughout at various plot improbabilities. I could not get my mind off tomorrow night. The best thing about going to the movies is "air-conditioning." The lineups are long and tiresome, but once you're inside it's like sitting in an icebox. You can feel your skin drying in the cool air. Of course, at the end of the movie, you must again encounter summer in New York. Even after dark, a thick heat still hangs over the city. Your clothes are again damp and clinging. This afternoon it rained suddenly and violently. The skies opened in a fierce brief downpour. People were running for shelter, holding sodden newspapers over their heads or standing in doorways. I stood by the window and watched the rain beating off the pavement and across the roofs of cars. The street was clogged with taxis and delivery trucks. It was like a tap of warm water suddenly opened. Then it stopped as quickly as it began and the road and sidewalks hissed and steamed. Yellow sunlight splashed across the glistening pavement.

Evelyn has given me several books of poetry by American women: Edna St. Vincent Millay, Marianne Moore, Louise Bogan. She also gave me some novels by Hemingway and Lewis and Thomas Wolfe, so I have plenty to read next week when I am recovering from whatever happens to me tomorrow night. Evelyn is a tough little bulldog of a woman and so clever and well read. She has a good heart. I have never met anyone like her. Nora is after me to come with her to the studio to see how they put the play on and I will one day, but not now, I am too nervous. I just want to read or listen to the radio. Nora returns in the late afternoon and before supper she likes a glass of beer and a cigarette. She drinks her beer while reading aloud from the script for the next day's program, walking back and forth from the front window to the kitchen with the cigarette in her mouth. She could strike one as very sexual in this pose. Strong good legs and bosom, and looking at her I wonder if there is a man in her life these days. There was always someone "on the fringes" in Toronto. The other day she made a passing reference to some "little recent heartbreak."

Saturday, July 27

Nora has gone shopping, thank heaven, and I am at last alone. She is driving me to distraction with her fussing. Since last night I have felt like screaming. It's worse than the actual pain between my legs.

"Are you sure you are going to be okay if I step out?"

"Yes, yes of course, Nora."

"Let me fix that pillow. Can I get you anything? How about a glass of ice water or some tea?"

The urge to scream is never far below the surface. It's a matter of control and small smiles.

"Nora, please, I'm fine. Just get on with what you're doing."

"You're sure now?"

"Yes, yes, I'm sure."

I love her, I really do, but she irritates me so easily. It was ever thus and ever will be, I suppose.

Now I must try to set down what happened last night. We were told to be at a certain address at eleven o'clock. It was up in a Negro section of the city called Harlem. It was a long taxi ride on a hot night with heat lightning. I counted the streets as the warm air from the open windows rushed against our faces. We kept the windows open because it was so stuffy in the car, but we had to hold on to our hats, mine a little Robin Hood thing that Nora had loaned me, and hers, a kind of fedora that mostly concealed her face. Nora had memorized the address because there was to be no evidence of an address on paper. In case we were found out, I imagine.

At 132nd Street we stopped for a red light and Nora pointed to a long lineup in front of a dance club. They were mostly white people.

"I've been to that club," Nora whispered. "They have wonderful jazz music."

The taxi driver misinterpreted her whispering and asked if we wanted to get out at that intersection, but Nora said, "No, please drive on to the address I gave you."

I wondered what the driver thought we were about, two white women alone in that part of the city at night. Or did he guess? Perhaps he had transported other hapless creatures like myself across his River Styx. All I could see of my Charon was a thick neck and a flat leather cap covered with union buttons.

The streets of Harlem were filled even at this late hour: a slow moving parade of dark people. I could smell fried meat and hear dance band music from the doorways of clubs. Clusters of men stood on street corners smoking cigarettes and talking to the women passing by in their brightly colored dresses. On this summer night, the people seemed to live on the street. Others leaned out windows and called down to passersby. It was all good-natured, a kind of carnival, and I could have enjoyed looking out at it under different circumstances. Beside me, Nora was twisting a handkerchief and I felt sorry that she had been dragged into this with me.

We turned down a side street and the driver had trouble with the number. He had to get out of the car and look at a darkened storefront. We were off the main avenue now and it was quiet and empty on that street. When he came back to the car, the driver said, "I'm not crazy about walking around up here." He was cross with us. We drove another block and stopped in front of a building. To give him his due, the driver got out again and checked the address. "This is it," he said. Nora paid him and she must have been generous because he thanked her before leaving.

So the taxi went down the street and we stood in front of the building, watching the taillights disappear. Nora pressed a buzzer and almost immediately a light appeared in the hallway. It was as if someone had been waiting there in the dark for us. The door was opened by a slender, lightly colored Negress. She might have been pretty had her face not been so badly pitted by some disease, chicken pox perhaps. Her cheeks were terribly scored and it made her look severe and disapproving. She turned out the hallway light and led us without a word to a small elevator, a kind of brass cage scarcely big enough for three. The woman had a sour winey smell to her. The elevator took us up to the third floor and we went down a hallway past office doors with frosted glass windows with the names of notaries and chiropractors and loan agencies. The shabbiness of the place distressed me; I had expected more from Evelyn's Park Avenue doctor. I saw myself dying horribly on a table of bloodied sheets behind one of those doors. To calm myself I returned to this thought: When this is over I can go back to my street and my house; I will feel again the coolness under the trees on my veranda; on rainy autumn nights I will enjoy the warmth of my kitchen.

The Negress opened a door that had no name on the glass and showed us into a small room which looked very like a doctor's or dentist's office. Wooden chairs. A bench with armrests. Venetian blinds. A pile of *National Geographic* magazines on a low table. A lamp in the corner casting a little yellow light. The window was partly open and I could smell the soft rank air from the alley below and hear music from a radio. After the Negress left, Nora and I sat on the wooden bench and she held my hand.

"Are you all right?" she whispered.

"Yes, I'm fine," I answered.

We could hear dance band music from somewhere and a little thunder and then it rained for a few minutes, just a shower. Nora whispered the names of the songs as they were played on the radio. She said it was a program she heard some nights. She told me she liked to lie in bed and listen to the dance band music that came from the big hotels downtown. She whispered all this to me hurriedly as though she were afraid she would run out of time before she could tell me these things about herself. And so she named the songs as they were played on the radio. "Under a Blanket of Blue," "The Touch of Your Hand," "Japanese Sandman." There was a lovely and sordid wistfulness to all this. The soft thundery air and the rain, the dance tunes. It seemed to infect Nora like a fever and she began to cry. I felt a catch in my own throat. Nora pressed the handkerchief to her eyes.

"This is so awful," she said.

"Yes, it is," I said.

I did feel such regret for getting her into all this. If we were found out, her career in radio would be over; there would be a terrible scandal and we would both be in disgrace. It was so horrible and yet we had to see it through. I felt a kind of despair then that passed between us. I think we both felt it. Perhaps it had to do with other feelings that must accompany this kind of experience. The feeling that something was about to be broken. When all was said and done, a human life or the beginning of one was going to be ended. The tramp's child and mine. I felt something about that. I don't know. I don't want to think about it right now. Sitting there on that bench, I wanted to tell Nora how it all came about. I wanted to tell her how the tramp had seized my wrists and whirled me about and flung his suit coat into the grass; how he had fallen on top of me after I stumbled and how he did what he did to me and how the walleyed boy had sat on the railway track and watched us. I wanted to tell her how impossible it would be for me to bear the offspring of such a man and perhaps I almost began to blurt out something. I think I said, "Nora, let me tell you," or "Nora, I want to tell you," but then we heard voices in the hallway, a man's and a woman's, and the door opened. A tall elderly man came briskly into the room and passed us. He barely glanced our way as he opened the door to the inner office. He had taken off his hat and was shaking the rain from it. I saw that he had a head of beautiful thick white hair and a slight stoop. A woman wearing a nurse's uniform then came into the room and smiled at us. She was stout, about fifty, with a broad, pleasant face.

"Hello there," she said. "Now which one of you is the patient?"

Nora seemed frozen with terror or grief, tongue-tied. I said, "I am."

The woman (was she really a nurse, I wondered) smiled again.

"That's fine then. Come along now, dear. The doctor will see you."

Nora squeezed my hand and I stood up and followed the woman into the room. There was a table and on it was a white sheet. Everything looked quite clean and I was grateful for this. The doctor's back was to me. I saw his rounded shoulders as he washed his hands at a sink in the corner. He had taken off his suit coat and was in his shirtsleeves. The woman took me behind a screen and handed me a cotton smock.

"Take all your clothes off, dear, and put this on. How far along are you now?"

I told her and she patted my arm.

"That's all right then. The doctor will look after things for you."

She was really very nice with her broad amiable face. Someone's grandmother, I suppose. So I was barefoot and naked beneath the cotton gown and I thought, I am dealing with this and it will soon be over and I can return to my life in Whitfield and no one will ever know what happened to me on that Saturday afternoon. Even the details will fade in time. Now and then in the years ahead, the memory will recur in dreams, and awaken me, or when I am an old woman, parting a bedroom curtain on a spring day, looking down on Church Street. But at least I will be able to live around those memories. The event will not have ruined everything. This is how I thought last night and it helped as I lay on the table. The doctor was still at the sink and I looked sideways at his rounded shoulders and silvery hair. Some terrible needs had brought him to this room by the barbecue restaurants and dance halls. I tried to imagine giving your life over to something like drugs or alcohol. How could it happen?

When he approached the sheeted table he wore a mask across his face, and all I could see was the silvery hair and the blue eyes and the large white hands. The woman too had now put on a little mask to cover her mouth and nose and so they stood above me. The doctor said nothing, but he patted my shoulder and nodded to the woman.

"Now we're going to give you something to make you sleep, dear, and when you wake up, you'll be as good as new," she said.

How could I ever be as good as new, I thought? She was only trying to make me feel more comfortable. I could see that, and I now had confidence in these strangers from another country who were going to make things right again in my life. The woman had placed a rubber cup over my mouth and nose and I felt suddenly closed in, mildly panicked.

"Breathe deeply, dear," she said. "Breathe deeply and count along with me. Remember when you were a little girl and skipped with your friends? One, two, buckle my shoe. Three, four, shut the door. Five, six, pick up sticks."

She was wrong about my childhood. I hated skipping. I used to watch the other girls, but I never joined in though I remember the songs. I wanted to tell the woman that she had misread me; that I was not that kind of child at all. I was too peculiar and aloof. I wanted to tell her all that, but instead, when I opened my eyes, Nora was holding my hand. For several moments I had no idea where I was, and Nora's voice seemed to come from the end of a long tunnel. It sounded so hollow and distant, though I heard every word distinctly.

"It's all right, Clara. It's all over now. We'll be going home in a few minutes."

I was looking up at her pale worried face. "Have they gone?" I asked.

"Yes," she said. "It's all over. The colored woman is going to call a cab for us. You must be very careful. There'll be some bleeding. We have to watch for hemorrhaging though the nurse said you'll be fine if you're careful. Plenty of bedrest for the next week, she said."

Then she left and I could hear her talking to the colored woman. I had a dull ache between my legs and there were napkins there. So the tramp's seed had been scraped from me. I would not bring his child into the world, but I could not help thinking what a curious mixture it would have been. Still I felt lighter and saw my life as filled now with possibilities.

The murmuring voices made me want to return to sleep, but Nora and the Negress came over to the table and helped me to my feet. I felt a rush of blood from within, as if I were a vessel of fluids that had been suddenly tipped and was now spilling. A faint sickness overtook me then as I sat on the edge of the table. I told myself that the next few hours would be difficult but they would have to be endured. There is so much to endure. Father used to say that. "You have to put up with things," he would say. "Every day brings something to put up with."

So, we walked slowly through the empty dark office building. Nora with her hat pulled down holding on to one of my arms and the Negress with her frowning pockmarked face and winey smell holding on to the other. We made our way into that cramped cage of an elevator and down to the first floor and out to the street where a taxi was waiting. The air had cooled and there was a faint lightness in the sky between the buildings. I was startled by that. It was nearly daybreak. Nora told me it was half past four. I was grateful to sit down and glad that I was well bandaged, for I didn't want to soil the seat of the taxi. We drove down Seventh Avenue in that half darkness between the end of night and the beginning of day. At the street intersections, the traffic lights were blinking and the driver didn't stop. There were almost no cars now, only a few taxis. I saw some colored people gathered outside a club and a man in shirtsleeves and a derby hat sitting on a curb: down a side street an old peddler was adjusting the harness of his horse and wagon. By the lighted windows of all-night restaurants, people were eating and looking out at the street. Those are some things I saw as we drove downtown early this morning.

Friday, August 2

A week of rest and recovery. I have been reading Louise Bogan's poetry and Thomas Wolfe's new novel *Of Time and the River*. It's very good though I don't like it as well as *Look Homeward, Angel.*

In the afternoons I listen to Nora's program. How strange to hear her voice on the radio! It is Nora, of course, but then it isn't. After a few minutes she is someone else, a woman named Alice Dale, likable and wise, concerned about her headstrong younger sister who has fallen in love with a teacher at the business school where she is training to be a secretary. The teacher is married, but Effie is determined to be "with the man I love." There is a quarrel at the kitchen table and the kindly old aunt and uncle are fretting after the young woman storms out of the house. The announcer with his rich beautiful American voice then poses a question and offers an invitation.

"Will Alice's heartfelt talk with the young and willful Effie save her sister from a disastrous turning in her life? Tune in again tomorrow when the makers of Sunrise, the soap that awakens your skin, invite you to walk once again past the white picket fences and front porches of Meadowvale to 'The House on Chestnut Street.'"

And then Elgar's *Salut D'Amour* played on the organ. It is surely all nonsense and yet I could see the house, the curtains on the windows, the aunt and uncle at the kitchen table. And Nora is utterly convincing as Alice Dale. She is very, very good.

Monday, August 5

Beginning to feel more myself again. Yesterday Nora, E.D. and I spent the afternoon in Central Park. A bright day but it has cooled off in New York, and we sat on benches under the trees eating ice cream, watching strolling families and lovers. Nora wants me to stay until the middle of the month, but I am determined to go home next week. I was happy there under the trees listening to Nora and E.D. talk about their program, Evelyn grinding a cigarette under her shoe and lighting another, as she talks about putting the listeners through "the emotional wringer."

Everything is grist to her mill as I suppose it is for anyone who writes, whether it's poetry or radio serials. E.D.: "Did you see that piece in yesterday's *Herald Trib*? About the woman who stole from the collection plate to buy groceries? Just a small piece on the back pages. This happened somewhere in Ohio. They were going to arrest her, but someone intervened. I'd like to work something like that in. A woman in the town is hard up and tries to steal something from the offering plate. Maybe her husband is sick. Or better still, why not have her young and unmarried and pregnant." E.D. gave me a wry look and shrugged. "So she's desperate. And Alice is the only one who sees her steal the money. She follows her from church and discovers she's living in some ratty place. Brings her back to Aunt Mary and Uncle Jim. A temporary thing, but she's a good kid. Her name is Margery or Madeline. Something like that. Effie gets jealous because of all the attention. What do you think, beauty?" We get up and walk under the dappled sunlight, peering through the leaves, and talk some more about this Margery or Madeline.

Wednesday, August 7

Today I went along with Nora to the studio at Rockefeller Center. The actors stand in front of microphones with their play scripts. Behind a glass partition, a man in short sleeves signals them and oversees things. Other men open and close doors, use wooden blocks, tread on light steps, play recordings of automobile engines. It all looks so contrived and pedestrian, and yet from the loudspeaker come the sounds and voices of people in this mythical town. When you close your eyes, as I did for a moment, you can see them clearly. It's a kind of auditory legerdemain. Nora looked pretty and capable standing with her script before the microphone in a polka-dot dress and white shoes. The program's announcer kept looking at her. He is perhaps in his late thirties and has the weak, handsome face of a matinee idol. He couldn't take his eyes off Nora, and looking at him, I wondered if there was something going on between them.

Sunday, August 11

Yesterday Nora took me to the Automat on Forty-second Street. It is an enormous restaurant with hundreds of tables but the food is kept in locked glass cases along the walls. To get your sandwich or piece of pie, you must insert a nickel or dime into a slot. I found it a very strange way to eat, but New Yorkers seem to take to this kind of thing as if it were perfectly routine. I wonder if all restaurants will be like this in ten years.

Later we went to Radio City Music Hall and saw a vaudeville show and a picture. Then we talked far into the night, lying there side by side in her funny little pullout bed. Nora is doing well down here, but she is also discontented. Turning thirty has left her troubled; she would like to marry and have children before it is too late. She hinted that she and the announcer have been "flirting" a bit. Nothing serious. Besides, he's married and so that could lead nowhere. At one point, Nora got up for a glass of water and then returned, falling into bed and staring at the ceiling as though entirely fed up with things. I remember her doing this at home after an argument with Father: storming into the room and collapsing on the bed, her sudden weight jarring the book I was reading. Last night as I lay there, she seemed embittered. I am going home on Monday and she may have felt (and I could hardly blame her) that in return for all she had done, she was at least owed an explanation. She said, "I wonder what I would do if it happened to me."

In the light from the window overlooking the street, I could see her angry little pout; she used to put on the same face when she felt unjustly dealt with by Father.

"Men just walk away from these things and leave the dirty work to us. I'll bet the bastard who got you pregnant is now snoring away beside his little wife. He didn't have to take a taxi up into darkytown in the middle of the night, did he?" I could see she wanted me to reveal the identity of the villain. But my heart was not open to confession. I wasn't about to tell Nora the sordid details of my encounter with the tramp. She wanted a love story: assignations, letters, meeting in cars on country roads, whispered embraces and the fluttering of hearts in hopeless passion. But since it wasn't like that, the tale was beyond me.

"One day, Nora," I said, "I will tell you all about it."

Whitfield, Ontario
Saturday, August 17, 1935

Dear Nora,
I wanted to write you before this but I have been busy with the house (dusty) and the yard (untidy), though Mr. Bryden thoughtfully cut the grass in my absence. I also overworked myself a bit and for a little while on Thursday felt feverish and faint. So I took to my bed and pretended that I was merely enduring "the vapors" of a spinster lady in her middle years. Now, however, I'm feeling hale again. You will find enclosed a money order for my train fare to New York and back. Again, I cashed in the sleeping-car ticket so that amount is included as well.

How can I begin to thank you for everything you've done over the past month? I'm certain that you and Evelyn Dowling literally saved me from ruin. I can't imagine what would have become of me without your help. So, Nora, I am in your debt now and forever.

Everyone in the village has plucked me by the sleeve at the post office or butcher shop to ask about my trip to New York City. It has made me, at least temporarily, quite the exotic traveler. Everyone is agog (don't get to use that word very often) when I tell them that you are now on the radio in New York. My, how that impresses them! Cora Macfarlane: "I always thought Nora would make something of herself. I said that to people when she used to do those nice recitations at the Christmas concerts. And sing? Why she had a voice like a bird!" So there you are, a heroine in your hometown. Everyone wants to know when they can hear your program and I said I thought that it might be heard sometime this fall through one of the Toronto stations. Was I right about that?

My trip, of course, made today's *Herald* under the rubric of *Whitfield Notes*. Here it is in all its glory!

> Miss Clara Callan has returned after spending the summer weeks visiting her sister Nora in New York City. Miss Nora Callan is now appearing in the radio show "The Home on Chestnut Street."

Well, they got some of it right anyway. In the post office yesterday, the odious Ida Atkins pestered me to write something for the church bulletin. "My impressions of New York City." I wonder what she would think if I were to describe a certain hot and thundery Friday night in Harlem. I could, of course, mention that Harlem is named after a city in Holland (they enjoy such details), but I didn't see any Dutchmen that night, did you?

As you can tell, I'm feeling quite gay and buoyant. What happened to me, Nora, was such a burden, and now that it's been lifted, I feel renewed and eager to get on with things: to get back to school, to ordinary routines, to life however pedestrian and mundane it might be. I know that in a few weeks (or a few days) I will sink, like everyone else, into the petty griping that accompanies daily life wherever it is lived. But right now I take delight in waking, in the opening petals of a flower, in playing my piano; everything is charged with a special music. With what I might call "The Perfectly Ordinary Day." I had hoped to write a poem about how it takes deliverance from disaster to make us feel grateful for that perfectly ordinary day. But alas, I can't seem to find the words. Well never mind—if I can't write poetry, at least perhaps I can try to think and feel like a poet.

I must make some supper now and then put my feet up. The

summer is drawing to a close. The Exhibition opens a week from today and I have agreed to go with the ladies on the twenty-ninth for an outing. But I do enjoy the Ex. Remember when Father would take us for the day? I began to look forward to it as soon as school was out. About the middle of August has always been the happiest time in the calendar for me. Anyway, we are going down on the twenty-ninth for the day.

I shall drop E.D. a note tomorrow and thank her for everything she did. I found her rather remarkable, though her destructive habits were a little unnerving to a puritan bumpkin like me. From the bottom of my heart, Nora, thank you again for everything.

Clara

Whitfield, Ontario
Sunday, August 18, 1935

Dear Evelyn,
I should have written before this, but I have spent the last week trying "to put my house in order." I do, however, want to thank you for everything. I really don't know what I would have done without you and Nora. I live in a village of six hundred souls and of course everyone knows your business. I simply could not have survived here and this is my home; this is where I live and I can't see myself anywhere else. So, I am extremely grateful to you for your help and generosity.

I suppose I may have struck you as a bit standoffish, but you can put that down partly at least to the unusual circumstances surrounding my visit. I am not as timid as I may have appeared, though I am the older, quieter, more reserved one in the family. Still you mustn't necessarily think of me as a dry spinster schoolteacher. Oh, I would like to live at least in part like some of the people I read about, perhaps like Madame Bovary or poor Anna Karenina. But I have no courage for those kinds of adventures and, more important, little opportunity, despite what happened to me.

I think Nora is very fortunate to have you as a friend. Thank you too for the meals and the flowers and the books. I particularly enjoyed Louise Bogan's poetry. How I wish I could write like her! But I seem only to have the impulses and sensibility of a poet; I merely lack that other thing—what is it called? Oh yes. Talent!

Thank you again, Evelyn, for everything and do take of yourself.

Sincerely, Clara Callan

P.S. Are you absolutely sure that I can't send you some money? It must have cost a good deal, and I feel bad about your paying for it all.

Sunday, August 25

I was reading on this warm, still afternoon when a cicada began to shriek. It was not the insect's usual cry from the trees, but something else, urgent and piercing. The sound of a creature imperiled. When I went around to the side of the house, I saw it in the sparrow's mouth. The bird flew off at once, carrying aloft the insect's rasping death cry. For a moment, I heard it in the big maple tree in front of the Brydens' and then it was all drowsy silence once more. What a monster the sparrow must seem to the insect! I wonder what Emily Dickinson would have made of this. She would have written a poem about it. Sitting at her little bedroom desk, dipping her pen into the inkwell and imagining what it would be like to be a cicada in a sparrow's bill.

Monday, August 26

I met Marion outside the post office today. She is just back from the cottage and was full of questions, a little too excited to wait for answers.

"Did you see any radio shows in New York, Clara?"

"Well, yes. As a matter of fact—"

"Rudy Vallee is at the Exhibition. Wouldn't it be something to get in to see him?"

"Well, I don't know—"

"I can hardly wait for Thursday."

Are the ladies all going to hear Rudy Vallee? It seems improbable.

Friday, August 30 (1:30 a.m.)

A remarkable thing happened only a few hours ago. I saw the tramp. I feel like Hamlet when his father's ghost revealed the truth about his death. What did the prince say?

O villain, villain, smiling damned villain!
My tables—meet it is I set it down
That one may smile and smile and be a villain.

And I saw him smiling tonight at the Exhibition grounds. On the midway. He was working at the Ferris wheel, hopping about with an oil can in that nimble-gaited way of his, agile and quick as a monkey among the gears and levers of the machinery, chattering to the man operating the engine. I stood transfixed, my view blocked now and then by passersby, but there he was again, the sharp and flinty profile in flat cap and overalls. It was him all right and I could scarcely breathe for a moment. This was eight o'clock or nine o'clock, I don't know. I was too beside myself at the sight of him yapping away at the other man. Telling some kind of story or joke. Marion wanted to see Rudy Vallee. I told her the lineup was a mile long and we'd never get in, but I felt sorry for her too. We had come down to the midway at my behest. Marion was prepared to humor me if I would go along with her afterward to hear the crooner. The others were still in the buildings, inspecting the washing machines and vacuum cleaners. But I have always loved the midway. Even when I was a child, Father would indulge me, though he hated the whole business. Its seedy charms were lost on him and lost on Marion too. But she had been stalwart about it and so we had walked under the lights by the tents with the painted dwarfs, and the Giant Man-Killing Octopus, the chimpanzees in checkered suits, and the fellow who spoke for Eno, the Turtle Boy: "He walks, he talks, he crawls on his belly like a reptile." I was happy there in my late-summer happiness, there among those sordid wonders.

And Marion, game to the end, had hung on to me through all this, her bad foot doubtless tired and throbbing. Now she wanted to hear her singer, but I was steadfast too, rooted to the ground by the Ferris wheel, watching the tramp leap across the guy ropes and poke at the engine with his oiling can.

The great wheel jolted to a halt, the seats rocking back and forth, and I looked up at the August sky darkening now, astonished anew that he was there. My tramp, my nightmare, and only yards away. The other man was lighting his pipe and then he eased the lever forward, and the wheel again began to move. Then stopped, and two girls got out, their seat taken by a young man and his sweetheart. The wheel again churned forward and I heard the tramp say something to the engine man, but his words were lost in the grinding noise of the machinery. Marion was tugging at my arm like a cranky child, but I said to her, "Let's take a ride on the Ferris wheel." I might just as well have suggested we take off our clothes and jump into Lake Ontario.

"Clara, I'd be frightened to death in that thing."

I told her I was tired and wanted to sit down for a while, hoping thereby to make her feel stronger and whole; I was the flagging one, not she.

"We can't, Clara. We'll be late for his second show."

But I was having none of it. I had seen the tramp and my heart was racing. "Very well, I'll go by myself."

"Clara, what's got into you anyway?"

"I want to ride on the big wheel."

And so I joined the lineup and there was nothing Marion could do but accompany me. I knew she was too timid to stand by herself in the midway. So we were settled finally by a rough-looking young man into a swaying seat. He dropped the safety bar across the front, and we were carried aloft with Marion's fingers digging into my arm and her cries of "Oh! Oh!" accompanying us skyward. She was frightened, of course, but confounded too. Imagine that such things should come to pass! I guessed that that was what was going through her mind. And I too was astounded to find myself there wheeling around in the sky. At the summit we plunged, as we had to do, and Marion screamed.

Then we rose again, passing the tramp who was wiping his hands on a piece of waste and staring out at the crowd. Looking down at him as we climbed, I wondered what I could do about it. What could be done about the tramp? I concluded that nothing could be done. There he was, but the time for doing anything had long passed. Nothing could now connect that man with what had happened to me three months ago by the railway tracks near Whitfield, Ontario. It was my fault entirely because I chose not to tell anyone, and we must live by our choices. The tramp would carry on with his various labors, laughing and joking with his wide monkey mouth. Not even divine retribution would strike his black heart.

Those were my thoughts as the rough-looking fellow lifted the bar and helped us onto the platform. Marion was delighted with her adventure.

"That was something, wasn't it, Clara? I never thought I'd see the day when you'd get me on that thing."

As we walked away, I looked back once more at the tramp who was smoking a cigarette and coiling a length of rope, chattering again at the engine man. The lineup for the second Rudy Vallee show was impossible; it snaked across the fairgrounds with no end in sight, mostly young people. Marion and I had ten or fifteen years on them and I felt foolish. They had set up loudspeakers so we could hear the great man singing about love, forever and ever. Marion was stoic about not seeing him and I think that her foot was sore. We joined the others at the Food Building and drove on home arriving just an hour ago.

I don't know why I did what I did yesterday. What was I hoping to accomplish? Still I did it. I took the train down to Toronto and returned to the Exhibition. It is Labor Day weekend and so it was very busy. By late morning the buildings and fairgrounds were jammed. But no sign of the tramp. I walked by the Ferris wheel and the pipe-smoking man was at his levers, but he had another fellow helping him. Yet it was early and I wondered if the tramp came to work late in the day. So I left and spent some time in the Automotive Building, admiring the new motorcars and listening to men ask questions about them. Everyone stood abashed and respectful before these gleaming machines, and the salesmen in their blazers had set aside their newspapers to answer the hesitant questions about torque and horsepower. They knew that none of the men asking could afford a new Packard or Studebaker, but they were good-natured fellows and fielded all questions.

In the early afternoon I returned to the Ferris wheel, filled now with screaming youngsters circling in the gray close air. Still no tramp, but I was determined to wait. Around two o'clock the pipe-smoking man was replaced by another and made his way through the crowd. I hurried after him along a path behind the sideshow tents. I could hear the shuffling feet and the murmuring voices from the other side of the canvas as people moved past the cages of snakes and monkeys. I called out, "Excuse me," and he turned a surly face my way. I was sympathetic to his confused and angry look which seemed to say, who are you and what is it now? He was a man used to trouble but tired of it all the same. Yet I could see his surprise at the respectable-looking woman standing behind the monkey tent. I was surely no carnival tart. He took the pipe from his mouth, the baffled, unfriendly face composed into a stare.

"I'm sorry to bother you," I said. "I'm looking for a man who might be working at the Ferris wheel and I noticed you there a moment ago. I am a nurse and the man's sister is a patient at the hospital where I work. The woman is gravely ill. She has no family except her brother and she has expressed a desire to see him. He's in his thirties, dark-haired, with a wide mouth. A friendly man, according to the woman, and filled with stories. She told me he was going to look for work at the Ferris wheel down here. That's what she told me. It's really very important that he come to the hospital to see her before it's too late. Can you help me?"

This outlandish story had presented itself as I was calling to the man. I don't know where it came from. Who knows where such tales abide and why they make their appearance on demand? He continued to stare at me.

"I don't know anybody like that," he began, "unless you mean the fellow who worked with me yesterday. Charlie! An awful gabber. I couldn't shut him up. Is that who you mean?"

"Yes," I said, "Charlie. That's his name. Can you tell me where he lives? He moves around a lot according to his sister. Will he be back to work today?"

The man sucked on his pipe.

"No, no, no. He just came by yesterday morning and asked if there was any work. Turned out my helper was sick so I took this man for the day. But he wasn't much good. I paid him off last night. He told me he knew all about four-stroke engines. Why, that man didn't know any more about four-stroke engines than probably you do. I had to let him go. About all he could do was use an oil can. A comical fellow. Liked to talk."

The pipe-smoking man didn't know anything more about Charlie.

"Not even his last name?"

"Nope. He just came by and I took him because I needed someone. But like I said, he wasn't much good."

So there was nothing more to be done, and I may have felt some relief in that. On the train home I thought of how foolish I had been to go back there and hope that I could find something useful. And what if I had? What could I have done? Then I started thinking that maybe it wasn't the tramp at all; maybe my eyes had played tricks on me in the summer darkness of Friday night. All the way home I doubted whether I had really seen the tramp, and it made me feel better about not being able to do anything. Yet now I really do believe it was him.

135 East 33rd Street
New York
August 24, 1935

Dear Clara,

Thanks for your letter. For goodness' sake, take it easy on yourself. You shouldn't be cleaning a house after what you went through. Why don't you hire some girl in the village to help you with that kind of thing? Anyway, thanks for the money for the train ticket, but it really wasn't necessary. For the life of me, I can't understand what you've got against sleeping on a train.

I am glad to hear, however, that you are feeling "gay and buoyant" because I'd heard that women often become depressed after those operations. So I hope the blues don't hit you. I suppose you're just glad that it's all over, and I can certainly understand that. You've always kept everything to yourself, that's your nature of course and I can appreciate that. But I just hope that you don't keep everything bottled up forever. Sometimes you have to talk about what happened or it will just kind of fester inside you. What I'm thinking about here is the man. I hope you are over him and don't become involved again. After what you went through, the heel doesn't deserve another chance, so I hope you will take that advice in the spirit in which it is offered.

I can imagine the fuss the people in Whitfield made about your visit to New York. If they only knew the reason, huh! Anyway, Cora Macfarlane is full of it. That woman never had a kind word to say about me when I was going to school. She always thought I would come to no good. Not for a moment would she ever have believed that

"I would someday make something of myself." What baloney! She was always complaining to Father that I was bothering her Ralphie. You remember Ralph Macfarlane? That drip! He used to sit beside me and stare at my legs. But his mother was so worried about her Ralphie. He is in Toronto now, isn't he? And married? It makes you wonder.

By the way, and I meant to say this right off the bat—we are going full network next month and the agency has sold the program to a number of Canadian stations including Toronto, though I can't remember which one. So, you can tell the good folks in Whitfield that they can tune me in and let Cora Macfarlane put that in her pipe and smoke it!!!

Have to go now. Les is taking me to the new Ginger Rogers movie at the Loew's. I get such a kick out of looking at her in those gorgeous gowns. You're probably thinking that it's now my turn to get mixed up with a married guy, but don't worry, I've been burned before. This is just a date. Once in a while it's nice to go out with a man. I like the smell of their shaving lotion and the way they can steer you through a crowd. Those are little things I miss. Anyway this is not serious. I told Les that it's just a friendly date and not to get his hopes up for anything "hot and heavy." Please take care of yourself, sister!

Love, Nora

P.S. I was talking to Evelyn and she said that it might be a good idea for you to have some kind of examination in a few weeks. Just to make sure everything is okay "down in the wheelhouse," as she puts it. Maybe you could go to Toronto and have that done. It's always better to be safe than sorry.

San Remo Apts.
1100 Central Park West
N.Y.C.
25/8/35

Dear Clara Callan,
My, aren't we formal and "standoffish" when we apply our signatures to letters to friends! Well, Clara Callan, I am glad that you are safely back in your little village of "six hundred souls" and are busy "putting things in order." Why do I imagine that you spend a good deal of time "putting things in order." Not that I couldn't use a little bit of that around here (thank God for Eunice). But you do strike me as the type of gal who is inordinately fond of tidiness, though obviously you have an intriguing secret life.

Never mind, I am only kidding. This is just old half-sloshed Evelyn speaking and you mustn't take offense. Let me just say this and I mean it. I very much enjoyed meeting you even under the difficult circumstances surrounding your visit. Yes, you are a tidy severe person and English or Canadian or Canadian-English or something. But you are also quite a nice person and the funny thing is you don't realize it. I hope you have been told by someone besides me just how nice you really are. There now, you are shocked, but you shouldn't be. You see yourself as the dry spinster schoolteacher, but you are obviously much more than that and you should know it. What do you do for amusement on, say, a Wednesday night in that village?

You and that sister of yours! What a pair! And how different! Yet you complement each other so remarkably well. Let me tell you about Nora and me since I could see by your furrowed brow that you were trying to puzzle out what was going on between us. Nora is beautiful in her own way; she turns men's heads, and women's too, believe me. She is also a wonderful trooper with the proverbial heart of gold. She is tough but innocent. Of course, she can be an utter birdbrain. She is far too simplistic and actually believes in the stuff I write for her. She thinks it helps a lot of people get through their day, and for all I know, she may be right, though God help the nation if she is. But Nora is also shrewd and honest. The radio business is filled with ambitious but dishonest people, but even the most corroded hearts down here like your sister.

Never sell Nora short! I saw you looking at her a few times and probably thinking, "My, how my sister has become a vulgar little American broad!" Of course, you wouldn't have put it in so many words, but you know what I mean. And yes, it's easy to see Nora as just a pretty little thing acting in this dopey radio show for housewives. But the fact is that she puts so much of her own goodness (I can think of no other word) into those fifteen minutes every day, that the damn thing sounds almost authentic. Innocence like that can be truly frightening. Well, I guess you can now see why I am so fond of her.

Now to other things. I'm glad you enjoyed the poetry books. I like Bogan too. She writes with a clear unsentimental voice and that is what appeals to me in her work. Millay's latest poems are a little spongy for my taste. You would probably enjoy Elinor Wylie. And let's not forget the boys! How about Eliot and Pound? Have you read anything by them? Or Wallace Stevens? He's interesting and intricate. A little cerebral for me but he'll put your brain to work. Maybe you could look for some of their stuff in Toronto. What a funny name for a city by the way! Is it Indian or what? And how far away from this city are you? Nora keeps reminding me that Canadians do not live in the bush, and of course I realize that, but I just wondered how close you were to bookstores and concerts and things like that. I was only up to Canada once. I was twelve. Good Lord, that was thirty-five years ago! My father, a kind, gentle wonderful man (unfortunately I take after my mother), took me up to Montreal on the train and then we had a boat ride down the St. Lawrence River. We stayed in a big hotel on a cliffside in Quebec City and I thought it was all thoroughly enchanting. It was like living in a castle and the French-Canadian maids were so nice to me, though I'm sure I must have been an awful brat. But that's my only experience of your fair country. Perhaps one of these days I will get up to that village of yours and see how it matches Meadowvale, U.S.A.

Allow me one last word. I was only too glad to help out last month and not for a moment should you feel indebted. As kindly old Aunt Mary says, "What are friends for after all?" Keep in touch, Clara Callan.

Love, Evelyn

P.S. I don't know if your sister has told you, but we'll be on the Canadian airwaves next month. Further evidence (as if we needed it) of the decline of Western civilization.

Friday, September 5

The first week of school in, and as I left, Milton was whistling in his office, happy to have the first few days over and done with. Milton is looking tanned and robust from his summer at the cottage, and he seems altogether more confident than he did this time last year.

Met Ella Miles who was moping in the schoolyard. She has not been happy in Milton's classes these past two years, and now it seems customary for her to begin each September with a litany of complaints about Milton's teaching, followed by a carol to those rapturous days when she sat at the front of my Senior Second row. Those days, of course, were not as blissful as Ella remembers, and she often tried my patience. Ella has a nasty side, a cruel spirit, though I chose to overlook it most of the time because she loved words and she wanted so much to please me. Perhaps I felt sorry for her and her mother working at McDermott's, dusting those coffins and throwing out the dead flowers. There is no doubt about it; Ella was a favorite and I let her get away with things.

"Do you remember, Miss Callan, when I won the Recitation Prize?"

"Indeed I do, Ella." And I did.

Whither, O splendid ship, thy white sails crowding,
Leaning against the bosom of the urgent West,

That fearest nor sea rising, nor sky clouding
Whither away, fair rover, and why thy quest?

Twenty-four such lines delivered with proper emphasis and without error in the town hall on a hot June night. No mean feat for a ten-year-old, and she has never forgotten the excitement of winning something.

"I liked your classes so much, Miss Callan. I wish you taught the senior forms instead of Mr. McKay."

But Ella is no longer the blond little girl with the scruffy ears who likes reading poems and writing stories about animals. Behind the simple dress, a girl is turning into a woman. I could see it too in her pale bitter look, that power to bestow or withhold. Already a little sexual creature. She will be a handful for Milton this year.

Whitfield, Ontario
Sunday, September 8, 1935

Dear Evelyn,

It was good to hear from you. I suppose you are right. I have always treated Nora a little too disdainfully, in the manner of older sisters everywhere, but perhaps because of my nature which leans toward the judgmental. I always thought Nora's work in radio shops and so on was not as high-minded as teaching. I'm afraid I always saw her as a shopgirl and amateur actress, and I was wrong to look at her that way. She worked much harder than I ever have and has been more successful than I could ever hope to be. As you rightly point out, she has succeeded in a difficult and competitive business, and lately I have begun to wonder if all along I wasn't just jealous. I always thought Nora took too many chances and was riding for a fall. Perhaps I was too influenced by my father who was also not terribly sympathetic to Nora's ambitions. To be honest, Father didn't care for Nora as much as he did for me. I was his favorite and I saw that from very early on. Now, however, I could be just jealous of her confidence and accomplishments. This innocence you mention often put me on the wrong track. I think that's what you may have been referring to, and you're probably right. I suppose that kind of close observation of another person is part of what makes you a writer, isn't it?

You're correct too about my being a bit fussy. I can't seem to help it and it sometimes worries me a little. I doubt that I will ever marry. To begin with, there is no one within shouting distance. I can't see myself married to some young farmer in the township, bearing a brood of six sons and daughters, baking pies and canning fruit on September afternoons. I shouldn't say I can't see myself doing all that. In fact I can, but I don't think it will happen. Of course, there is a side of me that would like that, but on my own terms. More fussiness, I suppose. I think I can make a good life for myself here with my teaching and my house. But there are things that tear away at me sometimes. Longings for I know not what. Well, enough of that.

You asked me what I do on Wednesday nights here in Whitfield? Well, let's see. You might find me reading some awful library novel by Louis Bromfield or Pearl Buck. Or washing my hair. Sometimes I play the piano. I have spent hundreds and hundreds of lovely wasteful hours dreaming across the keyboard. I was once considered to be "quite accomplished." What that means in these parts is moderately talented. It is the talent of the woman who is asked to accompany the soloist for "The Holy City" at a wedding or the carols at the Christmas concert. I don't play nearly as much as I used to. So there you have my Wednesday nights and something tells me that they are not that different from most people's. Don't most of us live out our lives in fairly quiet and simple ways?

I used to go to church, and I miss that. I wasn't active in church things like the Women's Auxiliary and the Missionary Society, but I always looked forward to the Sunday service. I used to go with my father and we sat four rows from the front and I liked everything about it except the mingling at the end by the church door. I always wanted to get away from that. But during the service I enjoyed the hymns and the readings and even Mr. Cameron's gentle sermons. I loved all that since childhood, and believed that God was listening to us there each Sunday morning in Whitfield, Ontario. Then one Sunday last winter, I just stopped believing, and this has been a great loss to me. Far greater than I might have imagined. And I can't retrieve my faith. It has vanished as surely as one's belief in Santa Claus or the tooth fairy. Do you still believe in God, by the way?

When I look back on this letter, I can see that I've been rambling, and I'm tempted to tear it up and start again, but I simply haven't the energy. Some things have happened to me this year that I am still trying to deal with and someday perhaps I will find the courage to tell someone. Meantime, please forgive this rather incoherent letter. It was very good to hear from you, Evelyn, and I hope I may again soon.

Clara

P.S. Yes, I have read some of T. S. Eliot though I couldn't make head nor tail of his poem *The Waste Land*. I suppose I'm just not smart enough. I will look for books by Pound and Stevens the next time I am in Toronto, which, since you asked, is a two-hour train ride from here.

P.P.S. Toronto is an Indian word for "meeting place." How about Kalamazoo or Milwaukee as "funny" American place names?

135 East 33rd Street
New York
September 15, 1935

Dear Clara,
How are you feeling anyway? Haven't heard from you in a while and thought I'd drop you a note. I'm a little bleary-eyed today and didn't even make church this morning. Last night we had a party at Evelyn's to celebrate our first week on the network, and I had a little more

champagne than was probably good for me. It was a swell evening except at the end when Les, who insisted on bringing me home in a cab, decided to make a fool of himself outside my apartment building. First he wanted to come up for a drink, and I said no it was late and not a good idea anyway. Then he started going on about how much he loved me and couldn't live without me. Brother! Right there on the street at two o'clock in the morning. Finally I got rid of him, but I can't imagine how he is going to look me in the eye tomorrow morning after that performance. Give a normally nice guy a few drinks and he turns into this many-handed monster who won't take no for an answer. I'm really furious about this though I blame myself too. I should never have gone out with him in the first place. But I liked the guy and I thought I made it clear that it was just friendship. On Thursday night we had tickets for "The Fleischman Hour" and we went to the show and had a wonderful time. Went for a bite afterward and it was terrific. He was a perfect gentleman. Now this!!! As you can tell, I'm really disappointed in him. And the party at Evelyn's had been so much fun! I don't know. It seems that men, however nice they seem to be, have only one thing on their minds. And the married ones are the worst!!!

How about you? I hope your love life is more tranquil these days and that in any case you are being "careful." How is school with dear old Milton McKay? Is he as boring as ever? Honestly, I don't know how you can work with somebody like that, but I guess you must be used to him by now. Well, I have to get busy and read over tomorrow's script. This headache is just about gone. Who invented the aspirin tablet anyway? He deserves a gold medal. Big crisis coming up this week in the show. Maddy, the pregnant girl Alice caught stealing money from the church's collection plate, disappears!!! The boy, who is probably the father of the child, has been around the house several times and it looks as if he has persuaded Maddy to run away with him. Effie is glad she's gone because she is jealous, but Alice and Aunt Mary and Uncle Jim are worried about her because she is so frail and vulnerable. Anybody in Whitfield caught the show?

Love, Nora

P.S. Do you remember Jack and Doris Halpern? Got a nice letter from them. They are living in Chicago now where Jack works for NBC. Doris is expecting, lucky girl.

San Remo Apartments
1100 Central Park West
N.Y.C.
22/9/35

Dear Clara,

Thanks for your letter about life in Whitfield, Ontario. I have been unable to locate it exactly on the map of the world, but I'll take your word that it exists and is, in fact, a two-hour train ride from Toronto. And touché about American place names!

You asked if I believed in God? Well, it's not a question you are asked every day. Only certain types of people want to know the answers to such questions and it would seem that you are one of them. Anyway, your question set the memory wheels in motion and I thought of when I was a girl at this Episcopalian boarding school for well-to-do young ladies in the green hills of Connecticut. I had what you might call a religious experience there. I had another kind of experience too, but maybe we'll leave the recollection of that for another day. Both of these momentous events occurred when I was an overweight and very serious thirteen-year-old.

On the faculty of Eden Hall was this wonderful old dame, Miss Barrett. She looked exactly like your standard-issue girls' schoolteacher of the time: a tall henna-haired spinster with glasses on a chain across her flat chest. Eden Hall was a very religious school in those days; we had chapel every day and twice on Sundays. We also had a regular class in Scripture taught by Miss Barrett. She talked about God as if He lived next door. One winter night I was walking back from Study Hall to my dormitory. It was one of those clear midwinter nights and I stopped to look up at all these stars. I was the kind of fat, sensitive kid who would do that. I was standing there admiring all that celestial glory when Miss Barrett arrived from behind a tree. She was wrapped up in her long coat and tam and gloves and carrying binoculars.

"You enjoy looking at the heavens, do you, Dowling?" she asked. *Looking at the heavens!* I really liked the sound of that expression. I can't remember what I said, but I recall Miss Barrett saying, "Did you know, Dowling, that great men have looked at such skies through the ages and have been both consoled and terrified by what they saw."

Good old Barrett. She had this terrific voice and there in that icy clear night it was coming through to me. This is what she quoted to me.

> Within its deep infinity I saw
> ingathered and bound by love in
> one volume the scattered leaves
> of all the universe.
>
> —Dante Alighieri, 1265–1321

> The eternal silence of these infinite spaces terrifies me.
>
> —Blaise Pascal, 1623–1662

"There you have it, Dowling," she said. "Nearly four hundred years separate the observations of two men who looked at much the same sky. Binding the scattered leaves of all the universe into one volume. There you have the medieval mind, Dowling. But Pascal sees only a vast loneliness. And there you have the difference between the medieval and the modern mind."

How that stuck with me. That stuff about the scattered leaves bound by love and then the vast loneliness that followed. I remember looking up those old guys, Dante and Pascal, in the library and memorizing those quotations. It started me thinking about God and all the rest of it. I am not quite as sure as you seem to be. I'm sitting on the fence and giving Him the benefit of the doubt.

You ask what consoles me. A bottle of Gordon's gin helps at times, though it's not really to be recommended in the long run. Good books, of course, and music and all the rest of that art stuff.

There's a poem by Wallace Stevens called "Sunday Morning." I was thinking of it when I read your letter. The woman in his poem sounds a bit like you. I think it's in a book called *Harmonium*, but I can't find my copy. I may have loaned it to someone. I'll look for one in the bookstores on Fourth Avenue and if I find a copy, I'll send it along.

Love, Evelyn

Whitfield, Ontario
Sunday, September 22, 1935

Dear Nora,

Yesterday I received your dramatic account of how you thwarted the advances of Mr. Cunningham. Clearly he is smitten. I noticed his adoring gaze on the day I visited the studio. Well, I suppose you are lucky that he came to his senses.

You have become quite the celebrity up here. People have been stopping me on the street to say, "Was it really Nora I heard the other day on that radio show? What a lovely program and she sounds so real." Or this, "And to think that the little girl with the blond curls I used to see going off to school is now on the radio in New York," etc., etc.

I want you to know, Nora, that I have to endure a fair amount of this guff, and I am holding you personally responsible for my actions on that day when I lose all patience and throttle a fellow citizen who is wondering whether Uncle Jim's spell is serious, or when Effie is going to ruin her life by running away with the business college teacher.

A terrible storm this past week. I have never seen such wind and rain and it might not be worth mentioning were it not for a casualty: that enormous oak tree near the Presbyterian church. You surely remember how people would come to the village to take snapshots of it. Mr. Grace told me it was at least two hundred years old. Well, it was split apart last Saturday night by wind and now men are busy with axes and saws cutting away at the great heart. A grim sight and I felt a little sick as I watched yesterday afternoon. I know the wood will go to the poor, but I will miss that old tree.

In your letter you asked about my love life. I have no love life, Nora. Please do not imagine that I have been carrying on some torrid affair with a traveling salesman. It has not been that way at all. Perhaps it would have been better if it had. You needn't worry that I will turn up again on your doorstep. That chapter in my life is mercifully closed. Say hello to Evelyn for me.

Clara

Tuesday, September 24 (7:40 a.m.)

Awakened at two o'clock this morning and imagined a cycle of poems about the rape and its aftermath: how it came about on that spring afternoon; how I took a taxi ride on a hot summer night in New York City; how I saw Charlie again at the Exhibition. So I scribbled for two hours in the night, my fingers cramping. Then I fell into bed tired and deliriously happy. Three hours later, as I read my words, I am repelled, sickened at how they fail to do what I wanted them to do.

Whitfield, Ontario
Sunday, October 6, 1935

Dear Evelyn,

Thank you for sending me Wallace Stevens's book. I've read "Sunday Morning" at least a dozen times. It is a remarkable poem.

"Divinity must live within herself." He follows that with a colon and then lists several emotional states that are all too familiar to me. "Gusty emotions on wet roads on autumn nights." "Gusty" is perfect, a surge of feeling akin to happiness. In fact, I have walked on wet roads on autumn nights and felt just like that. But so, of course, have millions of others down through time. It is humbling to recognize that one's private and peculiar moments are only part of a general pattern shared by countless others.

I see many echoes of Keats in Stevens's poem. It was good of you to send me this book, Evelyn. Thank you again.

Clara

135 East 33rd Street
New York
October 6, 1935

Dear Clara,
What a day! Just back from Evelyn's where I spent the afternoon trying to get her to eat something. She's in bed with a bad cold and just so croaky and crabby. A regular terror. You've never seen her like this, but she's a sight to behold! Sitting there in bed with her writing board and her gin and cigarettes. When I went over there about noon, I walked right into the middle of a fight between her and Eunice (her maid). Eunice had been trying to get her to eat something, but Evelyn was just being difficult. She had thrown a kind of tantrum (there was toast and egg on the floor) and Eunice had put on her coat and was leaving.

"That's it, Miss Callan. I'm not working for that woman anymore. I been in the family thirty-three years, but I'm not putting up with her anymore."

After she left I tried to reason with Evelyn, but she just waved me off. She didn't seem in the least concerned.

"Oh, don't worry about Eunice. She'll be back. She's done this before. She knows what side her bread's buttered on."

And she was right. Eunice came back just before I left. She was pretty sore, but she'll stay. Apparently this warfare has been going on for years.

Evelyn won't admit it, of course, but it's not just the cold that's making her so grouchy these days. It's her love life. I don't know if you got the signals when you were down here, but Evelyn likes women, not men. That's just her way and I don't hold it against her. She tried it out on me one weekend at her mother's place in Connecticut, but I soon set her right about that. Anyway, last month she took up with this young woman, June. Don't ask me where she met her, but she's certainly crazy about her. You should see the presents! This June is a dancer in a Broadway show. She's from Texas (you should hear her!!!) and nearly six feet tall. Only twenty years old, but a tough number, believe you me. She has Evelyn wrapped around her little finger (which isn't so little).

June hasn't been around to see Evelyn while she's been sick, and I think this is what has really upset our friend although she won't admit it. She keeps offering excuses like, "Oh, Junie can't afford to catch my cold. She could lose her place in the line."

But I think Evy is just sick with disappointment that this girl hasn't even taken the trouble to phone. It's pitiful to see an intelligent woman like Evelyn so wrapped up in this kid.

What's the old saying about it never rains, but pours. Just as I had Evelyn calmed down and eating something, our producer, Howard Friessen, phoned to say that Graydon Lott has disappeared. He's our Uncle Jim on the show. According to his wife, he went for a walk after breakfast and hasn't returned. She thinks he's fallen off the wagon and is now on a bender that could last for days. Graydon once told me he's been dry for two years. Told me he quit drinking when they did away with Prohibition. He said drinking was more fun then. But now we can't find him and so Howard has all kinds of people out looking for him in the bars along Forty-second Street. But just in case they can't find him, Howard asked Evelyn to rewrite the scripts for the next few days. Oh boy! Our Evy wasn't exactly too thrilled about that. I was glad to get away, believe me. I'm nearly dead on my feet, so I'm going to have a bite and go off to bed. It's just been one of those days, Clara. I'm sure things are a little quieter up your way.

Love, Nora

Whitfield, Ontario
October 15, 1935

Dear Nora,

Perhaps I shouldn't have, but I found your last letter quite funny, if only because it points out the gap between what really goes on behind the scenes and what people hear on the air. What magicians you people are! I wonder what your listeners would say if they had even an inkling of the shenanigans that go on behind the scenes. In any case, I hope poor Evelyn has recovered and you have found the unfortunate Mr. Lott. I like to think that he sought refuge in the bottle for those terrible platitudes that Evelyn forces him to utter. I remember at least two from last summer when I watched one of your programs. "As long as we all pull together, we'll get out of this." And something about "the Lord hating a quitter." Uttering such statements every day might even drive me to drink and it might go a long way toward explaining why our friend Evelyn likes the bottle so much. Anyway, I hope things have righted themselves and are back to what passes for normal in your life.

I don't know if the New York papers bothered to mention it, but we had an election up here yesterday and the Bennett Conservatives were soundly beaten by Mackenzie King's Liberals. I don't know if they can do anything about getting men back to work, but most people seem to think that they can't do worse than the Tories. I believe it has been that kind of response; one born more of desperation than genuine commitment. Well, winter is just up ahead and I have been getting ready. The coal was delivered last week and I am preparing to do battle. This year, however, I feel more confident about handling that furnace. I am well, by the way. Nothing seems to have been damaged and I am back to "normal routines." And that is very reassuring. Take care of yourself.

Clara

Sunday, October 27

Last night I dreamed of Charlie, the tramp. Not Charlie, the funny little celluloid tramp in his oversized shoes and derby hat, but my Charlie in his greasy overalls and suit coat. We were riding in the Ferris wheel and he was embracing me, singing over and over his infernal little love song. "I want to _____ you so bad, Missus."

As the wheel turned downward, I saw Marion looking at us and so was the pipe-smoking man, though it could also have been Father. I am not sure. Father used to smoke a pipe. I awakened then and lay in darkness thinking about Charlie. I imagined him born in the same year as Marion and I: 1903. On a farm somewhere north and east of here where the land is hilly and the soil poor. I saw ten or twelve children in an unpainted farmhouse up a lane.

Charlie's father was a lazy man but likable enough when sober. On Saturday nights, however, he likes to drink, and then he turns quarrelsome and vindictive at the kitchen table, prophesying ruin on all those who have rebuked him over a lifetime of grievance and error. The mother and the children keep their distance. Later, when the boys get older, there will be ugly fights, with some taking the father's side and some against: there will be swollen jaws and blackened eyes; someone's arm will be broken; another's fist will go through a window right up to the forearm, shredding nerves along the way, leaving a withered hand. A chaotic household whose weather is nearly always turbulent and unpredictable. How could it be otherwise among so many vicious hearts? They are a shiftless lot. Not worth a nickel. A bunch of damn fools. Those are the verdicts of neighbors, but uttered only among themselves. Who wants his barn burned down, his well poisoned? Who is anxious to find his best cow at the bottom of a pond? Minor villains to be sure, but you had to be careful what you said around them. They could be comical and lively at a dance, but the best advice was always to leave early. I imagined Charlie as one of the youngest; he had to make his way around that kitchen table. Perhaps that is where it started, that jokey, wheedling manner. When two of his brothers go off to the war, he wishes he too could go on the adventure. He follows the wagon down the lane, the old man holding the reins, the two brothers sprawled in the back with their cardboard suitcases. They promise to bring back a German for him as a pet.

"We'll keep him in the woodshed and feed him turnips. Maybe hitch him to the plow."

Charlie stands for a long time and watches the wagon disappear in the dust of the concession road. When he starts back for the house, he skips and hops about, a restless grasshopper of a boy with long legs built for dancing and a slyness beyond his years.

In a few months one of the brothers returns. The army doesn't want him. Something about an officer's wristwatch. No one knows exactly what happened and no one wants to. The other disappears off the face of the earth. What happened to him? No one knows. One afternoon two men come to the farm in a big military car and ask questions, but nobody knows the answers.

The next year Charlie leaves the little country schoolhouse for the last time, fed up with sitting and schoolbooks. He doesn't like farming. He likes town life. Hanging around the feed store where he makes men laugh with the faces he pulls and the tricks he can do. He can do a backward somersault, for one thing. And step-dance! Those feet just fly. But he can't stay with a job. He is restless and easily bored. When the Depression comes along, it doesn't bother Charlie; in fact, the tramp's life suits him: riding the freight trains, a morning's work here and there, a sandwich at the back door (housewives like his deference and exaggerated courtesy). Always on the move is my Charlie; a friendly, unreliable, thoroughly vicious man, and lying in my bed early this morning, I was thankful that his worthless seed was scraped from my womb three months ago.

Friday, November 1

Last evening I made a pan of fudge and had plenty of apples on hand for the children who came to the door, thirty-two in all. Stayed awake until well past midnight, but nothing untoward on my property. Heard what sounded like an automobile backfiring in the night and learned this morning that Norbert Johnson had discharged a shotgun at some boys.

Sunday, November 3

Where does Charlie meet the boy and why would he choose such a pitiful companion? But a man like Charlie needs someone to boss around and kick. And one day he sees him on the side of a township road sitting in the stiff, dry grass.

"Restin' your dogs, are you? What's your name, son? Mine's Charlie. Want to tag along with Uncle Charlie? Travel first class or stay at home. That's what I say. What do you say, boy?"

Donald, looking up through his one-eyed world at this quick-footed whistling man who can't bear stillness or silence. Always yapping or firing stones at crows on fence posts or barking dogs. A kind of ugly affection emerges between this pair, and I imagine sex acts brutal and swift. In abandoned barns and under bridges in the shadowy light of late afternoon. Panting and horrible, the dissolute life of byway and lane.

And Charlie is forever scolding the boy who seldom gets anything right. Watching from atop the boxcar as Donald struggles to grasp the ladder.

"You'll lose a foot someday, you stupid bugger."

135 East 33rd Street
New York
November 17, 1935

Dear Clara,

I'm sorry I haven't written for a while, but time just seems to whirl by and another week is gone. It's hard to believe that I've been down here nearly a year now. Where does the time go? We're all pretty thrilled with the latest Hooper ratings which have us third among the most-listened-to daytime serials. Only "Vic and Sade" and "Ma Perkins" were more popular last month. I'm getting bushelfuls of mail.

Everything at the studio is back on an even keel, thank goodness. Evelyn and her Texas playmate are all lovey-dovey again and Graydon is back on the wagon. Like you, my love life at the moment is nonexistent. Les and I have decided to be just friends and that means no dating. There are certain men that you just can't go to the movies or have a drink with, because sooner or later you'll get involved. Do you know what I mean? Sooner or later, you'll feel this attraction and then, before you know it, you're in over your head. And it's just not professional to start that kind of thing with a guy who works with you and is married to boot. I have to hand it to Les. He was very apologetic about his performance that night outside my apartment, and he's decided to pay more attention to his wife and kids. We're both glad nothing happened, though I can't say I wasn't tempted.

So my only love life at the moment will be on "Chestnut Street." Evy has decided to give Alice a beau, so next month listeners are going to meet Cal Harper, a handsome young doctor who is just starting up a practice in Meadowvale. What happens is that Effie has an attack of appendicitis and after the operation she wakes up to see this terrific-looking guy who's been caring for her. Of course, Effie falls instantly for him. The business teacher is long gone in case you're wondering and you probably aren't. But it looks as if Dr. Cal is more interested in Alice. So you can imagine the conversations that will take place around the kitchen table in the Dale household. I don't know if I'll get to marry the guy, Evy isn't saying. Anyway, I think it's an interesting wrinkle in our little story of American life and it should help to keep the listeners tuned in and our sponsor happy. The Sunrise people say that sales have increased over forty percent in the last three months.

How about you? Is everything the same up there? Would you consider coming down here for Christmas? Apparently the Amazon will have a week off and is going back to Texas. Evelyn is after me to go to her mother's. But I just don't feel comfortable there. Yet I don't like the idea of being alone here either. What about coming down for a few days? I would really love to have you, so think about it, okay?

Love, Nora

Sunday, November 24

Went with the Brydens yesterday to the Royal Winter Fair hoping that I might see Charlie cleaning out a cattle stall or feeding someone's prize hens. The foolishness of that idea was soon evident: the stern-looking farmers at the fair would never entrust their livestock to the likes of my Charlie.

Whitfield, Ontario
Sunday, November 24, 1935

Dear Nora,

I suppose a fictional romance is better than nothing, and you will obviously be doing very well for yourself. Handsome young doctors certainly don't grow on trees. The closest I have been to doctors recently was yesterday. And they were veterinarians. Several were standing around Betsy, a lovely little Jersey cow who, from her mournful gaze, was evidently costive. The vets were solemn, wondering what syrup to administer or whether more dramatic treatment was necessary. The worried owner looked on. All this drama took place at the Royal Winter Fair where I found myself in the company of the

Brydens. "A little outing," in Mrs. Bryden's words, and it was very good of them to take me along. Proximity to animals (except poor Betsy who was mooing most piteously) can induce a kind of bovine calm, and I felt something like that as I walked around the flanks of those great beasts with their warm homely smells. It made me think that perhaps I could have had a kind of happiness married to Randall Wilmott. Do you remember him at all? A tall, bony youth who had a crush on me in high school. His father farmed two hundred acres south of the village and, of course, Randall is there now. He married a girl from the township and they have five or six children. I see him and his wife sometimes in the village on Saturday afternoons; she is fingering the bolts of cloth at the Mercantile and pale bony Randall is studying the jackknives in the glass case by the cash register. He still looks at me with his goofy grin. "Hello there, Clara!" A pleasant gentleman. In those days I thought myself far too grand for such a humble plowman, but now I think maybe I could have been contented frying Randall's eggs and going out to the barn with scraps on a winter afternoon to feed the hogs. Maybe, but maybe not too. Anyway, I had a pleasant time yesterday at the fair and we got back before the weather turned around. It started to sleet in the night and I was glad to be home.

I don't think I can make it down to New York for Christmas. It gets complicated at this time of year because of the furnace. I could probably get Joe Morrow to look after it for me, but I don't think I want Joe tramping through the house when I'm away. I gather there is no possibility of your coming up here for the holiday. I suppose you don't get enough time off from your program with Christmas in the middle of the week this year. Well, perhaps next year. Say hello to Evelyn Dowling for me. For a while there we were exchanging letters, but I suppose she is too busy to keep up a correspondence. Take care of yourself, Nora.

Clara

125 East 33rd Street
New York
Deccember 8, 1935

Dear Clara,

I sent off your Christmas present yesterday and hope you like it. You better!!! The store guaranteed delivery in two weeks, so let me know if it doesn't arrive by then. Also make sure that *everything* works and nothing has been damaged in transit. The store *guaranteed* safe shipment and I want to hold them to that.

I'm still undecided about the holiday (you're right, we are only off two days, Christmas Eve and Christmas Day), but I am definitely not going with Evelyn to her mother's in Conn. I love Evy dearly, but she is too sour for my taste this time of year. She is forever going on about how Christmas is just a pain in the keister, but I don't see it that way at all. I have always loved Christmas and I refuse to be cynical about it. On Friday after work I walked over to Macy's and looked at their windows. I saw all the people standing there staring at the decorations and I thought, sure it's commercial and all that, but it's also giving people a real lift. Of course, the funny thing is that for all of Evelyn's griping about the holidays, she has written the most beautiful Christmas episode for "Chestnut Street." She showed me the script. Alice has invited Dr. Cal for Christmas dinner because he hasn't any family in town, and at the end of the dinner, Uncle Jim gives this little talk about family and Christmas and how important they are. It is truly inspiring and that is from our cynical old Evy!

I met an interesting man this past week. His name is Lewis Mills. I don't know if that name means anything to you, but he is an author. Evelyn knows about him and says he is a big-shot intellectual who writes for magazines like *Harper's* and the *New Republic*. I don't read them so I don't know, but she described him as a literary and social critic. He certainly loves to criticize, and he doesn't seem to think much of radio. He was in the studio last week watching us do our show. He's writing an article and said he was interested in "the phenomenon of daytime serials." He wanted to ask me some questions, so we went out for lunch. We didn't agree on one thing, but in a way, I think we like one another. The next thing you know, he invited me to dinner. Took me to the dining room of the Plaza. Talk about swanky!!! To tell you the truth, I found him kind of scary (he's so intelligent), but nice in a way too. He is quite a bit older than me and a very sophisticated man. Not really my type at all, but you never know about these things, I guess. Anyway, we're having dinner again tomorrow night. Nice change from my usual hot-plate cutlet!!!

Love, Nora

Sunday, December 15

Yesterday I had a kind of seizure in Toronto. It could have been more embarrassing than it was, but I must try to get a better grip on myself in crowds. And there were such crowds in the Toronto stores yesterday. I had finished my shopping and the last thing I bought was a copy of *True Detective* and I now believe that the magazine may have had something to do with my spell there on Yonge Street. Yet how could I resist the cover with its advertising of one of the stories: "'*I shot him and I'm glad.*' Rapist's Victim Faces Electric Chair After Fatal Shooting in Cold Blood."

I was saving that for the train ride home. And then I don't quite know how it happened. I had come out of a United Cigar Store and was walking south. I wanted a cup of tea, but the restaurants were all so busy. I found myself looking at men's faces on Yonge Street. I was looking intently at the faces beneath the caps and fedoras. I was studying them, but I had to be careful because I didn't want them to notice. Was Charlie somewhere among those faces, wandering the streets of the city? And so I looked at those faces on Yonge Street, wondering how many of those men had entered women against their wills. In the backseats of cars after the Saturday night dances, the pint bottles of liquor half-filled with ginger ale passed back and forth. Then the kisses and the pawing. Or the Sunday afternoon walk through the woods, the embraces in the cool shade under that big tree, the glimpse of the garter belt and the bare thigh, the hand pushed away from her underwear again and again.

"Come on now, Mary, please! You know you want to. Come on now, damn it!"

At the corner of Yonge and Richmond (I think) I stopped, overcome and a little dizzied from all those pictures in my head. I had this little spell or seizure there on the street, leaning against a store window. I felt sick to my stomach. Dropped one of my parcels. I must have looked a sight. A woman stopped and picked up my package. A middle-aged woman with a kind, homely face. She had a faint mustache and the buttons of her coat were oddly mismatched. I noted that.

"Are you all right, dear? You look all in."

"Yes, I'm fine," I said. "I'll be all right, thank you."

"You should sit down and have a cup of tea, dear. There's a Child's just up the street. Would you like me to take you?"

"No, no thank you, I'm fine."

Others were staring at us as they passed and a few feet away a Salvation Army woman took no notice of us whatsoever. She was busy shaking her tambourine by the glass kettle half-filled with coins. I thanked the mustached woman and walked on shamefaced. Found refuge finally in a movie theater where I sat in darkness, looking up at the lighted screen, watching the blond-haired woman in her evening gown and her skinny little cohort in his tuxedo dance together on top of a piano. Or maybe several pianos. All that jazzy footwork and those sprightly tunes helped, and I was soon feeling myself again.

San Remo Apts.
1100 Central Park West
N.Y.C.
16/12/35

Greetings from Gotham,
Hope this finds you well. Are you a Christmas person, by the way? I'm not. Can't stand the forced jollity and spurious goodwill demanded by the season. Of course, this may have to do with the fact that I spend the hallowed day with my Ma out in Connecticut. We usually manage to get through it, but just barely and with the help of a pailful of martinis. What do you do up there anyway? Ski? Skate? Skedaddle about? What? Since you've given up on church, you must find it all a bit tedious.

I cannot resist a little gossip. Your sister is now moving in some fairly sophisticated company. Has she written to you about Lewis Mills? I understand you don't have a telephone and all I can say is how wonderfully eccentric of you! So has she written yet about Mills? He's been hanging around the studio for the past couple of weeks watching us "put on our show" and making notes for an article he's writing on radio serials. When Howard Friessen asked me about this last month, I was skeptical, to say the least. Howard doesn't know Mills's work, but I do. He has a sharp eye for nonsense and writes "feelingly" about the excesses of American public life. He did a commendable job on the Fascist radio priest, Coughlin, for the *New Republic*, but nobody in the agency except me has read it. Howard and the others just think it will be great publicity for our program, but I am not so sure. He may do a hatchet job. What they don't seem to get is the fact that Mills *hates* radio: thinks it's the beginning of the end of civilization. I'm inclined to agree with him, but I keep a zippered lip. After all, it's "me bread and butter." Anyway, Mills has been sniffing around the studio these past couple of weeks and seems to enjoy the company of our Nora who, I must say, looks absolutely ravishing these days. She's had her hair cut even shorter and she now looks about twenty years old. Just the way Mr. Mills likes them, I'm told. I understand the great man was taking her to the "theeaytuh" last night. I'm afraid to tell her, since it's a good way to lose a friend, but Mr. Mills is reputed to be quite the ladies' man. He has been twice married and the consort of many. Word has it that he's bedded most of the lady poets in town. Personally, I can't see the attraction. He is three years older than yours truly (I looked it up) and is most assuredly no Adonis. Mr. Mills looks more like a two-legged version of your English bulldog with a face that is (I admit) unmistakably masculine, even though he is always scowling. He has this absolutely massive head (all brains, I guess) and he is as bald as our famous eagle. On the other hand, I am told that he can be quite the charmer. There has to be something. In any case, Nora seems very taken with L. Mills. I only hope the poor child doesn't fall too hard and end up badly bruised.

Have you ever read Pepys's diary? It's been a favorite of mine for years, and I saw this edition in Scribner's the other day and thought of you. The old gent's comments make for great reading on long winter nights, and I think this is a rather handsome edition. So, I'm sending it along with my very best wishes for the new year, Clara Callan.

Love, Evelyn

135 East 33rd Street
New York
Monday, December 17, 1935

Dear Clara,
I just felt like dropping you a note so I hope this reaches you before the twenty-fifth. Gee, I wish we could be together at Christmas. I really miss you, sister of mine. Has your present arrived yet, I wonder? You better like it.

I think I mentioned a week ago that I met this man Lewis Mills. He is a journalist and author, and he's writing an article about our show. Well, the long and the short of it is we've become "good friends" and have gone out a few times together. On Saturday night he took me to *Porgy and Bess,* the new Gershwin show. The entire cast was colored and boy could they sing! Then we went out for a late supper. It was quite the evening.

Lewis is a fascinating man, Clara. You would really like him. He seems to have read every book that was ever printed, and he can talk about everything from opera to baseball. I told him right off the bat that I am no intellectual, and he needn't expect me to keep up with him, but he just laughed and told me not to worry about such things. But of course, I do. I feel so dumb around him. So I guess you are wondering what's the attraction? To be honest, I don't know. He's not handsome, that's for sure. He's nearly fifty years old and about as tall as me but heavyset. Not exactly overweight, but just kind of packed together tightly. He would make a good wrestler. He has no hair to speak of and he's nearly always frowning and kind of grumpy. You should see the waiters in these restaurants hop to it when Lewis walks in. But he has a wonderful smile (on the rare occasions when he decides to use it), and his manners are impeccable. I suppose I would describe him as impressive. The funny thing is there is a kind of sexiness to him too.

I also think that behind all his stern disapproval (he really is worse than Evelyn when it comes to criticizing things) there is a very vulnerable and childlike quality. I don't know. I just find him very fascinating to listen to. And there is a sweetness about him too. The other night we went for a walk and I wanted to see the Christmas windows in the department stores on Thirty-fourth.

"Oh, not there, Nora," he kept saying. "Not there."

But he went along, and when we got there I tried to point out to him how thousands of people stand in front of those windows and dream of a better life for themselves. People just get a terrific kick out of those things, and he should try to be more tolerant of stuff like that. And he looked at me and gave me that rare smile and said, "Maybe I should try to see some of this stuff through your eyes, Nora."

And I said, "Maybe you should, Lewis."

He's invited me to Christmas dinner with some friends and I'm nervous about that. I can just imagine the kind of people who will be there: writers and book publishers and college professors. At first I said no because I didn't think I would fit into that kind of company, but Lewis was so insistent that I finally agreed, and now, to tell you the truth, I'm scared half to death. I don't know where any of this is going to go, Clara, if in fact it goes anywhere. At the moment, I am just taking it day by day. We are not sleeping together, if that's what you are thinking. I wouldn't rule it out however because I find Lewis, oh, I don't know, attractive in his own way. Laugh if you like, but I can't help it. Enjoy the holidays and wish me luck at that dinner party!!!

Love, Nora

Saturday, December 21

At my door at eight o'clock this morning, two men from the railway express, setting down a huge wooden crate on my veranda. Clearly, it could not get through the door. What am I to do about this, I wondered, but the men were good enough to dismantle the crating, prying the boards apart with their crowbars. And there for all to see, and worthy of at least three exclamation marks, was Nora's Christmas present!!! An enormous radio, a Stromberg-Carlson encircled with a red bow, and with more knobs and dials than a motor car. According to the instruction booklet, I can now listen to programs from as far away as Paris and Berlin. I can now listen to Herr Hitler in the flesh, so to speak. The console also has a turntable for playing phonograph records and Nora has included an album of Rubinstein playing Chopin.

The men were more than a little taken with this engineering marvel. As one fellow put it, "Isn't it a beaut?"

She certainly is and it must have cost Nora a small fortune. There followed a flurry of anxiety about where to put it. The front room is too small, and it occurred to me that my poor piano, dusty and neglected somewhat these past few months, might resent this brash, handsome newcomer. I settled finally for a corner of the dining room, and spent the rest of the day reading the booklet and fiddling with the dials. A couple of hours ago I began to pick up squawks in various foreign tongues. Bless Nora's heart, but when will I find the time to give this thing its proper due? Standing in its corner, it seems to command attention, a minor household god to whom obeisance must be paid.

Whitfield, Ontario
Thursday, December 26, 1935

Dear Nora,

Many thanks for the radio. What magnificence! As always, you are far too generous and my gifts to you (I hope both the blouse and skirt fit) now seem humble indeed. But it is a wonderful present and thank you again. At first I didn't know where to put it; the front room seems too small with the piano there, and so I settled finally on a corner in the dining room where it doesn't look entirely out of place, though I am not exactly happy with it there either. That was a long ugly sentence, wasn't it? I'm half-thinking of selling the piano. After listening to Rubinstein play Chopin's nocturnes, I wonder why anyone with limited talent like mine would even approach them. Well, I shall see.

The Brydens had me over for dinner yesterday, and I was glad to be with them. It's odd but this Christmas I seemed to miss Father more than even last year. I don't know why. Anyway, it was good of them to think of me.

Then Marion came by this afternoon for a visit, the Stromberg-Carlson inspiring her usual vocabulary for surprise and admiration. Marion still sounds as she did a dozen years ago in high school, still encountering life's wonders and vicissitudes with her little store of childhood exclamations like "Holy Cow" and "Gee Whiz" and

"Gosh," etc. She listens to your program religiously and wonders if you have a photograph of yourself or of Effie. Like the movie stars you see in Woolworth's. She also wanted to know if you had met Rudy Vallee in your travels, and if so, what is he really like? If you can answer these questions, you will make Marion's life even more radiant.

How did things go at your dinner party with Mr. Mills and his intellectual friends? Did you manage to avoid getting a word in? I would think that the best policy on such occasions (mind you, I have little experience) would be to nod knowingly and offer some bland comment that could not possibly suggest contradictions such as, "Yes, you have a point there," or "Well, that's certainly possible."

I'm anxious to know how it went. Your Mr. Mills sounds like an interesting but unusual consort. I'm wondering just what you have in common. He is certainly not the sort of fellow you've gone out with in the past, but then perhaps that fact alone is what makes him appealing. I just hope, Nora, that you don't come out of this with another "busted heart." You know how hard you tend to fall. Is it worth warning you to be careful and take your time with Mr. Mills? Probably not. I was about to say something, but I'm sure you would only be annoyed with me. What, after all, do I know about men? And you're right. Not much. Anyway, Happy New Year! And thanks again for the radio!

Clara

Whitfield, Ontario
Sunday, December 26, 1935

Dear Evelyn,
Thanks so much for Mr. Pepys's diary, which I am thoroughly enjoying. He has a wonderfully accurate eye for the world around him, and I am learning a great deal about what it must have been like to have lived in London two hundred and seventy years ago. I am also listening to the radio these days, thanks to Nora who sent me this extravagant present—a Stromberg-Carlson, on which I can hear everything

from that madman in Germany to the perilous adventures of the folks on "Chestnut Street." Speaking of which, I was home last Tuesday and so I heard kindly old Uncle Jim's Christmas Eve peroration on the season. You'll be happy to know that my face remained quite stony throughout, except for an occasional guffaw. Well, all right, maybe not a guffaw. I'm sure, however, that there wasn't a dry eye in the village, or probably across our two great lands. You certainly know how to tap into the great spongy heart of the people. That is a compliment by the way, and the "spongy" is yours, is it not?

I had a rather feverish letter from Nora who seems very taken with her Mr. Mills. Like you, I hope she doesn't come down with a terrible thud. Mills sounds to me like the sort of man who has other things on his mind besides the opera or the Italian campaign in Ethiopia. Ah well, Nora has been down this road before. I hope 1936 is a good year for you, Evelyn. While I am at it, I might just as well hope the same for myself. It has to be an improvement on this one.

With best wishes, Clara

1936

135 East 33rd Street
New York
January 5, 1936

Dear Clara,

Happy New Year!!! And many thanks for the skirt and blouse (perfect fit!). I'm glad you like the radio. Ain't it a beauty? I'm enclosing a dozen signed agency photographs (they make me look kind of glamorous, don't they?) and you can give one to Marion or anyone else who asks. You can also inform her that unfortunately I haven't met Rudy Vallee, and so I can't tell her what he's like.

I'm very happy these days, Clara. The program is going well (did you hear any episodes over the holidays?) and there's a very sweet man in my life. Many people (Evelyn, for instance) think Lewis is some kind of ogre, but they don't know him at all. In fact, he's extremely considerate and loving. There is a public side to him that can be pretty frightening, I admit, but in private he's just a very sweet man and the most interesting person I have ever met. The Christmas dinner, by the way, was just a lot of fun. I didn't find it heavy going at all. In fact, I felt very much at home with Lewis's friends.

On New Year's Eve, we were invited to a big party at this book publisher's, but we decided to be alone. We walked over to Times Square to see the new year in. At first Lewis nixed the idea: "All those people, Nora, please!" He can get like that, all choosy about mingling with the "peasants," but I told him it would be fun and it was. Lewis is a bit of a snob, I must admit. He went to Princeton University and has spent most of his life around intellectual people. I told him he has to get out and see what makes ordinary folk tick. He admits that he doesn't know enough about how the average Joe lives. He knows all about political and economic ideas, but he doesn't understand much about ordinary life. Anyway, he enjoyed himself or at least was sweet enough to say he did.

He's going to California next week to talk to some people in the movie business. This is for another article he's writing. I don't know when the piece about our program will be published, probably not until the fall. It looks as if I have this intellectual guy for a beau, Clara. It's really something, isn't it?

Love, Nora

Monday, January 13

For the first time in five years I have missed a day of school. I have been ill since Friday with a terrible grippe. Mrs. Bryden dropped in this morning with some broth and poor Marion trudged through the snow to bring me Saturday's paper and letter from Nora. I rewarded her with a studio photograph which shows Nora smiling coyly, the childish signature scrawled across the bottom.

"Gosh, she sure looks glamorous, doesn't she, Clara?"

I have to admit she does.

Marion said she didn't know what she would do without the radio. "It sure helps to pass the time," she said.

I hear that expression more and more. When people are playing euchre or assembling a jigsaw puzzle or listening to the radio, they say that they are passing the time. As if time were something to get through and be done with. But if one regards time as finite, then would one not want to slow it down somehow and savor its every moment? Impossible, of course, but that might be an ideal worth striving for. Marion, of course, may well be waiting for earthly time to pass so she can get off to Heaven where presumably time is not a major concern.

Tuesday, January 21

The King is dead. I heard it on the radio last evening and it was all the talk at school and on the street. The children are anxious to know if they will get a holiday.

Saturday, January 25

Stormy and cold. In all its fury, the fourth season is upon us. The village is snowbound; even the train had trouble getting through this evening.

Tuesday, January 28

National holiday to commemorate the King's funeral. Mrs. Bryden told me she got up at four o'clock this morning to listen to the service from London. Still stormy and very cold. This is one of the worst winters I can remember. The monster in the cellar devours coal by the shovelful. At this rate, I will have to order another ton to see me through to spring.

135 East 33rd Street
New York
February 2, 1936

Dear Clara,
It's been ages since I've been in touch and I apologize, but the days just seem to fly. How is everything with you? Boy, you're having some kind of winter up there, aren't you? I've been reading about it in the *Trib*. It's been pretty cold and snowy down here too. Got a note from Evelyn the other day (she's been working at our agency in Chicago for a couple of weeks), and she said she had never seen so much snow. She also mentioned that the Halperns (remember Jack Halpern who brought me to N.Y.) have a baby boy and they are just thrilled.

What do you think of our new King? Isn't he handsome? I'm sorry his father died, but Edward is more suited for the times. This is one area where Lewis and I can get into a squabble. He is very anti-English and thinks the idea of a monarchy in this day and age is ridiculous. He doesn't mind making fun of the Royal Family and that just rubs me the wrong way. We've had a couple of pretty good tussles on this subject, but then I guess you can't expect two people to agree on everything. What about you? Writing any poetry these days? Drop me a line, why don't cha?

Love, Nora

P.S. If you need any more pictures, let me know. The agency sends out about three hundred to listeners every month. Isn't that something?

Whitfield, Ontario
February 9, 1936

Dear Nora,
Thanks for your note. You are certainly right about the winter. I've never seen anything like it; day after day it snows and every weekend there seems to be a storm. It gets you down a bit and it's certainly hard

on coal. I'm going to have to order more to get me through to spring. About all I seem to do is shovel myself out in the morning, battle my way through snowdrifts to school and then shovel the front walk again when I come home in the afternoon. It's all a bit discouraging. I just don't seem to have much news for you. I was down with a terrible cold early in the new year, but I have recovered and am once again as healthy as a horse. Getting through a winter like this is not as difficult physically as it is mentally. No, I am not writing any poetry these days. Inspiration seems to have dried up, though I have several ideas for poems. I am just so infernally lazy and lacking in ambition. I'll write again when I am more cheerful.

Clara

Sunday, February 16 (3:10 a.m.)

A few hours ago I had a dangerous and foolish little adventure that left me thinking about Mother and how she died. For years, I wondered whether she stumbled accidentally in front of that freight train or stepped deliberately into its path. And tonight, for the briefest of moments, I think I understood how easy it is to let go.

Another storm began late yesterday afternoon and all evening the wind rose. By ten o'clock I could not see across the street for the blowing snow. Throughout, I felt such a restlessness: I was reading a bit, fiddling with the radio stations, going down to the cellar to check the furnace. About eleven o'clock I decided to go for a walk. An absurd idea in the middle of a blizzard, and I cannot explain why I gave in to such blind will, but give in I did, and dressing warmly (I had at least enough sense for that) I went out into the night. At first, I felt sheer exhilaration at the commotion of it all, emboldened in that white and howling air. Keeping to the middle of the road I walked toward the train station. I would go no farther, for beyond lay the township roads and open fields with the full force of the westerly blowing across them. As I moved toward the edge of the village, there was nothing but a wild whiteness and here and there a house light glimpsed through the snow. Most people had sensibly gone to their beds to sleep away the storm.

When I saw the outline of the station, I turned and started back. I was warm enough in my coat and tam, a scarf covering most of my face. Then quite suddenly I lost my way, or my sense of direction failed me. In any case, I stumbled and fell into the roadside ditch. I did not hurt myself for the snow was soft, but nevertheless I was upended and I turned over on my back. I was now below the road, listening to the wind, feeling the snow sift across me. It was filling the ditch, but I was sheltered from the wind and feeling almost—what is the word—languorous, no, stuporous might be closer to describing my state. I had no desire to move and as I brushed the snow from my eyes, I thought of how easy it would be to lie there unseen until it no longer mattered. Was I too "half in love with easeful Death"? Had Mother also felt this way on that summer morning thirty years ago? One doesn't need the songs of nightingales "to cease upon the midnight with no pain." That much I realized lying in that ditch three hours ago. What roused me I cannot say. I only know I did climb out and with difficulty found my way through all that swirling snow back to the dark shapes of trees and houses. And how delicious to come in from the cold, to taste a cup of hot cocoa and to feel the warmth of flannel on my skin. I must be the most foolish woman in the province.

135 East 33rd Street
New York
March 15, 1936

Dear Clara,
I'm sorry for not writing before now, but you know how the weeks go by, and you don't realize how much time has passed. Anyway, here is something that I want you to think about. Lewis is planning a trip to Europe this summer. He's been asked by a magazine to write a series

of articles on European politics and he thinks that maybe later on he can publish them as a book. So he is going to visit Italy, France and Germany and he has asked me to come along.

I talked it over with Evelyn and she said that the agency would probably not be too happy about me being away for several weeks. She could, however, write me out of the script for a while, though any longer than three or four weeks and we might lose what she calls "listener identification." So I decided maybe I would just visit Italy and Lewis could go on to France and Germany on his own. I've always wanted to see Italy and so then I thought, well, it's the summer and why not ask Clara to come along? Lewis will be busy throughout the day interviewing people and it would be more fun if I had someone like you for company. We could have a swell time sightseeing and having lunch together. So, what do you think? Lewis wants to leave about the middle of July and he is going to Italy first, so we could be back no later than the middle of August. Don't you think it would be terrific?

Last night I told Lewis that I was going to ask you and he said, "Fine. Sure, bring her along." Now you don't have to worry about costs. I'll pick up your fare if you can look after your own spending money. So there you have it, a chance for a free European holiday. Will you think *seriously* about it and let me know as soon as you can? Lewis wants to make arrangements as quickly as possible because the Olympic Games are on in Germany this summer and Europe will have a lot of visitors. So let me know, okay? Evelyn says hello!

Love, Nora

P.S. Is the new Chaplin picture playing in Toronto yet? If you can get a chance to see it, do so because it's very good. Paulette Goddard is wonderful and of course Chaplin is Chaplin.

Saturday, March 21

A jaunty letter from Nora who is going to Europe this summer with her Mr. Mills. She wonders if I would like to come along. To Italy! Well! Land of Michelangelo and Raphael, of Corelli and Puccini and Dante. Wouldn't Nora be surprised if I accepted her invitation? Yet, things are so very unsettled over there. There could well be a war if you can believe the radio and newspapers. I can't imagine being caught up in a war. But do I not need an adventure? Is it not time to see the world?

Whitfield, Ontario
March 22, 1936

Dear Nora,

Thank you for your letter with its invitation to go to Italy with you and Mr. Mills this summer. Allow me to surprise you by saying that I would be happy to go, and I look forward to it. There now! Have you fully recovered, or are you still on the floor? I hadn't thought a trip to Europe would be in my plans, but this seems like a good opportunity to see that part of the world, and it would be a shame to pass it up. And who knows? Perhaps I shall meet a handsome count and become a devout Papist and mother of twelve, living in my villa and overseeing the laborers in the vineyards.

I wonder about the possibilities of trouble over there. Aren't you a little concerned about the situation? Germany seems determined to provoke the French, and, of course, if anything comes of that, you can expect England to get mixed up in it. I'm afraid I have become a great listener of the radio news and it is all bad. Another war over there seems altogether likely these days. Perhaps, however, they are exaggerating things. What does your Mr. Mills think about all this? Since he intends to write about these matters, I would imagine that he's given it all a good deal of thought.

Can you tell me what dates you have in mind so that I can begin to plan. It's months away, but you know how I am and I can't help it. What sort of clothes ought I to bring? What does one wear aboard the ship? I imagine that Italy in August is quite hot (sounds wonderful to me right now). I will look for some books in the Linden library on climate and customs, but anything you can tell me about the place would be helpful. It is really very kind of you, Nora, to offer to pay my fare, but I would feel much better if you allowed me to pay at least half. Then I wouldn't feel like such a sponger.

We still have plenty of snow, but with the strengthening sun and milder winds, it is melting fast and soon there will be green leaves and violets in the woods and trilliums underfoot. Hurrah for spring!

Clara

135 East 33rd Street
New York
March 29, 1936

Dear Clara,
How happy you've made me! It's good to know that you're coming to Italy with us and it's even better to hear you sounding so gay. It must be the spring weather and I can certainly understand that. What a winter you've put up with!!! I've told Lewis that you're coming along and he was happy to hear it. The more the merrier! He's looking forward to meeting you (I've told him all about you) and I'm sure you'll find him an interesting person, to say the least. When you first meet him, you might wonder what I see in him. He's a grouchy and complicated man, but he can also be charming and considerate when he's in the mood. He is also very affectionate (if you get my meaning), though you wouldn't know it to look at him.

I told him of your concerns about a possible war in Europe, but he doesn't think it will happen. He says the French will back down on this Rhineland business and the Germans will get their way. According to him, Hitler has as many friends in France and England as he has in his own country. He also said the Olympic Games are taking place in Germany this summer, so they're not going to start a war in the middle of all that. I don't know much about these things, so I'll take his word for it.

Lewis tried to get tickets on the Italian liner *Rex*, but it was already booked for the dates he wanted, so we'll be going on an American ship (but with an Italian crew) called *Genoa Princess*. It's not nearly as expensive as the *Rex* and it's fairly new. If you want to pay half your fare, fine, but it really isn't necessary. We're leaving on Saturday, July 18, and you and I will return on August 24, so you'll have time to get ready for school. Lewis, of course, will go on to Paris and Berlin. I told Evelyn and Howard Friessen, and while the agency isn't exactly happy that I'm going to be away so long, Evelyn has assured them that she can "write the show around me." I don't know what will happen to Alice during those weeks, but leave it to Evy, she'll come up with something.

Now about clothes—I wouldn't worry. If you come down a few days ahead of our sailing date, we can find some things for you. Leave it to me. I don't imagine there'd be too much in Linden Ladies' Wear that would be all that "chic" on the promenade deck of the *Genoa Princess*. Lewis is now working on an itinerary and it looks as if we'll be visiting Rome, Florence and Venice. Just imagine, Clara!!! Four months from now, we'll be in Rome. We'll have lots of time to look around for your count or duke or prince. Why settle for anything less than a prince?

Love, Nora

Friday, April 17

The entire village is listening to the drama of the three trapped miners in Nova Scotia. The poor men are two miles beneath the Atlantic Ocean and have been down there now for five days. That is so hard to believe. After listening to the radio news this evening, I lay in bed seeing those men in all that darkness, breathing coal dust with the weight of the ocean above them. I suffered an attack of nerves there in the darkness and had trouble breathing. I have had these attacks before, but never one so acute. Finally, I had to turn on the bedside lamp. Slept then for a while. Children too are caught up in this drama and Milton made himself the most popular man in Whitfield, among the schoolchildren at least, by bringing a radio to the school. This afternoon we all listened to the announcer describing how the rescuers are trying to reach the men.

Monday, April 20

The miners are still alive and are actually being fed soup through a tube that has been threaded down a hole. Amid so much gloomy news these days, this is a remarkably heartening story.

Thursday, April 23

After 240 hours underground, two men (one of them a doctor) have been rescued. It was the most exciting event I have ever listened to. Assigned a composition for the pupils in Senior Second. Asked them to write on the rescue of the miners and the role that hope and courage play as qualities in daily life. When I told Milton, he was so taken with the idea that he decided to assign the same to his Senior Fourth. We decided we would give prizes to the winners.

135 East 33rd Street
New York
April 25, 1936

Dear Clara,
Have you been following the story of the miners up in Nova Scotia? Wasn't that something? I'm so glad they got those fellows out. It was in all the papers down here.

Speaking of stories, Evelyn has come up with a wonderful idea for the show while we are off gallivanting in Europe this summer. And maybe it would be a good idea if you didn't mention this to anybody in Whitfield, because we want to make the show as realistic as possible. What's going to happen is that Alice will suffer this minor accident (actually she is going to slip on the library steps and fall, hitting her head). She loses her memory and wanders away. Our dependable down-to-earth Alice just wanders away because, of course, she is not herself. Where has she gone? Everyone in Meadowvale is looking for her. What has happened? Has she been harmed? These are some of the questions listeners are bound to be asking themselves while you and I are having fun in Europe. Then Aunt Mary and Uncle Jim hire a private detective to find her. He turns out to be a handsome guy, but a bit of a scamp, and, of course, Effie falls for him.

By the time I get back, Alice will be found, just how and where we don't know yet, neither does E., for that matter. Then Alice will have to untangle Effie's affair with the private detective. Dr. Cal, of course, will help her. Everyone now thinks that Alice's disappearance will be a great boost for the summer audience, which tends to drop a bit. It turns out that going away in July may be the best thing for the show thanks to Evy's imagination. So, can I please ask you not to say who you are going to Italy with? Maybe you could tell people you are traveling with an old friend from your Normal School days or something. I hate to ask you to fib like this, but I'm sure you understand. It's just that people take the program so seriously that we have "to keep their illusions intact," to quote E. Hope you're well and looking forward to this summer as much as I am.

Love, Nora

Whitfield, Ontario
Sunday, May 3, 1936

Dear Nora,

Fear not, sister. Your little secret is safe with me. The ladies of Whitfield can look forward to a summer fraught with delicious anxiety over Alice's whereabouts while you and I and Mr. Mills cavort in Signor Mussolini's land. Actually, I haven't yet told anyone that I am going to Italy, but when I do I will say that I am traveling with a group from my Normal School days, class of 1922. We are the ones who, after years of frantic searching, have yet to find husbands and are now not likely to (alas); to console ourselves we are going to Italy to gawk at churches and galleries and eat ice cream. How does that sound? You must not for a minute worry about asking me to fib. I am really capable of the most outrageous lies, and there is something undeniably intoxicating about deceiving the Ida Atkinses of this world.

Our spring has been cool and damp and I long for sunlight and warmth. But everything is greening and rather wonderful. Yes, all of us listened to the Moose River Mine cave-in and it was heartening when those men were saved. A bit of good news for a change. All one hears on the radio these days is the threat of another war in Europe. I hope Mr. Mills is right about things over there. Best as always,

Clara

Saturday, May 16

"Let us talk about happiness," I said to Marion this afternoon. She had come around with some cake for me. Mother Webb, it seems, had been baking all day. Pies and cakes and tarts, a veritable bakery's output. So Marion had brought some of her mother's cake and I was grateful. I made some tea and we sat at the kitchen table. A nondescript day of cloud and showers. Happiness had been on my mind for days: its various aspects, its defining elements and so on. Why are some people happier than others? Could happiness more or less depend on one's disposition? A beggar, for example, may be cheerful and a wealthy man morose according to their temperaments. Even so, circumstances must surely play a role. Unless you are a madman or a saint, it would be hard to be happy if you were deprived of warmth and shelter and food; if you were in constant pain or had no expectation that matters would improve. All this was going through my mind when Marion came by, making her way along the hall, punishing my floorboards with her preposterous tread. Her dark bangs were damp from the rain and she looked both pitiful and lovely sitting down beside me.

"Let us talk about happiness," I said. "What makes you happy, Marion?"

Her beautiful dark eyes widened at once in wonder and alarm. What was Clara up to now? Was this another of her little games? *Honestly, Clara, I never know how to take you.* I could see that statement in her face. And why wouldn't she be suspicious? How many times since childhood have I been cruelly playful with her?

"Let's write a letter to the Prince of Wales," I remember proposing that one listless summer afternoon on the veranda steps. We were twelve or thirteen. Together we would write a letter to the handsome young prince who would be our next King. A look of adoration in Marion's eyes. "Oh yes, Clara, let's."

Her job was to make a list of questions for the prince, and she sat all afternoon beneath the maple tree with her paper and pencil. I went into the house and Father asked me to do something; I've forgotten now what. But when Marion showed me her questions, I only shrugged. By then I had lost interest or perhaps even forgotten about the project.

"I don't want to do that now. When you really think about it, Marion, it's a stupid idea."

I'm sure I said something like that before her crushed and tearful look.

It was hardly surprising then to watch her slowly weigh my questions this afternoon. "What do you mean, Clara? I don't get it."

"There's nothing to get," I said, helping myself to another piece of matrimony cake. "It's just a simple question. Well, maybe not so simple," I said.

"What in the world are you talking about?"

Yes! What in the world was I talking about? Besides, I already know what makes Marion happy.

—singing in the choir of Whitfield United Church on Sunday mornings
—the novels of Ellen Glasgow and A. J. Cronin
—Rudy Vallee crooning "My Time Is Your Time"
—"The House on Chestnut Street," "Just Plain Bill," "The Goldbergs," "Vic and Sade," "The Fleischman Hour"
—sitting in the kitchen with me on Saturday afternoon eating matrimony cake

I then told her that I was going to Italy this summer with some old chums from Normal School.

"Gosh, Clara. Italy!"

"Yep."

"I'd be so frightened to cross that ocean."

"Me too."

"Then why are you going?"

"Just for the hell of it."

"Clara, really!"

Monday, May 25

Dear Charlie,

It's a year now to the day. Remember? No, of course you don't. How could you be expected to remember fifteen minutes from a busy year? Oh, you may vaguely recall ____ing some woman in a ditch by the railway tracks, but so what? It wasn't the first and it won't be the last, will it? But I remember, Charlie. I remember that cool sunlit spring day and you walking toward me along the railway tracks and the boy with his bad eye and broken shoe. You came upon me like that, and I remember how you burned my wrists with your grip as you twirled me around in that grass. And now I am wondering how many others like me will lie awake at night and curse the hour you wandered into our lives?

Who will it be today? I see a fifteen-year-old girl and the farm where her father has hired you for a few days. And don't you get along well with the family! You're such a polite and amusing fellow. "He'll be all right if I tell him what to do." The words of the girl's father to his wife. They let you sleep on an old sofa in a corner of the barn.

"Why this is just fine, Missus. Don't you worry about me. I'll just be as snug as a bug here. It's all a workingman needs." And the girl is taken with you, isn't she? She's not very bright and she hasn't any friends and she likes to have you around. She likes your kidding when she's feeding the chickens. "The Exhibition! Sure I been to the Exhibition. Why, Thelma, you should see the rides they got down there! They got a Ferris wheel. You ever seen a Ferris wheel, Thelma? Why it must be the biggest in the world. And you know what, Thelma? I worked on that Ferris wheel last summer."

You can charm a simple girl like Thelma, can't you? And when all is said and done, you're not such a bad-looking fellow when you're scrubbed up and wearing a clean shirt. That wide monkey mouth is always full of jokes and stories. And today Mr. and Mrs. have gone into town for the afternoon. You watch the truck go down the lane, and then you watch Thelma at the clothesline, rising on her toes to pin the sheets. And isn't that a pretty sight, the backs of those bare legs and the round little rump in the cotton dress! Why, yes it is, and when she is finished you call out, "Come down here for a minute, Thelma, I got something to show you." And here she comes, wary but fascinated too. And you show her the little bird you whittled from a stick last evening. “Look at that now! Isn’t it pretty? I wish I could make it sing for you, Thelma.” That line surely beguiles the girl, and before you know it, the tomfoolery begins.

Everything starts with the tomfoolery, doesn’t it? The banter and the laughter and the tickling. “I’ll bet you got a funny bone somewheres, Thelma. I’ll just bet you have. Now where is that old Mister Funny Bone? Where is he hiding?” So Charlie’s courting dance begins and just listen to Thelma’s laughter. And why not? Somebody is paying attention to her. A little harmless fun on a spring afternoon when there is no one else around. “Give us a little kiss, Thelma. You’ll like it. You just see if you don’t.” That prying wheedling voice and those bony wrists of yours. Around and around and around you go there in the dust of the farmyard. And how in the world did things come to this pass? There you both are on that sofa in a corner of the barn, the dusty sunlight in the doorway and isn’t that just a glimmer of fear now in Thelma’s eyes? She wasn’t quite counting on this, was she, Charlie? Being pulled down on the musty old sofa next to you? But the line has been crossed, hasn’t it? The line was crossed when you stood there looking at the backs of her bare legs ten minutes ago. And you are not a man who takes no for an answer, so we might just as well get on with this, right, Charlie? “There now, little girl, it’s going to be just fine. You’ll like it. We’ll have some fun here, yes we will. Oh my, look at this now. Yes, yes, I’m gonna ____ you, Thelma, and you’re gonna love it. Yes, yes, you will, you pretty little thing.”

Do you know what you are, Charlie? You are a grief-monger, purveying sadness and remorse across the land. In my dreams, I have seen you bent across this girl or someone like her, and I have brought the ax down upon your skull (waking once with such a cry because my hand had struck the wall). Oh, in my dreams I have done you in, Charlie, murdered you with mattock or coal shovel, dragged your body into bushes where only flies and maggots would ever find you. Yet none of this will happen. You will die a peaceful man in some far-off year (say 1977), a skinny frail old fellow in a charity ward, fussed over by the nurses who love your joking manner. That's how it will end for you, Charlie. There in a narrow hospital bed with clean sheets, surrounded by attentive women who see only "a sweet old guy who always has a smile and a story." But not all your stories get told, do they, Charlie?

Saturday, June 27

Where has the last month gone? Yesterday was the end of another school year and now I am ready for my summer adventure. Ida Atkins stopped me on the street this afternoon. She crowds you so when she talks. The rankness of her breath. Spring onions from her garden for lunch.

"I've heard of your holiday plans, Clara, and I'm delighted for you. Perhaps an evening next fall you'll tell us all about your trip. I'm sure the ladies would enjoy hearing about it."

What did I say to that? I may have agreed to speak to the Women's Auxiliary or the Missionary Society. Something. It was all a bit indeterminate. The woman flusters me so. But what of that? It's weeks and weeks away and today is my birthday. Today I am three and thirty as the poets used to say. My life must be half over now and what have I accomplished?

Whitfield, Ontario
Sunday, June 28, 1936

Dear Nora,

It's ages since I've been in touch. What are you up to these days? I hope that all is well and that our travel plans are still in force. By my reckoning (as you can tell, I am already adopting the argot of the seafarer), three weeks from today we should be aboard the *Genoa Princess*, outward bound for Naples. If this be but a dream, please so inform me. If it's all true, I am planning to leave Toronto on Tuesday,

July 14, arriving in New York the next morning. Is that all right with you?

Clara

135 East 33rd Street
New York
Saturday, July 4, 1936

Dear Clara,

I am *really* sorry not to have written before. Honestly, I don't know where this spring has gone. I even forgot your birthday!!! I'll make it up to you when you get down here, believe me. We'll go on a real shopping spree. I have been awfully busy with the program and then it seems that Lewis has to say goodbye to just about everybody in New York. So a lot of people have been taking us out to dinner or throwing parties.

I have been a little preoccupied lately (another reason I haven't written, I guess). These days I sometimes don't know where I stand with Lewis. Not perhaps the best situation to be in when you're planning a holiday with somebody. Boy, am I glad you're coming along. I'm not suggesting that Lewis and I are breaking up or anything, but there is no denying that things are a little unsettled at the moment. I have told you about his sharp tongue and I recognize that he is a very intelligent man and has mixed all his life with brainy people. I told him right off the bat that I was not the college type, and he accepted that. I have always said that you have to accept people for what they are and not for what you think they ought to be. And I have never pretended to be anything other than what I am. Everything else between us has been wonderful, especially you know what! That part has been just fine.

It's when we are talking about things that sometimes there is trouble. Lewis can be damn cruel. Mind you, I knew that from the first day when I had lunch with him in the cafeteria at Radio City. But he was always pretty good about saying sorry and how he didn't mean it and I could accept that. But he can be really mean! The other night at this restaurant, we were sitting around after dinner with some people talking about this movie and I said how much I enjoyed it. All right, it was a corny movie. I could see that, but it was also kind of sweet and had a nice story. Well, that set His Lordship off, believe me. He started going on about how "Nora, of course, is in the sentiment business with her little radio show" and all that. I just got up and left. He came out and I was waiting for a taxi and he said, "What are you doing embarrassing me like that in front of my friends?" Imagine! Embarrassing him? What about me? I said to him, "I'm not taking any more of your guff about my job, Lewis. If you don't like what I do for a living, too bad." I guess we made quite a scene there in front of the restaurant. Anyway, I went home by myself. I was in tears. He phoned the next morning and apologized, blamed it on the drinks, and that's part of it, of course. He's usually okay when he's not drinking, but put a couple of whiskeys into him and look out. So we made up, but that's just an example of the kind of thing that sometimes goes on between us.

A couple of weeks ago at a party I met one of his ex-wives. Can you imagine going to a party where you run into one of your beau's ex-wives, but that happens all the time in New York, which in many ways is a very close little world, especially among the artsy and writer types. The ex-wife is also a writer and a bit of a mess from what I could see. Lewis practically ignored me at this party while he talked to "Peggy" who was having some kind of emotional trouble. Seeing her psychiatrist and all that. And drinking buckets as far as I could tell. You should have seen the look she gave me across the room. It was as if I was this little backwoods peasant from the forests of Canada. Oh, I'm sorry to go on like this, but I wanted to explain why I have been so preoccupied.

Maybe getting away from New York will be good for us. When Lewis and I are alone everything is usually fine. The thing is I'm still very much in love with him. Right from the start I could see all his faults, his grumpiness, his snobby attitude, his short temper and so on. But I have always been prepared to take a person as they are. You have to take the bad with the good, don't you?

Anyway, you get the general idea, so enough of this. We'll have fun on our holiday, don't you worry. We're sailing on the eighteenth and you are going to be here on the fifteenth, that's a Wednesday. Clara, could you do me a favor? Wednesday is a workday for me, and I'm always a little nervous before the broadcast, so could you find your way to the taxi stand at Penn Station and just give the driver my address? It's only a few blocks away. Make sure you have a little American money, but it's only a forty-cent cab ride. If the train is late and I'm not here when you arrive, just ring the superintendent's buzzer and Mr. Shulman will let you in. I have told him all about you, so don't worry about being left out on the street. Just make yourself at home. Put your feet up and turn on the radio. At three o'clock there is a really good program!!!

It's the American holiday weekend and this afternoon Lewis and I are going to friends of his out in New Jersey. Some place called Sea Bright. I like the sound of it anyway, and it will get us out of the city and the heat. It's hot as Hades down here, so be prepared.

Love, Nora

P.S. Yesterday Evelyn reminded me to pass along her good wishes. She is looking forward to seeing you again and is planning a little party for us. Ciao! That's Italian for "cheerio" or "see ya," according to His Lordship who is busy these days with his dictionaries and phrase books.

Saturday, July 11

This has been the hottest week on record in Ontario according to today's *Herald*. It was 100 degrees in the driveway today. Thirty people in Toronto have died from this heat and hundreds are sleeping in the parks. What must New York be like? In her letter Nora says it's "hot as Hades" but doesn't elaborate. She is too busy chronicling the woes of life with Mr. Mills. It doesn't bode well for a holiday. I don't care to be around quarrelsome lovers with their sulks and tears and recuperative embraces. All that emotional theater can be wearing to an onlooker. Nothing I can do about it, of course. A book left on the veranda last night with a note from Marion wishing me a safe and happy journey. She is off to Sparrow Lake first thing in the morning.

The book is called *Death in Venice* and in her note Marion hopes "it will be a good read on the ocean." She must have bought it in a secondhand bookstore in Toronto. It has no wrapper and it feels unread; the pages are stiff; it smells a little musty as though years ago its owner, perhaps one day after Christmas, started the book and then, disappointed by the absence of blood and corpses (What the hell! This isn't a mystery book), put it aside and forgot about it. So it became part of a rich man's library, and then was sold finally to one of those shops along Queen Street. Marion was no doubt taken by the title and thought it was a crime novel. A good read on the ocean. In fact, the book is anything but a mild crime novel and I read it at a sitting this afternoon. It's a brilliant story about an artist in crisis. An aging writer, vaguely dissatisfied with the course of his life and the demands of his art, journeys to Venice for a holiday and falls in love with a beautiful boy. The entire experience, unconsummated and unheralded, enthralls, bewilders and destroys him. An extraordinary book. Thank you, Marion. Mann's observations on those of us who live alone seem accurate to me. He writes,

> The experiences of a man who lives alone and in silence are both vaguer and more penetrating than those of people in society; his thoughts are heavier, more odd and touched always with melancholy. Images and observations which could easily be disposed of by a glance, a smile, an exchange of opinion, will occupy him

unbearably, sink deep into the silence, become full of meaning, become life, adventure, emotion. Loneliness ripens the eccentric, the daringly and estrangingly beautiful, the poetic. But loneliness also ripens the perverse, the disproportionate, the absurd, and the illicit.

Wednesday, July 15 (New York)

From about midnight we moved through heavy rain, but everything had cleared up by the time I arrived at Penn Station. The morning was fresh and cool, and tired though I was, I felt exuberant as I looked out the taxi window at the streets of New York, cleansed and glistening in the sunlight. I was thinking, of course, of how different everything is this year from last, when I had arrived feeling so burdened and perplexed, frightened for my life in fact. Nora was here when I arrived, but she is now at work and I am sitting by the window on this glorious summer afternoon, watching the people pass below on Thirty-third Street, listening to the honk and blare of the cars and trucks, the muffled racket of the elevated train on Third Avenue.

Directly below me a smartly dressed light-skinned Negro couple are having some kind of disagreement, the man putting forth his position with gestures, ingratiating himself with the lady. There is a kind of rakish glamour to this pair, the man in his suit and straw hat, his two-toned shoes, and the pretty woman in her flowered dress, the long hair straightened and gleaming with oil. As he helps her into a taxi I catch at least a little of his predicament as he raises his voice in mild exasperation. "Don't you understand, woman? I got to get back my equilibrium." What a good phrase! Get back my equilibrium.

Thursday, July 16

Met Lewis Mills tonight. The three of us had dinner in a fancy restaurant near the park, and Mills met us there, rising from the table as we entered. He was friendly enough, holding on to my hand perhaps a little too long as Nora introduced us.

"Ah, our traveling companion, the sister I've heard so much about."

A mild satirical tone in his voice. Mockery, even kindly meant, is probably second nature to him. He's an intellectual bruiser, one of life's critics, charming and convivial when things are going his way, abrasive and difficult when crossed. I think I could see a little of all that in him tonight. He fussed over Nora in his mildly critical style.

"Are you going to have the oysters again, sweetie? You raved about them the other night."

Had Nora gone a little overboard in her enthusiasm for the oysters "the other night"? And was he now reminding her with the use of that verb?

Mills is a stolid handsome man with a perfectly round bald head. There is a no-nonsense air and look about him. He is used to having his way with women and that can have its appeal, I suppose. Perhaps it's what attracts Nora whose taste in men usually runs toward the matinee idol. No point in appearing like a total bumpkin, so I asked about the elections in November. "Would Roosevelt win again?"

"In a landslide," said Mills, who just last month attended the Republican convention in Cleveland and didn't think much of either Mr. Landon, or his vice-presidential choice, a wealthy Chicago newspaperman. "The Republicans keep shooting themselves in the foot," said Mills. "They can't read the mood of the country. They pay too much attention to the big shots in their party and not enough to the little guy on the street. The little guy loves FDR."

He asked me many questions about Canada and the King government. He's a very well informed man, intelligent and imaginative, and despite his sometimes overbearing manner, I found myself liking him. When we got back to the apartment, Nora showed me L.M.'s magazine article on radio. She wasn't happy with it.

"Lewis thinks we should be listening to highbrow stuff all the time, but ordinary people deserve to be entertained too. Not everyone likes the opera or lectures on dead writers."

Nora was tired and out of sorts tonight and I didn't argue with her. After she went to bed I read Mills's piece. Entitled "The Demotic Voice," it is highly critical of programs like "The House on Chestnut Street." Mills grudgingly admits that such programs employ "gifted people and a great deal of craft goes into even the most banal offering." But he objects to radio's simplified view of life and laments the increasing commercialization of popular culture. No wonder poor Nora didn't think much of it.

Friday, July 17 (6:30 p.m.)

Went shopping with Nora this afternoon after her program. The big department stores like Macy's and Gimbels are very busy and there is such a quantity of goods on display. Little evidence of hard times in Manhattan! Went to a big bookstore on Fifth Avenue and bought cheap but good copies of Keats's letters, Boswell's *Life of Johnson*, a collection of Heine's poetry and *A Brief History of Modern Italy*. Nora bought a copy of *Gone With the Wind*, the Civil War novel that, according to her, "everyone in New York is reading." It would certainly appear so judging from the bookstore windows which are filled with copies. Tonight a party for Nora at Evelyn's.

Saturday, July 18 (1:30 a.m.)

Difficulty sleeping, so have got up to sit by the window. The big city seems to be settling down for the night. A police siren now and then, but only faint traffic noise from the avenues nearby. L.M. is picking us up at noon, and in twelve hours we'll be aboard the ship.

A party tonight at Evelyn's and she greeted me with a great hug and kisses. I was looking forward to a conversation with her, but she was preoccupied with her "friend" the dancer June who drank too much and became ill. She's young, only twenty or so. Very tall and blond and beautiful. Striking might be a suitable cliché to describe her. E. spent most of the evening with her in the bathroom. Or so it seemed to me. The young woman is from Texas, and before she got drunk I had a little talk with her, but for the life of me, I could scarcely understand a word she said. She might just as well have been speaking in a foreign tongue. The people at the party were lively and open, but I am so awkward at these things, while Nora moves through the crowd with such ease. I did, however, enjoy meeting some of these people. Graydon Lott is a sweet and gentle man and Vivian Rhodes, who plays the mischievous and careless Effie, is in fact a rather bookish woman who is married to a professor of classics at Columbia University. He sat in a corner all evening drinking soda water and I believe that he, along with Mr. Lott and I, were the only non-drinkers in the crowd. Everyone was talking about the Civil War book with the room divided between those who had read it and those who were now doing so. "Don't, don't tell me what happens." At midnight Evelyn brought out a cake in the shape of a boat with "Bon Voyage, Nora" on the icing. Nora gave a fine little thank-you speech. How at home she is among these friendly and likable Americans! I confess to a pang of jealousy as I watched her cutting the cake. To have so many people wishing you happiness surely counts for something. In the taxi back to the apartment, I asked why L.M. had not come along to the party.

"He would have been there if I'd asked him," she said. "He would have enjoyed standing around and sneering at all of us. That's why I didn't ask him."

Even allowing that she was a little tight, I was shocked at the bitterness in her voice.

*Saturday, July 18 (*Genoa Princess, *5:30 p.m.)*

A rich glowing afternoon on the Hudson River. It's exhilarating to be moving on water. My little room (cabin) is quite comfortable and has a small round window (porthole) overlooking the water. Without it, I would feel a bit smothered in this space. L.M. and Nora next door. L.M. is busy reading newspapers; he brought a stack of them aboard the ship. Civil war has broken out in Spain, and L.M. is devouring any news he can find on this. Nora and I went for a walk around the upper deck (promenading) and she told me that she can't get a word out of L.M. because he is so absorbed in this Spanish business. After our walk, we had tea and biscuits in the lounge. Dinner will not be served until eight o'clock, a nuisance to a rustic like myself who is used to earlier meals. I shall have to fill up on biscuits. The ship is American, but the crew is mostly Italian, and the stewards make a fuss over the female passengers. They are handsome young fellows in their fancy getup, helpful and flirtatious, proud as peacocks. Several women in the lounge reading *GWTW*.

Sunday, July 19 (7:00 a.m.)

Awakened an hour ago and stared out my little window at the sea. When I went on deck it was deserted, except for an elderly man dressed all in white. He was briskly walking about, stopping now and then to fan his arms like propellers, or sink to his knees and rise again several times. He looked a little angry doing this, which I thought a pity on such a lovely morning with the sunlight sparkling on the sea. Nothing now but water and sky as we move between them.

(4:30 p.m.)

Spent an hour in the lounge this afternoon with L.M. Nora was off playing shuffleboard. She has befriended some wealthy young Americans of Italian descent, a playful group it seems. L.M. came into the lounge and, after looking around in his surly manner, came over and sat down with his newspapers. Ordered a large gin drink from the steward. In his shirt and tie and linen suit he looked flushed and distended. I wondered if his bowels might not be doing their job. Pleasant enough however. Nodded at my book of Keats's letters as if they were an agreeable companion to a schoolteacher's sea journey. Appraised me with his shrewd, intelligent eyes. He is excited over the outbreak of war in Spain. Called it a "fight between Church and the Communists. And the Church will win," he exclaimed. "Franco will get all the help he needs from Germany and Italy."

I played the innocent female, mildly distressed by the situation. "Do you think we'll be in any danger? Don't we have to go right by Spain, so to speak?"

An indulgent smile. L.M. likes to be asked questions. "We do, indeed, Miss Callan. Or, I hope I can call you Clara. Yes, we have to sail right past Spain at Gibraltar. Your grasp of geography is a good deal sounder than your sister's. This morning Nora had Spain situated a little too far to the north. Around Belgium, I think."

"I'm sure you're exaggerating, Mr. Mills."

Another smile. "Perhaps a little. And it's Lewis. Please! We're on a trip together, Clara."

Always that hint of sexual playfulness in his voice. Yet he looked hot and ill at ease in the wicker chair, fanning himself with his Panama hat and sipping his gin. It seemed as if he hadn't yet figured out how to deal with me or perhaps with many things. I wondered if he had been to Europe before.

"Not since the war," he said and then after a while, "There will be no danger. After all, we're flying the American flag. Both sides will leave us alone. The last thing either wants is an international incident involving the U.S.A. We Americans are still very much a question mark to Europeans. They still don't know which side we'll throw our support behind."

I asked him about his plans in Italy.

"I'd like to see how that country is working under Mussolini," he said. "God knows they've had time now. If you can believe what you read, he's done some great stuff. So, I'd like to know whether

Europe's future is in Fascism or Communism. I'd like to get some kind of handle on that. Certainly, Fascism has lots of friends and not just in Italy or Germany or Spain. There is more support for Fascism in France and England than most people think. By most people, I'm referring to Americans. So, I'd like to see how it has affected everyday life. I'm going to be talking to people who have lived in Italy for several years: writers, painters, a few professors. I'd like to interview Santayana, the philosopher. He lives in Rome these days and I think he would have some interesting things to say about it all. He's an old man now, but apparently still very alert. But I don't know if I can get to him. I didn't get an answer to my letter. I'd also like to talk to Pound, the poet."

I enjoyed listening to L.M. and as he talked he seemed to relax. Perhaps he had unloosened a button or two or maybe it was the gin. He ordered another and talked about how Europeans are more interested in politics than most Americans.

"It's closer to their lives. And they had the war to deal with. I imagine there are many who are scared to death of another one and will do anything to avoid it. A lot of the older people don't want to go through that again and Hitler knows it. That's why he got his way in the Rhineland and he's not finished either."

Another drink was placed before him. "What do you remember of the war, Clara? You would have been just a kid."

"Oh, soldiers in the village. Farm boys coming back from army camp all spruced up in their uniforms with their boots polished and their hair cut. I used to play the piano at school concerts and war bond evenings. 'The Minstrel Boy,' 'Keep the Home Fires Burning.'"

L.M. seemed delighted with these images. I looked out the window of the lounge. The day had clouded over.

"You Canadians," he said, "had it much tougher than we did. You really took it on the chin over there." He paused for more gin. "I was in it, you know. Not as a combatant. I was against the war on principle, but I joined the Ambulance Corps and got over to France in the summer of 1918. I was twenty-eight years old. I'm still not sure why I did that." In fact, he did look rather bewildered by the memory. "Saw some terrible things, Clara. Not as bad as being shot at, but bad enough. That's why I don't think there will be another war. Not a big one anyway. A lot of people over there don't want to go through all that again. Of course, it's more complicated now. There's this whole business with the Jews in Germany. I'd like to find out more about that, but the Germans have been stonewalling me. They want to give me the tourist's tour, I guess. They've had some problems with American journalists. They've kicked one or two out of the country so I don't know how far I'll get. Once I get these pieces written, I'd like to gather them into a book, maybe for next spring. I've already done some things, a piece on radio entertainment, you know, Nora's world. Another on the radio priest Coughlin and one on the labor leader John L. Lewis. Covered the Republican and Democratic conventions last month. I thought all this could make an interesting book. Call it *The Temper of the Times* or something like that. What do you think?"

I said it sounded interesting. It was raining now and I watched the drops, driven by a gust of wind, strike the windows and run down the glass. On the deck, stewards were folding up the canvas chairs and people were hurrying inside with newspapers and magazines on their heads. L.M. asked me what I wanted most to see in Italy and I told him the house in Rome where Keats died.

"Nora told me you write poetry. I'd like to see some of your work one day."

I told him there was nothing to see. "I only dream of doing it," I said.

He was about to add something when Nora came in from her shuffleboard game with a sweater tied across her shoulders, her hair damp from the rain. She looked pretty and erotic and L.M. rose to embrace her. There was talk of cocktails somewhere with her new friends. Nora and L.M. began to nibble at one another, and I thought of a nymph and a satyr at play. Agreed to meet them for dinner and they left the lounge arm in arm.

On my way to the cabin, I looked out at the rain beating now against the windows. A steward assured me that it was nothing. "A little squall, Signorina. It will soon pass."

And so it did. A moment ago the sun broke through the clouds and briefly colored the sea a light bronze. I keep imagining the depths over which we travel: the abyss that awaits the careless or unfortunate. I wonder how far it is to the bottom of the sea.

Tuesday, July 21 (midnight)

Nora and L.M. quarreled before dinner. Something to do with suitable or unsuitable clothing. Lewis a little tight and more than a little disagreeable. Of course, Nora can hold her own. Flashes of the temper I remember from childhood when she and Father would argue over the smallest things. They were in the midst of all this when they knocked on my door to take me to the dining room. Wasn't the least bit hungry. I can't get used to eating at eight o'clock and so I keep asking the steward for fruit and biscuits which I bolt in the late afternoon. Also the food on the ship is foreign and rich to me. Soups made from tortoises and strange fishes, guinea fowl, whatever they are. I suppose I am not made for the "high life."

Wednesday, July 22

All seems well again between Nora and L.M. Cooing and touching at breakfast (my best meal). A brilliant sunny day and the sea as flat as a plate. The days are now very warm. This afternoon I saw a faint smudge on the horizon. Smoke from another ship perhaps. A man and his little boy were examining it through binoculars, and after a few minutes the man shyly offered me the glasses for a look. But I could make nothing of this dark smear against the ridge of water and sky.

We introduced ourselves. Mr. Rossi is from Cleveland, Ohio, and is traveling with his seven-year-old son, Marco. They are going to see the child's grandmother who lives south of Naples. Despite the afternoon sun, Mr. Rossi was dressed like an English gentleman in blazer and white pants and straw hat. The little boy stood next to him unsmiling in a sailor suit and cap. An air of almost comical gravity surrounded both father and son. Life seemed to be a serious business with them and then I discovered that Mr. Rossi had recently lost his wife and the little boy his mother. She died two months ago in a motorcar accident, and so now they are going to spend some time with relatives "in the old country." Mr. Rossi emigrated thirty-five years ago at the age of fifteen and he has done well in the construction business. He has not been back to Italy since that long-ago day in 1901 when he sailed away with an aunt and uncle. His father is dead but he would like to bring his mother back to America for a visit, though he doubts that she will agree. "She loves her village and, of course, Il Duce. She thinks he is a saint."

Mr. Rossi told me about his wife whom he met in a diner where she worked as a waitress. In no time they had "tied the knot." This was only eight years ago. "I was too busy making money to look for a wife. And then when I found one, she was taken from me just like that." He made a snapping sound with his enormous fingers. She was struck by a car while crossing the street. "But, it was only a nudge that knocked her down and she struck her head. Killed like that and not a mark on her body, so help me God."

The little boy scarcely moved as he listened to all this, and I wondered how many times he had heard the story. Mr. Rossi carefully fitted the expensive-looking binoculars into a leather case and hung it around his neck. He struck me as a man who pays attention to details. He looked down at his son. "Would you like an ice cream, Marco?"

"Yes, Papa."

"Would you care to join us, Miss?"

I wouldn't have minded a bit, for I liked Mr. Rossi and Marco and the graceful, particular air about them. The sun, however, had given me a searing headache and I had to retreat to my cabin.

This evening there was a change in our seating at dinner, probably managed by Nora. We are now with her new friends, two couples in their thirties. They are in the restaurant business in Philadelphia and this is their third or fourth trip to Italy. They are cheerful, loud, self-absorbed people with numerous jokes about Italian men and their alleged virility. As the single woman at the table, I was good-naturedly warned to be on guard for my virtue. Laughter all around except from L.M. who seemed to be tiring of the shenanigans. He was beginning to take on what Nora refers to as "his bulldog look."

The captain, a hearty American in his smart white uniform, came by the tables, inquiring about our welfare. "How are we all getting along? Is there anything you folks need?"

One of the restaurant wives asked about the war in Spain. "Would we be in any danger?"

"Clear sailing all the way," said the captain. "You have my word on it."

At a nearby table, some elderly women were making a pleasant fuss over Marco, and for the first time Mr. Rossi looked happy.

Thursday, July 23

Nora at her shuffleboard all morning despite the heat. I have been reading Keats's letters. He is walking through Scotland with his friend Brown. Poor Keats has only three years to live. L.M. came by the lounge and said he was talking to one of the ship's officers, and we may be held up by this war, after all. Apparently Gibraltar has been attacked by airships. He asked me how I felt about being so close to an actual war and I only shrugged. I think he interpreted this gesture as indifference to danger, when in fact it was nothing of the sort. I am not a courageous person at the best of times; the shrug was only a reaction to my sense of unreality. I seem to exist these days in a kind of dream.

I am sitting in a chair in the middle of the Atlantic Ocean, reading about Keats tramping through Scotland.

Later

A hot night and many people are staying out on deck quite late. Some kind of auction in the ballroom and Nora and L.M. have gone to that. In these latitudes, the stars are immense and brilliant, a heavenly feast for the eyes. I wish I knew more about them. As I gazed upward, I thought of Evelyn Dowling's story about her old teacher setting up her telescope one winter night on the snow-covered playing field.

Watched a couple leaning against the railing. The woman kept up this high-pitched laughter. On and on it went, ending finally with, "Oh, Roger, you slay me!"

What an odd expression!

Friday, July 24 (4:10 a.m.)

I awoke two hours ago from a troubling dream which I wish I could recall, but the memory of it vanished upon awakening. The ship had stopped and I was aware at once of the stillness and silence. Have lain awake now these two hours, watching the stars, until one by one they have disappeared into the lightening sky. Just felt the vibrations of the engine and so once again we are under way.

(Afternoon)

It is so hot now that few venture out on deck. Like others, I am thirsty all the time, but one's thirst is quenched by the best lemonade I have ever tasted. The stewards will bring as much as you want. You must drink it quickly, however, for the ice melts so fast in this heat. Nora is spending the afternoons in her cabin reading *GWTW*. Looking out at the blazing, merciless sun, I thought of Coleridge's sailors. How terrible to suffer from thirst in such heat! "There passed a weary time/Each throat was parched and glazed each eye/A weary time, a weary time."

Saturday, July 26 (3:00 a.m.)

A hot and still and starless night. Only the whirring of the tiny fan and the faint vibrations from the ship's engine. Awakened a half hour ago by a "smothering seizure." I felt as if I were drowning in darkness. Had such difficulty getting my breath, but far worse was this terrible sense of loss and sadness accompanying this panic in the dark. Turned on the reading lamp and this seems to have helped. I think I will soon sleep again.

(3:00 p.m.)

The poor night's sleep left me nervous and unsteady, so I took some Sal Hepatica and stayed in my cabin for a good part of today. The stewards were very kind, bringing me fruit and tea. Nora too is unwell with her monthlies. L.M. is working on something. I saw him an hour ago at a small corner table in the lounge. His "bulldog look" said clearly "stay away." There is to be a masquerade ball tonight, though many seem too hot and fed up to think about going. The novelty of life aboard ship has passed, and most would probably like to feel again the earth beneath their feet. The recreation director, a bossy little man, has been bustling about all afternoon, knocking on cabin doors, trying to drum up business for his dance. Talked to Mr. Rossi who is distressed. It seems that children will not be allowed to attend and I gather that the R.D. was rather rude to him. A steward told me that we will see the Rock of Gibraltar tomorrow.

Sunday July 26

A misty morning with the sun a lemon-colored eye in the clouds. By nine o'clock, however, the sky was clear and the day hot again. Around eleven a flurry of excitement: Gibraltar could now be seen through binoculars, and so there was much rushing to and fro to find a spot along the railing. Nora, a little pallid and depressed, joined me on deck. She thanks God for *Gone With the Wind* which is keeping her occupied. L.M. "is too cranky for words."

(5:00 p.m.)

We passed through the Straits of Gibraltar. Mr. Rossi loaned me his glasses, so I could see the immense brown cliffs and the faint outlines of a settlement. There is a rumor that Loyalist Spanish gunboats are patrolling these waters, but we have seen nothing.

(Later)

Just before dinner we heard the drone of airplanes and people were looking skyward. One man claimed to have seen them, but for the rest of us, there was only the immensity of the darkening sky. I asked a steward how far it was to Naples.

"Nearly a thousand miles," he said. "We'll be there Wednesday afternoon."

The stewards and waiters seem unconcerned by these rumors of gunboats and airships and that at least is reassuring. And so now I am traveling over the dark water of the Mediterranean.

Monday, July 27

A long talk with Nora who is troubled by L.M.'s ill temper, which she attributes to no sex on account of her condition.

"I've never seen anyone so interested in doing it. You'd never know to look at him, would you?"

In the late afternoon an Italian warship steamed past with smoke billowing from her stacks; the sailors in their white uniforms and tasseled caps looked splendidly severe. Many aboard the *Genoa Princess* waved and cheered, but the sailors looked back at us impassively. At dinner, people talked about whether or not Italy would get involved in this war. L.M. thinks they won't, but believes they will help the rebels with guns and planes. All this talk about war has made the restaurant wives nervous and unhappy. Rain in the night. I was awakened by the sound of it against my little window.

Tuesday, July 28

Everything was still wet when I went out this morning at six o'clock. The deck was deserted except for Mr. Rossi who was leaning on the railing, looking out at the beginning of another hot day. We had the following conversation.

"I am so very nervous," he confessed. "Tomorrow I will see my mother for the first time in thirty-five years. I was only fifteen when I left with my aunt and uncle. What will Mama think when she sees me?"

"She will be very proud of you and Marco," I said. "After all, you have been a success in America and Marco is a handsome little boy."

Mr. Rossi looked as if he wanted to embrace me. "Do you think so? I could never do anything right in Mama's eyes. None of us could. How I wish my wife were with me!"

Mr. Rossi stared gloomily out to sea for the longest time and then said something like this.

"Mama was difficult and I will tell you for a fact that as a child I was frightened of her. We all were, my sisters, my brothers. Papa never said a word. He wouldn't contradict her. Of course, he was much smaller. It's true. My mother is a big woman, over six feet and maybe two hundred pounds. In the old days, she could lift a sack of grain like that." Again the snap of the heavy fingers. "And her temper! I have seen her handle men in the village. I watched her once. I was only five or six, maybe Marco's age. I watched her pull a man off the stone bench near the church where the men gathered to talk after Mass. He must have said something. Mama pulled him right off the bench and shook a fist in his face. I remember that as if it were yesterday. As a girl, she worked in the vineyards. Worked for my grandfather and better than her brothers too. She was strong. But any little thing could set her off. The whole village was afraid of her, I think. Even the priest."

Another pause. "I hope she takes to Marco. She is now much older, of course, but still fierce enough, according to my sisters who write. They say she can still get into her rages, and then look out. You must leave the house. She throws things. I'm afraid she will frighten the boy. He's a nervous child. Perhaps it was a mistake to return."

What a sweet and gentle man Mr. Rossi is! And while we talked, the little boy was asleep in his cabin, dreaming perhaps of his dead mother, or the fierce old tyrant who lives in a village south of Naples, with her bad temper and her pictures of Mussolini and the Virgin Mary on the walls. Perhaps Mr. Rossi has made a mistake in returning to his homeland, but it was not for me to tell him.

L.M. and Nora are both in much better spirits today; we are all looking forward to getting off the *Genoa Princess* tomorrow.

Wednesday, July 29 (Hotel Victoria, Rome, 11:30 p.m.)

An exhausting day! We docked at Naples around four o'clock this afternoon. Chaotic! So many people jostling you and everyone seemed to be shouting. L.M. kept bulling his way through all this with Nora and me in tow. A final look at Mr. Rossi, surrounded by weeping women in black; they must have been his sisters. The child was being passed from woman to woman and smothered with kisses; poor little Marco seemed dazed and unhappy. I looked for the legendary matriarch, but she must have stayed in her village. A nasty scene at the immigration counter, and for a few horrible minutes it looked as though we might not be allowed to enter the country. The problem was L.M.'s truculence. He seemed to be under the impression that the immigration people would recognize him as a distinguished guest, an American journalist who was doing them a favor by visiting their country. In L.M.'s view, they should have been appropriately cowed. Instead, they didn't care a pin for his reputation, and in fact were suspicious of both his credentials and his reasons for being there. The result—a huge fuss with glares and muttered threats about appealing to the American Embassy with heads rolling, etc., etc. On both sides of the counter, a great deal of masculine posturing that reminded me of the schoolyard at recess. My feet encased in new shoes were swollen with the heat and Nora too was suffering.

"Isn't this awful, Clara!"

More charging through the crowd to the railroad station with L.M. in the vanguard, followed by two frightened women and a poor hunchbacked porter pushing a barrow with our luggage. Resentful looks from all around us to whom we must have seemed hateful and rude.

Aboard the train for Rome in a first-class carriage, I watched L.M. who sat by the window glowering at the crowd on the platform: a stranger thrust suddenly into a foreign land and imagining sharp practice and iniquity everywhere. He is probably right, but I fear he will get us into trouble with his belligerent manner. There are so many men in uniform in this country: immigration people, customs officials, railroad police, soldiers, sailors, carabinieri, clusters of ominous-looking black-shirted young men; all of them look as if they expect to be obeyed instantly. This appears to be the face of Fascism, at least as far as I can tell. When we arrived in Rome, we had problems with the luggage. A piece belonging to Nora was missing.

Nora: "It's all right, Lewis. I can do without those things."

L.M.: "The country is full of goddamn thieves."

Thursday, July 30 (Hotel Victoria, 8:00 a.m.)

Dinner in the hotel dining room last evening was nourishing and good. They kindly made special arrangements for us since we arrived so late. The hotel people speak English and are very accommodating. Most of the guests appear to be English or American. Some Germans and Scandinavians. L.M. and Nora are across the hall registered as man and wife; apparently it is the only way to secure a room where they may sleep together. We are thankfully at the rear of the hotel and away from the noise of the street (Via Sistina). My room is small but comfortable. It overlooks a courtyard in the middle of which is an enormous plane tree whose trunk is enclosed by a wooden bench. I write these words at a beautiful little rosewood desk; here in this room, someone with talent and time might write a novel or a book of poems. We are going to see some of Rome today.

(8:00 p.m.)

The house where Keats died is not far and we plan to visit it tomorrow. The streets of Rome are colorful with flags and bunting on all the buildings in celebration of Mussolini's birthday two days ago. No one knows how old he is, and we were told that it is forbidden to inquire. Still fatigued from the journey and so have retired early.

Friday, July 31 (Hotel Victoria)

L.M. in a gay humor at breakfast. Had business to attend to today.

"You are on your own, ladies, so beware. Two Protestants in the middle of all this Catholic splendor. Try not to be corrupted."

He can be amusing, but I sense genuine hostility behind it all. He is an unhappy man and I don't think he really cares for women except in a physical way. Or he may just be bored with us. Nora seems increasingly bewildered by him, and I wonder if their affair has run its course. They are always sniping at one another. Today Nora asked the waiter for a boiled egg and this roused L.M. from his newspaper.

"Italians don't eat eggs for breakfast, Nora. The guidebook will tell you that."

"I only asked, Lewis. I didn't insist."

"Yes, but you must try to adjust to new surroundings, kiddo. Have you never heard the saying 'When in Rome, do as the Romans do'?" At the next table a man brayed with laughter.

"Well, I'm sorry if I'm not the swell traveler you are, Lewis."

"Don't worry about it. I'm just trying to save you embarrassment."

As we left, L.M. said, "If you're going to visit churches, ladies, put something on your heads, or they won't let you in."

"I read that in a guidebook, Lewis. I can read, you know."

We were glad to be on our own and so we visited the famous chapel in the Vatican, standing in an enormous lineup behind German tourists who were growling away and eating ice cream. Nora is taken with all this Catholic art, sentimental about the stained windows and statuary; she was forever lighting candles or kneeling at yet another plaster Virgin Mary, looking appealingly pious in her kerchief and sundress.

"What are you praying for, Nora?" I asked. "Anything special?" She bristled at that.

"Are you going to be sarcastic too? Don't I get enough of that from him?"

I said I was sorry and I was.

In Keats's house in the Piazza de Spagna, we climbed the narrow marble stairs behind some English schoolgirls who were chattering and giggling, hushed at by their teacher. We stared at the books and the manuscripts in their glass cases, and gazed at the stone fireplace with its strange carved heads. Finally, we stood by the deathbed and listened to our guide, a tall homely Englishwoman about my age, describe Keats's final hours: the poet clutching Fanny Brawne's cornelian, sipping milk brought by the faithful Severn, watching the winter sunlight move across the walls, listening to the voices from the street and the splashing of the fountain in the square. Then the cold sweat clinging to his brow, the mucus-clotted throat, the approach of the final darkness.

"Lift me up—I am dying—I shall die easy—don't be frightened—thank God it has come."

Through the waning afternoon light he lingered. But at four o'clock he heaved a sigh and departed this life.

At the end of the Englishwoman's recitation, many of the schoolchildren were in tears, and I was not far from them myself, marveling at the woman's passion for this morbid house and the sad tale she was obliged to repeat for visitors each day. I wondered about her life in Rome; here in this ornate Catholic city with her long Protestant face, her tightly bound hair, the large white hands clasped to her breast as she spoke, the shapeless violet-colored dress. Where did she return to at the end of the day? Did she live with retired parents or in a room alone with her books and a gas ring?

In the sun-splashed piazza, we again encountered the clamor of life and the young English girls, released from the gloomy spell cast by the guide, soon forgot their tears and busied themselves taking snapshots of each other by the fountain. Nora and I had lunch at a trattoria across the street. To please her I had a glass of wine.

"I'm so glad you came along, Clara. I don't know what I would have done if I'd been on my own."

I was glad I had come along too, and I was happy sitting there with my sister, sipping wine and looking out at the square in the Roman sunlight. From our table, we could see the entrance to Keats's house and we watched the Englishwoman come out and lock the door. I suppose it was her lunch hour. She stood by the doorway in her awful violet dress. Then a young man came by on a bicycle and stopped in front of her. He was twenty-five or so, and handsome enough for a painter's model, though poorly dressed in an ill-fitting brown suit that looked soiled. He wore cheap yellow shoes and bicycle clips and a "berretto," a kind of tam that seems popular here with workingmen. He and the Englishwoman embraced and kissed.

Nora (astonished): "Will you look at that?"

Myself (equally astonished): "Yes. Who would have guessed it?"

The Englishwoman was now sitting on the crossbar and the young man began to wheel her through the crowd. As he pedaled away, I caught a glimpse of bare ankles above the ridiculous yellow shoes. Nora thought he must be some kind of gigolo.

"How else could a woman who looks like that attract such a handsome guy? She has to be paying him. I actually felt sorry for her when she was telling us about the poet."

Nora sounded a bit vexed by it all. But I thought this: Perhaps she was paying him, but did it matter? Was she not having an adventure? At this very moment, she was confounding the expectations of others: of parents, of relatives, of schoolmates who had foreseen only a strict and virginal solitude for this woman. And I too felt chastened. Had I not also confined her to a room with only books and a gas ring? Or evenings alone with aged parents? This homely Englishwoman had triumphed over all our presumptions and was now pursuing a life of romantic adventure, reminding me that things are never as they seem, and that in fact we know very little about the lives of others.

Saturday, August 1 (Hotel Victoria, 10:30 p.m.)

Just in and glad to be alone after a tense evening amid L.M. and his Roman acquaintances. It began well with a good dinner near the famous Trevi Fountain. L.M. had invited a fellow American named Donald Packard. He has lived in Rome for years and is an expert on Italian Renaissance painting. He writes articles for art magazines and teaches at some kind of academy. Mid-forties, small and finely made, almost delicate, with a head of bright yellow hair which I'm afraid I stared at from time to time; it was so unusual, and it took me half the evening to see that it was a wig. An outlandish effeminate man with extravagant mannerisms and a cruel tongue. His friend was a handsome young Italian (did all foreigners have such companions in

Rome?). This Gino or Giorgio said little but seemed amused by us all; I'm not sure he understood much of what was said.

There was a good deal of drinking. Cocktails and then bottle after bottle of wine. It is all this drink that transforms people into such monsters. At first everyone is amiable and courteous, but as the evening wears on and people empty the bottles, things begin to turn. A chance remark or imagined slight or perhaps just rancid cruelty sours the air. And so it was this evening. At first the yellow-haired man wanted to know all about Nora's program and, of course, she went on and on about it. Nora couldn't read the signs around the table (Nora can never read such signs), and so she could not see that she was turning into a source of amusement for Packard who grew increasingly satirical.

"And so now your poor listeners don't know where you are? They still think you are wandering around the streets of this mythical little American town with this frightful amnesia occasioned by the fall down the library steps when, if the truth were told, you are right here in the Eternal City having a whale of a time. Have I got that much right so far?"

L.M. was enjoying this and it finally occurred to Nora that she was being mocked by this horrible little man. She grew increasingly flushed and so Packard turned on me, small white hand rotating the wineglass.

"And Lewis tells me you are a teacher in some hamlet in the wilds of Canada. I've never been to Canada, but I am told it's very English and very Puritan. I have it on good authority that as a people you are suspicious of vice and who can blame you? Do you have any artists there? Should I know who they are?"

And plenty more of that sort of thing. The evening ended predictably with a quarrel between Nora and L.M. Gino/Giorgio put us into a taxi and we returned to the hotel on our own. A tipsy and tearful Nora. "It's all turned out so badly, hasn't it, Clara? And for months, I looked forward to this trip."

Monday, August 3

Yesterday was gray and humid with the heat finally broken by an afternoon thundershower. Nora spent the day reading her book and I finished Keats's letters. Wrote a poem about the Englishwoman and tore it up. Today, we visited the Colosseum and I tried to imagine the ancient city of Caesars, but I couldn't make head nor tail of the ruins. L.M. busy interviewing various people and so we didn't see much of him. Just as well.

Tuesday, August 4

Nora claims she is unwell from something she ate, but I suspect she wants to finish *GWTW*. So I ventured forth on my own. This afternoon the streets were almost empty, and as I walked I could hear radios from open windows, the shouts of a crowd and the excited voice of an announcer. People were listening to the Olympic Games from Berlin.

After I came out of the Pantheon, I went down several narrow streets, turning first one corner and then another. Of course, I lost my way and my little map was useless. A hundred feet or so ahead of me, two scruffy-looking men were leaning against a building, smoking. They watched me approach. I felt a little panic then and turned around. When I looked back, they were following me, sauntering along. One of them waved and shouted something, and I felt a little sick to my stomach. Quickened my pace. I could hear a radio in that narrow street, but there was no one else except the two men and myself. Perhaps I was too nervous about everything. After all, I was in the middle of the city; I could hear the traffic from a street nearby, yet I had no idea how to get there. Those two men had unsettled me. I was saved then by a flock of priests. I heard the strangest sound (turned out to be the rustle of their cassocks) and then they came around a corner, a dozen or so in their black robes and sandals. They looked anxious to get past me, but I was trying my guidebook Italian on them, and they stopped to stare in wonder at this woman in the street. Under their soup-plate hats, their faces were palely severe as I tried to explain my predicament. Finally one of them beckoned me to follow, and so I did, this way and that, around corners and down alleyways, myself among these men of God (their large hairy toes in the rope sandals), until at last we came out onto an avenue of restaurants and stores. A few moments later inside a taxi, I looked out and saw the two men. One of them held up a hand, arranging his fingers in what I took to be an obscene gesture. He was grinning. Just like Charlie. I turned to watch the priests as they crossed the wide avenue, the last one lifting the skirts of his robe as he stepped over a puddle. Carnality and piety side by side on this Roman street.

At dinner, L.M. was in good spirits. He had received a letter from the philosopher Santayana who was not in Rome at all, but in Paris for the summer. Nevertheless, he agreed to an interview in a few weeks and L.M. regards this as "a coup." Santayana is a "cornucopia of knowledge." In his excitement, L.M. is oddly appealing; to be so enthusiastic about ideas is an attractive trait in a man. Nora and I were both rapt listeners throughout the meal. "Santayana has a great mind. Have you read *The Last Puritan*?" I haven't. "I can't wait to hear what he has to say about Hitler and Mussolini. Stalin. The man knows his stuff."

Wednesday, August 5

What a grimly bizarre adventure was in store for us today! It began after lunch when L.M. and Nora drank too much. L.M. started with martinis, which he claimed were the best he'd tasted since leaving New York. He went over to congratulate the bartender who had learned his trade in America. Everything was fine when we left the restaurant, but I sensed trouble ahead; L.M. was far too cocky and grand in the taxi. We looked out at the Piazza Venezia, the Quirinale, etc., with L.M. providing commentary.

"All these flags. The symbolism is very powerful."

"No more so," said Nora, "than the States on the Fourth of July."

To annoy her I'm sure, L.M. remarked on the Roman women. "Look at all these beautiful dames! I'll bet they're just dying to get laid by Il Duce. I'm told he has two or three different women a day. Takes them right in his office. On the floor apparently. Between meetings."

I could see the driver's eyes in the mirror looking back at us with dislike as we passed a yellow stucco mansion, its black iron gates patrolled by soldiers.

"The residence of Il Duce," said the driver in a tone so respectful that even L.M. was silenced.

On the Corso, L.M. proposed that we walk to the Borghese Gardens, though Nora complained of heat and fatigue. It was early afternoon and the hottest part of the day, perhaps not the best time for walking, but L.M. would not be swayed. We had not gone far, however, when he stepped into a pile of fresh dog dirt. He had been pointing to the statue of a man on a horse, some heroic figure whom he was at pains to identify and lecture upon. Hence, the misstep. I watched repelled as one of his expensive shoes sank deeply into the thick brown excrement. Looking down at his shoe so enraged the man that he began to curse the Romans for their slovenly public habits. It is true that dog excrement is everywhere in Rome; you have to be careful where you place your feet. But L.M. had clearly taken leave of his senses. Using the curb to scrape away at his shoe, he shouted, "Bastards, sons of bitches. Look at this _____ing mess!" I have never heard anyone carry on so in public. Nora too was appalled, though she sounded like some lady in a genteel English novel.

"Lewis, really! There is no need to behave like this. You're making a scene."

Crimson-faced with rage and drink, L.M. continued his tirade. "Look at the dog shit on the streets! It's everywhere for Christ's sake. A _____ing public disgrace! They brag about how progressive they are, but can't clean up after their _____ing dogs."

A shopkeeper in a long white apron came out from his doorway to watch all this, and soon he was joined by others. A small man, dapper in suit and tie, startled us by speaking English. "You should not talk like that against our country," he said to L.M. "You have no business talking like that. I have been to London. You also have the remains of the dogs on your streets."

L.M. stared at the little man in disbelief. He looked about ready to throttle him. "I am not an Englishman, goddamn it, I am an American."

"No difference," said the little man. "You are a foreigner coming to our country and making the criticism. What is a little dirt on your shoe? You are making something of nothing." He was growing stronger with indignation. "It is all unnecessary."

L.M. could do no better than, "Mind your own ____ing business."

Turning to the small crowd in front of the shop, the man began to explain what was going on, or I assumed that's what he was doing. Then a policeman arrived, a brutal-looking fellow with an unattractive, pockmarked face. Frowning at everybody. What is going on here, etc., etc. He and the little man exchanged rapid-fire comments and then the policeman said something to L.M. in Italian. The latter waved him off and continued to scrape his shoe against the curbside. The policeman then began to scold L.M., and the little man inclined his head backward, and with his right hand mimed the act of drinking. The crowd was made to understand that they were watching a drunken foreigner criticizing their city over nothing more than a little dog dirt. A good many glares directed at all three of us, and Nora was now tugging at L.M.'s arm. "Lewis, for goodness' sake, let's go. Just forget it and let's get out of here."

But the policeman placed a hand on L.M.'s arm. "You come."

L.M. shook off the hand. "Like hell!"

I noticed that the shopkeeper had disappeared, and he must have telephoned because a few minutes later a car arrived with two policemen. More heavy, sullen faces. We were told to get in the car, with L.M. protesting all the way. "You can't do this to us. We're American citizens." And so on. The three of us were squeezed into the back where the smell of L.M.'s shoe, caked and soiled, filled the little car. They took us to a police station on Via Settembre. I saw the words on the side of a building, September Street, and I wondered what time it was in Whitfield; by my reckoning, early morning and Mrs. Bryden would be in her garden. What preposterous things transpire in this world while we go about our ordinary business! At the police station, they thought at first we were English, which, of course, infuriated L.M. The English are presently not among Italy's favorite tourists due in part to England's opposition to the recent war in Ethiopia. The Italians still seem resentful about that. Once they learned that we were not English, they were more civil to us. Nora and I were seated on a long bench while L.M. was escorted into another room. A few minutes later the little man arrived and was hurried through to the same room. Around us, policemen were coming and going, heavy revolvers strapped to their belts. A woman was seated at a typewriter in one corner, and from time to time would look over at us with evident dislike. Now and then, from the other room, we could hear L.M.'s voice and the little man's and then a torrent of Italian. Nora looked bludgeoned by the whole experience, and I'm sure that I too was bedraggled. Yet in a perverse way I was enjoying myself. I saw it all as an adventure. I couldn't imagine that we would go to prison or anything. Then they brought in a young man. He was wearing only trousers, not even shoes. Between two policemen, he shuffled along in bare feet, his hands shackled behind him. At the front desk, he said something and one of the policemen abruptly struck him in the face. The young man's head snapped back, but he did not cry out. His nose began to bleed and the policemen pushed him toward another door. The young man stumbled and they more or less picked him up and carried him away. It was unnerving to see such rough treatment of another human being, and at that moment I began to feel less sure of everything. Perhaps they were manhandling L.M. too, though I had difficulty picturing it.

Nora whispered, "Do you think if I told them that I'm on the radio back in New York, it would help?"

"They don't speak our language, Nora."

We sat there until nearly eight o'clock. We watched the young woman put a cover over her machine and then pick up her purse and say good night to the policemen. As she passed by us, she stared down with such contempt that I felt like a common criminal. Through the tall windows behind the desks, the sky was darkening. Finally L.M. came out of the room. He was pale, but he still had his bulldog look. The little man was now all smiles and friendly gestures, so it was with relief that we could see matters had been resolved. The little man obviously enjoyed being the center of attention. He playfully wagged a finger at L.M.

"It is fortunate for you, Signore, that they did not apply the *olio di ricino*."

L.M. merely glared at him. I looked up *olio di ricino* (castor oil). Apparently (L.M. told us later) it is commonly used as a humiliating punishment for dissenters and troublemakers.

They telephoned for a taxi for us and how good it felt to be away from that uniformed brutality. Nora was holding L.M.'s hand and kissing him in the taxi.

"What happened, Lewis? Did they strike you at all?"

"No, no. I threatened them with the embassy. They're a bunch of ruffians. Country boys dressed up in uniforms. It was just a show for the crowd. I could have killed that old wop though. If it hadn't been for him . . ."

Perhaps, but L.M. doesn't seem to understand that he brought the whole business on himself with his outlandish behavior on the street. Dinner in the hotel was subdued. To Florence tomorrow.

Thursday, August 6 (Hotel Rio, Florence)

Train to Florence through the hot dry countryside. Many Germans on board, and I could sometimes make out a few words; they all seemed to be talking of the games in Berlin. Our hotel is near the Duomo.

Sunday, August 8

I like Florence with its red-tiled roofs and pretty churches, but like Rome, it is filled with soldiers and policemen. This afternoon a demonstration in the piazza in front of the Uffizi Gallery. Mostly young Italian men waving flags in support of the Spanish rebels under General Franco. A kind of angry patriotism flowing through the crowd, most of the ill feeling directed against England. A number of English tourists appeared nervous as they watched the rally.

Unpleasantness at dinner when L.M. got into a political argument with a man at the next table. I thought the man gave a good account of himself. Nora is very unhappy. Told me she can't wait to get back to New York. Yet I am enjoying all this. I don't like the soldiers and the policemen who seem to be everywhere, but ordinary people are friendly enough, and the cities are filled with beautiful buildings. There is also a vitality about the country that I like. I wonder if this is what attracted the Englishwoman to Rome.

Monday, August 10

Bags packed and waiting for the porter. We are to catch the train for Venice in an hour. A storm in the night awakened me from a dream in which I was surrounded by the priests in their cassocks and sandals. Among them was the Englishwoman's lover, the bare ankles showing above the yellow shoes. I lay awake listening to the rain, looking out at the tiled roofs lighted by the storm. From the open windows, the sound of water spilling from the drainpipes into the street.

(Hotel Lux, Venice)

The train climbed the hills of Tuscany, often disappearing into long tunnels and these gave me trouble. As we hurtled into those black spaces, the carriage lights dimmed and I felt a great pressure in my chest, a tightening of nerves. A kind of claustrophobia, I suppose.

Some of the tunnels seemed endless and then, just as I felt that I could no longer draw a breath, we were flung headlong into sunlight with green fields and the red roofs of farmhouses. At the station in Bologna where we changed trains the following:

L.M.: "Do you know who was born in this town, kiddo?"

Nora: "No, Lewis, tell me. You know everything."

L.M.: "Well, my little angel of the airwaves, this is the birthplace of the founder of it all. Without him you wouldn't have all those listeners on the edge of their kitchen chairs. Marconi was born in this city."

Nora (looking out the carriage window as if the people hurrying by had assumed a sudden and vast importance): "Really? Gee, I used to sell Marconi radios in Toronto."

Wednesday, August 12 (Hotel Lux, Venice)

Death in Venice today. Not the literary death from plague that awaits Von Aschenbach in Mann's novel, but actual death, sudden and dramatic in the Grand Canal near the Piazza San Marco. It happened after lunch. We were walking through the overcast afternoon, following some young Germans. They were boisterously enjoying themselves and then (who knows why?) one of the young men jumped or was pushed (playfully?) into the canal. Laughter from the others as the young man splashed about in the oily water. Soon, however, it was evident that he could not swim. We were perhaps forty or fifty feet behind them, but I could see that he was in trouble. Two others from his group leaped in to help and everything suddenly went wrong. It was going to be a more difficult job than they imagined because the young man was in a panic, fighting them off, his arms flailing about. For a moment, we could see only the tangle of arms, the thrashing water, the wet blond hair. Then he simply disappeared, nearly dragging one of the others with him. It all happened so quickly. One of the German girls clutched the sides of her head and began to scream, a terrible sound in the Venetian afternoon. Others pulled the two men from the water and in their sodden clothes they sat weeping on the canal wall. A policeman began to push people away from the edge of the water. A careless few moments and a young life was now over. Nora had tears in her eyes and L.M. put his arm around her. We walked to a small gallery, but we were too upset to enjoy the pictures. This somber mood prevailed at dinner as the conversation settled on the arbitrary nature of events, the randomness of fortune, a subject that has intrigued me since that day I stopped believing in God. Nora was adamant that events are foreordained by Him (her words); there is purpose and meaning even in calamity. If there weren't, how could life be endured? How indeed? L.M. read her mood (the feisty Nora) and was careful not to contradict her. I liked him for that. Why tamper with another's faith?

The talk then shifted to poetry and I said how much I liked Stevens's "Sunday Morning."

"I met Stevens once," L.M. said. "At a party down in the Village though the man is no bohemian. Did you know that he works for an insurance company? Three-piece suit, the whole kit and caboodle. Looking at him, you'd never know he was a poet. Of course, Williams is a doctor. These guys have to make a living too."

I would have enjoyed hearing more about Wallace Stevens and William Carlos Williams, but L.M. had moved on. Still, it was the most enjoyable meal that the three of us have had together on this trip.

The day after tomorrow Nora and I return to Rome and then to Naples to catch the boat for America. L.M. goes on to France and Germany. He is an interesting man, brilliant in his own way, but self-indulgent to a fault. He wears you down with his relentless opinions and his forceful nature. He is far too vivid to be lived with for long, and I think Nora realizes this now. I have enjoyed meeting him, but I will not be sorry to say goodbye. For the first time in weeks, I miss Whitfield.

Friday, August 14 (12:30 a.m.)

An hour ago L.M. made a pass at me, but I don't want to make too much of this; he was a little tight and he didn't persist. I had just finished packing for tomorrow and was getting ready for bed when I heard the knock. Thought it was Nora, but when I opened the door, Lewis was standing there in his rumpled linen suit, looking a bit down in the mouth, not a trace of the bulldog in his face. Wanted to come in for a minute and I asked him why. He said he wanted to apologize; he had behaved badly on the trip and now felt contrite. Before we parted in the morning, he "wanted things to be right between us."

I should have told him to go to bed, but I didn't and he came into the room and slumped in the green baize chair by the window. He said nothing but stared at the floor. Nora told me that L.M. suffers from spells of depression and had been seeing a doctor about this in New York.

Through the open window behind him, I watched the dark shapes of passing gondolas with their lanterns. After a while L.M. said, "Your sister and I are having a rough time of it these days, and it's made me miserable. I have a lousy disposition anyway."

I was wearing my dressing gown and I could see that he was looking at my feet and legs.

"I'm fond of Nora," he said. "She's a sweet woman."

His voice trailed away and he turned to the window to look out at the boats. All evening I had been thinking of the young German tourist. It was almost unbearable to imagine him lying under the weight of all that dark water. Then L.M. said, "You're so unlike your sister."

I told him that this was true, though not perhaps as true as he thought. In fact, we were alike in many ways. He wanted to know in what ways, but I didn't feel right talking to him about any of this. I wondered if Nora were now asleep. I hated the idea of talking to L.M. in my room while Nora was sleeping. So I told him that it would be best if he were to leave. He shrugged and then got up and stood there looking down at me. I was seated on the edge of the bed and after a moment he sat beside me. I was going to get up at once, but he put his arm around me and began to rub my neck. It was a clumsy gesture, foolish in the extreme, and he was saying something I couldn't catch. It might have been a line of poetry. I smelled the drink on him and oddly enough thought of Hamlet's words to his mother about Claudius. Something about paddling in your neck with his damned fingers. I wasn't about to play the hysterical old maid, but neither did I want his hands upon me, and he didn't pursue matters. Either he was too tired and discouraged or he didn't think me worth the struggle. Then, like some character in an old bedroom farce, Nora was knocking at the door. I could hear her voice from the hallway.

"Clara, is Lewis in there with you?"

When I opened the door she looked in and saw him sitting on the bed.

"What the hell is he doing in here?"

"Not what you might think," I said. "All is well and Lewis is on his way."

And so he was, quite subdued as he passed by her stare. After he left, Nora stayed a while, packing herself into the green baize chair, drawing her legs up and clasping her knees, just as she used to do on Saturday nights in our bedroom when she would talk about the cute salesman from the wholesale company or the shy young man in her acting class. She told me that she and L.M. were probably finished.

"The whole thing has just run its course. It's burned out," she said. "Lewis is just too demanding. I can't take any more of it. Let him go back to his brainy women. The night we had dinner in Rome with that awful little fruit? Remember? That was it as far as I was concerned. Lewis just sat there and laughed at me all evening. Well, to hell with him. There's plenty more fish in the sea. I'm tired of his sulks and his demands. Always after me to do unnatural things in bed. Brother!"

"What kinds of things?" I asked.

"I don't want to talk about it," Nora said, giving me a peculiar look of dislike. But why, I wondered, had she brought up the subject if she didn't want to talk about it? And why, for that matter, did I want to know?

Sunday, August 30

Arrived home yesterday and glad to be here. Marion looked in after church today, eager for news. "How was it, Clara? What did you see?"

Oh, I tormented the poor girl with larky tales of handsome men. Told her that I almost took a lover, there among the ancient stones of Rome. A swarthy young man who wore a black tam and rode a bicycle.

"Clara! You didn't!"

"Well, I might have. He was very good-looking."

"You are really something, Clara Callan."

"Am I really, Marion?"

Saturday, September 3

To Toronto on the train and then the streetcar to the Exhibition. Walked past the kewpie doll stands in search of my errant knight. There are women who work at these carnivals and I wondered about their lives: the rough lovemaking in the caravans behind the tents, the smell of onions and frying meat in the air, the cheap glitter of this world where men and women fight and couple and carry on as others do before they vanish into oblivion. No Charlie this year!

Tuesday, September 8

The scrubbed faces of the children on opening day. The smell of soap and ironed pinafores in the classroom. For as long as I can remember, I have always felt renewed at the beginning of another school year. What do I feel this year? I feel wayward. Here came the word out of nowhere. Wayward! I love its sound and may even have said it aloud this morning. Two or three pupils glanced my way, I think. While they were doing their first lesson, I looked up the word in the dictionary.

Wayward: 1. Disposed to go counter to the wishes and advice of others or to what is reasonable; wrong-headed, intractable, self-willed, perverse. 2. Capriciously willful; conforming to no fixed rule or principle of conduct.

Exactly. Sleeping poorly these nights. Mrs. Bryden asked after supper whether I was all right. Saw my bedroom light at three yesterday morning. Up, I suppose, for her nightly tinkle.

135 East 33rd Street
New York
September 12, 1936

Dear Clara,
I trust all is well and you're settled in for another school year. I'm back in business too and everybody was glad to see me. You should have seen the mail while I was gone! Well, Italy wasn't everything we thought it might be, was it? Some experience, huh? I might have known Lewis would behave the way he did. I could see signs of it long before we left New York. I guess I was just dazzled by the big-shot intellectual. But then I've always had bad luck with men. Why can't I just find a nice ordinary guy who wouldn't be so mean or such a show-off? Such fellows seem to have dropped off the face of the earth.

His Lordship sent me a postcard from Paris saying he didn't think we were suited for each other and thanks for the memories. Couldn't even face me to say goodbye. What a crumb! Him and his fancy friends! Remember that awful little fruit with the yellow hair in Rome? I should have slapped his face that night. Thrown his wig onto the floor or something. Oh well, we live and learn. Now that I'm back on the shelf, I'm spending my nights reading or listening to the radio. Evelyn is also feeling blue. Her showgirl friend from Texas "has taken a powder," to use Evy's phrase. She went back home after getting a letter from her high school sweetheart who said he was still in love and wanted to marry her. How about that? Anyway, Evy is pretty glum about it all and she's now talking about a change in her life. She is thinking very seriously of moving out to California to write for the movies. Apparently a number of the studios have been after her. Gee, I hope she doesn't go because I can't imagine living down here without Evy. At the same time, I hate to see her so unhappy. She really fell hard for that girl and she's taking all this badly. Why don't you drop her a line? She thinks the world of you, and I know she'd be tickled to hear from you.

Well, I have to wash my hair. Evy and I are going to the movies tonight. Any chance of you coming down here for Christmas? I'd love to have you and I know the three of us could have a great time. Why not think about it?

Love, Nora

Whitfield, Ontario
Sunday, September 20, 1936

Dear Evelyn,
I am writing this in the midst of a terrible storm. Such wind and rain! I feel like one of the three little pigs being blown at by the wolf. Thank goodness I'm the one in the brick house! This tumult must signal the turning of the seasons. We always have unsettled weather at the equinox, but this afternoon is unsurpassed in my memory. Sheets of rain against the windows and it seems to be coming at me horizontally rather than vertically. An astounding display of nature in commotion. Not a soul on the streets. Whitfield truly is the deserted village on this wet autumn afternoon.

I have been wondering how things are with you. No doubt Nora has told you of our Italian holiday. I don't think she enjoyed it as much as she thought she would. But then does reality ever meet our expectations? I, on the other hand, enjoyed it more than I dared to hope (the pessimist's occasional reward). Rome was so utterly different from anything in my admittedly limited experience that I was caught up in its vividness. I felt so alive there, even though I was often frightened by the sheer maleness of the culture. The streets seemed to be filled with young men in uniform prowling with a hungry eye, while the women covered their heads with kerchiefs and fled to the nearest church. But what churches and ruins there are to see!

Of course, speaking of maleness, we had the redoubtable Mr. Mills for company, and though Lewis Mills may be a brilliant man, he can also readily play the role of buffoon. Did Nora tell you of our singular adventure with the police in Rome? All of it brought on by Mr. Mills and his encounter with what dogs leave behind after dinner. How is that for a euphemism? Of course, we ended up in the police station. It was fascinating, but also more than a little alarming. At one point, I watched them bring in a young man; he was obviously poor and he certainly didn't look like a serious criminal. But the way they treated him was so brutal. It was perhaps a glimpse of how life is for some under Mussolini. Yet, the country has a compelling luster to it and the ordinary people were friendly and helpful. Certainly I shall never forget it. I saw an Englishwoman in Rome. At Keats's house, the house where he died. I pitied the woman, but then later I envied her. Ah well! Perhaps I will tell you about it another time.

Nora has mentioned that you might be going out to California to write for the moving pictures. Such a life seems to me impossibly remote and glamorous. For years I wasn't interested in the pictures, but lately (perhaps on Nora's urging; she seems addicted to them), I have been looking at some of them. After I have finished shopping in Toronto on a Saturday afternoon, I will sometimes go to the picture theater. We do not have such a place in the village and in the nearby town of Linden all the movies are about men chasing Indians on horses. When I am in Toronto and waiting for the afternoon train home, I particularly enjoy the gangster pictures. Not very inspiring, I admit, but entertaining. I suppose I am like one of those country dogs that for some reason will eat a mouthful of dirt now and again. I too seem to need to enter a world of vice and corruption. Does that strike you as odd? I sometimes wonder if that's normal. Not that I've ever made any great claims to being normal.

I've just been holding my breath as another of these great gusts has shaken the windows of this old house. I feel like jumping into bed and burrowing beneath the covers like a child. Well, never mind, this storm will pass as do all manner of things. In time. Do take care of yourself.

Kindest regards, Clara

Whitfield, Ontario
Sunday, September 20, 1936

Dear Nora,

Thanks for your letter. What a day we are having here! Such wind and rain! The heavens are truly in turmoil. It must have something to do with the changing seasons. I heard on the radio this morning that there have been many deaths from this weather down in your part of the world.

So, it's goodbye to Mr. Mills, is it? Well, I can't say that I'm surprised, and it's probably just as well, don't you think? L.M. is an intelligent and interesting man, but like all such rare creatures, he is difficult and ultimately incomprehensible. The way he behaved in Rome that day was inexcusable. I am sure you will be better off without him. Remember what I said on the boat ride back?

School has returned to its routines and Milton and I will have plenty of work to do this year. Well, there was another gust of wind against the house. I fear for the trees on our street though they all seem to be upright. But the roads and sidewalks are a mess, littered with leaves and fallen branches. However, I am warm and dry and hope to ride out this rough weather. Do take care of yourself.

Clara

P.S. As you suggested, I have dropped Evelyn Dowling a line.

Wednesday, September 23

Foolish, foolish, foolish! Why do I agree to do such things? Outside the post office today, Ida Atkins persuaded me to address the Women's Auxiliary a week from next Tuesday. It seems I cannot say no to this woman, and now I must invent some nonsense about traveling with my Normal School "friends." Then, I must face all those women.

Saturday, September 26 (5:35 p.m.)

Henry Hill lurching about and singing in the streets, still wearing Father's overcoat with its velvet collar. From the front window I watched him pass the house a few minutes ago. Manley and Melvin Kray and two or three other boys were taunting the old man and throwing stones at him. I got up to look at this after trying all afternoon to gather some impressions of Italy for this damn talk.

(11:15 p.m.)

Fell asleep too early and then awakened at ten. I could not get back to sleep and so I have been reading *Startling Detective*: "Mismatched Lovers Want to Die Together." A thirty-five-year-old woman in California runs away with a nineteen-year-old boy who worked for the woman's husband as an usher in a movie theater. The woman went to the movies several nights a week and the two became "acquainted." She persuaded the boy to murder her husband, and so he beat him to death with a hammer one night in the projection room. The pair fled in the family sedan, but the police caught up with them in a tourist court near the Mexican border. "I'm glad I did it," the woman says. "I don't care what you do with us now. I want to die with him. We want to die together."

Both of them sentenced to the electric chair. With dulled eyes the woman stares at the camera in her prison smock. The youth has a torpid, sexual look to him, slack-faced, defiled, brimming with seed.

San Remo Apts.
1100 Central Park West
N.Y.C.
27/9/36

Dear Clara,
Great to hear from you. Yes, we got that storm down here too. The tail end of a hurricane, it seems. According to the *Times*, the Empire State Building was actually moving in the gale. Apparently it was designed to do just that, but I find the idea a little horrifying. When you look up and see this huge chunk of steel and concrete and glass, you just expect it to stay in place when the wind is blowing. But, swaying back and forth! Jeez! Anyway, it was quite the blow and we had buckets of rain too.

For the past several weeks I have been suffering "the pangs of disprized love." My little June bug, all five feet ten of her, lit out for Texas where she was reared. She is going to marry some drip she went to high school with. I hope you don't mind my ending a sentence with a preposition. You have to be careful when you're writing a schoolmarm. Anyway, Junie left me and my heart has been rent in twain. Can you imagine leaving me for a Studebaker salesman? I could have shown her the world. Offered it, in fact, on a fairly good-sized platter. But no dice. Oh, the powerful appeal of the front porch and apron! Well, there is nothing to be done about these passions except try to get over them. Your sister and I have been commiserating with one another since her return from Europe. She's told me all about the trip and Mr. Mills's nutty behavior. What an experience for you both! Please do not judge all Americans by what you saw and heard from Lewis Mills. Believe it or not, some of us do manage to travel quietly and stay out of trouble when we go abroad. Nora said she didn't know what she would have done if you hadn't been along. Gee, I wish I had a big sister!

"The House on Chestnut Street" continues to garner any amount of lavish praise in the trade journals. *Radio News* called it "the best-written afternoon serial on the air." So there! Nobody is going to win a Pulitzer writing this stuff, but I'll take what I can get and it's always nice to be recognized by people in the industry. We are currently in the top five, but we can't seem to catch old "Ma Perkins." We've come close, but we can't close the gap. Exciting, huh? I've been busy with two other proposals: one, another weeper for the ladies of the afternoon, and the other, a detective show set in Manhattan. That one is more fun to write. I've submitted both to the agency, but haven't heard anything back yet.

Yes, I am thinking of going out to California. MGM has offered me a lot of money and I am thinking about it. In many ways, it's appealing. I feel I could use a change of scenery. On the other hand, I love New York and I know I would miss the place. So, I continue to dither. Dithery old Evelyn!

Nora said she asked you down for Christmas. Why not take her up on it? It would be fun to see you again. The three of us could do the tourist stuff: Macy's windows, Radio City, a Broadway show. Nora loves all that, and I love watching her love it. Love and chaste kisses, Clara.

Evelyn

Monday, October 5

A showery evening. I walked over to Ida Atkins's house to tell her that I can't speak to the Women's Auxiliary tomorrow night. I just can't do it. It's impossible. But the garage was empty and the house in darkness. Returned in damp clothes and spent the rest of the evening cobbling together some impressions of Italy: the Colosseum, the Sistine Chapel, priests, beggars, soldiers, the vineyards of Tuscany, the light on the stones of Venice. Horrible trite stuff! What can I say to these women that has any ring of truth? How will I ever sleep tonight?

Cobble: to mend or patch coarsely; to make or put together roughly or hastily.

Trite: hackneyed from much use. Stale.

Tuesday, October 6 (11:45 p.m.)

Marion has finally left; I didn't think she would ever go. Fussing over me as if I were an invalid. The tea I have drunk tonight should keep me awake for hours. When did I last sleep? It seems a long time ago. And tonight I most assuredly disgraced myself. Yet, may I now record that the memory of the various startled expressions on all those faces will sustain me over the coming days. No doubt my "performance" this evening is now on its way around the township through the telephone lines. Tomorrow across the fences and over the counters. Well, so be it. It has happened and nothing can be done to change matters. I have to wonder though (I'm sure others are doing so at this very moment), whether, in fact, I am having some kind of breakdown. But I feel strong and able enough, in command of my poor faculties. Here is the desk. There is the bed. These are my fingers holding the pen against the blue-lined paper under the light. Still I did behave in a most peculiar fashion this evening. Why did I say those things? I did intend to go through with it. I stood before them in the overheated church hall. It *was* awfully hot, or so it seemed to me. Of course, I was nervous, but it felt unusually warm. I remember someone opening a window before I started. And so I stood before them clutching my notes, "The waterways of Venice are unique and attract thousands of visitors to this fabled city each year," and I knew in my heart that things would go awry before the evening was over. *I knew it.* Ida Atkins was introducing me and I looked out at the pleasant, expectant faces of my neighbors. Why did I feel such anger? Contempt? When Father died, these people brought me plates of food and pressed my hand. They gave me scented handkerchiefs embroidered in black for mourning. We greet one another in the stores and on the street. Mrs. A. was going on about the Callan sisters and how proud the village was of our accomplishments. Nora was making such a name for herself on the radio in New York. But let us not forget that we still have Clara in our midst, a talented musician and a valuable mentor to our youngsters, etc., etc.

I stood before them trembling. "This past summer Clara traveled with some of her friends from Normal School, and now she is going to regale us with her impressions of the ancient world." *Regale!* When I picked up the glass, my hands were shaking. I spilled some water. They saw that. At least those near the front saw me spill the water. Looking down at my notes, I saw only swirls of black letters on the blue-lined paper. The words might as well have been in Hungarian. "Rome is a wondrous city indeed. And by the way, it is very hot during the summer." After that impressive topic sentence, I could think of nothing more to say. I must have stood there for how long? A minute perhaps? An awkwardly long time in the circumstances. The faces were looking up at me, the wind stirring the leaves beyond the open window. That dry, rustling sound. I heard that from the open window.

From her chair, Mrs. A. threw me a lifeline. "What is your most vivid memory of Rome, Clara?"

Yes, a vivid memory. I could think only of the Englishwoman in Keats's house. Her awful violet dress. I began something like this.

"Let me tell you. I saw a woman in Rome. She was English. She was telling visitors about the poet's last months in this house near the Spanish Steps. She was such a plain woman, tall and pale with a long English face and that purple dress. I felt sorry for her. You wouldn't have expected such a dismal-looking creature ... I know that sounds cruel ... but you wouldn't have expected. I wondered then how she had managed to end up there. I imagined her loneliness in that city of stones and sunlight. Her pale English homeliness in all that sunlight. Oh, I imagined so much about her. And then ... Well, how wrong can we be about others? I saw her leave the house. And a young man on his bicycle was waiting for her. She came out of Keats's house into the sunlight, and this handsome young man was waiting for her and they embraced there on the street. Such an ardent embrace! The Englishwoman leaned into the young man as if she wished to be devoured."

Did I really say those words? *Ardent*? *Devoured*? I believe I did.

They were staring at me now, of course; I had their puzzled attention, and I could feel the onset of laughter within me. Pointless to try to stop it. It's like a child who begins to giggle in the classroom. All you can do is ask her to leave. And so I continued. I told them that I wondered about this woman and her life in Rome. Where did she live? How did she get from some damp English town to this city of light? How could she endure telling visitors about the dying poet day after day? How did she meet the handsome young man on the bicycle with his brown suit and cap, his cheap yellow shoes? I told them that he didn't even wear socks. I had seen his bare ankles above those shoes. I told them I saw all this as he wheeled her away through the streets of Rome. The Englishwoman was clinging to the young man's neck and looked so happy. I suppose they went off to a room. I wondered about that too.

Mrs. Atkins now looked distressed, her face a picture of baffled dismay. That's perhaps a little precious, but it's true; she did look like that and I began to laugh. A few of them nervously joined in, but soon stopped. They could now see that something was amiss. Yet I couldn't stop laughing. I don't know why. I laughed and laughed and I can only imagine what I must have sounded like. A woman laughing alone in a church hall must be an affliction to the eyes and ears of the sober. I also told them (I may have shouted this, yes, I believe I did) that I had not traveled to Italy with any Normal School chums, but with my sister and her lover, who by the way, I said, made a pass at me in a hotel room in Venice.

Mrs. Atkins and the minister's wife, Helen Jackson, then came over to the lectern and took my arm and led me off to the vestry. Marion came along too and sat next to me and held my hand in that room that smelled of stale air and furniture polish. I had not been in the vestry since Father's funeral when Mr. Cameron had tried to speak some words of comfort before the service. Tonight the look of love and pity in Marion's dark eyes was terrible to behold. I could hardly bear to glance at her. From the doorway, I could hear the murmuring voices of the women in the hall. Squeezing Marion's hand, I told her not to worry. I told her that, appearances aside, I was sound as a bell. Yet I wonder if that is true. What I did this evening was ridiculous and tomorrow everyone in the village will know about it. Even now, as I write these words, wives are sinking into creaking beds beside their husbands.

"Clara Callan acted peculiar tonight. It was something to see."

"Who?"

"Clara Callan, the schoolteacher."

"What about her?"

"She was to give a talk on her summer holiday in Europe and she went on and on about some man and woman in Rome, Italy. The way she carried on! Why, she shouted and laughed. It was something, I can tell you."

"Why would she do that?"

"Well, how do I know why she'd do that? I just wouldn't have thought it of Clara. She's always been such a sensible girl. Maybe she's going through the change of life though she seems awfully young for that."

I can hear their voices. I am in their bedrooms.

Wednesday, October 7

Not a word as yet about last night. In the classroom, I was prepared for the sidelong glances of the curious, but life was just Wednesday morning. Not a hint of anything untoward in the children's behavior, no smirks or whispers from the upper-form children in the hallway. Milton acted as though he had heard nothing, but he is a Presbyterian, and news may not yet have reached their households. For a moment, sitting at my desk, I imagined it all as a dream. I hadn't carried on like that in front of the Women's Auxiliary; Marion hadn't given me that dark, pitying look and taken me home. But, of course, it did happen. It is a fact that will harden into village folklore with the passing years.

"Do you remember the night poor Clara Callan behaved so oddly in the church hall?"

"Yes. She told us how she met a man in Italy or something."

Sunday, October 11

This morning I found a note underneath the doormat on the veranda. Typewritten with the spelling in place. Except for Eyetalian, which is doubtless intended to be crudely satirical.

> To the Lady with the Phantom Lover
> We have heard about your mystery man from Rome. Does he visit you in the night on his bicycle? Does he climb the stairs to your bedroom and tickle your toes to wake you up? Be careful or you will wake up one day with a little Eyetalian.

Wednesday, October 14

This one under the doormat this morning.

> Rumor has it that your Italian Lover Man has been to visit lately, and leaves his yellow shoes under your bed. You are being very

naughty, Miss Callan. A little bird has told us that you are planning a spring wedding in the Roman Catholic church in Linden and the Virgin Mary will be there.

The notes are not illiterate and I'm inclined to believe that it's the work of a former pupil or perhaps two or three, a cabal of spiteful girls, perhaps in the Senior Fourth. Their mothers probably mentioned my performance last Tuesday. How many, I wonder, would have typewriting machines? It is so tiresome and dispiriting to look at such words on a brilliant sunlit morning in autumn.

Sunday, October 18

Another today. Thumbtacked to the back door.

> Miss Callan
> We note that the mystery man from Rome, Italy, has been visiting you again. Your love life is certainly a busy one, isn't it? We peeked in on you two the other night and my, my, what we saw! It might be proper, Miss Callan, to draw the curtains. We have to report that it was quite the sight to see you and your Latin lover with his long dark hair seated together on the piano bench. And both of you bare naked! What was he whispering in your ear while he stroked your flanks? Aren't you the lucky one to have such a handsome lover?
>
> Interested bystander

I am more than ever convinced that two or three girls are behind the notes. Thirteen- or fourteen-year-olds, filled with a vague prurience, giggling as they compose their sentences. I probably taught them two or three years ago and they still remember slights and scoldings, the failing grade on an essay. The Patterson girl comes to mind. Jean Patterson. She never liked me. I sensed her hostility the first day she stepped into the classroom. She is always around Louise Abbott and Mary Epps. Laughing and whispering in the hall. Milton has told me what a nuisance they are in class. When I think of it, Jean Patterson's sister attends the business college in Linden. She could very well have a typewriting machine at home.

Flanks: An interesting choice of word. Hard to imagine Jean Patterson's pedestrian mind coming up with it. Perhaps one of the others? Mary Epps lives on a farm in the township. "Flanks" might be a term she would contribute.

Tuesday, October 20

A visit after supper from Helen Jackson, who appeared suddenly at the front door looking ill at ease. I was not at my best this evening. The coal man had delivered today and since four o'clock I had been cleaning coal dust off the furniture and windowsills. And there was the minister's wife, perched on the edge of the sofa in the parlor. She seemed terrified of me and I can't say that I blame her. I must have been staring fiercely when she told me that she had written Nora about "your little spell two weeks ago. We're concerned about you, Henry and I."

"You wrote my sister? Why would you do that?"

"Yes, I did, Clara. I took the liberty. I got her address from Mr. Manes at the post office."

Bert Manes giving out addresses that he reads off the public mail? Surely that is against the law, but what can one do?

"I don't want you to think that I'm a busybody, Clara. I'm not that way at all. But I just thought your sister ought to know."

I had still not asked her to take off her coat. It was rude, but I couldn't help it. I was furious enough sitting there in my soiled housedress and slippers. The coal dust had been everywhere. I certainly wasn't expecting company.

"I've walked past your house so many times," said Helen Jackson.

"Trying to find the courage to knock on your door. Henry, of course, has been after me to see you, but I wanted to anyway. You seemed so confused and unhappy that evening."

"Confusion and unhappiness are often what life is all about," I said. "Don't you think that is true?" Now, when I think of it, that was perhaps an odd remark to make in a casual conversation. I am far too intense about such matters. Too much alone. Too much brooding. I can see how I must look to others. Still it's true enough, isn't it? Aren't we often unhappy and confused? What is so wrong with saying so?

"Perhaps," said Helen Jackson. "We could take the train down to Toronto. I like to look at paintings. We could go to the art gallery together some Saturday."

"I don't think so," I said. "I'm not much for that kind of thing. I like books and music."

She looked so dissatisfied sitting there on the edge of the sofa. A meek and pretty little woman. Married to the fiery minister and childless like me. All that tea pouring with the Ida Atkinses of this world. I didn't offer her any tea. I couldn't bring myself to go through with all that: boiling the water, putting out the best cups and saucers, the sugar bowl and cream jug. Couldn't and wouldn't. In the hallway as she left, she took my hand. Such small hands she has!

"I will pray for you, Clara. God always listens to those who ask for help."

"Well, I wish I could believe that," I said. "It would make things a great deal easier. But I don't believe it to be true and that is the great pity. As far as I am concerned, there is nobody listening. I'm afraid we are on our own, Mrs. Jackson."

"Surely that isn't true, Clara. If I believed that, my life would not be worth living."

She looked up at me and grasped my hand tightly. Such strength in that small hand. I felt awkward standing beside her under the hallway light. The beginning of gray in Helen Jackson's hair, though she can't be much older than I am.

"I wish you would drop by now and again for a visit, Clara. I know there are things we could talk about. Come when Henry is out, if that would make you feel better. Come and see me when the car isn't there."

I wondered about that remark as I watched her hurry across the street.

Thursday, October 22

To Miss Callan
What nights of bliss you must be enjoying there in your house all alone with your phantom lover. We cannot see into your bedroom but we can imagine ... Do you stroke his dark hair and swarthy skin as he leans across your bed at night? Do you sigh over his kisses when he takes you in his arms? Is it not wonderful to have such a phantom lover? To kiss you and tell you that you are not alone? Oh, you are so lucky to have your phantom lover, Miss Callan. Be careful however or one day we will see you pushing a baby carriage with a little phantom baby inside.

Interested bystanders

When do they put these notes under the veranda mat, I wonder? It must be very late. Do their parents not notice their absence? I must watch Jean Patterson closely tomorrow and see if I can detect anything in her expression. I am convinced that she and her friends are behind all this.

Friday, October 23

Jean Patterson and Mary Epps passed me in the hall this morning on their way to Milton's room. "Good morning, Miss Callan." I merely nodded. Duplicity can bear an innocent face even in the young. This afternoon a letter from Nora filled with concern about my "spell." She also sent me a book. *Live and Learn How to Live* by Dr. Ralph Crispin, whose picture is on the back wrapper. A plump cheerful-looking fellow who is the minister of some large church in Los Angeles, California. I have had such a time this evening glancing through Dr. Crispin's pages. Some chapter headings: "Wake Up and Sing, Don't Mind the Stormy Weather"; "Look at the Forest, But Don't Miss the Trees"; "You Can Do It If You Want To"; "God Loves a Happy Person."

I will write Nora about all this, but tomorrow when I am, and if I am, feeling calmer.

135 East 33rd Street
New York
October 17, 1936

Dear Clara,
Yesterday I received a letter from a Mrs. Helen Jackson, the new minister's wife. She was writing about a talk you gave to the Women's Auxiliary on our trip to Italy last summer. She said that you had a spell or something, became sick with nerves. I have since telephoned her. Clara, I do wish you would have a telephone installed. Why do you resist such an obvious convenience in today's world? I will be more than happy to pay the monthly charges. In any case, I telephoned Helen Jackson. According to her, you seemed to go to pieces that evening. She sounded very nice and she's concerned about you as are others in the village. She feels, and I certainly agree, that you spend far too much time by yourself. You seem to have just your work and that old house to look after. You really ought to make more of an effort to get out and meet people, Clara. It would be good for you. Everyone needs friends. I don't know what I would do without Evelyn. I wish you would take advantage of Helen Jackson's offer of friendship. Why not invite her over from time to time? You'll probably find out that you have a great deal in common. She certainly sounded like an educated woman to me. You are just too stubborn in your insistence on being alone and independent. You should make more of an effort

to get out and meet people. As Dr. Crispin says, "No man is an island." I'm sure he meant that to apply to women as well. I'm worried about you, Clara. Please let me know how you are.

Love, Nora

Whitfield, Ontario
Sunday, October 25, 1936

Dear Nora,

Your letter arrived on Friday, but I put off replying because I was annoyed by it, and I still am. I think it was presumptuous of Helen Jackson to get in touch with you. I suppose her heart's in the right place as is yours, of course, but I wish people wouldn't fuss over me. Please keep the following in mind:

1. I don't want a telephone in my house.
2. I don't want to "make more of an effort to get out and meet people."
3. Helen Jackson leads a more pathetic life than you imagine I do.
4. Dr. Crispin is full of shit.

Clara

Monday, October 26

I stayed up until two last night, sitting in the dark by the front door hoping they might come by. What foolishness! At two o'clock I climbed the stairs to bed and today I paid the price. So did the children, for I was fretful and cranky.

135 East 33rd Street
New York
Saturday, October 31, 1936

Dear Clara,

I was going to ignore your letter, but I don't see how I can. After all, *I am your sister.* We are pretty much on our own in this old world, Clara, and so it seems to me that we should look out for one another. Helen Jackson was only trying to be a good neighbor. I will tell you something—your last letter doesn't leave me feeling very confident that you are quite yourself these days. What is the matter anyway? If you can't tell me, who can you tell? I have to say this too. Last summer on our trip, I noticed that you were behaving oddly. I know you have always been a quiet broody type of person, but last summer you just seemed so remote from everything. Even Lewis remarked on it. On the ship you wouldn't join in on any of the activities, even though there was something for everyone. They even had a book club. Do you remember how I urged you to join that and talk to other women about books you've read? But all you wanted to do was be off by yourself reading or sitting in the deck chair staring out to sea. You just sat there for *hours* staring at the ocean. I don't call that normal, Clara. I think you need to talk to somebody about all this, and if not me, perhaps a doctor. Evelyn has her problems and she sees a doctor every week about them. It's not all that uncommon nowadays. Maybe you could arrange to go down to Toronto on Saturday mornings or something. I would be more than happy to help because those kinds of doctors can be expensive. I'm really serious about this, Clara. I just don't like the sound of your last letter. I sent you Dr. Crispin's book in the hope that you might have found it helpful. Okay, there are things in it that you might not agree with, but that book has helped thousands of people get through their days. He was interviewed on the radio the other night and he talked about the thousands of letters he has received. Are you so special that you can ridicule him with rude language?

Here is something I would like to do and I hope you have no objections. I have asked Evelyn to write me out of the script for a few days over Christmas so that I can come up to Whitfield to see you. We'll spend the holidays together. I want to see our little village on Christmas Eve just as I remember it with the snow falling and the band playing at the skating rink. Do they still have skating parties? Remember how we used to lie in bed and listen to the band? On a clear night, we could just faintly hear it from the bedroom. If I were behaving myself or you were in the mood, you would make up a story to tell me. I'd like to do that again, and I'd like to keep you company over the holidays. I'll probably arrive on Christmas Eve (a Thursday) and I'll likely stay until the Sunday or Monday. I hope you like the idea. We should have a swell time together. Evelyn sends her best.

Love, Nora

San Remo Apts.
1100 Central Park West
N.Y.C.
8/11/36

Dear Clara,

Surprise, surprise! Remember me? Evelyn Dowling, Nora's pal. She told me you've been under the weather, so to speak. It must be catching, because so have I, and I'm seeing a quack about it. He calls himself a psychiatrist and every Wednesday afternoon he asks me questions about days of yore when I was a fat cuddly moppet living with Mommy and Daddy.

Your sister wondered if I had any words of wisdom to pass along, but I really don't, beyond saying that women who live alone should probably buy a cat or something. In my case, I'd need a large one, say a leopard or a panther. Maybe one of those roaming about the place would help concentrate the mind (thank you, Dr. Johnson). We single ladies seem to be susceptible (whew, all those sibilants crowded together) to some kind of malaise in the air, particularly as old man Winter approaches. Of course, we don't have the husband and his goddamn slippers and the kiddies to deal with (thank heavens), though I imagine that that kind of clutter in your life could take your mind off certain things. Like who the hell am I, and what am I doing here? And how am I going to get through the next thirty years?

You'll have to forgive me, kiddo, for going on like this. I guess I should be consoling you and here I am whining away. But it's a wet Sunday afternoon in New York and I've seen all the movies. There is nothing on the radio and I'm too tired to read. Besides, I'm sick of words, the thousands of hackneyed ones I churn out each week, and even the other ones, better arranged in books by more talented people. The truth is I've been trying to do some real writing lately. By real writing, I mean stories. But they always turn out to be pale and very sickly imitations of Dorothy Parker or Dawn Powell. There is always something missing. It's probably called talent. But put me down in front of my trusty Smith-Corona and ask me to crank out another episode of "Chestnut Street" or "Manhattan Patrol" (a new cop show I'm writing), and voilà—there you have it, ready for the oven.

I've come to the conclusion that I suffer from a corrupted imagination and there doesn't seem to be much I can do about it. I suppose Nora has told you (maybe I already have) that this corrupted imagination of mine has been noticed by various and sundry moguls out in Hollywood where such imaginations are much sought after. So, I have had a few offers and I have to say I sometimes feel tempted. By way of temptation these moguls offer to pay hilariously vast sums for my services, and on days like this, I can see myself under the palm trees. I also understand that Hollywood is filled with psychiatrists and beautiful women and sometimes they are one and the same. Well, we shall see what the new year brings.

You must write and tell me how life is unfolding in that picturesque Canadian hamlet of yours. Are the people as gosh darn nice as the folks in Meadowvale, U.S.A.? Nora talks so much about Whitfield that it has become Meadowvale for me. Please don't tell me that you have an actual Chestnut Street (I have been afraid to ask Nora) or I'll probably cut my throat. Why not drop me a line when you have a moment?

Fondly, Evelyn

Tuesday, November 10

Nothing for over two weeks. I thought they had grown tired of their game, and then today a letter actually sent through the post. *Ruckus. Raptures. Ardently. Luxurious.* They must find such words in magazines.

> Dear Miss Callan,
> A little bird has told us that your phantom lover has returned from the land of the Latins. We understand he favors Saturday night visits and stays over. And so it was last Saturday night that we heard your commotion. What a ruckus you two kick up! Such shrieks of delight as he chases you around the house. It must be fun playing hide-and-go-seek bare naked! And when he catches you in his arms—what then, Miss Callan? What raptures as he embraces you ardently in his strong arms and covers your face with kisses. And as he carries you up the stairs to your bedroom, your mind gives way to luxurious thoughts of love as he lays your bare-naked body across the bed. Oh, Miss Callan, you mustn't. You shouldn't. Ohhh.
>
> Fascinated bystanders

Whitfield, Ontario
Saturday, November 14, 1936

Dear Evelyn,
Thanks for your letter. You may have been feeling a little melancholy on that wet Sunday, but your letter was certainly amusing. Isn't it odd

how, even when we are not feeling quite ourselves, we can still transcend our feelings through words. I suppose this is what poets and novelists and playwrights do only in a more concentrated and artistic way. I like to imagine Shakespeare, for example, inventing Falstaff on a day when his spirits were especially low. Or writing the final act of *King Lear* in a particularly sunny mood.

Anyway, it was kind of you to think about me and write. Nora worries so. She thinks I am by myself too much and am therefore turning into a funny old maid in my father's house. There was a minor episode last month at one of the local churches that may have furnished her with evidence for these suspicions. I foolishly agreed to talk to the Women's Auxiliary about our trip to Italy last summer. And something happened, I'm still not sure what, but I lost my way during this talk. Perhaps I just realized the sheer fatuity of what I was trying to do. So I went on and on about a man and a woman I saw in Rome. This particular man and woman had formed the most interesting memory of my entire trip and I suppose I began to laugh at the absurdity of trying to explain something that is perhaps unexplainable to certain people, and of course it all came out badly. I must have sounded hysterical. I can see how those women might have thought that. The new minister's wife was so alarmed by my performance that she saw fit to get in touch with Nora. But I must record here and now that I feel as sane as one can feel if one is fully conscious on this benighted planet.

There has been, however, a troubling offshoot to this episode. For the past month I have been receiving poison pen letters in which I am imagined to be having a torrid love affair with an Italian! My "phantom lover," as he is called by the letter writers, implies that I am a frustrated victim of sexual fantasies. How diabolical these brats can be! I am unable with certainty to prove the authorship of these scurrilous little notes which arrive every so often under my doormat, but I suspect two or three of my former pupils who are now in their entrance year (I teach the four junior forms). They are playing out some kind of schoolgirl fantasy, the erotic daydreams of thirteen-year-olds, perhaps as revenge for slights of long ago. That's my theory anyway. The notes are a bit unsettling. It's never pleasant to be made fun of, but I hope eventually to get to the bottom of it all. What I shall do about it then, I am not quite sure. But enough of all that, and by the way, please don't mention any of this to Nora. She is already far too needlessly concerned about my "mental condition." Take care of yourself and write now and again. I do enjoy your letters.

Clara

Monday, November 16 (7:22 a.m.)

A strange and troubling dream which I feel almost ashamed to record. I sometimes wonder if, in fact, I am not a little mad. For the first time in months, I dreamed of Charlie. He was pursuing me through the rooms of this house, yet the images were indefinite and at times indistinct. We seemed, for instance, scarcely to be moving. It was as if we were floating, our bare feet not touching the floorboards of the hallway and rooms. I did not seem to be afraid. In my bedroom, we were both naked and then he seemed to be the young man from Rome and yet he had Charlie's wide monkey mouth and grin. I could no longer stay in bed or endure the darkness, so I turned on the bedside lamp and sat in the chair by the window. I must have been there two hours or so before I fell asleep (my neck now aches from the way I slept). I awakened at first light and through the window saw the faint grayness and the dark branches.

135 East 33rd Street
New York
Sunday, November 29, 1936

Dear Clara,

I haven't heard from you for ages. Hope everything is okay. I'm still planning to come up for Christmas and I've looked into the connections. I'm taking the evening train out of Penn Station on the twenty-third and I'll arrive in Toronto the next morning. I thought I'd spend the day in the city looking around and maybe call on a couple of old friends and have lunch with them. Then I'll catch the Linden train. Does Bert Manes still pick up the mail and drive passengers into the village? If he doesn't, would you mind asking Joe Morrow to come down to the station for me? Of course, I'll pay him. I just don't feel like toting two bags all the way home. I'm really looking forward to an old-fashioned Christmas with you. Hope there will be lots of snow. Are my old skates still in the basement? I thought I might go for a skate if they have ice at the rink by then. Busy down here as usual, and I've been offered some freelance work in the new year. I'll tell you all about it when I see you. I'm worried about Evy who is awfully blue these days. She is just in a real funk. She's nice enough to me, but she bites nearly everyone else's head off if they cross swords with her. Brother, can she be mean!!! I think she's just lonely. Well, who isn't, huh?

Our traveling companion from last summer has published this article in a magazine down here. It's all about the war in Spain and European politics. He mentions the streets of Rome, but he doesn't bother to write about how he behaved one day. Remember? It just proves that what you read isn't anything like what actually happened. He makes himself out to be a hero, telling off the police, blah, blah, blah. We don't even get a mention, and it's probably just as well. It's almost as though we never even went along with him. He talks about that man with the yellow hair making fun of a radio actress, but she is at another table. It's me, of course, only he makes it sound like it's another person. I'd like to think he was sparing my feelings, but what I really believe is that His Lordship didn't want to admit that he was traveling with a lowbrow like me. According to the magazine, a number of these pieces by him are going to be published in a book next spring or summer. Big deal!!!

Do you think the King is really going to abdicate? In today's *Trib*, there's a big picture of him and Wallis Simpson. What do people up in Canada think about all this? I'll bet they're not too happy with the situation. Just imagine though—giving up the throne of England for the woman you love. You have to admit, Clara, that's awfully romantic. See you Christmas Eve.

Love, Nora

Monday, December 7

As I was about to leave today, Ella Myles came into the classroom to ask for help in an essay competition. She doesn't feel comfortable talking to Milton. I wonder she can talk to anyone; she is such a grave, quiet and shy creature. Her dark blond hair has been cut severely across her brow, butchered really by her mother's scissors. A pale unhealthiness to the girl. It's as though she exists on white bread and milky tea. A damp, unclean smell. The mother should talk to her about personal hygiene. Ella stood by my desk and showed me the advertisement in the Toronto paper. The competition is sponsored by one of the banks. A twenty-five-dollar prize for the best essay. Open to all members of the entrance class across the province. Five hundred words. The predictable topics: The Responsibilities of a Good Citizen; The Future of the British Empire; The Miracle of the Airplane; How the Railways Made Canada. Which one should she choose? A vein throbbing in her slender throat as she asked.

The poor child doesn't stand much of a chance in this; her sensibility is far too dreamy and lyrical. That's why she didn't win our little essay competition about the miners last June. These topics call for closely reasoned arguments and logical development of a thesis. It's just not in her gift. If they were asking for a short story or a poem! But I couldn't bring myself to discourage her. We decided on the responsible citizen topic and I loaned her a little book of essays to study, though I doubt whether Chesterton and Leacock will interest her very much. The deadline is February, but she wants to work on this over the holidays. Swore me to secrecy, of course.

An awful fuss on the radio about the King and his American lady friend. It looks now as if he is going to abdicate and marry this woman. Nora, along with millions of others, will be agog.

Tuesday, December 8

I have to do something about all this. When I arrived in the classroom this morning, I saw the piece of paper sticking out of the dictionary on my desk. They now feel bold enough to enter my classroom. The children were crowding into the room, and I felt such an urge to run. I have never felt this before. I saw the day and week ahead and heard a kind of roaring in my ears. Hurried off to the lunchroom to compose myself, but Milton was still in there finishing his morning cup of tea. His broad back was to me and he turned, embarrassed and red-faced. "Oh Clara, good morning! I thought you were in class by now. We're late, aren't we?" Felt sick to my stomach over everything. Can Jean Patterson and her friends hate me so much that they put words like these between the pages of my dictionary?

> Dear Miss Callan,
> Another visit on Saturday night from your dark and handsome lover with his yellow shoes and bicycle. We watched the both of you. We can see inside your mind. We watched him remove your clothes. Ah, there he is as you touch yourself in that forbidden place, Miss Callan. Oh, that is naughty of you. And now he is kissing your breasts. His lips are now upon them. Then he moves across your body. Down, down across the whiteness of your belly. There, there, there, there. Doesn't that feel good, Miss Callan?
>
> Jealous bystanders

I have made a serious mistake and in the days ahead I will surely pay. And I was so certain. After supper I walked over to the Pattersons', determined once and for all to sort out this business of the notes. I knew Jean attended Girl Guides on Thursday evenings, and I wanted to talk to her mother alone. That too may have been a mistake. Mrs. P. was understandably surprised to see me. She had sat near the front of the church hall that night, and I remembered her look of astonished distaste at my performance. In the hallway tonight, she was smiling fiercely, almost a grimace. "Why, Miss Callan, what a surprise!" Yes, a surprise. Jean's older sister Carol was home listening to dance band music. "Carol! Turn that off, for heaven's sake!" Through the doorway to the front room I could see Carol swinging her legs off the couch.

In the front room she gave me a brief, interested look. The weird Miss Callan whom she remembers only as her crabby junior-form teacher. Carol was a lazy, stubborn child and we didn't like one another. She is now at business college in Linden, a younger version of the mother, full-bosomed in her sweater, a pretty, childlike face. Mrs. P. had hung up my coat and now fluttered into the room, a chesty little wren of a woman. Years ago she had designs on Father, and for a few horrible months I imagined the worst, this dumpy widow with her two brats as my stepmother. Now we sat facing one another; Carol had fled upstairs and I could hear the clatter of a typewriter. Mrs. P. maintained her tight little smile. I could only imagine what was going through her mind. I no longer taught either of her daughters, so what was I doing there clutching my envelope of notes? And so I began with something like the following:

"Mrs. Patterson, I am sorry to have to say this, but I believe Jean and some of her friends have been writing notes to me." A puzzled frown, and I continued. "These are notes of a personal nature, I'm afraid."

"I see," said Mrs. P. "And what makes you think that Jean may be responsible for writing these notes?"

Her face was now a mask of dislike and suspicion. And what indeed had made me think so? I had no genuine evidence.

"The notes," I said, "have been written on a typewriter. I have always suspected that Jean disliked me. Perhaps she still harbors some resentment for the grades I used to give her."

"I'm sure that isn't true, Miss Callan." A chilliness to her voice and who could blame her? "Jean is not like that at all. She does not bear grudges. I have never heard her say an unkind word about you."

I had to carry on now. The fat, as Father used to say, was in the fire. "I don't think Jean was alone in this," I said. "The Abbott girl may have been in on it and Mary Epps. The three of them stick together."

"We do not own the only typewriter in the village, Miss Callan."

"Perhaps not, Mrs. Patterson, but Jean seems the most likely person. I would like to get to the bottom of this. These notes have been terribly upsetting to me."

The typewriter had stopped. I had not heard Carol coming down the stairs, but she now stood at the entrance to the front room.

"I am sure," said Mrs. P., "that you would like to get to the bottom of this. But you are very much mistaken in accusing my daughter. What are these notes about, may I ask?"

I felt myself faltering then, but what could I do but go on. "I'm afraid," I said, "they are rather salacious." Another mistake. They didn't know the meaning of the word, and they hated me for using it. I could see the hatred in their faces. There I was, the schoolteacher showing off her knowledge of fancy words. Why had I not simply said *rude* or *offensive*? Carol was leaning against the wall with her arms folded across her chest.

"I am sure you are mistaken about all this," said Mrs. P. "I can't for the life of me imagine Jean writing notes to you anonymously. Of course, Jean is not here to defend herself and, by the way, I think that is very unfair of you, Miss Callan. The child should be allowed to defend herself. You schoolteachers can be very unfair about these things. You don't give your pupils a chance to speak for themselves."

"I wanted to talk to you first," I said.

"I don't understand any of this," said Mrs. P. "May I see one of these notes, Miss Callan?" I handed over one of the least offensive and Carol moved to her mother's side. Both read of my "phantom lover." As she read, Mrs. P. muttered, "Ridiculous. I can't believe Jean had anything to do with this."

I blundered on. "You were there that night, Mrs. Patterson. You heard me. You could have told Jean."

"And what if I did?" said Mrs. P., looking up at me sharply. "I must say you acted very strangely that night, Miss Callan. What if I did tell my daughters? That doesn't prove that one of them wrote this note or any of the others."

Carol then uttered the terrible words. She had taken the note from her mother and was reading it again. "This note was not typed on my machine, Mother, and I can prove it. If you and Miss Callan will come up to my room, I can prove it."

Mrs. P. looked understandably satisfied with this turn of events. "Well that certainly sounds like a good idea."

Climbed the stairs following Mrs. P.'s sizable bottom, an intimation of catastrophe in the very air I was breathing. Difficult to put into words the emerging despair enveloping me. Into the little pink bedroom with its pennants and pictures of movie stars, the teddy bear on the bed. Carol sat down at the desk and rolled a piece of paper into the machine. The sound of her tapping was like nails in my skull. She handed her mother the piece of paper. "Mine is a Royal," she said. "I'm pretty sure that note to Miss Callan was typed on an Underwood. We have Underwoods at the college. You can see the difference in the lettering."

Mrs. P. holding both pieces of paper, unmistakable triumph in her face.

How hateful we look in such circumstances! I am sure that I have arranged my features in just that way after discovering a pupil cheating or lying.

"Well," said Mrs. P., "this certainly proves that Jean had no part in the writing of these notes. You can see for yourself, Miss Callan," she added, thrusting the pages under my nose. And indeed I could see that each had been typed on a different machine.

"Yes," I said. "I can see that. I am sorry, Mrs. Patterson."

"I would think you should be, Miss Callan. It's a terrible thing to accuse a child of something like this without proof. I certainly intend to talk to Mr. McKay about this."

"As you wish, Mrs. Patterson," I said, or I think I did. By then I had perhaps fled from Carol Patterson's pink bedroom, hastening down the stairs and out the door into the night. An ignominious retreat. That was hours ago. Will I sleep at all tonight?

Friday, December 11

As I expected, Milton called me into his office at recess this morning. Mrs. P. had telephoned and Milton looked flustered, face reddened with embarrassment. He was listening to the news on his small radio and he didn't bother to turn it off; a man with an English accent was going on about the King who was to address the Empire at five o'clock today. Milton was half-listening to this larger drama, wishing probably I were somewhere else. Maybe Timbuktu. Yet he treated me as gently as you would a madwoman who might suddenly decide to hurl a book across the room. Oh, I am doubtless exaggerating, but he did seem to regard me with a wary eye.

"It's a terrible thing to receive anonymous letters," he said. "I once had some poison pen letters sent to me. It was my first school in Pine Falls. I found out they came from a girl I gave a bad grade to. It's always girls who do these things, isn't it? You would never get a boy writing anonymous letters. It's just not something boys do."

Milton frowned, irritated at that moment perhaps by the very presence of females in the world: spiteful schoolgirls, nagging mothers, capricious teachers, wealthy socialites who turn the heads of kings. He mumbled something about exercising more caution in the future and left it at that. Returned to his radio news. Milton's primary strategy in dealing with problems is to do nothing, hoping that in time they will go away or be forgotten. It used to annoy Father, who said that Milton would never make a satisfactory principal for that very reason. Yet, I was grateful. Perhaps all this will pass over.

Listened to the King announcing his abdication but turned him off after a few minutes. Couldn't stand the sound of his tinny little English voice going on about "the woman I love."

San Remo Apts.
1100 Central Park West
N.Y.C.
13/12/36

Dear Clara,
I'm sorry not to have answered your letter sooner, but I've been fighting a cold and feeling generally lousy. I seem to be on the mend now, getting back to my old self. That's not a particularly appealing sight, but at least it's me.

It's too bad you're plagued with those letters, sent no doubt by some rotten little girls. Or maybe they are not so little? My goodness, the things that go on in idyllic villages like yours! I am sure you'll forgive me if one of these days, our Alice starts receiving poison pen letters. So you started laughing in the middle of this talk you gave to the Women's Club or whatever you call it? Hell, that isn't a sign of craziness, it's a display of sanity. In the middle of it all, you realized the entire absurdity of the situation. Sometimes all we can do is laugh, right? They should have been on their feet, applauding you. In any case, I wouldn't worry about these notes. Why not just throw them in the garbage? Don't even read them. Whoever is responsible will get tired of the game in time. They always do. Speaking of writing, I just finished the Christmas week episodes of "Chestnut Street." (Your sister has decided to visit an old woman who is alone and friendless at Christmas and so she is out of the script, visiting you, I understand.) And so Uncle Jim, played by that merry old drunk Graydon Lott (I believe you met him last summer at my place) will give his annual peroration around the stuffed turkey to Effie and Aunt Mary. How we should all be grateful for the good Lord and everything he gives us in this little corner of America where folks know the meaning of love and trust and neighborliness. "And seldom is heard a discouraging word/And the skies are not cloudy all day."

So what do you think of England's Eddie taking off with our American babe? She's a high-stepper that one and the little prince may have his hands full. Your sister is all broken up about this, but I think it's hilarious. Little England seduced by America. I see a lapdog being climbed on by a big mongrel bitch. How is your love life? Do you have a love life? I myself am going through a dry spell. Bah humbug as old Scrooge would say. Happy 1937!

Evelyn

Saturday, December 19

Bought a Christmas tree this afternoon and left it in the backyard for Nora. She will want to decorate it when she arrives and so I got out the old boxes of tinsel and colored balls. Christmas concert this evening. Ella Myles read a poem about the three wise men. She was pretty and nervous, in a blue dress. Very severe, but she read well. I watched her mother in the audience and then walked home under a star-filled sky. Nora will be here this time next week.

Christmas Eve (11:30 p.m.)

Nora now asleep in Father's room. She arrived yesterday afternoon in a brilliant-green coat and matching hat. Perfumed. Very smart. Joe Morrow brought her up from the station in his truck and carried her luggage into the house, casting glances at this marvel, scarcely believing, I'm sure, that such wonders could step off the afternoon train. She is not the Nora he remembers and he told me so. Still in her coat, Nora walked through the house as though she were buying the place.

"Oh, Clara, you haven't changed a thing! It's just as it used to be when I would come home on Saturday nights."

Nora wanted snow falling through the yellow light of the street lamps and the music of sleigh bells. But it was not to be. Not this year. Just a mild cloudy evening with coal smoke in the air. A green Christmas, I'm afraid. "Oh, well," she said. "We can't have everything. So let's have a drink."

We sat at the kitchen table and she poured herself a little whiskey. "What would poor Father think," she said. "His youngest daughter drinking whiskey at this kitchen table." I didn't tell her, but I don't think he would be as surprised as she might imagine.

She has spent today among her admirers. The whole village knows she is spending Christmas with me and so she has gone forth to receive their praises, stopping in at the Brydens' and the Macfarlanes', at the post office and the Mercantile, to chat about Alice and Effie and Aunt Mary. After supper we decorated the tree while she went on about Edward and Mrs. Simpson. What did he see in her? She wasn't even pretty, etc., etc. I kept waiting for questions about the church hall episode, but so far nothing; she is still too caught up in her triumphant return.

Sunday, December 27

Nora's visit has not been the success she wanted it to be. She came up here ostensibly to see if I still had all my marbles, and I don't think she has entirely made up her mind about that yet. Today, before she left, we had our talk. For a moment, I was tempted to tell her what really happened, but then Joe was at the back door and we had to get Nora's things into the truck. I watched Joe carefully take her arm and escort her down the driveway, Nora stepping carefully through the snow that was finally falling at the end of her holiday. Waving from the doorway, I thought of how little we understand one another. Thought too of her comment about my muttering in the kitchen this morning. She said she could hear me upstairs. I wasn't aware that I muttered in the morning, but I suppose I do.

1937

Saturday, January 9

A blustery day and I spent a good part of the afternoon visiting Marion, who is ill with a grippe. When I got home about four o'clock, Ella Myles was waiting on the veranda, shivering in a thin jacket, a little tam on her head, but no stockings or mittens. She wanted to show me her essay for the competition. Silently I cursed her mother for allowing the child out on such a day, half-dressed like that. Stoked the furnace and then made some cocoa. We had that with biscuits, seated near the heating vent in the front room. While I read "What Makes a Good Citizen," Ella wandered about the room, stopping by the window to stare out at the snow and the bare trees, turning then to inspect my furniture, touching a lamp here, an armchair there, the piano. It was as if she were delighted to be here in the tidy comfort of Miss Callan's house on a winter afternoon.

Her composition was lazily written and full of errors, but when I suggested ways to improve things, Ella merely shrugged. I could see that she was tired of the whole enterprise and would settle for nothing but approval. She will very likely throw it into the wastebasket when she gets home and that would not be a bad idea. There is an undisciplined side to Ella, and I probably overvalued her sentimental verses in the Senior Second form. Milton has told me how poorly she is doing in the entrance class.

She asked me to play something for her, and so I did the best I could with Dvořák's *Humoresque* and one or two of Mendelssohn's songs. She loves MacDowell's "To a Wild Rose." The dreamy little tunes seemed to entrance her as she stood by the window. I think she was just bored and lonely today. Letter from Nora who has taken up with another man. Or the same one she was seeing a year ago. I am losing track of her various encounters.

135 East 33rd Street
New York
Sunday, January 3, 1937

Dear Clara,
Happy New Year, and for a start, let me apologize for grilling you like I did that last day before I caught the train. I'm sorry, really I am. How you choose to live your life is really none of my business. It's just that I worry so about you. I can't help that, can I? After all, I'm your sister and I love you. I know we don't talk much about love in our family. We never have. I don't think I ever heard Father use the word. But we do love one another, don't we? And when you love someone, you worry when they are unhappy or troubled. So really it was love that was behind my questions that day, but I could see you were getting annoyed with me and so I'm sorry. I just want you to be happy, Clara.

Do you remember Les Cunningham, the announcer on our show? He's always been a little sweet on me and we went out together for a while. It was all strictly kosher, as they say down here. But now Les is thinking of getting a divorce, and so we have more or less drifted back together again. He told me how much he missed me over the holidays and so we've started dating again. Nothing serious, but it's sure nice to have a fellow on your arm when you go to the movies. I just wish you could find someone too. Evy sends her love and so do I.

Nora

Whitfield, Ontario
Sunday, January 10, 1937

Dear Nora,

Thanks for your New Year's wishes which I hereby return tenfold. Don't concern yourself unduly about the "grilling" you gave me on the day you left. Perhaps I deserved it. When all is said and done, I am a peculiar cuss, and there doesn't seem to be much I can do about it. It's my disposition to be morbidly curious about certain things and that can sometimes make life awkward and uneasy. Can't be helped, I'm afraid. I just have to live with my temperament and do the best I can.

You say you want me to be happy? Fine! How? When? For how long? We all have happy moments, and these depend, I suppose, on our tastes and inclinations. Emily Dickinson made much of her happiness out of the careful observance of small daily events: a bird on a winter branch, the color of a morning sky. The Marquis de Sade was otherwise stimulated. Isn't it largely a matter of this disposition I referred to? Whether, in general, we feel hopeful or despairing, confident or fainthearted? Look at you! Off you went to New York and made a success of yourself! You were confident and hopeful because it is in your nature to be that way. I would have perished in a week down there. Does that make you a happy person? I don't know, but I would guess that you may be inclined to be happier or more optimistic than I am. But in my own way, I am happy enough, Nora, so you mustn't fret about me. Say hello to Evelyn.

Clara

Wednesday, January 20

After weeks, I thought it was over, but today this—wedged beneath the front door. The night's snowfall had covered the writer's footsteps.

> Miss C
> A little winter bird has told us that your phantom lover has returned, and so we peeked in your front window the other night. The things we saw! The two of you running around the house naked and playing hide-and-go-seek. We saw you crouched behind the armchair by the piano. We saw him creeping across the rug toward you. What embraces there on the rug in front of the piano! How he covered you with kisses, Miss C! Aren't you the lucky one.
>
> Bystanders

Friday, January 22 (4:30 a.m.)

It came to me upon awakening a half hour ago. Perhaps I dreamed it, I'm not sure. But lying there in the darkness, I knew. Knew, as I know I'm alive, that the writer of those notes is Ella Myles. I was foolish to think that a dull creature like Jean Patterson has the erotic imagination to write such things. Ella is the author of this perfidy. But she grew too bold, wanted details: "the armchair by the piano," "the rug in front of the piano." It was clever to use the plural of *bystander*. Make it look as if more than one person were involved. Since Ella has no friends at all, the trail would lead to others. What a little dissembler she is, and I thought she liked me! I think now of the Saturday before last when she took everything in, as she drank her cocoa and walked about the front room. I wonder why she hates me so, or is it just a thirst for narrative invention, the creation of something beyond her dismal little world? Whatever her motives, it was wicked of her to create these preposterous fantasies in which I am made to look so pathetic. She must have typed them on the office machine at McDermott's while her mother dusted the coffins. No point in going back to bed now. I am as wide awake as I can ever hope to be. But it will be a long day.

Monday, January 25 (6:00 p.m.)

Ella has just left and I hope that is the end of it. Perhaps coming back to the house and doing what we did was a little self-serving on my part, but I wanted to show the girl that I am not the pitiful specimen she portrayed in her notes, but someone who also has an inner life. Perhaps I was mistaken in doing so. I wanted to have it out with her about these notes, and so I asked her to see me after school in my classroom. She came at four-thirty. The school was empty. She stood before my desk, and I think she knew what our conversation would be about, though she displayed no feelings whatsoever about being there; just the usual, lame, washed-out look. Sleep-crust still along her eyelids. Did she never wash her face? I could see the weakness of her drunken father in the habitual slouch.

"Stand up straight, for goodness' sake, Ella!"

Oh, the hectoring teacher in me and I felt ashamed of my temper! She straightened her spine a little then, but stared out the window. The light of the winter day was pale as water.

"Have you been writing notes about me, Ella? Leaving them on the veranda or even here, in this dictionary, on my desk?"

She turned and gave me a narrow shifty look. I had seen this look many times before.

"Notes, Miss Callan? No. Why would I write notes about you?"

"I don't know," I said. "Perhaps because you don't really like me. Or maybe because you didn't win the essay competition in June. Maybe no reason at all. Maybe just for something to do. To amuse yourself."

She said nothing but returned again to looking out the window.

"I can prove you wrote these notes, Ella. You wrote them on the office typewriter at McDermott's while your mother was busy working. How would you like it if I showed these notes to your mother?"

A shrug. Infuriating.

"I may show them to Mr. McKay too. You could be expelled for this. You could lose your year." That, of course, was nonsense; I could never bring myself to show such notes to Milton. "I thought we were friends, Ella. And then you write these notes in which I am made to look foolish and pathetic."

The wretched child continued to gaze out the window. With a decent haircut and a good scrubbing, she might be presentable enough to entice a boy to hold her hand and walk her home from school. Take her skating.

"Have you nothing to say about any of this?" I asked.

Then she turned to me and the words rushed forth. "You're wrong about last June, Miss Callan. Who cares about writing compositions anyway? I don't. I don't care about any of it. Go ahead and kick me out of school. See if I care!"

"But why did you write those notes about me, Ella? That's all I'd like to know."

A shrug. "It was something to do," she muttered.

"Something to do," I said. "Just that?"

"I guess so."

It was then that I had my little inspiration. I suppose I wanted to impress upon her the idea that people aren't necessarily what they appear to be; that it's a mistake to make assumptions about people you think you know. So I asked her to come home with me. Of course, she frowned at the suggestion. Puzzled. "Why?"

"I want you to do something for me," I said.

"What?"

"Come along and you'll see. Oh, don't worry, Ella, I'm not going to punish you."

And so the two of us walked through the cold afternoon to this house, wordless and alone with our thoughts. In the kitchen I handed her the envelope of notes.

"Sometimes," I said, "I write poems, but there is always something wrong with them. They never quite say what I mean them to say, and then I think of how many good poems there already are in the world, and I realize that what I've written doesn't add very much to what's already been said. So I just throw the poems in this stove. That way, at least, they will be useful. In their own small way they will help to keep me warm. So I try to make use out of something useless. Now I want you to do the same thing. I want you to think of these notes, Ella, as your own dark and rather hateful little poems and get rid of them."

I said something like that, something confessional and perhaps I shouldn't have. Children don't like adults to uncover their feelings and they are right. It looks eccentric and weak, self-indulgent. I may have done exactly the opposite of what I intended. Well, it's done and she did as she was told. I took the lid off the stove and we stood there side by side as Ella fed the notes one by one into the fire. We watched together as the paper curled and browned, the words disappearing in smoke. The flames were leaping from the mouth of the stove as she finished. But not a word of apology from the girl for what she did to me.

Saturday, January 30

Went to Toronto today on the train and bought half a dozen detective magazines. Then I went to a movie theater and watched a story about a woman who survives a train wreck. She suffers from amnesia, however, and is cared for by a handsome doctor who falls in love with her. The woman tries to remember her former life, but she can't recall a single hour and so she marries the handsome doctor and goes off to Europe on a honeymoon. Then her memory suddenly returns. This happens while she and the doctor are walking one afternoon in the Luxembourg Gardens in Paris. She sees a small boy playing with a boat by the edge of a pond and her past life comes flooding back to her. She remembers her own son, only six years old when last she saw him, and a daughter and, of course, another husband. Her life of romance and adventure with the handsome doctor has been shattered by the sight of the little boy and the boat.

In the darkened theater a hundred or so of us watched this woman's life unfold. The moving pictures have a life of their own; they draw you in and transport you to another world. When you are watching them, you are scarcely aware of your own existence. Of course, you must deal with all that when you come out of the movie theater; there you see it again: the soiled snow underfoot, the candy wrapper, the crying child tugged along by its mother.

Tuesday, February 9

Last night I read this in one of the magazines. There were two sisters who lived on a farm in Arkansas. After their mother died of influenza, the father arranged for a neighbor woman to come in to look after the house and the two little girls who were only seven or eight years old at the time. After a while the father began to have relations with this woman. In the night the sisters could hear them in the next room. This went on for several years, and then the father began to bother his daughters, one after the other. In time, a child was born to one of them, but it was so badly deformed that it lasted only a few hours and then was buried in the woods nearby. The father looked after that.

When the sisters were eighteen or nineteen, they murdered their father and the neighbor woman. They killed them one night with an ax while they slept. After the sisters were arrested, there was some dispute about who actually wielded the ax, but it didn't matter to the authorities. Both sisters were electrocuted. For the longest time, I lay awake thinking of the horror of that night in Arkansas: the sisters making their way toward the sleepers, the first blow from the ax, the half-awakened cries, the second blow severing life. The mess of it all: the blood-soaked bedclothes and splattered walls.

The sisters dragged the bodies to the farmyard for burial. Their father weighed over two hundred and fifty pounds and the neighbor woman was also immense. Shoveling dirt over the bodies behind the barn and then cleaning everything up and going to bed. Or maybe they sat at the kitchen table and drank some coffee. Sat there in silence until daybreak. It happened while the rest of us went about our lives. It is happening now somewhere.

Saturday, February 20

Went to Loew's theater and saw *Dancing Lady* with Joan Crawford and Clark Gable.

Saturday, February 27

Saw *Beloved Enemy* with Brian Aherne and Merle Oberon. On the train home I was the only passenger in the coach for the last thirty miles. The conductor was dozing in his seat and the wet snowflakes clung to the windows. I wanted the train ride to last for hours.

Saturday, March 6

Saw *When You're in Love.*

Sunday, March 7

Marion has not been well all winter and today I learned from Mrs. Bryden that she has gone to stay with an aunt to convalesce. The aunt is a retired nurse and lives in St. Thomas. Marion came by yesterday with her mother and father to say goodbye but, of course, I was in Toronto. Haven't heard from Nora in weeks. I should write, but I have nothing to say to her. And apparently she has nothing to say to me.

Saturday, March 13

Saw *Camille* at the Loew's theater.

Saturday, March 20

Went again to Loew's. It is handy and I can't be bothered looking for other theaters in which to pass an hour or two. Something today called *Great Guy* with James Cagney and Mae Clark.

Saturday, March 27

The Last of Mrs. Cheyney with Joan Crawford and Robert Montgomery.

Saturday, April 3

Felt too sluggish and out of sorts to go down to Toronto.

Saturday, April 10

I met a man today. At the end of the picture (a musical absurdity with those two warblers, MacDonald and Eddy), he spoke to me. I had come out onto Yonge Street, my eyes narrowing in the afternoon sunlight, and then this voice beside me.

"Excuse me, Miss!" I turned. A man in his early forties perhaps. Not even as tall as I am, but pleasant enough looking. Neatly dressed in suit and topcoat. Fair with gray eyes and a thin sand-colored mustache. He touched the brim of his homburg. The word *decorous* came to mind. I thought perhaps I had dropped a glove. Around us others were stepping into the street with the dazed look of afternoon movie watchers. Then the man said, "You weren't here last Saturday. I was looking for you."

I thought at first glance he had mistaken me for someone else, but how could that be? We were face-to-face there on the street. He was smiling. "My name is Frank Quinlan. I have seen you at the movies for the past several weeks and then you missed last Saturday. I was looking for you. I hope you weren't ill."

He was looking at me. What did he mean by that? I told him that I didn't know what he was talking about.

"Look," he said. "Please don't be alarmed. I realize that my speaking to you on the street like this is unusual. I mean no harm, believe me."

I must have been frowning, but he continued to smile. "You come early," he said. "You always sit in the same seat. I'm four rows behind you." Then he asked me to join him for a cup of tea at Child's up the street.

"But I don't even know you," I said. "Why would I do such a thing?"

"Well," he said and looked away for the briefest moment before smiling at me again. "I just thought it might be enjoyable for the two of us to have a cup of tea together. Surely, there can be no harm in it."

I found his looking away like that affecting. And the manner in which he said "well," as though he expected improbable encounters like this to be forever resisted. That won me over in a way. Certainly he didn't look in the least sinister, and so I surprised myself by going along with him. I remember thinking as we walked up Yonge Street that no harm could come to me in a restaurant. In Child's I told him that I could not stay long. "I have to be at the railway station by a quarter past five," I said.

He asked me then if I was going on a trip.

"Why no," I said. "I don't live in the city."

"I see," he said. "And you come in every Saturday to go to the movies."

Then I said, "I also visit my aunt who is ill." The lie came so easily to my lips that I scarcely missed a heartbeat in uttering it. But I said that because I did not want to appear pathetic in his eyes; I did not want to be seen as a woman who comes all the way into the city to go to the moving pictures by herself. I also lied about my name. I told him it was Carrie Hughes and that too came as easily and quickly as the name I gave that doctor on Sherbourne Street when I was pregnant.

"Well, Carrie Hughes," he said. "It's a pleasure to meet you."

How odd it feels to have someone call you by a name you have just invented! Yet I felt strangely alive at that moment. It was as if I had taken on another life, even though I felt mildly ashamed to be lying to this man who seemed decent enough.

"Do you mind if I smoke?" he asked. And when I said I didn't care, he filled a small brown pipe with tobacco and lighted it; the smell of the pipe smoke drifted across the table as we drank our tea. And all the while I was thinking what on earth am I doing here with this man? Yet it was interesting that he had chosen me. We talked about the movie and agreed that it had all been very silly. I said I preferred the melodramas and he said he did too. He told me it was wonderful to have someone to talk to after seeing a picture.

"I get tired," he said, "of walking out by myself every Saturday afternoon and no one to share a thought with."

I don't think I believed him then, and I'm not sure I believe him now. He seems altogether too presentable, this small, neat, handsome man. He must be married. He wanted to know where I lived, but I was circumspect, inventing a little life for myself even as I spoke. I found I enjoyed doing this. I told him I was from Uxbridge and my aunt lived on Huron Street; I was thinking of the boardinghouse I lived in years ago when I went to Normal School.

"Why don't you have something to eat before your trip back?" he asked. "A piece of pie, Carrie?" But I told him it was late. I was petrified at the thought of missing my train. Frank Quinlan (if that is his name) looked at his wristwatch. "I'll take you down to the station in a taxi," he said. "You won't be late. I promise."

And so he did. We talked a little more about movies we had enjoyed, and afterward we went down Yonge Street in a taxi and I thought to myself, I am sitting in a taxi with a man I didn't even know this morning.

"Will you be coming into the city next Saturday, Carrie?" he asked, and I felt so utterly dishonest having him call me by that name.

"I might be," I said and hated the suggestion of coyness in that answer, for I knew very well that I was going to.

"I wish you would," he said. "Perhaps we could sit together."

I could see the taxi driver's eyes in the rearview mirror. What was he thinking I wondered? Probably that I was the kind of woman men pick up in movie houses! But, why should I have cared what a taxi driver thought? Why did that matter? I told Frank Quinlan that in all likelihood I would be at the movies next Saturday. We were then in front of Union Station, and I had climbed out of the car and was looking in at him. I thought of my shabby coat. I have been intending to buy a new coat now for weeks, and yet there I was in that old thing. How down at the heels I must have appeared!

"I would really like to see you next Saturday, Carrie," he said. "Please come. I'll be looking for you." His face was upturned to mine under the hat. But I was so afraid of being late for my train that I didn't even say goodbye. Carrie Hughes indeed!

Thursday, April 15

A visit from the school inspector today, a new man, a Mr. Gibson. Milton was in a state. The inspector was not pleased with Milton's preparation for the senior classes. At the end of the day, Milton sat in his office, looking discomfited. I made him a cup of tea to settle his nerves. As for my classes, Gibson seemed pleased. A tall, humorless man, he stood at the back of the room for half an hour making notes. But I have endured many such visits, and I gave him a good performance. If you are prepared, there is nothing to fear from the Gibsons of this world. That is Milton's problem as a teacher; he just makes things up as he goes along. Father used to remark on it. My pupils sensed the importance of the visitor and were very helpful, thrusting their hands into the air at every question. I was proud of them.

Finally, a letter from Nora. All about her new boyfriend and their weekend together. How casually she enters into these arrangements! I wonder if I should mention Mr. Quinlan. "Nora, I met this man last Saturday in a movie theater on Yonge Street and he would like to see me again." What would she think?

135 East 33rd Street
New York
April 11, 1937

Dear Clara,
I guess I'm the one who owes the letter and it's been months, hasn't it? Gee, I'm sorry, I should have kept in touch before this, but the days just fly past, and half the time I don't know whether I'm coming or going. Now it's very late on a Sunday night, but I wanted at least to get this off to you, so you'll know I'm still in the land of the living. Les just dropped me off. We spent the weekend in Atlantic City. It's kind of a strange place to go this time of year. Most things were closed and the weather was absolutely lousy, cold and damp and foggy. But so what? We had fun and we mostly had the place to ourselves. We stayed in this old hotel and there were only three or four other guests. We walked along the boardwalk in the mist and fog and then came back to this old hotel for drinks. I guess you could say it was romantic. Les's wife and kids were visiting relatives in Philadelphia, so that's why he had the weekend to spend with me. He still hasn't moved out of the house, but he's thinking of it. I know, I know. I remember saying some time ago that I wasn't seriously interested in him, but now I'm not so sure. Les kind of grows on you. He's very easy to get along with and he's so good-looking. You should see the green stares I get from other women when we're out together ("dancing cheek to cheek"). Anyway, we'll see. I don't think his wife

wants to give him a divorce. She is going to battle him all the way and Les is not much of a fighter. He's maybe just a little too easygoing and Miriam (wife) more or less rules the roost. So things are a bit up in the air at the moment. Some days I think I'd marry the guy if he asked me. Other days, well...

How are things with you? Do you have any plans for the summer? I mention this because Evy and I were talking the other day about the Dionne quintuplets. There's a big splash on them in *Life* magazine and we were looking at the pictures. And I said how much I would like to see the little girls. They are on display at their home and thousands of people visit the place every year. Then Evy said why not, and maybe Clara could join us. Evy said she could borrow her mother's car, "a sturdy old Packard," and we could drive up to Whitfield and then on to the quints' place. She wanted to know how far Callander is from Whitfield, but I wasn't sure. You know what my geography is like!!! But it doesn't really matter. It can't be all that far and we could take a week and just be on our own (no men included, right?). So give this idea some thought, will you? Have to go to bed now or I'll drop. Let me know how things are going.

Love, Nora

Saturday, April 17

I saw Frank again today. Decided as I was walking up Yonge Street at a quarter past one. Would I see *Waikiki Wedding* at the Imperial or *Lost Horizon* at the Loew's? Five minutes after I arrived in the theater, he sat down beside me.

"Well, Carrie, I'm glad you came."

Again, it was strange to hear my imaginary name, and I felt so guilty lying to him like that. I was glad when the lights went down. When the feature began, I had trouble concentrating. Some people were fleeing a political crisis in China. They got into an airplane, but it crashed in the mountains of Tibet. From time to time, I glanced at

Frank's profile and at the businessman's hat in his lap. An ordinary, pleasant-looking man watching a movie. He seemed absorbed, but once he caught me glancing at him and he smiled. I had agreed to meet a man I don't even know. And where do such things lead if not to a hotel room on some rainy afternoon? How did the Englishwoman in Rome meet her lover? I wondered. At some point he must have introduced himself. "Would you join me for a cup of coffee, Signorina?" Or, "May I show you the way to the Protestant cemetery? It is not far." There has to be a beginning, and when others invite us into their lives, we must, of course, choose. And I had now chosen.

We went again to Child's and talked about the film. I can scarcely remember what I said. Frank told me he goes to the movies to get away from things. What things, I wonder? Family? Business? There is trouble in his life somewhere; I can hear it in his voice and see it in his eyes. And he seems such a kind and gentle man. At one point he said, "You come a long way to see a picture, Carrie. Is there no movie house in Uxbridge?"

"No," I said.

"But of course you visit your aunt too. How is she, by the way?"

I had forgotten the invented aunt and I think he sensed I was lying.

"She's recovering," I said.

"Good."

Afterward we again got into a taxi and drove down to Union Station. In the car, he asked me what I liked to do besides watch movies. I told him I liked poetry and music and he said, "I thought you might." The smell of his pipe filled the taxi. "What about next Saturday?" he asked. "Will you be in town? Please say you will." He had taken my hand and his fingers were gently pressing mine and I said yes, I would. Then on the street, I waved goodbye to him.

Whitfield, Ontario
Sunday, April 18, 1937

Dear Nora,

I too am sorry not to have written before this, but I seem to have been busy with this and that. We are having a gentle, mild spring up here and everything seems to be coming on early. The trees are already in their fresh new green and it makes me so happy just looking at them. Mr. Bryden has already spaded his garden and hopes to put things in the ground as early as next week. He asked me if I was going to put in a garden this year and I said I didn't think so. He looked disapproving. "When your father was alive" and so on. But I just haven't the heart to stand in the garden on a hot summer day pulling the weeds that invariably overtake things. Gardening is just not in my blood, I suppose.

I hope you're happy with Mr. Cunningham. He's a different type from Lewis Mills, isn't he? That is probably a good thing. L.M. was an interesting man in many ways, but he clearly wasn't your type as I'm sure you now realize. Is his book out, by the way? I wouldn't mind reading it if only because I was briefly acquainted with the man, and I think it would be interesting to read a book by someone you once knew, however fleetingly. If you see a copy in one of the bookstores, would you pick it up for me and send it along? I doubt whether any of the stores in Toronto would carry it. I'll reimburse you, of course.

Nothing much new in my life. I have got into the habit of going down to Toronto most Saturdays on the train. It makes a change. I walk about the stores though I'm not much of a shopper, as you know. Then I generally see a picture before I catch the train home. It's an outing and something to look forward to through the week. I am quite contented with my lot in life at the moment, and so you mustn't worry on my behalf. It has just now started to rain. A spring shower that will rinse the air and nourish Mr. Bryden's freshly turned garden. Boys will look for worms for fishing. I love rainy afternoons like this. I may take Father's old umbrella and go for a walk under these heavy gray skies. I think I would like that and I shall mail this letter on the way. Do take care of yourself.

Clara

Saturday, April 24

Frank and I saw *Top of the Town*. Pleasant nonsense and it seemed to be over in no time at all. When we came out, it was raining quite hard and I was hatless. By the time we got to the restaurant, I looked a sight. I used some paper napkins to dry my face and Frank was amused by me. His beautiful hat was stained, but he didn't seem to mind. The restaurant was crowded but the waitress found us a booth. I think she recognized us from other Saturdays, and I suspect she knows we are not married and may be up to something. In the booth Frank took my hands and rubbed them. "I think we should get to know one another if we are going to the movies together. Tell me about yourself, Carrie. You seem to be such a quiet and serious person."

"Serious?"

"Yes. Serious. There's a certain gravity about you. I like that, by the way. You're not frivolous. You think things through."

"I tend to, yes."

"What we are doing now," he said. "Meeting like this without knowing too much about each other. You're thinking that through carefully too, aren't you? Wondering if all this is proper and correct. Right?"

"I suppose I am, yes."

"I don't think you're married, so either you live alone or with your parents?"

"No no, they are both dead."

"Ah, I see. I'm sorry." He was studying me as he smoked his pipe. He is not afraid to look me in the eye. I don't mind him doing that. In fact, I rather enjoy it. I am getting used to his gray eyes.

"You work then," he said. "Let me guess. You are a secretary perhaps. Or maybe a librarian or schoolteacher?"

"Perhaps I am," I said and smiled.

He remarked on that. "You have smiled at last," he said. "My grave young friend has smiled."

"Not so young," I said.

"Of course, you're young. You are what? Twenty-eight or -nine? Perhaps thirty?"

"I am thirty-three." It was only my second truthful statement to him.

"Thirty-three is a good age," he said. "I'm forty-six."

We sat in silence for a while drinking our tea. Around us people were coming in out of the weather, shaking the rain from hats and umbrellas. I was happy to be in that crowded restaurant with this man among the other moviegoers and shoppers. I thought, This is how people go about their lives while I am home. And now I was a part of all this Saturday afternoon life. Then Frank told me he was married.

"I'm sure you must have guessed that," he said. "My wife and I have not been close for years." He looked out the streaked window of the restaurant at people hurrying past. "This started some time ago. After our last son was born. She seemed to go into decline. She has seen doctors about it."

Then he told me that he has four children. Michael is twenty-three and lives in Kingston. I have forgotten what he works at, but he went to Queen's University. He may be an accountant or a bookkeeper. The other three still live at home. Theresa is twenty, and Frank says she doesn't know what to do with herself. One minute she wants to write a novel, and the next minute she wants to go off to Spain or China and save the world. She takes courses at the university. I gather she has been a difficult child to raise, but from the way Frank talks about her, I think she is her father's favorite. Anne is eighteen and thinking of entering the religious life this summer. That is how he phrased it, "the religious life," by which I take him to mean that she intends one day to be a nun. The youngest child, a boy, is only eleven and I have forgotten his name.

Frank was forthcoming about all this. He also told me about the family business. They are coal merchants and seem fairly well-to-do. Frank has two older brothers in the business, and their offices are on King Street. "So there you have it," he said. "I want to be honest with you, Carrie. I am not a very complicated man. I work in an office. I look after my children. I tolerate my wife who is not well and who no longer cares for me. I go to the movies on Saturday afternoons because I am unhappy and I want two hours to myself. Edith thinks I am working at the office, but I don't believe she really cares where I am. When I'm not around the house, she finds it easier to drink. She's usually asleep in her bedroom by the time I get home. Then she drinks some more before dinner and falls asleep early, waking in the middle of the night to read or wander about. She drinks then too."

"Why does she drink so much?" I asked. "Why is she so unhappy?"

Frank took his time replying. "I don't really know," he said finally. "Her father was a drinker. Perhaps it's in the blood. I'm worried about Michael too. When he comes home for a visit, I can smell it on his breath."

In the taxi to the train station, Frank took my hand and asked if I would be there next Saturday and I said I would. So now I am seeing an Irish Catholic who has four children and a troubled wife. I like Frank Quinlan and I must stop lying to him.

Saturday, May 1

Today he did not appear, and I felt such a letdown sitting there alone in Loew's theater that I could have wept. I know I was very close to tears, and then before the newsreel began, this happened. The lights had just dimmed and I was watching the usher with his flashlamp bending across the seats in front of me talking to women who were sitting alone. There weren't many. Then the young man approached me and whispered, "Are you Miss Hughes?" I was going to say no, but then I remembered my foolish imposture and said yes and he gave me an envelope. I knew it had to be from Frank, and all through the picture (I can't even remember the name of it) I clutched the envelope and wondered what it contained. I was sure that he no longer wanted to see me and I tried to think of what I may have done to discourage him. From among others, he had chosen me, but then I had done something to make him change his mind. What? Such disappointment there in that darkened theater this afternoon! Then, once on the train, I opened the envelope, and like a schoolgirl who has been passed a note, I have read his words a hundred times.

> Dear Carrie:
> I am sorry, but I can't make the movies today. I am at the office and Theresa just telephoned. Something has come up at home and I have to be there. Please forgive me. I'm going up to Loew's theater now (it's nearly twelve o'clock) and see if I can get an usher to deliver this for me. I hope you're wearing the same coat, because I have to tell him what you look like. I will see you next Saturday. Please don't disappoint me!
>
> Fondly, F.

What happiness I felt upon reading those words on the train this afternoon! I cannot continue to lie to him, and when we meet next Saturday, I will tell him who I really am. I wonder what the trouble at home was; probably something to do with the neurasthenic wife.

Wednesday, May 5

After supper I walked west of the village along the township road. The evening sky was streaked with red and gold. As Miss Matheson and Miss Weeks would have said, "God is unfurling His banners." In the summer of my tenth year, Father sent me to a Bible camp on Lake Couchiching run by the Methodist church. At the end of the day, we gathered on the shore of the lake, a hundred little girls, to watch the brilliant sunsets; and always Miss Matheson or Miss Weeks would announce that God was unfurling His banners. And I would think of Mother somewhere behind those sun-touched clouds with God.

A hundred yards or so ahead of me on the road were Ella Myles and Martin Kray. I had seen them walking together earlier in the day and felt downcast by the sight. Of all the boys in the village, she has settled for Martin Kray, a seventeen-year-old tough who is just back from a year in reform school at Bowmanville. But perhaps no one else expressed interest in her. At fourteen the heart is hungry for affection and will find it where it can. But I fear he will hurt her, perhaps get her into trouble. I watch them walking ahead of me arm in arm, a moment of happiness for both of them under the spring sky. Wondered too what Frank might be doing at that hour of the day. Wondered what Edith Quinlan looks like. He said, "She's usually asleep in her bedroom," so they must sleep apart now. Oh, Miss Matheson and Miss Weeks, sleeping now yourselves alone in narrow plots! If you could only know the tangled thoughts and wishes of all those little girls who passed and still are passing by this way!

Saturday, May 8

Today we saw the newsreel of the German airship that burned last Thursday somewhere near New York. The announcer was weeping and we saw the huge ship engulfed in fire and smoke. How terrible to be trapped in all that! Around me people were transfixed by the images. Yet how quickly we all soon forgot the tragedy of those lost lives. Within a minute we were laughing at the antics of a cat and mouse and last Thursday's dreadful accident had vanished.

I am doubtless too morbid about such things and Frank reminded me of this in a gentle way. We were in the restaurant and, amid the clatter of the plates and cutlery, I was talking about the people in that airship; how a week ago they were making plans and so on and now everything was over. He took my hand in both of his and told me I was too serious about such matters, but he liked that side of me anyway. Then I told him my name was Clara, not Carrie, and I lived in Whitfield, not Uxbridge; that I had no aunt and I was sorry for having deceived him. I said I came down to Toronto on Saturdays because I was tired of seeing the same faces every day. And then Frank did something; he kissed my hand there in the restaurant. I remember the waitress was laying the cups of tea before us and she was smiling. She was envious of me, I think, and it was wonderful to be sitting there and having my hand kissed like that. I very nearly missed my train.

Before we parted, Frank said, "Why don't we do something different next Saturday? We could go for a drive in the country. I could come up and get you." But I am afraid of gossip in the village and so suggested that we meet somewhere along the way, and that's what we are going to do. He will drive up from the city and meet me at Uxbridge station next Saturday morning. It then occurred to me that someone on the train from the village would see me meeting him and that would set tongues wagging, so we agreed that he would stay in his automobile until the train left the station. Frank also gave me a book today. *Favorite Poems Through the Ages*. I was touched that he remembered I liked poetry.

135 East 33rd Street
New York
Sunday, May 9, 1937

Dear Clara,
Thanks for your letter. My, don't you sound gay! It must be this spring weather. This afternoon Evy and I went walking in Central Park and was it ever lovely! The trees and flowers are all out now and

young people are lying on the grass (Ha, ha). Evy and I just walked and talked about everything—the show and where it should be going over the next few months, and this new program that she's writing. There's a part in it that she thinks I could do. It's a detective show and she says it has a little zip and bite and she hopes she can get it past the agency. They don't like anything too unconventional. Evy is quite lonely these days. It's hard for women like her to find suitable companionship. It's not that there aren't plenty of lesbians in New York, it's just finding the right one. Well, when I think of it, I guess it's no different with normal women. Anyway, she is quite restless these days and is talking again about going out to California. A number of the studios are after her.

We're still planning to come up to Canada this summer, and we thought the last two weeks of July would be best. Evy will write me out of the script for that time and so we'll drive up to Whitfield in her mother's Packard. How about that? We'll pick you up and then go north to see the little girls. We'll stay in awful tourist courts and eat terrible food in roadside diners and generally have a whale of a time. What do you think? Doesn't it sound like fun? I hope you are still on for this adventure because I'm sure looking forward to it. Drop me a note one of these days. It's great to hear you sounding so cheerful.

Love, Nora

P.S. Wasn't that an awful tragedy the other day with the Hindenburg burning over in Lakehurst? It was in all the papers and on the radio.

P.P.S. Evy heard that Mr. Crumb's book will be out this summer and I'll get a copy for you.

Wednesday, May 12

The new King's coronation and so we got a holiday. At five o'clock this morning, people were listening to the ceremony from England.

Houses are adorned with flags and this afternoon there was a parade and a tree planting at the fairgrounds. Unfortunately for the revelers, it rained off and on most of the day.

Friday, May 14

Today, a letter from Frank.

305 King Street East
Toronto, Ontario
Tuesday

My dear Clara,
I'm writing this during my lunch hour. My brothers were after me to go out with them to the hotel for lunch (we generally go to the King Edward two or three times a week), but I would much rather sit here at my desk and think about you and of how happy I am that we have met. I hope, by the way, that you can read my handwriting. I haven't practiced my penmanship for years. Miss Haines does all my letters on the typewriter.

What shall we do on Saturday? Would you enjoy a picnic lunch or would you rather a meal in, say, a hotel in one of the towns along the lake? Cobourg or Port Hope? I can't imagine it would be very grand, but we could try a hotel dining room. I think that would be best, don't you? We'll try some old hotel where the roast beef will be overcooked and the gravy salty and they will give us some terrible rice pudding for dessert. But we won't care about any of that because we'll be enjoying one another's company. I have so many questions I want to ask you. Who are you, Clara Callan, and why have I been so fortunate to meet you? I know you will tell me the truth about yourself because you're not the sort of person who lies (not for very long at any rate), and I find it refreshing to know someone who so values honesty. I can see it in your clear, dark eyes and your grave expression. Now, you may think that's an odd statement since I am a married man, and if we are to go on seeing one another, I will have to invent another life for myself, and that, of course, will involve deceit. It has to, I'm afraid, or others whom I care about (my sons and daughters and, yes, Edith in a way) will be badly hurt. So I can see no way around that. Yet it seems to me that when you are lucky enough to find someone who you think is good and true, then the lies you tell others are forgivable. That may sound strange, but I think it's true.

Well, my dear, I am certainly looking forward to seeing you on Saturday morning, and I shall be waiting in my car at the Uxbridge train station. According to the schedule, your train arrives there at 10:10 so I shall be there waiting. My car, by the way, is a dark green Pontiac sedan (though I can't imagine there will be many others there), and I will be behind the wheel reading a newspaper. Isn't that how it is usually done in the movies? I very much look forward to our day together, my dear, and I hope you do too.

Fondly, Frank

P.S. I never bothered to ask whether you have a telephone, and when I tried information for your region, they had no listing. Don't you find the lack of a telephone a terrible inconvenience?

Saturday, May 15 (2:00 a.m.)

A fitful sleep because of a toothache that started after supper and now has wrenched me awake. I have tried cloves and a hot towel to my face, but nothing seems to appease the wretched thing. I will have to see a dentist in Linden soon. This neglect of my teeth; it's gone on for years and now I am paying for it, as pay we must. It's a wonder they are as presentable as they are. And so I lie in bed and read F.'s letter for the twentieth time. He called me "my dear" twice. Staring at the clock face and waiting for daybreak or sleep. I will surely look a wreck by morning.

Yesterday morning I took the train and got off at Uxbridge station. I wore a skirt and blouse and tied a sweater around my shoulders though the day was mild. There was no one else from the village on the train and I felt wonderfully alive and whole except for the cursed toothache. "There are always ants at the picnic," as Father used to say. From the window of the train, I could see Frank sitting in his dark green car and I felt so happy seeing him there. It was as if I hadn't really expected him to appear, but there he was. When I got into the car, he smiled and squeezed my hand. His car is new and I could smell its newness. He told me he has had it less than a month and enjoyed his drive up from the city. We drove out along the highway past villages and farms. I could smell the earth. I worried about making conversation, but talking comes easily to Frank. At one point he rested his hand on my arm and looked across at me. "I'm glad you decided to come, Clara," he said. And I was glad too. We stopped by the side of a road and walked along a stream, listening to the water rush over the stones. That gurgling sound and the smell of lilacs and I felt so wonderful except for the toothache which pestered me like the devil. Frank asked if he could kiss me and I was worried that my mouth would taste awful, but then I thought perhaps it wouldn't matter and it didn't, I think. *His* mouth tasted of tobacco. His lips were softer than I imagined and his mustache felt odd against my lips, but I liked it. Holding hands, we walked back to the car like schoolchildren, and I thought of Ella and her young man on the township road.

"Is there anything the matter?" Frank asked. "You seem preoccupied, Clara."

I didn't want him to think that I found his company tiresome, and so I told him about my toothache.

"Ah, well then," he said, brightening. "We must do something about that." He seemed charged suddenly with energy and I get the impression that Frank is one of those persons who like to have things to do. He was now all business. "We'll find a druggist in the next town."

"It isn't necessary," I said.

"Of course, it's necessary. You don't have to suffer with a toothache in this day and age. You need looking after, Clara," he said. "Everyone needs looking after once in a while."

As we drove along the highway, I thought about that and had to agree. We all do need to be fussed over now and then. In the next town we parked the car and walked along the main street like a married couple. Frank insisted that I take his arm and I did. Then we went into a drugstore and Frank said, "My wife has a toothache. What have you got for that?" It felt so peculiar hearing him say "my wife," but the druggist didn't bat an eye. He sold us some drops which took away the ache in no time. I felt so relieved to be free of it that I wanted to kiss Frank again there on the street.

In the dining room of the hotel we were the only patrons except for a frail elderly man in a suit who sat at a corner table. The waitress served us a full dinner with soup and roast beef and potatoes and gravy, just as Frank had predicted in his letter. When I reminded him of this, he laughed. "Well, yes," he said. "I have eaten in these places many times."

I'm afraid I left a good deal of it on my plate. Frank put it down to my toothache, but really I was too nervous to eat much. I imagined the old man in the suit eating his dinner in this hotel dining room every day at twelve o'clock. I saw him as a widower, a wealthy merchant or perhaps the owner of a local mill. I imagined him having no family and living in a large brick house with a turret somewhere on a leafy street and coming to this hotel every day at a quarter to twelve for his roast beef. And one day he would surprise everyone by leaving his fortune to the pretty young waitress. And again it felt strange when the waitress asked Frank, "Would your wife like some pie?"

When we came out of the hotel it had clouded over, and Frank said, "Let's go to the movies," and we both laughed because it seems that this is what we end up doing on Saturday afternoons wherever we are. So we lined up on the main street with all the children and moved along into the little theater which was crowded and noisy with all those youngsters shouting and climbing over the seats. Amid this clamor Frank and I held hands. When the cartoon lighted the screen, the children settled down, and we all sat and watched Mickey Mouse and then the fat and skinny comedians and then a picture with cowboys and Indians fighting one another. From time to time Frank squeezed my hand and once he leaned across and kissed my cheek.

When we came out into the warm gray afternoon, I was afraid I would miss the train, but I didn't. Frank had studied the schedule and knew exactly when it would arrive. We were there in plenty of time and by then it had started to rain. In the car he kissed me many times and I felt a little flushed and breathless and my tooth (damnable tooth) was beginning to throb again. I watched the rain beating on the platform while Frank embraced me and called me his darling. "Oh, my darling Clara," he said. "I am so glad I've met you."

I don't know what to make of it all. Should I try to make anything of it? Frank is a married man with a family. Yet I feel so wonderfully happy and reckless with my life at the moment. Yes, it is reckless of me. I know that, and all the way home as I looked out the train window at the rain slanting across the freshly seeded fields, I thought about my recklessness. I won't see Frank next weekend because the family opens up the cottage on Victoria Day weekend. It's up in Muskoka and it's a family tradition and so he can't possibly get out of it. What shall I do next Saturday?

305 King Street East
Toronto

My dear Clara,
How wonderful it was being with you last Saturday! And how I miss you now as I sit in my office. Everyone has left and now and then I get up and stand by the window. How I wish I could just get in my car and drive up to see you! It's such a beautiful evening and I just heard the

bells from the Anglican cathedral down the street. This has all made me feel so lonely for you, Clara. Do you miss me too a little bit?

Wasn't last Saturday fun? Going to the movies like that with all those children. I wonder what people I know would think of such a day. Not much, I imagine, and yet I so thoroughly enjoyed it. What I especially liked, however, was our walk by that little stream and the smell of lilacs and your hand in mine. And our kisses at the Uxbridge railway station. Let me tell you, my dear, that you have made a lonely man very happy, and I do look forward so much to seeing you again. You are quite a wonderful woman and you don't even realize it, and I want to shower your face with kisses and hold you close to my heart. I don't care if that sounds corny, it's how I feel and you must believe it. I am so glad I found the courage to speak to you that day outside Loew's. Of course, I know how complicated all this can be, but surely it's worth it. Don't you think it will be worth this bit of happiness that has come into our lives?

Well, I must be getting on home soon, and so I had better close. I shall miss you this coming weekend, but as I told you, it just can't be helped. We've been opening up the cottages on Victoria Day weekend since I was a very small child, believe it or not. There are now actually three cottages on the property, my brothers and I and our families each have one (I was left my parents'—the original). So there will be a lot of people up there. We are a kind of clan and there will be a good deal of talking and drinking as we open up our summer places. By Monday night, we will have had enough of one another and some of us probably won't be talking to others for a while. It's a tribal weekend and can't be avoided. But please remember that I shall be thinking of you while I am up there. Can we meet at Uxbridge station again on the twenty-ninth? We'll go for another drive and perhaps try another town. Please write me here at the office and mark your letter personal. I wish you would think about having a telephone installed. Would it not be much simpler to pick up a telephone and talk to each other? But never mind that now. Do please think of me and *write*.

Fondly, Frank

Saturday, May 22 (3:00 a.m.)

Awakened again by this cursed tooth. Three o'clock! By now a familiar hour. A dead hour. The hour of the dead. About ten years ago the band at the skating rink used to play a pretty little song on Saturday nights. "It's three o'clock in the morning." A lover's song, lamenting the end of an evening together. But three o'clock in the morning is also a time for death. I once read in a magazine that more people die at three o'clock in the morning than at any other time. In hospital wards and cottage bedrooms, old men and women are now clutching rosary beads and praying for deliverance. According to that magazine, it has something to do with the blood pressure sinking in the middle of the night and the body's defenses surrendering. But perhaps it is just the sheer bleakness of the hour which dismays the spirit and discourages the sick. One often awakens and hears across the fence that old Mrs. Somebody "passed away in the night."

Whitfield, Ontario
Sunday, May 23, 1937

Dear Frank,

I am writing this on my veranda. It is just after two o'clock on a perfectly lovely spring afternoon, and I am wondering what you are doing at this very moment. Are you out on your lake in a canoe (please be careful), or are you surrounded by family and relatives after lunch? Cold chicken and potato salad? By two o'clock the meal is over and the women are cleaning up. You and your brothers are smoking out on a lawn overlooking the lake, sitting in those uncomfortable chairs that have been in the boathouse all winter. The children have dusted them; it was one of their chores this weekend. You and your brothers are making plans for the summer. You are listening as your brothers talk, but not really listening because you are thinking of me. Isn't it foolish of me to imagine that you might be? Oh, what do I know about your cottage weekends anyway?

I only know that I miss you here and now. This very minute. As I sit on my veranda and listen to the leaves stirring. Watch the sunlight spilling across the grass, hear an automobile clattering by, raising dust. What I wouldn't give to see you drive up right now and take me away to some town where we could walk along the streets arm in arm. Go into the Chinese restaurant for a cup of tea. No one would know us. We would be just another couple passing through their town. We could stroll by the river (my little town has a river), and lean against the railing of the bridge and look down at the water passing beneath us. We could tell one another what we like to do best on rainy afternoons or winter nights.

Oh, Frank, I am not at all certain whether I am happy or miserable by all that's happened in the past six weeks. It was six weeks ago yesterday when we met. I don't expect you will remember that. I have the notion that men don't pay much attention to such things, or do they? I don't know much about men, as I'm sure you have gathered by now. So am I happy or miserable? Both, I suppose. It's an impossible arrangement as you well know, and yet I am glad I am in the middle of it. At least I think I'm glad. I will see you next Saturday, won't I? Please don't disappoint me by saying that you won't be there. By writing on company stationery to tell me that upon sober reflection, after a weekend at the cottage, surrounded by family and friends, etc., etc., you have decided that this is all too complicated and a terrible mistake. I am sure it is, but perhaps we have to make terrible mistakes to truly live. There, I have split an infinitive. See what you have made me do. A schoolteacher splitting an infinitive! Let me say again how much I miss you on this perfect afternoon. This lovely, lovely afternoon. Please be at the train station next Saturday.

Fondly, Clara

Sunday, May 23

Wrote Frank, but it is a foolish letter. Too overwrought. Too presumptuous. I sound like a lovesick schoolgirl. I won't mail it. Marion came by as I was writing. She looks much better than she did last winter and seems her cheerful self again. Went on and on about how she and her aunt enjoyed Nora's program and could I possibly get an autographed picture of Nora for her aunt? Listening to Marion, I wondered if she ever had sexual feelings. She surely must have had. It's a pity she has never met a man. Under those severely cut dark bangs, her face is quite lovely. Limpid brown eyes and beautiful skin that darkens a little each summer. I have often wondered if she didn't have some Mediterranean or Celtic blood in her. It is her lameness though that has kept them away and she has resigned herself to this. After she left, I wrote Nora.

Whitfield, Ontario
Sunday, May 23, 1937

Dear Nora,

It's probably time that I dropped you a note. It's a perfectly lovely Sunday afternoon and I'm writing this on the veranda. Marion Webb has just left after her "little visit." Poor Marion! She is just the same as you probably remember her. Older, of course, like the rest of us, with a touch of gray in her hair now. Still in love with Rudy Vallee and one of your biggest fans, as I'm sure you gathered last Christmas. Marion virtually lives in your mythical Meadowvale. "Do you think Alice will really marry Dr. Harper? Oh, I hope so, Clara, but I keep thinking something will come along to ruin it. They seem made for one another. He's such a nice man. And a doctor too. But do you know what? I think Effie is jealous of Alice. I wouldn't put anything past Effie."

You may tell Evelyn, for me, that she is a sorceress bewitching the women of America (and Canada) with these tales of thwarted love and mysterious happenings.

How are you and your announcer getting on these days? Is there any chance that he will leave his wife (speaking of "real-life dramas"), or is it all hopeless? Or does it matter? I suppose in the circumstances, you just carry on from day to day. In that sense, you are lucky to live in a place like New York. You can imagine the fuss there would be in this village if I had a lover! Yet I sometimes think it would be bracing to shock them all with some kind of amorous adventure. Many here, of course, believe that my only adventures are in my head. But we probably all need someone in our lives, don't we? It's easy to grow stale, become mere creatures with undernourished hearts. They say that love nourishes the heart. Well, I am going on, aren't I? It must be this spring weather. You have to admit that this has been a glorious spring. I just hope that you and Mr. Cunningham are happy. Maybe one day I too will find someone. You never know. Do take care of yourself.

Clara

P.S. Have you and Evelyn decided on a firm date for your visit this summer en route to the quintuplets?

Tuesday, May 25

Milton went off to Toronto to attend a conference, and so I had to deal with the senior forms as well as my own. I set various tasks but some of the girls (Jean Patterson and company) were disruptive. A good deal of whispering and note passing, most of it concerning Ella Myles who sits by herself at the back of the Senior Fourth row. She used to be right in front of me when I taught her. It was clear that Patterson and her friends were making fun of the girl, and dear God, it isn't hard to ridicule her. Ella now smears her mouth with lip rouge and wears a horrible pink sweater that shows her breasts. How can her mother dress her like this? Thin bare legs in soiled ankle socks. She even wears cheap perfume. She looks like a little tart, and the other girls kept glancing back at her and whispering. It got on my nerves. Then, just before lunch, Ella had had enough and swore at them. Uttered that ugly word right there in the classroom. Even the boys were startled. I had to say something, and so I told her to stay after school. But then she hardly listened to me. Slumped in the desk she stared out the window while I talked. I told her this was her entrance year and she was clever enough to do well. She could go on to the collegiate in Linden and get a job and make something of herself. Mere words in the wind. After she left, I stood at the window and watched her saunter across the schoolyard toward Martin Kray who was leaning against a tree smoking a cigarette. Watched him take her hand, a clumsy gallant, and off they walked together. Soon they will be down along the township road, looking for a meadow to lie in, hoping the rain will hold off for a few hours. It left me a little heartsick, and then I remembered that it was two years ago on this date that the tramp raped me. I hadn't thought of him for weeks, but now he is here again, poisoning my day.

305 King Street East
Toronto, Ontario
Tuesday

Dearest Clara,
I am a little disappointed in you, my dear. I thought there might be a letter waiting for me this morning. I asked Miss Haines to check both deliveries carefully, but nothing. Ah well! Perhaps you had other things to do over the weekend, and in any case, I forgive you. My dear, I have missed you so much this past week. I have been thinking about you all the time. Yes, even up at the cottage while everything and everybody buzzed around me, I was thinking of you.

I can hardly wait until Saturday to see you. It's just a few dozen hours away. That is how I am looking at it and that way it doesn't seem so long. I hope this reaches you by Friday, so you can see how very much I miss you. Don't you think it would be a good idea to have a telephone installed? I am thinking of how grand it would be to pick up the telephone and hear your voice. I hope you'll think about it. Till Saturday then.

Fondly, Frank

Wednesday, May 26

I have finally made arrangements with a Dr. Watts in Linden. Mrs. Bryden gave me his name and says he is reliable and inexpensive. I am to see him next Wednesday at five o'clock and that time will work well because Mr. Bryden drives to Linden every Wednesday for his service club supper and I can go along with him. What a mistake I made in selling Father's car! I could have learned how to operate it, and had much more freedom of movement. It will be such a relief to have these teeth fixed, but I hope he doesn't have to pull any. I don't think I could bear that.

Sunday, May 30

Frank comes from an Irish Catholic family and so does his wife. I was interested in her "problems," but Frank was reluctant to talk about them except to say that they no longer love one another; they merely "share a house." Then he said, "We no longer sleep together, if you know what I mean." Yes, he means they no longer have relations, though I didn't say so. Poor Edith Quinlan. And now I am seeing her husband. I am "the other woman" that I have read about so many times in those magazines. I don't want to think about Edith Quinlan, though I keep seeing her as one of those pretty, dark-haired Irishwomen whose looks begin to fade in middle age. I know she has dark hair because Frank said his eldest daughter Theresa "has dark hair just like her mother when she was twenty-one." Frank likes dark-haired women. He has touched my hair several times and said how much he likes it. Yesterday he said he wished it were longer and he would like to see it "spilling across your bare shoulders." Then he laughed and said I was blushing and that "it becomes you."

All this over dinner in another hotel dining room. We were seated at a corner table by an enormous rubber plant, the leaves speckled with dust and insect droppings. The sunlight came through the tall windows. Along a wall was a terrible painting of Indians welcoming a locomotive and the Fathers of Confederation in frock coats and top hats. A radio was playing sentimental music. I felt so happy being in that awful dining room. We were talking about religion. I've forgotten how the subject came up, but Frank told me he believes in God. I expected that, but it always interests me to hear this. How I envy Catholics their faith! It is so accommodating. Catholics commit sins and then expect to be forgiven. Frank was surprised to discover that I no longer believe in God. I said to him, "How I wish I could! It would make everything different."

He smiled. "Different in what way?"

"Well," I said. "Surely believing in God gives your life a purpose, some shape or direction. It seems to me that without God, we are just putting in time. And then time becomes so urgent, a source of anxiety because, of course, our time will eventually run out."

Oh, I went on about this. Perhaps I talked too much about God and Time, but I couldn't help myself. I think about these subjects so much, and like most people who live alone, I overdo it when I have an audience. It felt peculiar to be talking about God and Time in the dining room of a small-town hotel at twelve-thirty on a Saturday afternoon, looking up at that terrible mural and listening to "Blue Skies." Frank told me that he could not imagine a life without God. For him, God was simply *there*. Doubting His existence was out of the question. How could a person not believe in God? I could see that I puzzled, maybe even disturbed him a little by all this. He smoked his pipe and looked grave. I asked him if seeing me didn't make it difficult for him.

"Will you not have to tell your priest about us when you go to confession?" I asked.

Then Frank said something wonderful. He said, "I suppose I will, but what has that got to do with my belief in God? To tell you the truth, I don't think God really minds about us. Surely He has more important things to think about than two people who are trying to find a little happiness on this earth?"

I liked that answer, but I sensed that Frank was growing uncomfortable with our conversation. I don't believe Catholics think much about God. He is simply there and they accept that and get on with their lives. I wish I could do that.

After dinner we went for a drive and then at the station, before we said goodbye, there were more kisses and we grew quite fervent. That is an old-fashioned word to describe our embraces, but it is the only one that comes to mind. His fervent kisses! I felt rushed and breathless beneath them, and a man on the platform was watching us, so after a while we stopped. Frank asked me what I thought of the idea of spending more time together. He said he could probably get away for a Saturday night and we could go someplace. That will mean sleeping with him. I said I would think about it. We are to meet again next Saturday at the train station.

Wednesday, June 2

My first visit to Dr. Watts. What an ordeal! Several of my teeth need filling, but it looks as if I won't lose any, thank goodness. Watts scolded me mercilessly as he prodded and drilled and tapped away. "Why on earth did you let these teeth get into such a state, Miss Callan?"

I suffered in silence under his ministrations, but the drilling brought tears to my eyes. I'm sure I'll hear that infernal instrument grinding away in my sleep tonight. And this will have to go on for another five or six weeks! Something to look forward to each Wednesday. Yet it must be done, and there is a certain grim satisfaction in getting on with it.

135 East 33rd Street
New York
May 30, 1937

Dear Clara,

Well your last letter was certainly worth a few laughs. Of course, you're right about New York in a way. It's certainly easier "to have a friend over," but you'd be surprised how nosy the neighbors can be. Les and I are pretty careful about all that. As for your question about us, I don't know where this is all going. Nowhere probably, and when I think about it too much, it gets me down. So I don't think about it too much. Les is very attached to his children (a boy and a girl around twelve and thirteen), and I know he can't stand the idea of giving them up, so I don't think he'll ever ask his wife for a divorce. Anyway, I'm not sure I'm in love with him. He's swell company and handsome as the dickens, but there's something missing. I can feel it. It's funny because Les is considerate and kind to a fault. He's a little vain, of course, but what handsome guy isn't? Yet sometimes I actually miss being with grumpy old Lewis. Can you imagine that? Lewis was always lecturing me on this and that, and cheating on me all the time. I now know that for a fact. But there was still something about him that I just don't feel with Les. I can't figure it out.

Speaking of men, you don't need to tell Marion Webb, but Alice isn't going to marry Dr. Harper this week. There will be no June wedding for Alice Dale in spite of the bushels of mail we've been getting congratulating us. And presents too, believe it or not!!! Tea towels from a lady in Kentucky, bedsheets (imagine) from someone in Indiana. A creamer and sugar bowl from a listener in Toronto. It's crazy. We give this stuff to the girls in the office. Our ratings are so high at the moment that the producers want us to keep everything "on the boil" for a few more weeks, maybe months. So there will be complications. Evelyn hinted on Friday that Doc Harper is probably going to have a car accident on his way to the ceremony (she has been told she cannot kill him off, he's too popular). Anyway, we'll know tomorrow for sure and it should keep them listening and the Sunrise people happy.

I guess next week there will be a real wedding. According to today's *Trib*, Edward is marrying Mrs. Simpson next Thursday. Wouldn't you love to be there? Of course, Evelyn knew all this and that's why our on-air wedding was planned. Clever, huh? Anyway, take care. We'll be up on Friday, July 9, and leave the next day or maybe Sunday for Callander. Okay? I'm really looking forward to seeing those little girls, aren't you?

Love, Nora

Saturday, June 5

Went to Uxbridge station this morning, but Frank wasn't there and I was stuck for the day. It was raining and no train until late afternoon. Infuriating! I spent the day in the library inattentively reading Sinclair Lewis's *It Can't Happen Here*. Not very good and all I could do was look out from time to time at the wet street and watch the people hurrying past. I was, of course, an object of interest for the locals who cast furtive glances my way as they checked out their week's reading. Commotion from the basement where the children were playing some games, but at least the library provided a refuge from the weather. I don't know where else I could have gone to pass the time. Anyway, why wasn't Frank there? He is usually so reliable. I keep wondering if he had an accident in this rain. Perhaps I should have a telephone installed. By now he could have called and told me what happened.

305 King Street East
Toronto, Ontario
Sunday

Dearest Clara,

I'm writing this in a hurry at home and I will try to mail it this afternoon. I'm so sorry about yesterday. You must have been stranded in that village all day, my poor darling, and it was so wet. But I couldn't get away because my youngest child, Patrick, had an accident on his bicycle. He was hit by a car backing out of a driveway. This just happened down the street. We know the driver, an elderly man, and he's terribly upset by what happened. I suppose he didn't look behind him, but Patrick can be careless on that bicycle. He just goes like the wind. Anyhow, the man backed into him and Patrick struck his head on the sidewalk and we had to rush him down to St. Michael's. This all happened yesterday morning just as I was about to leave. What a frightening experience it's all been! We spent the entire day at the hospital, Edith, myself and Patrick's sisters. The doctors have told us that they think he'll be all right, but a head injury is always a worry. As you can imagine, his mother is beside herself and I am concerned about her too. She is fragile in emergencies like this.

If you had a telephone, I could have called you about all this. Won't you consider putting one in? I can just picture you going all the way to Uxbridge yesterday and then being surprised and disappointed that I wasn't there waiting for you. My darling, I am so sorry but, of course, you will now understand the predicament I was in. I have to run now because we are going back to the hospital. So I'll say goodbye and mail this with many, many kisses. Shall we try then for next Saturday at the same place? Things should be settled down by then. I miss you so much, my darling girl.

Fondly, Frank

Wednesday, June 9

Frank's letter arrived, but I had just enough time to pick it up at the post office and get over to Mr. Bryden's office. The letter "burned a hole in my pocket" all the way to Linden and I could only just manage a glance at it before Watts began his weekly torture session. I have decided to have a telephone put in the house, and I am going to get in touch with the Bell people tomorrow.

San Remo Apts
1100 Central Park West
New York
6/6/37

Dear Clara,

On Friday your sister read parts of your recent letter in which you suggested that I, poor little me, was "a sorceress bewitching the women of America." I am taking that as a compliment, though sometimes when John Barleycorn and I get together for a little talk (like right now, for instance), I get somewhat lachrymose. There! You like words, so you can have that one. It's not every day that one gets to read the word *lachrymose* in a letter. Now I get this way when I think that maybe I'm wasting my time entertaining the housewives of the nation with the intrigues surrounding Alice and Effie and dear old Uncle Jim and Aunt Mary. Sometimes, in fact, I feel I'd like to burn Meadowvale to the ground and leave not a stick standing.

At such times, I think of others who are doing more important things. Like those high-minded folk who are going off to Spain to fight the Fascists. I wish I had the courage, but the truth is, I don't. I like my steak and gin and cigarettes too much. Anyway, I'm too old to wrap bandages. If it comes to that, I don't know how to wrap bandages and doubt whether I could ever learn. All this comes to mind because yesterday on Fifth Avenue, I was accosted by an earnest young man and woman who were soliciting for the Republican cause in Spain. They rattled their little cardboard box and pressed a pamphlet into my unwilling hand, lecturing me on the complacency of the American people while the suffering of our Spanish comrades, etc., etc. Well, I fished fifty cents out of my purse, which was generous, I thought, though it only earned me a scowl from the young woman. They gave me quite the little harangue there, and listening to them I got the feeling that on another day in another country, this pair could cheerfully cut my fat, bourgeois throat. To care that much about something! For a minute or so, those youngsters made me feel (never mind that I am a sound, upright, tax-paying citizen) that my life is by and large worthless because millions of workers in Spain and around the world are enchained and suffering, etc., etc.

Well, a couple of gins soon fixed that, but those two Stalinists did unnerve me for a minute or two. I know that what I do is essentially frivolous in the grand scheme of things. Isn't that true of most people's jobs? Not yours, my dear. The good teacher may actually do something worthwhile in this tattered old world. If only someone would show this poor cynic a better way! And if only the Communists had better-looking gals working for the cause, I might consider joining ranks. I jest, of course. But they all look so dowdy and unkempt. I felt like saying to that young woman yesterday, "Why don't you do something with your hair, Missy?"

Never mind. We do what we have to do in this old world. How are things with you these days? It looks as if we will be seeing you next month. With Nora guiding me (a somewhat unnerving thought, right?), your nearsighted correspondent will try to avoid other vehicles as she steers dear Mother's Packard northward into the wilds of Canada. Should I bring warm clothes? Fur hat? Mittens? Oh, don't take me seriously. I know it's summer up there and it will probably be as hot as blazes. I think I told you once that as a child I went up into Quebec on a trip with my father, so I know a little about traveling in those parts. So, here's to Adventure and Northward Ho!

Regards from the Sorceress E.

Sunday, June 13

Yesterday was fair and warm and we had a picnic. It was my idea and Frank was delightfully surprised. I didn't want to hurt his feelings because he has been so generous with meals, but I am tired of those brown hotel dining rooms with their awful pictures and dusty philodendrons. So I made sandwiches and we bought cold ginger ale at a store near the station. Then we drove to the brook where Frank first kissed me, and we took the car blanket and sat under a tree. Frank talked about his youngest son who is home now recovering, thank goodness. Then I told him I was having a telephone installed this coming week so we could keep in touch, and this appeared to make him so happy that he kissed me while I was still eating my sandwich. We laughed at that. And have I ever been as happy as I was yesterday afternoon looking at Frank's eyes and listening to the water as it rushed over the stones in that stream?

Frank asked me about my life, and I told him about Nora in New York and my ordinary days as a schoolteacher in Whitfield, my walks and the music I used to play and the poems I used to write. He said he would like to come up and see me in my house.

"I have to be careful," I said. "In small places like Whitfield, people talk. It's all they have to do really and so anything is an excuse for gossip. A stranger's car in your driveway, a man entering your house, it's all noted and remarked upon. Some already think I'm a bit peculiar." I thought he might ask why, but he didn't.

Frank then began to caress me and I felt warm and nervous. I lay there looking up at the trees and their fresh leaves and through them the sunlit sky. I was being touched and my eyes closed under Frank's kisses and warm tobacco breath. He told me I reminded him of the movie actress Claudette Colbert. "You look a bit like her, you know."

"Nonsense," I said, though I was happy enough that he said it.

"There is a resemblance, Clara, believe me."

Then under his kisses I grew anxious. It came unbidden this anxiousness, for I remembered the tramp stepping through the long grass and seizing my wrists and whirling me about, flinging me finally to the ground and covering me with his body. Pressing against me as he did with the oily machine stink of his overalls and the foul-mouth smell of him. The feel of the grass against my neck may have done all this. I don't know, but I grew fearful and I asked Frank to stop touching me. His gray eyes seemed to grow milky. "What's the matter?" he asked.

I wondered then if I should tell him what had happened to me two years ago on an afternoon like this, but I worried about what he might think of me. To be taken like that by a passing tramp! I sensed he might feel a kind of disgust with it all. With me perhaps. Even if he didn't mean to feel that way, he might. And once I told him, it could never be changed. It would be a part of his view of me forever. So I didn't tell him and there was tension between us. He sulked a bit like a disappointed schoolboy, so I told him that I had little experience in intimate matters and this was no place for it anyway. We could hear the sound of passing cars and I said that perhaps children might come along. We were not all that far from the road; everything would be rushed and unsatisfactory. I think I was so afraid of losing him then that I hardly knew what I was saying, but finally he took me in his arms and held me.

"You mustn't worry about that, darling girl," he said. "You're perfectly right. We must find some place where we can be alone and have plenty of time." He suggested a motor court. "We must arrange something" was how he put it.

"Yes, I would like that," I said and so we agreed to meet again next Saturday. I didn't tell him that it would probably be a bad time of the month for me, though perhaps that will hold off until Sunday or Monday. I couldn't bring myself to talk to him about that, though now I feel I should have. I should have told him that next weekend will be my time of the month. I should have done that.

Whitfield, Ontario
Sunday, June 13, 1937

Dear Evelyn,

Thank you for your letter. Never has the road to dissipation been so amusingly described. I think too that I can see you arching your eyebrows at the two young Communists on Fifth Avenue. I don't know much about the Communists. We have them up here, of course, and they sometimes cause trouble in labor union rallies and so on. But they seem to confine their activities to towns or cities. They don't appear to be very interested in farm and village folk. I am really not very interested in politics, particularly in the politics of extreme positions. Last summer in Italy I saw enough young men bullying people with their uniforms and flags. It seemed to me then that the Fascists like nothing better than pushing people around, and I imagine that the Communists are no different. In that sense you are probably right when you mention that "on another day and in another country, this pair would cheerfully cut my fat, bourgeois throat." I think they are a bit like the fanatical preachers who used to come through the village when I was a child. They would set up their tents on the fairgrounds and draw in people from the countryside, mostly Baptists from around Linden (a nearby town and county seat). I only went once because my father disapproved of evangelicals. He thought they preyed on impressionable hearts, and as in most of his evaluations about human nature, he was correct. But I do remember how earnest and intense that preacher was and how he promised salvation for the elect and damnation for the unsaved. He terrified me, but also made me ecstatic with promise for the future. I imagine your young Communists are something like that in their own way. They want everything turned upside down and a new order proclaimed, only here on earth. I don't know if it's working in Russia. Perhaps it is and certainly some of the things they are fighting for are worth the struggle. But they seem to want to change everything so fast and so violently, and I can't believe any good will come of that approach.

Well, enough of my preaching. I am looking forward to seeing you next month, and you are right, it will very likely be "as hot as blazes" up here if last summer is anything to go by. Today, however, it is a perfect, balmy seventy-five degrees by the thermometer mounted outside my kitchen window. A light wind stirs the leaves. I am writing this on the veranda and there go the United Church minister and his pretty little wife on their Sunday promenade. They no longer visit me since I stopped going to church. But it is all a peaceful prospect before me. Nothing like your mythical Meadowvale with all its intrigues and adulteries. My little village is nothing like that. Or is it?

See you next month. Say hello to Nora for me and tell her that I am well and will have a surprise for her next week. She loves surprises and this one will especially please her.

Clara

Wednesday, June 16

On the way home from the dentist's today, Mr. Bryden said, "You remind me of your mother, Clara. When I see you reading on the veranda, or walking home from school, I see your mother again. You have her ways."

I was interested in this and asked him to tell me more about her, for she is now such a distant figure to me. I seem to see her only in outline, a slender dark-haired woman, almost girlish, still wearing an apron as she sat reading. He told me that from the first day she set foot in the village, every young man set his cap for her. "She was," he said, "such a pretty little thing and so different from the other girls."

"How was she different?" I asked.

"She was like no one I had ever met," he said. "She was like a poet, I suppose, or an artist. Always a bit dreamy in her ways. She would go off walking by herself. Or read. She was always reading. She boarded that first year down at Mrs. Hallam's by the Presbyterian church, and you would see her on the veranda there reading. All the young fellows would walk by for a glance at her. Your father was bowled over by her. We all were in a way, though of course, I was married by then and happily married too. Don't get me wrong, Clara. But your mother was just a very special kind of person, I thought. We all envied Ed when he caught her. We were surprised too, for as you know he was a good bit older than your mother. We thought he was going to be a bachelor for life. We didn't think he stood a chance with Ettie Smith who was only nineteen or twenty at the time. But your father was a fine figure of a man all the same and they made a handsome couple."

Then he told me about my brother's death and how it seemed to push Mother beyond herself. I found that an interesting phrase to describe distraction or derangement. "She was never the same after the little fellow died of fever that spring," he said. "That would have been in 1904. Good heavens, thirty-three years ago and it seems like yesterday. You were only a baby. You were lucky you didn't catch it. You stayed at our house. Mrs. Bryden looked after you. After the little fellow died, your mother was lost. Even though she had you, she was lost. I could see it in the way she carried herself about the village. Then your mother and father had Nora and at first we thought she'd got over things. But she never really did."

It was strange to hear all this from Mr. Bryden, this lawyer and neighbor whom I have known (and not known) all these years. I believe he has been carrying all this feeling for Mother and now was glad to reveal it. As I was getting out of the car, however, he placed a hand on my arm and said, "Of course, I'm sure you understand that all this happened many years ago and I'm very fond of Mrs. Bryden and always have been. Just so you're clear about that."

Friday, June 18 (5:00 p.m.)

The Bell people have just installed the telephone. I don't like the looks of the thing on the kitchen wall, but I suppose I will get used to it. It startled me so when it first rang though they were only checking the line. I thought of reaching Frank, but I expect he has now gone for the day. I have decided to wait until Sunday to surprise Nora. In a way, this is a ridiculous expense because aside from Frank and Nora, I can't think of anyone else to telephone.

(10:00 p.m.)

What I don't like about this telephone is the constant ringing. What a nuisance when you are settling down to read or listen to the gramophone! I could not get a private line, and so I am sharing with the Macfarlanes and the Caldwells. The man explained that my ring is two short and one long whereas Cora Macfarlane's is two short and two long and the Caldwells is something or other. I suppose I will get on to it in time, but I don't much like the idea of others listening in on my conversation. The telephone man said that most people are polite about that, but I have to wonder.

Sunday, June 20

Yesterday was unsettling. I met Frank as usual at the station and he was affectionate, delighted to see me. We touched and kissed in his car, and then we took some back roads southward toward the lake. I asked about Patrick and he said that he was okay though he still has terrible headaches. He also told me that his oldest daughter is giving him trouble though he didn't elaborate. I gather she is a high-strung and difficult young woman. Listening to him, I realized how free I am from the vicissitudes of family life.

After an hour or so, we pulled into a tourist court near Port Hope: a dozen white cabins overlooking the lake. It was just before noon and we were the only car. Frank looked across at me and smiled. "We can go into town for dinner afterward," he said. I felt so miserable then because I had to tell him that we couldn't rent one of the cabins; it was not the right time for me. This put him into a sulk. "You might have told me this," he said.

"Well, I have told you," I said, "and there is nothing that can be done about it. Nature will have its way." I don't know why I added that. It sounded so foolish and pretentious. Neither of us wanted to talk about it, and so we sat watching the sunlight on the lake. I could feel the heat of the sun through the glass. Frank was wearing a short-sleeved shirt and I looked at the hair on his arm and I wanted him to hold me, but he seemed too much within himself, irritable with disappointment.

Then a woman with a mop and pail came out of one of the cabins and looked our way before going up a lane toward a house.

"We better go," Frank said. And so we went into Port Hope and had our dinner in a restaurant. I felt the day was ruined and it was all my fault. I should have told him before and so in the restaurant I said I was sorry. He brightened a little after that and at the station we parted with some kisses. It seems that we will not be able to see one another for two weeks. Frank must take his family up to their cottage next Saturday. They spend the entire summer in Muskoka and Frank goes up most weekends. I wondered how we would find time to see one another.

"We'll find time," he said, but he sounded unhappy about it all. I gave him my telephone number and he said, "Well, that at least is something." It was not a good day for us.

This evening I telephoned Nora and how she went on! "Is that really you, Clara? I can't believe I'm speaking to my sister on the telephone." And on and on she went. I couldn't shut her up. The call must have cost me the earth. She told me that she and Evelyn will be here on the ninth of next month.

This telephone rings all the time. I wondered if the members of the other two households had nothing better to do than talk at all hours of the day and night. Then a half hour ago (10:15), as I lay cursing the endless rings, willing both families into perdition, I realized that it was my ring, two short and a long. Rushed downstairs to hear Frank's voice. He told me how sorry he was for the way he behaved yesterday. It was so wonderful to hear his voice. He promised to make things up for me, and we agreed to meet a week from next Saturday, the third of July, at Union Station. His wife and youngest son will be up at the cottage that weekend.

"We can go someplace where we can be completely by ourselves," he said.

And I said, "Yes, let's do that, Frank."

After I hung up, I wondered if someone had been listening.

Friday, June 25

School is over for another year and Milton and I had games and treats for the children. The entrance class have been writing their examinations at the town hall and this afternoon, on my way home, I met Ella Myles and asked her how the examinations were going. She gave me a wry crooked little grin. "I'm not writing the exams," she said.

"Oh, Ella," I said. "I'm sorry to hear that. You should have tried at least."

A moue of disdain from the painted mouth. I feel the child is lost.

Saturday, June 26

This afternoon Mr. Bryden told me of a motorcar for sale. I had almost forgotten that on a Wednesday drive to Linden, I had mentioned my interest in buying a car. He told me of a widow on the twelfth concession, a Mrs. Creeley, who is selling the farm and moving into Linden to be with her married daughter. She wants to sell her late husband's car, and Mr. Bryden thinks it is in good condition, and that Joe Morrow would be willing to take me out tomorrow afternoon to look at it. The widow is asking three hundred dollars, which is a great deal of money, but an automobile would make things so much easier. I would no longer have to depend on that train.

Sunday, June 27

I bought the car, perhaps as a present to myself, for today is my thirty-fourth birthday. This afternoon Joe drove me out to the Creeley farm. The widow is a big woman with a large red face and a friendly manner. She allowed us to take the car for a drive. It's a black Chevrolet coupe, only three years old. "She's a good little car, Clara," Joe said. "She's worth the money, but if it was me, I'd offer her two hundred and you'd probably get it for two fifty." But the suggestion made me feel vaguely guilty. It would be like taking bread from a widow's mouth although Mrs. Creeley looked well off enough. So I asked Joe, "Is it worth the three hundred?"

"Oh hang, yes," he said. "She's worth every nickel of that."

"Then I'll give her the three hundred," I said.

"Suit yourself, but if it was me, I'd try to beat her down."

But I was not interested in "beating her down," and so Mrs. Creeley and I agreed on things and Joe will go out tomorrow to pick up the car. He is going to give me lessons in operating it, and I told him I would give him fifty cents for each lesson. He didn't want to be paid, but I'm using his time, so I feel I owe him for that.

Nora phoned this evening to wish me happy birthday. She had been trying to reach me all afternoon, but couldn't get through. "You'll have to tell those people to stop hogging the line," she said. It's interesting that after nearly three years in New York, Nora still uses old-fashioned expressions from her childhood. Perhaps we never entirely abandon these locutions from our past. But I can't see myself telling Cora Macfarlane "to stop hogging the line." Then I told Nora that I had just bought a car and that flummoxed her.

"You bought a car?"

"Yes, I did. A Chevrolet coupe. Three years old."

"Well, I'll be damned. What has got into you lately, Clara? A telephone and now a car? It's too early for the change of life, isn't it?"

"Much too early," I said.

Monday, June 28

My first lesson! After supper, Joe and I went out along the township roads and he showed me how to shift the gears. As many times as I used to watch Father moving the gear lever, I never paid much attention to how it was actually done. For an hour or so, Joe and I bucked and stalled our way along the roads. Had anyone been around, it would have been comical to witness; as it was, only a few cows raised their big homely faces to study this mechanical ineptitude. Joe is wonderfully good-natured about it all.

"Don't worry, Clara," he keeps saying. "You'll get the hang of her before long."

Friday, July 2

Another driving lesson and this evening I managed to get the car into third gear and actually drove some distance along the township road, almost as far as Linden. I was so proud of myself and Joe was pleased too. When I got home, it was still light and I was standing in the kitchen feeling utterly triumphant when suddenly it all vanished and I was overtaken by nerves. It was like the shadow of a cloud crossing a field. I sat down at the table and very nearly wept. This was an hour ago, and I have been trying to think of a reason for all this. I now believe that, without realizing it, I have been worrying about tomorrow and how things will go between Frank and me. We are going to "sleep together" tomorrow and I have had no experience in that. I am afraid that I will be tentative and uninviting and he will be disappointed, perhaps even repelled by me.

Sunday, July 4

This is what I was thinking yesterday in the room of the tourist court as I stood in my new wrap behind the venetian blinds and looked out onto Lakeshore Boulevard. I could hear faintly the cries of the bathers at Sunnyside. It was so hot in that room. The little fan on the bedside table hardly helped at all. And standing there I thought this: I am in a motor court with Frank on a Saturday afternoon. We have been intimate and now I am standing in this hideous wrapper. I bought it hurriedly in a store on Queen Street while Frank waited in the car. I hadn't thought to bring anything and so I needed something to cover myself with or walk around in. The wrapper is absurdly vulgar, yellow with large mauve flowers. If I had said to the salesgirl, "Give me something to cover myself with after I go to bed with a married man this afternoon," she could not have chosen a more appropriate garment. My emblem of illicit happiness. In it, I feel like one of those women in the detective magazines who leave a husband and run off with a boyfriend to rob banks and live in cabins on the edge of highways. But I have another woman's husband, and so I wondered what Edith Quinlan was doing at that moment. Was she washing the lunch dishes and looking out the cottage window at her youngest child as he played in the water? Was she worrying about his headaches? Frank was sleeping. He had dropped off as if plunging down a cliffside into unconsciousness. At first I was awkward about it all; I know I was, though he said I was fine. Yet I wonder. It is something to take off all your clothes in front of another person. It takes some getting used to. But he kissed me all over and I felt a kind of deep longing within, though I was nervous too, remembering the tramp in the grass by the railway tracks. But Frank covered me with kisses and I remember saying, "I don't want to become pregnant, Frank," and he said, "Don't worry, darling, I have something," and he reached over and put a rubber on himself. He made me watch him and asked me to touch him and I did. And what an odd-looking thing it is! Stupid, yet playful. As if it possessed a life of its own, as in a way, I suppose, it does.

Then Frank said, "We must get used to one another, darling," and he touched me. After a while he entered me and I watched his eyes widen. It hurt me a bit until I felt him whole within me and so he began to kiss my breasts and throat. That was lovely. How I enjoyed those kisses! Then he told me to put my legs around him and I did and he again began to move and so perhaps did I. And always he was whispering endearments which I enjoyed as much as anything. It was the closeness that I loved and the endearments. I felt utterly overwhelmed by it all and then he began to move more quickly, and I sensed that I was losing him. Yet I held him fast and watched and felt my racing heart. Our bodies were so slippery and I thought this: Human life begins with a woman's legs around a man's body. She receives his seed and this too is how I became. Mother and Father once lay like this on some long-ago September night in 1902. My brother was sleeping in a crib in a corner of the room, and perhaps they tried not to awaken him as they moved within one another. And so I became.

After Frank released himself, he seemed to shudder and grow youthful. When he opened his eyes, I thought I could see him at sixteen, callow and filled with yearning. He kissed my shoulder and called me his darling and loved one and I felt a deep happiness holding him like that. When he fell asleep, I placed my hand on his chest and felt his heartbeat subsiding. That was as good as anything because I was as close as I would ever get to this man whom I met outside a movie house thirteen weeks ago. This Catholic coal merchant and father of four. What would his daughters think if they could see us like this? I wondered. Yet I was happy enough to assume the role of trollop, for like the Englishwoman in Rome, I too now had a lover and on my lips the very word itself was enkindling. *I have a lover*. Like poor Emma Bovary looking in the mirror after her first encounter with Rodolphe.

Later in the afternoon we went out to a roadside diner and had hamburgers and coffee, and then we hurried back to our room and made love again and it was better than the first time. In the night,

Frank put quarters into the radio, and we listened to dance band music and then a news announcer talking about the woman flyer who crashed in Hawaii. She was trying to go around the world in an airplane. What a thing to undertake!

Before we fell asleep, we made love again. Then this morning Frank told me that he had to go to Mass. He wanted to catch "the ten o'clock at St. Michael's." It left us a bit rushed, and I had so wanted to lie in bed with him longer.

As we drove through the empty Sunday morning streets of Toronto, I reminded myself that this was how it would always be, and that I must not give in to self-pity. I am not eighteen years old. I am thirty-four and I have chosen to become involved with a married man. And so there will always be this hurrying from one place to another, with a run in my stocking and that look from the desk clerk as we go out the door. These things will always be and I must accept them or stop seeing him.

On the train I sat across from Hazel McConkey, who was returning from a week of looking after her grandchildren while "Mel and Ebbie have a little holiday." She fanned herself with some kind of pamphlet and talked about the "kiddies." Did she notice how swollen my mouth was from kisses? How my throat was still flushed? But I don't think Hazel McConkey is capable of imagining me naked beneath a man in a motor court. She did, however, want to know what I was doing on the train on Sunday morning. I told her I had been visiting an old friend from Normal School days. Those imaginary friends from long ago do come in handy.

Wednesday, July 7

Another trip to Dr. Watts and another driving lesson after supper. Joe says that in two weeks or so, I should be ready for my test. "You'll have to give her a try then, Clara." In years to come, I think I shall always remember these long, summer evenings in the little Chevrolet on the gravel roads south of the village. I shall remember Joe's large hand on the steering wheel, his tobacco juice spurting out the window, his patience and kindness.

Frank has just phoned me to tell me how much he enjoyed the weekend. "I did too," I said. We have agreed to meet again on the seventeenth.

Friday, July 9 (11:00 p.m.)

As I write this, it is warm and still, with a good deal of heat lightning and distant thunder. I had a supper of cold cuts and potato salad ready when Nora and Evelyn arrived about six o'clock (they are now sleeping). E. arrived in trousers and lavender shirt. On her head, a white cotton cap with a little green window in its peak. She looked like a yachtsman at the wheel of her Packard, which now sits in the driveway and has been a cause for wonder all evening among the village children. Both guests were hot and tired and a little cranky after their drive up from Buffalo where they stayed last night. Dispositions improved, however, after E. made some of her famous gin concoctions.

Sunday, July 11 (North Bay)

Yesterday we motored up here with "Captain Dowling" at the wheel while "Nora the Navigator" sat by her side studying the road map. I had the entire backseat to myself and felt like Cleopatra on her barge. "Fetch me my adulteress's robe, Charmion!" Evelyn kept up a steady patter about the countryside: the rocks, the lakes, the endless forest. It does look like the land God gave to Cain. Nora excited about the quints and she talked too much about the death of the American woman who had been trying to fly around the world. We are staying in a cabin on a lake near the town. Evelyn is entertaining company with droll and sardonic observations on nearly everything. Yesterday evening, she got a little tight and took snapshots of Nora and me with her Kodak. I hate having my picture taken, but you can't refuse Evelyn, and so Nora and I stood next to the big car and on the steps of the cabin.

As we lay in our bunks last night, Evelyn said she was reminded of boarding school and she told us stories about old classmates and teachers. I lay there watching the lightning across the lake. Someone nearby was playing a car radio and I thought of Frank and wondered what he was doing at that moment. Then Nora and Evelyn began talking more about people from their pasts who had been close to them. Evelyn mentioned a girl at her school whom she had secretly been in love with; she had been bridesmaid at the girl's wedding years later and still wrote to her in Australia. But never did she reveal her heart and she sounded unhappy about that. Then Nora talked about a man in Toronto whom she thought she once loved, but he went out west before she could tell him how she felt. It was someone I had never heard of and this surprised me, for I thought she had told me everything on those Saturday nights when she came home on the train. It was as if they had forgotten I was there, or perhaps they thought I was asleep. For a brief moment, I wanted to tell them about Frank, but I'm glad now that I didn't.

In the middle of the night, there was a tremendous storm with several fierce strikes close by. We all got up to watch. The sky was filled with lightning and the thunder was deafening. I think Evelyn was a little frightened by it all though she joked about it. "You Canadians sure know how to put on a show for a New York girl." Perhaps we were all a little shaken by the tumult and relieved to see it pass.

This morning we drove to Callander for a look at the five little girls. Nora was beside herself with excitement, and Evelyn took pictures of the signs and souvenir shops. There was a long lineup with crying children and mothers and men smoking. It was a gray warm day with the threat of more storms in the air and the body odor and bad breath in that lineup gave me a terrible headache. There is something fundamentally wrong with lining up to gawk at these youngsters as if they were freaks in a carnival show. I felt foolish about it all. We saw them finally in a kind of compound. They were playing with sand pails and shovels and there were little swings and a teeter-totter. A nurse was in attendance. In the lineup, we inched forward behind a plate-glass window and gazed in at the five of them in their overalls. Around me the whispered trite expressions of wonder. "Gosh, aren't they adorable!" "Oh, look at them! They are so cute."

After this, Evelyn said she needed a drink though it was only eleven o'clock. We ate lunch and supper at a log cabin restaurant and went to sleep early. I think we were all a bit dispirited by the vulgarity surrounding the quintuplets. There were more thunderstorms in the night and I lay in my bunk, aching for the sound of Frank's voice and the feel of his kisses on my throat.

Monday, July 12

A long drive home through the little towns celebrating "the glorious twelfth" with bunting and parades: elderly women in white dresses and bugle bands. We took side streets to avoid the commotion and got turned around a few times. I could not help thinking how ironic that I was desperate to phone my Catholic lover on this of all days. If poor Father only knew! Evelyn was feeling unwell (too much drink?) and after supper went right to bed. Nora and I sat on the veranda and talked until past eleven; this affair with her announcer friend is going nowhere and now she has had two or three "nasty calls" from the man's wife. These have upset her and she doesn't know where to go from here. She longs for marriage and children—"just a quiet normal life." Yet I wonder if either of us will ever have that. I wanted to tell her about Frank, but I couldn't bring myself to admit that I too am caught in this marital flytrap. It all seems a bit hopeless when looked at late at night.

Tuesday, July 13

Nora and Evelyn left about ten o'clock; they plan to sightsee in Toronto and Niagara Falls over the next day or two before returning to New York. Before she left, Nora told me that Lewis Mills's book will be out sometime this month, and she will send me a copy. After they left, I phoned Frank at his office. It was so good to hear his voice. We are to meet this Saturday and then he is spending two weeks at the cottage. What shall I do for the rest of July?

Sunday, July 18 (10:00 p.m.)

Frank has just dropped me off, and I could see Mrs. Bryden at her front window watching us. Soon she will want to know who was driving me home at this hour and so on. More lies. Yesterday morning we returned to the cabins near Port Hope. We scarcely left the place all day; just two brief walks along a road by the lake and into town for something to eat. Our bodies again so slick with perspiration. It must be like this on honeymoons when newlyweds discover one another. How wonderful and frightening it all is! Last night we both awakened at the same time and became so caught up in ourselves that Frank did not bother with a rubber and I didn't care. It was foolish of me, but I remember thinking at the time, It doesn't matter, it doesn't matter. I think I said that to him in the midst of it all. But, of course, it does matter. It matters a great deal and now I am a little concerned; not much, for I think I am all right at this time of the month, but we simply must be more careful. An instant of carelessness and my life will be turned upside down. How quickly it could all change! I don't know what I would do if I became pregnant again. I could not go back to Nora for another "operation," and I'm sure that, as a Catholic, Frank would oppose it anyway. What then? Have a child and give it up for adoption? Unimaginably complicated. We must be more careful. Yet how transporting erotic love can be! Is it because I have come to it so late in life that I feel this way? Yet the young also become unhinged by it. What of Ella Myles and that awful Kray boy? They too must be lost in all this rapture. A man and a woman with their clothes off—it is nothing less than unconditional surrender to the senses.

Thursday, July 22

Relief this morning. I was fairly certain I would be all right, but it's good to have it confirmed. So I shall live to love another day and how childishly happy I have been through the hours of this ordinary midsummer Thursday! A mouthful of egg at breakfast, the light through my kitchen window, the clatter of a lawn mower and everything registered in a higher key.

This afternoon a chat with Mrs. Bryden across the fence. It went like this:

"We haven't see much of you lately, Clara."

"Well, I've been rather busy."

"Mr. Bryden tells me that you've finished with the dentist now. I'm sure you're glad that's over."

"Yes, I am. It was something of an ordeal."

"And what about the car? Will you be driving that soon?"

"Yes. Joe is giving me a final lesson after supper and thinks I should be ready for the test next week."

"Well, that will be nice for you, Clara, having your own transportation like that. I see you got a ride home last Sunday night."

"Yes, I did. An old friend from the city."

"Isn't that nice?"

This evening Frank phoned from a public booth up north to say that he had written me on Monday and I should get the letter by tomorrow or Saturday. He sounded so happy and full of endearments. I think, however, that someone was listening to us. Very likely Cora Macfarlane or one of the Caldwell girls.

Muskoka
Monday

Dear One,

How I miss my sweet Clara! Do you know that I cannot get through an hour of the day without thinking of you? This morning, for example, I took Patrick fishing. We got up at five and the lake was so beautiful and still. We could hear the loons and the sun was only a red eye rising through the mist. We rowed out several hundred yards and dropped our lines. It was a wonderful moment with my son there on the lake on a fine summer morning, and yet, my darling, I was far, far away in that little room with you and covering you with kisses. How delightful you were and what heaven it was to wake up and find you there beside me! What pleasure we took in each other! Don't you agree? Please tell me that you were as happy as I was in that cabin last Saturday?

Can we return there on the seventh of next month? I know it is a long time away, and I hate these intervals between meeting one another, but I just don't see any remedy for it at the moment. I can't ignore family things, especially this coming weekend because we are having a get-together this Saturday with my brothers and their families. My daughter Anne is going off to the convent next week, and we won't be allowed to see her for six months, so everyone will be here to celebrate her vocation. Even my oldest son, Michael, who isn't fond of family gatherings, is coming up from Kingston. He and Anne have always been close. She is the only one in the family Michael seems to care about. Anyway, it will be a busy time, but I want you to know that my thoughts will be with you always.

I'm writing this in the car in a nearby village where I have been sent to fetch supplies. So I must now mail this and get back. Please take care of yourself, and I will see you on the seventh. I cover you with kisses, my darling Clara.

Love, Frank

Saturday, July 24

This evening I sat on the veranda and thought about Frank and his family "get-together." I wondered what he was wearing. A short-sleeved shirt probably and I pictured the fine hair on his arms. And a week ago at this time we were lying in one another's arms.

Across the street the Reverend Jackson and his wife were taking their evening promenade. Bats were swooping in the darkening air (the days are getting shorter) and Helen Jackson was leaning against her husband's arm. I wonder if they will make love tonight. Henry Jackson seems to be such a cold man when he isn't in the pulpit hectoring his congregation. I can't image him being as passionate as Frank. I think Henry Jackson would be ashamed to be ardent. He will no longer walk on this side of the street past my door; perhaps he feels that a heathen like me may contaminate his soul. The sight of the Jacksons on this summer evening left me feeling a little "blue," to use one of Nora's favorite words. And here is something else. Why has the urge to write poems dried up within me? I thought love inspired poetry, yet I feel emptied of any words that would make sense.

Tuesday, July 27

Absurdly proud of myself today. At 3:25 this afternoon in Linden, I was granted permission to operate a motor vehicle on the streets and highways of this province and presumably the rest of the Dominion. Hurrah! The test was not nearly as difficult as I had imagined, and Joe had prepared me well. He was so proud of me. "There now, Clara, you could do it. Didn't I tell you so?" Yes, he did, bless his heart! He gave me the confidence I needed. To celebrate, I bought Joe his supper at a restaurant in Linden. Poor Joe; he appreciated the gesture, but he was plainly ill at ease in that restaurant with his hot beef sandwich and raisin pie. I drove the Chevrolet home and it is now safely stowed in the garage. In a fit of foolish pride, I phoned Nora with my news. That call will cost me.

San Remo Apts.
1100 Central Park West
N.Y.C.
21/7/37

Dear Clara,
I thought I should drop you a note (seeing as I was supposed to have been properly brung up) to thank you for the hospitality. I enjoyed my little visit to the "True North strong and free." A little quaint in places but, in most respects, not unlike our own fair republic. Toronto reminded me a bit of, say, Hartford, Conn. You don't have your own Wallace Stevens in one of those insurance buildings, do you? You don't expect much to happen in such places, just folks getting on with their dull, decent lives. But that village of yours? Are you sure I didn't invent it? It seemed to me that I had pictured just such a place when I sat down to imagine "Chestnut Street." All those Uncle Jims and Aunt Marys behind their curtains, and I'll bet they are nearly as nice as mine! Just plain folks with all their bitchiness, nosiness, guilt tremors, backbiting gossip and general all-round orneriness. In other words, the salt of the earth. I'm not saying we don't have such people in this city of ours. We do, a few million of them as a matter of fact. It's just that you're not bumping into them all the time. You can safely ignore your neighbors and get on with your life. I suppose an intelligent woman like you learns how to handle all that rancorous intimacy, but it would drive me nuts. I suppose you have to be born into it.

I expect you have been talking to Nora by now about the cute little tykes and the souvenir shops up in that town we visited. Speaking of carnivals, I really enjoyed Niagara Falls. That place is wonderful, and as I walked around and looked at the jumbo waterfall and everything, I was reminded of what Oscar Wilde said about the place. Something about the falls being the second biggest disappointment of the honeymoon.

"Chestnut Street" continues to roll along as does my little nighttime mystery show. Our Nora is in the swing of things, standing by that microphone with script in hand, "enduring the thousand natural shocks that flesh is heir to." Anyway, I've got her doctor back to her. Poor Dr. Harper does have the worst luck. And so he had this nasty car accident on the way to the wedding. But Alice is now by his side at the hospital. And we are left only with a nagging question these days? Was the doctor's car tampered with? Did Alice's sister Effie have something to do with that? Will Alice and Dr. Harper ever find true happiness in the wedded state? Will I ever win an Irish sweepstake? Stay tuned and buy some of our soap!

In "real" life, Nora and her announcer friend are having some problems too. He doesn't know whether to divorce his wife or go back to her. The wife is a nasty piece of work, believe me, and Nora will have her work cut out for her with this dame. Les just doesn't know which way to turn these days, and you can see the look of puzzled distress on his big handsome mug. All the girls around the place are crazy about him. He's a bit of a chump, but nice enough. Les can wear a suit and he's got a cute little Don Ameche mustache. He'll never win any prizes for brains, but I don't think Nora is exactly interested in his brain.

I just hope Les treats her better than Lewis Mills, whom I saw yesterday by the way. This was in a swanky restaurant on Fifty-fourth Street and he was "dining" and "hand-holding" with his latest conquest, a young, pretty Vassar type (maybe Hunter College). Short dark hair and very shapely legs. She's supposed to be the latest hotshot poet around. She has at least twenty years on Lewis Mills, who really is an old goat, God bless him. Someone once told me that he'd had an operation somewhere (Switzerland) for monkey glands. I don't think I believe that, but I do remember Nora saying that he wore her out with his "demands." Well, I certainly wouldn't mind having a little Hunter College hotshot of my own. Ah well, perhaps in due course.

It was great seeing you again, my dear, and I hope that in the not-too-distant future you will find your way down here to wicked old Gotham.

Best always, Evelyn

Friday, August 5 (midnight)

In less than twelve hours I will see Frank again. It seems ages since we were together though it's only three weeks. I've told him to phone after ten o'clock when the lines are generally free and so he called two hours ago to say how much he's looking forward to tomorrow. As we began to speak, I distinctly heard a click on the line. I can't bear the thought of those Caldwell girls listening and giggling over Frank's expressions of love. It makes everything ludicrous and shameful. It will be awkward, but this telephone will have to be removed.

Sunday, August 8

I was going to drive down to Port Hope and meet Frank there, but I became a little nervous at the prospect. Perhaps next time. So we made our usual arrangements at the Uxbridge station. And what a joy to be again in our little motor court by Lake Ontario. We were both so consumed in our need for one another that I feared others might hear us. There was a family in the next cabin and we could hear them talking and moving about with their young children; the usual family fussing over what to do. Should they go down the road to the lake or into town? Should they bring bathing suits or not? Could they buy a brick of ice cream somewhere? "I want an Eskimo Pie," said a small voice. We went into Port Hope for supper and then saw a movie about the Irish politician, Charles Parnell (Clark Gable), and his paramour Kitty O'Shea (Myrna Loy). Parnell's affair with O'Shea brings about his political ruin, and on the way back to the cabin, Frank kidded me about the seductive power of women. He called me his Kitty O'Shea, but I don't think our passion for one another will bring down a government. At which he laughed, "You never know, Clara."

He was in such a good humor all evening and when we returned, the cabins were all in darkness. I am afraid, however, that the people next door may have been kept awake by our cries in the night. We couldn't help ourselves and after a while we decided we didn't care. Is this not what tourist courts are made for? And if they make them with such flimsy walls, will strangers then not hear sounds in the night? Certainly the woman gave me a good looking-over this morning while we were putting our bags into the car. I thought I could detect the following: curiosity, envy, resentment, perhaps a kind of guarded admiration. I noticed her eyes scanning my hand for a ring. It felt quite wonderful standing there in the morning sunlight after a night of love, feeling the woman's eyes upon me. Each day I seem to be getting better at playing the "fallen woman." On the way to the station, Frank told me that we can't be together next weekend because he must again go up to the cottage. This provoked a quarrel between us. It was my fault really, because I mildly protested that our time together was so far apart. This seemed to set him off. "I can do nothing about that, Clara," he said. "In the summer I have to spend my weekends up there. You know that. It's expected of me. You have no idea what I had to go through to arrange this weekend. The damnedest lies I had to tell." I was surprised by his outburst. He had been so happy all weekend and now this sudden exasperation. Still I foolishly persisted.

"But when can we see one another again?"

"I'm not sure," he said.

We left it at that and then I mentioned the possibility that someone might be listening to my telephone while we were on the line and this set him off again.

"Why not get a private line, Clara?" he said. "Good heavens, it only makes sense. Do you want me to help you pay for it? Is that it?"

"No, no, of course not," I said, but I was stung by his implication that I am close with money. Perhaps because it's true.

At the station he was affectionate again and murmured apologies into my shoulder. I told him about my driving license and this seemed to cheer him up. We parted on good terms and so I am glad that our little storm cloud has passed. I must get used to the idea that lovers sometimes exchange harsh words. It's just that I hate quarreling so much.

Monday, August 9

Nora sent me a copy of Lewis Mills's *The Temper of Our Times* with a note.

"It's pretty good, I guess. I only read parts of it. If only the guy hadn't been such a crumb!!!"

Chapters on Roosevelt, the union boss, John L. Lewis, the radio priest, Coughlin. An interview with George Santayana. A profile of Italy under Mussolini (no mention of the Callan sisters, thank goodness), a chapter on French Fascism and one on Hitler's Germany (the weakest, I think, a little haphazard and hurried-sounding). But overall, it's an intelligent and informative book. Picture of L.M. on the dust cover, staring at the camera. Wearing his bulldog look.

Friday, August 13

Yesterday I drove to Toronto to be with Frank. It came about this way. Late Wednesday night he phoned to tell me how sorry he was about last Sunday in the car. Said he "needed to be with me desperately" before he faced another weekend at the cottage. I was nervous driving into the city, but I persevered. We met at Loew's in the late afternoon and then had sandwiches and tea at Child's. Then we went to his office building on King Street.

It was nearly eight o'clock and everyone had left for the day. We made love, first on a sofa in a corner of his office, but that was unsatisfactory; the couch was too hard and narrow and so we put some clothes and rugs together on the floor. I remember looking up at the fading light of the August sky through the window. As he released himself, Frank bit me on the shoulder and that is still very sore. To be honest, I didn't enjoy his rough and anxious lovemaking though I didn't say anything. We parted with many kisses and agreed to meet again next Wednesday. At first I was frightened driving home by myself at night, but out in the countryside I began to enjoy the experience. It became exhilarating. With the windows of the coupe rolled down, I could smell the cropped hayfields. I was totally disheveled and sodden, rank with the smell of sex and returning from my lover. The car lights blazed a narrow yellow path along the dark road homeward. Intensely happy.

Thursday, August 19

Another "amorous adventure" yesterday. Again we met in the movie house and made our way to his office building. We didn't even bother to eat. How anxious we were to shed our clothes, casting them aside like children, embracing one another naked, beside ourselves with passion. We both seem to be in the grip of some kind of carnal delirium. I do believe that it is a form of madness. I told Frank not to be so rough and he did apologize, but he was so rushed and frantic in his lovemaking. I find it uncomfortable on the floor and there is, after all, something rather squalid about it. Things I remember: Frank's pounding heart, the sky darkening through those high windows as I looked across his shoulder, the grinding of the trolley car wheels along King Street, the ticking of the clock by Frank's desk.

As I left him, it began to rain, but I enjoyed being safe inside my little car, going home through the wet dark night. I felt sore and bruised, but happy. I told Frank that next week I would be having my period, but he said there was no reason why we could not still meet. "We'll go out to dinner," he said. "I'll take you someplace nice."

What a wonderful idea!

Tuesday, August 24

Frank phoned at suppertime to say that he cannot meet me tomorrow. It has to do with Patrick, a softball game or something. I thought the family was still at the cottage, but I hardly listened, so deep was my disappointment. He wouldn't be there. What difference did it make why? As we talked, somebody else was on the line, I am sure of it.

Later I drove into the countryside and parked by a field to watch the swallows. A late summer evening with a moon rising and the hayfields in silvery light. The days are getting shorter and I must begin to think of school. Milton has given me a copy of the new curriculum and I will have to get used to this grade system. Gone forever is Junior First. Now, it is Grade One. Senior First is Grade Two and so on. I suppose I shall get used to it.

Monday, August 30

Intense heat all over the province and in fact across the entire eastern half of the continent. Nora phoned this evening to say how stifling it is down there. Everyone she says is fleeing to air-cooled movie theaters.

Terrible news for Jack and Hilda Parsons; their youngest son, Harold, has come down with what they think is poliomyelitis. He was taken to Toronto on the weekend and is now in an iron lung. They fear paralysis. Eleven years old and he could be crippled for the rest of his life.

Thursday, September 2

When we met in the movie house yesterday, Frank whispered, "I have a surprise for you today." Throughout the picture (*The Good Earth*) we held hands and then we took a taxi to the west end of the city. I thought we might be going out for dinner, but at the corner of Dufferin and King streets, we got out and Frank told me we were going to a hotel. "No floor tonight, my darling," he said.

Perhaps not, but what a hotel to take me to! A beverage room on the main floor with some rough-looking women going in and out; the smell of tobacco smoke and beer, the usual shifty-eyed clerk and hangers-on in the lobby looking us over. Frank didn't seem to mind, but I felt ashamed standing there while he signed the register and those men stared at me.

The room on the second floor was small and stuffy. Frank opened a window and we sat on the bed. We could hear people walking down Dufferin Street on their way to the Exhibition, and sitting there, I felt suddenly let down by everything: the shabby hotel, the Exhibition (for I thought again of Charlie and wondered if he were working down there again), the braying female laughter from the beverage room below us. In the lobby, I had seen a woman going into the beer parlor, a woman in a red sundress with a heavy mantle of dark hair across her bare shoulders. She had thick muscular legs. I imagined it was she who was laughing.

Frank began to kiss me and we took off our clothes. He said, "I know it's not the King Edward, darling, but you must understand. I have to be careful. Certain people in this city know me and it's not as big a place as you might think."

I'm afraid I was not very good at anything last night. Frank kissed my entire body and that was delicious; I wanted to give way, but I could hear that woman's laughter from below, and I kept wondering where she lived and what she had done that afternoon. Had she gone shopping for bread and milk? Dressed a child? Was she a prostitute? Now she was in the beer parlor in her sundress with her painted mouth and the thick dark hair on her bare shoulders, surrounded by men. How unseemly and covert my life has become! Then Frank asked me to do something that I did not enjoy. I did it to please him, but I did not like it. At the end of the evening, Frank said, "We won't come back here if you don't want to, but we can't use my office because my brothers will be back this weekend and they work late. It's getting on for our busy season."

He seemed to be out of temper with me, and so I told him the hotel would be fine, but that Wednesday nights would be difficult for me once school resumed.

"Well then," he said. "I suppose we can go back to Saturday afternoons or something. Once we close up the cottage, I'll be in the city on weekends." We were both a little cross with each other.

Friday, September 3

Hot weather continues. Milton phoned this morning to say that school opening may be delayed a week because of this constant threat of poliomyelitis. Apparently, the Toronto schools are waiting for the weather to break. Milton is going into Linden tonight for a board meeting and will let me know tomorrow.

Sunday, September 5

Cooler weather at last, and Milton phoned to say that classes will begin as usual on Tuesday. But I can only think of Frank and of how much I want to be with him, even in that awful hotel. I should be preparing lesson plans. I have been so negligent this summer. I haven't opened a schoolbook since June.

Monday, September 6

Nora phoned this morning. She and Mr. Cunningham had a "swell time" together this weekend; they went to some resort. I could not help feeling a little angry and jealous as I listened to her. Nora lives in an immense city where a woman can do whatever she likes with her life. Here it is "What will the neighbors think?" as Father used to say. What indeed? And wouldn't it be restful not to care?

Then Frank phoned at suppertime and I was overjoyed to hear from him. He had just brought his family down from the cottage and was calling from a pay booth. He told me how much he missed me, and how much he was looking forward to seeing me on Wednesday night. He sounded so eager and affectionate that I became overwrought. I began to weep, there on the telephone. Told him I loved him so much and I knew that I was being silly, but I couldn't help myself. I know others were listening, Cora Macfarlane or those Caldwell girls, but I didn't care. What a grip all this has taken on my feelings! I must be the talk of the village.

Tuesday, September 7

Somehow I got through the day and it was not as bad as I had feared. This new grade system is simpler and should not be a problem. Getting back to work has been a relief. But I see Frank tomorrow night.

Saturday, September 11

I have taken a few days to think about what happened last Wednesday night. In the hotel room, Frank did something that bothered me. He had thrown his jacket over a chair and was sitting on the bed. We had talked about my drive down to the city, and of how difficult it was going to be now that I was back in school.

"Yes, yes, my darling," he said. "I understand all that and we'll work something out. You mustn't worry."

He then fell silent, and leaning back on his elbows, smoked his pipe and regarded me. His gaze was so intent that I wondered if I had done something that displeased him. Finally I said, "What's the matter, Frank? Is something wrong?"

"Not at all," he said, smiling. "Nothing's the matter. It's just that I want to show you something. Do you think you'd mind?"

"Why should I mind?"

He tapped his pipe into an ashtray, reached over for his jacket and withdrew a package of photographs from one of the pockets. "I thought," he said, "it might be interesting for us to look at some pictures together. They're a little racy, Clara. Are you sure you don't mind?"

"What kind of pictures are they?" I asked.

He came around to the other side of the bed where I was sitting.

"We'll look at them together and you can tell me what you think."

In the first photograph, a naked woman was on her knees in front of a man and she had taken his organ into her mouth while another naked woman fondled the man from behind. The other pictures also involved the man and the two women in various obscene postures. I found them both astonishing and revolting. As we looked at them,

Frank kept saying things like, “What do you think of that, darling? Wouldn’t that be fun? Wouldn’t that be exciting to try?”

“What do you mean?” I asked. “Another person? With us?”

He shrugged. “Well, why not?”

I didn’t know what to make of it all. The pictures aroused Frank, but only left me vaguely disgusted, and the idea of another woman sharing our intimacy was unthinkable. I wondered if Frank no longer found me desirable. Was I too dull for him? The experience upset me and I’m afraid I was ill at ease and unromantic. The whole evening was ruined and Frank could not conceal his disappointment.

“All right, Clara,” he said. “This is clearly a waste of time. You’re like a board tonight.”

But in that hotel room I felt so cheap and those pictures were so revolting. I don’t know what to make of it all. He said he would phone me, and I told him to be careful about what he said on the line. “Oh, that again,” he said peevishly.

“Frank,” I said. “Let’s go back to the little motor court by the lake. We’ve been happy there.”

“Perhaps,” he said. “We’ll see.”

I haven’t heard from him since. I wonder if I should write and tell him how I feel.

Sunday, September 12

Spent all morning composing this letter and then didn’t feel I could mail it. This afternoon I wrote another, almost word for word, and sent it.

Whitfield, Ontario
Sunday, September 12, 1937

Dear Frank,

I am marking this letter personal and trusting to the professionalism of your secretary to pass it on to you unopened. For several days now, I have wanted to write to you or talk to you about what happened last Wednesday night. Please believe me when I say that I want you to be happy with me. I want that more than anything in the world. And I think of how happy we have been in one another's arms, and, Frank, I want that to continue. But I cannot bring myself to imagine another person sharing our intimacy. That is such a repugnant idea to me and please don't think I am being merely prudish. It is more than that. What we have together is so special to me that I can't bear the thought of soiling it with mere sexual games. Please try not to be angry with me about this. It's the way I am and I cannot change my nature. I want to please you in any way I can, but it must be just us, we two, together, alone. I want to be with you.

Love, Clara

Friday, September 17

No word and I can think of nothing except that I have turned him away forever. I feel distanced from everything around me. A terrible day at school and finally at five o'clock I phoned his office. The secretary told me he wasn't in. She was not the same woman I have spoken to before and she was very rude about it all. "Mr. Quinlan is not taking personal calls during business hours," she said in this snippy voice. Has he given this woman instructions not to take my calls? I should never have mailed that letter. I have driven him away.

Sunday, September 19

I have done nothing all weekend but walk about the house in this ridiculous wrapper. The phone keeps ringing and always it's for the Macfarlanes or the Caldwells. Frank has walked out of my life without a word of explanation, and I feel as hollow as a reed, walking from room to room. Last night Marion phoned to ask if I wanted to go to the movies with her and her parents over in Linden, but I couldn't face them.

After church today, Mrs. Bryden looked in because she hadn't seen me all weekend and wondered if I were ill. But I just want to be alone. A pile of scribblers on the dining-room table to mark and I haven't even glanced at them.

This evening Nora phoned. She was having a party for Evelyn's forty-ninth birthday. I could hear the music and laughter and Nora was in high spirits.

"How I wish you were down here with us today, Clara!"

"Yes. Well ..."

Evelyn came on the line, but I could scarcely concentrate. They all sounded so gay on this lovely September evening that when Nora was saying goodbye, I began to weep. Carried on like a madwoman there on the telephone and, of course, this sent Nora into mild hysterics.

"Clara, for heaven's sake, what's the matter?"

Lamely I told her not to worry, I would write. But I felt disgusted with myself. I'm sure I ruined her party. That was hours ago and it is now nearly midnight. I can't believe I'll sleep a minute.

Monday, September 20 (4:22 p.m.)

How a mere day can make a difference in our outlook and expectations! I am writing this hurriedly, but perhaps at least these few poor words will remind me on some bleak Monday ahead that our fortunes can quickly change and for the better. All day I went through the motions, wondering whether I should tell Milton that I had a doctor's appointment in Toronto tomorrow. I thought of going down there and waiting for Frank outside his office building. Try to talk to him about all this. But I didn't and now I am glad, for as I got in the door, the phone was ringing and it was Frank. He has been on a business trip to Montreal. Told me he left instructions with the girl in the office to tell me this, but she didn't and what does it matter now? Yet that woman cost me a weekend of despair, damn her eyes. Frank apologized for all this and told me how much he missed me and could we meet tonight somewhere? He made no mention of my letter and I am just as glad. I am now going to have a cup of tea and drive to Uxbridge station to meet him.

Tuesday, September 21 (8:35 p.m.)

So tired and just now, at the door, Mrs. Bryden and the minister's wife canvassing for the Parsons. Harold is coming home from the hospital next week. I was happy enough to contribute, but desperate to see them go. Yet they lingered with Mrs. Bryden studying my face, as if expecting to find there the secrets of my life.

"You looked tired, Clara."

Is it any wonder? I got in this morning at four o'clock, as she well knows. I saw her light come on as I pulled into the driveway. The village is talking about me; I can sense it in people's looks. Finally got rid of them and then phoned Nora.

"Where were you last night? I tried until midnight to reach you. What's going on, Clara? Are you all right now?"

"Yes, yes. I'm fine, Nora, thanks. I'm sorry I carried on like that last Sunday. It was nothing. A mountain out of a molehill. I'm ashamed of myself."

"I'm worried about you. You don't sound yourself."

"Don't worry about me, Nora. I'm fine now, really."

I can scarcely remember anything I said to the children today. Imagine coming in at four o'clock on a Tuesday morning! Imagine making love in the backseat of a car on the side of a highway! When I think of what might have happened I can only shudder. In love we abandon reason and embrace risk and sooner or later ... Last night was a close call.

We met at the station and I followed Frank to the little river where we met months ago. We parked and I got into his car. The wind came up and it began to rain, a season-turning storm. But it was delicious there in the warm car in one another's arms. Frank insisted that we take off our clothes. I was reluctant, but the idea was exciting and so we did. We lay there making love until midnight. Perhaps we even slept a little, I don't recall. We had just put on our clothes (thank the gods of good fortune) when a policeman came by. I shall not soon forget the sight of him getting off his motorcycle. The huge figure in a rubber cape, shining a light into the car, the rain slanting through the beam of his flashlamp. That voice on the other side of the glass.

"What the hell are you doing out here at this time of the night?"

I was terrified, but Frank wasn't in the least intimidated. I suppose his manner, his clothes, his car were all reassuring; the policeman could see we weren't hooligans. Frank told him we were trying to sort out some domestic problems. The policeman told us to move along and we did. But what if he had come by only a half hour earlier and found us naked? How could we have talked our way out of that? I was so nervous I stalled the car several times before I finally got under way. What a strange, happy, frightening experience!

Saturday, September 25

Frank phoned last night to say that he cannot meet me in Toronto. He and his brothers are taking the train to Sydney, Nova Scotia, to see about coal purchases for next year. He'll be gone a week and said he would try to phone. Perhaps it's just as well. These days I feel languid and spent. And so, a little holiday from love.

Wednesday, September 29

Frank phoned this evening. He was in a hurry and I can't remember what he said. It was just good to hear his voice.

Friday, October 1

This came in today's mail. For the past hour I have sat at the kitchen table with this before me. It is so hurtful to read, yet like a child picking at a scab, I return to it again and again. I'm sure I now know these awful words by heart.

44 Eden Avenue
Toronto, Ontario
Tuesday, Sept. 23

Dear Miss Callan,

I want you to know that you are not the only woman in my father's life. You are only one among many whom he has "entertained" in various hotel rooms around this city. I am sure he has told you how much he cares for you. Well la-di-da, but you needn't waste your time believing him. He is certain to tire of you one of these days, just as he has tired of the others.

My mother suffered through this for years. My sister Anne and my brother Michael are also well aware of our father's "habits." Patrick, thank goodness, is still too young. I am not sure what you do, but I am guessing (judging from the letter you wrote) that you are either a schoolteacher or a secretary. Those are the kind of women he seems to prefer. Did he pick you up at the movies on Saturday afternoon? That is how he meets women. I followed him once many years ago. I was twelve years old, Miss Callan. I sat at the back of the theater and watched my father leave with a woman. Can you possibly imagine how that felt at twelve years of age? Miss Callan, my father preys on women like you and then abandons them when he becomes bored.

All this is shameful to me, my mother, my brother and my sister. It is the main reason why Anne is now in a convent. She cannot stand being at home around him. My brother Michael too. He knows all about our father and stays away. I could tell you other things about my father, but I won't. My sister and I have wished many times that he would be taken from us by accident. I still live at home because I feel a great obligation to my mother who has suffered all these years because of my father's weakness for women like you.

You should know that I have written letters like this to three other women over the past few years. If you are wondering how I got your name, I can tell you that I sometimes work in my father's office when Miss Haines is on holiday or ill. I answered the telephone the day you called and my father was in Montreal. I also opened your letter because I wanted your address.

I hope you will come to your senses and realize that my father is not for you. I could tell you of another woman who had a nervous breakdown after involving herself with my father. Don't let this happen to you, Miss Callan. You have been warned.

Yours sincerely, Theresa Quinlan

Sunday, October 3

Frank called this afternoon. He got back from Nova Scotia last night and was in his office "catching up on the paper." He talked about his trip and how much he missed me while I stood by the telephone rigid with nerves, listening for the slightest hint of falsehood or insincerity. Because of that damn letter, I am wretched with suspicion. I asked if it was safe to write him at the office.

"Of course you can write to me," he said. "I love your letters. Just mark it 'personal' and Miss Haines will pass it along to me unopened."

I said I would write him today because something important has come up, and it was better discussed in a letter.

"Well, of course, darling, if you would prefer to write. By all means, please do."

I am sure Cora Macfarlane must love to hear me called darling by a strange man. After he called, I went for a drive in the country to calm myself, but it was a mistake. I couldn't concentrate, and at one point I nearly went off the road. Before I knew it, the car was slewing about in the gravel and I was fortunate not to overturn. Had to stop by the side of the road to collect myself. All I could think of was that young woman reading my letter. That was unconscionable; I don't care what kind of difficulties she has had with her father.

Spent all evening on various drafts of this letter. The one I sent was much like this though I took out some of the rhetorical (hysterical?) questions.

Whitfield, Ontario
Sunday, October 3, 1937

Dear Frank,

All this is difficult and it will soon be evident why I could not speak about it on the telephone this afternoon. While you were away, I received a letter from your daughter, Theresa. It was a cruel and disturbing letter, and I have to wonder how much of it is true. Apparently your daughter was at the office while you were away. She answered the telephone one day when I called; I thought she was a new secretary. Unfortunately, that was the week when I chose to write you, and it seems your daughter opened my letter. I find that utterly unconscionable, Frank. That letter was meant for you. It was about us. To imagine your daughter's eyes upon my words to you is shameful to me. I can never forgive her for that. It is all so maddening.

In her letter she said that you have had other women in your life; that I am merely one among many; that you pick us up in movie theaters and take us to hotel rooms. How could she know all that, Frank, unless it is true? I don't know what to think about any of this. I would like to see you and talk to you about all this, but I am frightened of what I will hear. Suppose it is all true and I am just another of your hotel-room women?

Frank, I would like nothing better than to hear you tell me that none of this has happened, and that whatever feelings we have between us are honest and good. I know that in a sense we are both living a lie, but

I can't stand lies, Frank. I like to think I can tolerate many weaknesses in another, but not deceit. Your daughter accuses you of chronic unfaithfulness. To her, you are nothing more than a philanderer. Is this true? Am I just another "fling" for you? She went so far as to warn me against you. It was a terrible, hurtful letter, Frank. I don't know what to think. Can you write to me please!

Clara

345 King Street
Toronto, Ontario
Thursday

Dearest Clara,
What can I say after reading your letter except to suggest that you are being unfair. After all, you have heard only one side of things. Your letter is filled with accusations and comments that are hurtful to me too, Clara. And everything is based on what my oldest daughter has told you. What about the times we spent together? Those wonderful times that we have both enjoyed. Do they not count for something?

I am sorry that Theresa opened my mail. I did not think she would go that far. I gave her a job for a week while Miss Haines was on holiday. Theresa was at loose ends, and I thought the office routine would settle her down. I never for a moment thought she would interfere with my personal mail. You are right, of course. It was unforgivable of her to read your letter. Why did you write me, by the way? I wasn't expecting a letter from you now that you have a telephone.

Well, what's done is done, though it is a shame that Theresa has come between us like this. I should tell you a little about my oldest daughter. She has always been a problem for her mother and me. For years now, we have had medical treatment for her, but she can be difficult. She gets tired of a particular doctor, or he says something that upsets her, and she doesn't go back. We find out about it weeks later. She is twenty-one, but she still sometimes behaves like a twelve-year-old. Theresa is a very high-strung young woman, and her mother and I have tried to make her a happier person, but without much success, I'm afraid. Theresa is very intelligent, but she can't seem to find her way in anything. She has been to university, but she left without a degree. Then she thought she wanted to be an artist so she took up painting. Then it was novel writing. She just never finishes anything.

She also tends to exaggerate things. She has done this since she was a child, always inventing stories. I suppose she wants to make life more interesting and exciting. Given all this, I think you can see that Theresa is not a very reliable witness to my personal conduct. There is also a great deal of spite in Theresa, I'm afraid, and it's often directed at me. I don't know why.

She is correct, however, when she says I have known other women. I don't deny that, though I can't recall the subject ever coming up between us. I am sure you understand that for many years now, my wife and I have not had a normal life together. In the past, it is true I have sought out other women. I have my needs, Clara. But I chose to speak to you that day outside Loew's theater because I thought I saw another person who was as lonely as I was on that Saturday afternoon last April. I hope you believe that.

I can understand how hurt you must have been by my daughter's letter, but I hope now that you can see that it came from a young woman who sometimes has trouble with the truth. Now that you have heard my side of things, please let me know how you feel about all this. I miss you.

Fondly, Frank

Wednesday, October 13

After receiving Frank's letter yesterday, I phoned him at noon. We agreed to meet this Saturday at Uxbridge station, but I am already sorry I agreed to this. Something has happened; the poison from his daughter's pen has infected us. I sensed it in his voice. Yet I so want to see him.

Sunday, October 17

I do not know what to make of yesterday. We met at the station and I followed Frank in my car to the little motor court by the lake, but they had closed for the season and so we drove into Port Hope and registered as man and wife at the Queen's Hotel. Much cleaner than that place in Toronto. In the room we spoke not a dozen words to one another, and I do not know where the afternoon and evening went. We lay in that room as though drugged. We slept a little. We must have done. Then we ate supper in the dining room and returned to the third floor. I remember thinking, What do I care if he has done these things with other women? It is enough to see him and touch him and feel his heartbeat next to mine. It was as if nothing had come between us. Not once did we mention his daughter or her letter. It seems so odd to me now that we could put all that aside and carry on as if nothing had happened. It's all my fault really. The truth is I was too frightened to mention it. I did not want anything to interfere with our happiness in that hotel room. He wants me to come to that awful place in Toronto next Saturday and I suppose I will.

Thursday, October 21

Milton called me into his office after classes today. He looked flushed and uncomfortable, drawing little figures on the desk blotter with his pen.

"Now, Clara, I hope you don't think I'm being unreasonable. I'm trying to be fair about all this, but there's talk. You know how people talk."

He was looking down at the desk blotter all this time. Couldn't or wouldn't meet my eyes. Of course, we were both embarrassed;

neither of us can talk about such things without flinching. He has had phone calls from parents about "my excursions down to the city on weekends."

"They're upset, Clara. They don't think it's right. I understand he's a married man. Now, don't get me wrong, it doesn't bother me. But some of the parents are upset about it."

He kept taking the top off his fountain pen and then screwing it on again. Over and over. It got on my nerves watching him. I could see that he wanted to be rid of me. He probably felt that he had discharged his duty. I could hear them saying, "You should talk to her, Mr. McKay." Now he had done that and could he please go home to his supper? Milton is a gentle, nice man who doesn't want any trouble and now I am complicating his life. He is a little baffled by it all. Yet I sensed he was both curious and sympathetic. Curious because now he must reckon with another side of me; I am not exactly the kind of woman he thought I was; I am perhaps more complex than he imagined. Sympathetic because he likes me and he knows that I like him and we have worked well together these past two years. I am sorry that I am making life difficult for Milton. If only others would mind their own business, but that is a faint and pious hope in Whitfield.

Saturday, October 23 (7:30 p.m.)

Have just returned from Toronto after spending the afternoon with Frank in that hotel. For the first time, I felt distanced from him and I feigned passion. Feigned! Yes, that's the word. I felt guilty because he becomes upset if he thinks I am not enjoying him. But sometimes I just want him to hold me. I cannot get used to these antics of his. "Let's try this, let's try that."

Today, he again mentioned the idea of another person in the room with us. He knows a woman who does this sort of thing. A telephone call and she would be there. I thought of the woman in the red dress with the thick legs. I told him he was being ridiculous. What kind of woman did he think I was? I was sharp with him, and while I went on about it, he lay back on the bed smoking. When we parted, we said little to one another and I have seldom felt so empty.

Friday, October 29

Nearly a week now and not a word. Both of us are either too stubborn or too proud to talk. The coal people came from Linden and have just left. Six tons now in the cellar, so at least I'll be warm this winter. As it all rumbled from the truck through the cellar window, I thought of Frank and his family business. The least he could have done was send me a truckload of winter coal. Doesn't the disobedient child get a lump of coal in her stocking, damn it? Just before six I tried his office, but Miss Haines said he had left for the day.

Sunday, October 31

This afternoon I drove out to the cemetery and tidied up Mother's and Father's grave. A wistful lovely afternoon, surely one of the last days of fall. Later I made candy for the children who will be visiting this evening. Before supper I sat down at the piano and tried my hand at a little étude by Arensky. Fumbled it badly and felt gloomy, almost sick with longing and loneliness.

Whitfield, Ontario
Saturday, November 6, 1937

Dear Frank,
I tried to reach you by telephone last Friday, but apparently you had left for the day, so I thought I would drop you a note. Frank, I do not think that I am a cold person. At least, I certainly don't mean to be, but you must be patient with me. I have come to all this very late. There is nothing that I want more than to be with you. I do miss you so, but I

am confused and unhappy by what's happened between us. Please don't shut the door on me like this. The way you left me two weeks ago today—not even a kiss. That was so unlike you. Have you grown tired of me? I have to know, Frank. I have little experience in these matters, so you must tell me. I am writing because I am afraid of making a fool of myself on the telephone. Please write.

Love, Clara

Sunday, November 7

I am glad I didn't mail the letter. Its air of helplessness, the cringing tone. What would he think of me? How we abase ourselves before another! And for what? A look? A touch? A kind word? A kiss? Abject surrender. I feel so stupid and heartsick about all this. In the evenings I can do nothing but listen to the radio. I cannot read a novel because if it is any good at all, it will only remind me of how truth and pain live side by side. I cannot listen to music, for I hear only loss. Art demands that we pay heed, but I want only diversion. I'm like one of Ulysses' sailors, "Only let me taste the fruit and forget."

So I listen to the melodramas, losing myself in "Big Town," "The Shadow," "Gangbusters."

"Come out with your hands up, Rocky!"

"You'll never take me alive, copper."

Gunshots ringing through my poor old house. And two hours of my life gone!

Whitfield, Ontario
Monday, November 8, 1937

Dear Nora,

I wanted to talk to you yesterday when you called, but I don't want the whole village to know, and thanks to Cora Macfarlane and the Caldwell girls, my business on the telephone quickly becomes the stuff of breakfast conversation around Whitfield. So here is what I have to say. I have made something of a fool of myself over a man, and since that character of yours, Alice Dale, is always dispensing advice, maybe I could benefit from some of it. All right, that was sarcastic and uncalled for and I'm sorry. I would truly like to hear what you think.

Here are the facts. F. is a forty-six-year-old businessman who lives in Toronto. He is married and the father of four (ages eleven to twenty-three). He is also a Roman Catholic. How we met is neither here nor there, but we have been seeing one another, mostly on weekends, since April. This, of course, has resulted in intimacy. How could it not? So F. and I seemed to be in a kind of love (I write these words with diffidence and uncertainty because I am far from clear about what love between a man and a woman really is). That was a terrible sentence, but never mind. We both seemed to have enjoyed the physical side of it, though I am no longer even certain about that. F. has strange urges and I wonder if I am too reserved for him. You would never know it to look at him. He is rather small and fair (my hands are bigger than his), and in his suit and homburg, he looks like and is in fact a respectable businessman. There is even a faint resemblance to that movie actor Richard (?) Ronald (?) Colman. I am just wondering if there is more to this than afternoons in bed. I am not sure, but I think so. I know that I miss him. Even now as I write these words to you.

Because of his family, our times together have been so brief that it's difficult for me to know how I truly feel about him. These last few months seem to have gone by in a blur, a matter mostly of waiting from Monday on for the weekend. The abysmal disappointment when he can't see me. What a dreadful business it all is, Nora! But surely you have been through this kind of thing. Now there is more. A month ago I received an extraordinary letter from F.'s oldest daughter. She knew of our affair; in fact, she seemed to know a good deal about her father's adulterous life. According to this girl (young woman—she is twenty-one years old), F. has had many such affairs, and I am just another one of his floozies. She warned me against him. Yet, as I read her letter, I couldn't escape the feeling that she was in some way disturbed. There seemed to be an unhealthy intensity in the way she wrote about her father. It was a frightening letter.

I wrote F. about all this and his reply seemed to make sense. If anything makes sense in all this. But he did not deny that he had known other women. Apparently he and his wife have not been intimate in years. F. also cautioned me not to trust his daughter's word. According to him, she suffers from a nervous condition (confirming my suspicions) and she has been seeing various doctors. She is, however, far too headstrong to stick with any treatment. In F.'s view, the girl has an overactive imagination. She has dabbled in painting and novel writing. It all sounds a bit sordid, doesn't it? And I suppose it is; certainly F. and I have met in some doubtful places.

Nora, it's difficult for me to write to you about all this, but I needed to talk to someone. There is really no one around here whom I can confide in; Marion is a good friend in many ways, but her entire notion of what a man and a woman do together is a schoolgirl's fantasy of romance and earnest feeling. She would only be embarrassed if I told her any of this. Mrs. Bryden and Milton McKay have gently hinted that I am endangering my reputation by seeing a married man in Toronto. There has also been some talk apparently about my suitability as a teacher in the community. So there you have it.

I wrote F. a week ago (I no longer trust the telephone), but I haven't heard from him. Perhaps he has decided to end this, though it seems so callous not to say goodbye. Perhaps, however, when you grow tired of someone, you don't say anything. You just walk out of a life. I don't know what to think anymore. Could you drop me a line with your thoughts on all this? Please don't telephone.

Clara

135 East 33rd Street
New York
November 14, 1937

Dear Clara,

Whew! When I read your letter I had to sit down and make myself a strong cup of coffee. Is this really my sister? I said to myself. It sounds more like something in the movies, or even on our program. It's really funny, but at this moment Effie is also having trouble with a married man. Brother, what a coincidence!!! But in a way it shows how programs like ours are not just the fluff that smart-aleck critics say they are. Shows like "Chestnut Street" really do reflect real-life situations, and believe you me, I get the mail to prove it. Anyway, what to do? You are going to have to write your own script for this one, Clara, but here are my thoughts.

First of all, stay away from married men!!! I know, I know, the pot addressing the kettle, etc., but I'll come to that in a minute. You don't stand a chance with a married guy, Clara, especially a Catholic. They don't believe in divorce, and to get a marriage annulled, or whatever they call it, I think you have to go all the way to Rome and ask the Pope or something. But even if this F. weren't Catholic, you probably aren't going to get anywhere with him in the marriage department. Men may hate their marriages, but that doesn't necessarily mean they want to get out of them, especially if they have kids. Men really feel guilty about leaving their kids. Les is like that. He's always going on about his son and daughter. So I would say, give him up, Clara. I can tell that you really like this guy, and it's going to hurt, but in the long run, it's the only move you've got. Now you might think, How can she say that when she's seeing a married man herself? Well, down here it's a little different. You better make that a whole lot different! In the first place, I don't live in a village where everybody knows what I do with my life. I say hello to my neighbors and go out in the morning to work and that's that. If I want to have somebody over for the evening, that's my business. But look at your situation! You said yourself that everybody in Whitfield knows about you and this F. Why so coy, by the way? Doesn't he have a name? So now even your job could be affected. Your job, Clara!!!

The other thing about Les and me that makes it different from your situation is that we have come to this arrangement. We're not really in love with one another. We're just, well, close. We like going to the movies and the clubs and the other stuff too. We have a lot of fun together. But I now know that it's not going anywhere and that's okay. I've accepted that. Sooner or later, we'll call it quits and just be friends. Now and then I get a nasty phone call from his wife, but so what? Women like me will always get nasty phone calls from wives. So what I'm involved in is nothing half as complicated and crazy as this affair with your Canadian version of Ronald Colman. You say that he has "strange urges." I don't like the sounds of it. I put up with some of that with Mr. Mills. What is it with these guys anyway? They want you to put on black underwear and sit in a rocking chair while they do it to you. I don't get it.

As for this daughter of his, she sounds nuts to me. Has it occurred to you that there could be something between her and the father? It's been known to happen, Clara. Remember the Pollits who used to live down near the old sawmill? All those girls were supposed to have done it with old Nathan Pollit. Disgusting when you think about it, but it probably happens in well-to-do families too. For your own sake, you better start forgetting this guy and consider yourself lucky that you're not coming out of it with another problem. You don't want to go through all that again.

Listen, I have a suggestion. Why not come down here for Christmas? A change of scenery can do wonders. Evy is always asking about you. It will take your mind off all this. So think about it, okay?

Love, Nora

Whitfield, Ontario
Sunday, November 21, 1937

Dear Nora,

Thanks for your letter. I'm sure you are right; it would certainly make things less complicated if I just forgot about Frank. There! That is his name. But isn't forgetting someone you really care about easier said than done? The trouble is that every time the phone rings, I jump. And, of course, with this damn party line, it rings all the time. But then I think to myself, What if he calls someday? What will I say to him? The truth is that I'm afraid that what I will say will be, "When and where do you want to meet?" Of course, it makes little sense to feel this way about someone who can never be a permanent part of your life. But how do you turn off feelings? Tell me that and I will die a happy woman. At least twenty times a day I see his face: I see him when I'm washing the supper dishes or reading the *Herald* or staring out at my pupils. His face just swims up out of nowhere before my eyes. It's probably a kind of sickness and perhaps time will cure me.

I don't think I feel like coming to New York for Christmas. You're right. It would be a change of scenery and probably good for me. But even the idea of packing a bag or changing trains leaves me bewildered and gloomy. I'm afraid I would be terrible company. So thank you anyway, but I don't think so. Maybe next year.

Do you remember Henry Hill, the old man who lived for years in that abandoned boxcar down near the trestle bridge? Some boys found him dead last Sunday by the side of the road. Heart failure or too much drink, no one really knows. Poor old Henry, alone in that boxcar winter and summer, stealing vegetables from gardens. Such a strange way to live! When Henry was sober, he was gentle, almost courtly in manner. I went down to McDermott's on Tuesday night to pay my respects. Only three or four old men in attendance, and I'm sure they must have wondered what I was doing there. It will be bruited about the village as another example of my eccentric character, I suppose. But I liked Henry and often wondered how he came to live in that boxcar and have stones thrown at him by village children. And there he was, peaceful at last in his casket, wearing Father's old blue suit. I don't know if I told you, but after Father died I gave his clothes to the church rummage and Henry got most of them. I once wrote a poem about him wearing Father's overcoat, the one he bought months before he died, but wouldn't wear because he thought it made him look too much like a dandy. Do you remember? Anyway, Henry is gone and will no longer have to endure the derision and the stones. Thanks again for your letter, Nora.

Clara

135 East 33rd Street
New York
November 28, 1937

Dear Clara,

I just think you're making a terrible mistake staying in that house over the holidays. All you are going to do is brood over this guy. Are you sure you won't change your mind and come down here? Honestly, Clara, you sound so morbid. Going on about Henry Hill. He was just a dirty old man who used to get drunk and show his thing to children. Why on earth you would go to the funeral parlor to see a man like that is beyond me. When you do things like that, you can't blame people for thinking you're odd. You have to pull yourself together, Clara, and get out of that gloomy mood. Frankly, I don't want to hear about Henry Hill lying in a casket wearing Father's blue suit. It's just too morbid for words. You could come down here and have some fun. We could go to Radio City and see the Christmas show. It would cheer you up. Instead, you are going to sit around that big house for two weeks and mope. It's unhealthy, Clara. I'm sorry to sound so cross, but your letter upset me. I suppose I'm not in a very good humor myself these days. On Friday at the script meeting, Evelyn told us that she will be leaving the program at the end of January.

She's been offered a job out in Hollywood. I am going to miss her so much. She's been a wonderful friend to me. I don't know what I'll do without her. So I guess that's why I am a little testy. It's been a bad week all around. I'll phone you next Sunday.

Love, Nora

Sunday, December 19

To Toronto on the train yesterday with Marion who wanted to see the store windows and buy Christmas presents. I went along reluctantly. Eaton's and Simpson's were so crowded, but everyone made way for us as Marion, ungainly but steadfast, lurched from counter to counter. People are generally kind and accommodate the crippled. It is perhaps their singular advantage over the rest of us. Marion displays the patience of the ages in choosing gifts, and she seemed to be buying for the entire village: a scarf for a fellow chorister, a hockey puck for the boy who delivers the *Herald*. She can spend fifteen minutes fingering handkerchiefs before selecting one worth ten cents. And amid all this cheerful commerce and goodwill, my dreadful, stony heart. Overcome finally, nearly maddened in fact by impatience, I concocted a story about seeing a friend in a music shop and arranged to meet Marion for lunch in the tearoom at Simpson's. She agreed but only after I promised to go with her afterward to see *Snow White and the Seven Dwarfs*.

"I know it's supposed to be for children, Clara, but grown-ups are going too. I'm told it's wonderful."

So where did I flee if not to King Street and the building where Quinlan Fuels has its offices? Standing across the street in the cold, brittle air, I stared up at the third-floor window, the very window I looked out from as I lay beneath him watching the evening sky darken last August. It now seems a lifetime ago. And what did I expect yesterday morning? After all, it was Saturday. Would he not be at home? Or

Christmas shopping like the rest of Toronto? Or taking another woman by the arm into the lobby of that hotel?

Walking back toward Yonge Street, I asked myself these questions. Was the experience worth all this vague sadness that will not go away? Was it like this too for the Englishwoman in Rome when her lothario grew tired of that pale flesh and returned to his Anna or Maria? Perhaps women like us should leave well enough alone; perhaps we should never engage in the carnal wars which always end with ransacked hearts and the marauder's departure. Perhaps such adventures suit more fiery spirits, and women like us should settle for the afternoon hour at the piano, the evening service, the Sunday drive, the rituals of a homely passage toward senescence. Marion Webb and I hand in hand in the county home.

Took refuge from these sober reflections in a used bookstore where among the encyclopedias and heartless romances I found a novel whose title intrigues me. *The Postman Always Rings Twice*. From the looks of it, a mystery, but better handled than most if the first few pages are anything to go by. The main character's name is Frank. On the inside cover the words, "Gotham Book Market, 155 Broadway." How did the book find its way from New York to Toronto? In any case, I bought it for twenty cents.

After lunch Marion and I sat with hundreds of children and watched the dwarf movie. Entrancing in its own way and the color is extraordinary. Yet I wonder if children who see it will ever again read *Snow White* in quite the same way and with quite the same magic?

Have just now finished some Christmas cards including one to Frank. "I hope you have a happy Christmas and best wishes for 1938. Love, Clara." The innocuous and banal words of the defeated who hopes to stir just a spoonful of guilt in the heart of the marauder.

A year ago the house was filled with Nora's chatter. People dropped in to see Alice Dale in the flesh. "Can it really be you I hear every afternoon, Nora? My goodness, I wouldn't miss 'The House on Chestnut Street' for the world." This year, the solitude of the gray day enclosed and comforted me. There are worse fates than being alone, especially when accompanied by a good book. I spent the day in a roadside diner in California where the discontented young wife and the handsome drifter are planning to murder her husband. This is what happens when you no longer believe in the divine origins of the day. Once upon a time I could summon forth the wonder of the old narrative: the weary carpenter and his wife struggling through the narrow crooked streets of Bethlehem, turned away by surly innkeepers, arriving finally at a stable; the shepherds coming down from the hills to pay homage to the child in the straw. Today, I settled for adultery and murder in California. Sat all afternoon in my yellow-and-purple dressing gown, eating crackers and drinking tea, the voluptuary at home. At four o'clock Mrs. Bryden came to the door to invite me to dinner.

"You can't spend Christmas all alone, Clara. We have a huge goose. More than enough."

I begged off, hinting darkly at the fluids that gather within a woman and upset her equilibrium! As the Negro man said to his lady friend on a New York street, "Don't you understand, woman? I got to get back my equilibrium." To each his equilibrium!

Looking around the house, Mrs. B. uttered a small cry of distress.

"Not even a tree this year, Clara!"

"Not this year, I'm afraid. I suppose I'm not feeling very festive."

Mrs. B., however, was not to be denied. "I'm going to bring you over something later. You have to eat. It's Christmas Day, for heaven's sake. You can't just have crackers and tea on Christmas Day." Yet I sensed her relief that I am no longer returning from trysts at ungodly hours of the morning. She now regards me as a repentant sinner who is slowly and painfully recovering from the errors of her past. This notion provides her with the license to indulge me. Frowning over my slovenly habits, but feeding me on feast days. Later she brought over a plate of goose and turnips and potatoes, and I ate it all ravenously, turning the pages of Mr. Cain's book with greasy fingers, reading right through until Frank gets the hot seat.

Nora phoned around ten o'clock. She was at a party; I could hear the laughter and jazz music. But Nora was penitent and teary, going on about how cruel she must have seemed in her last letter. Drink brings out the worst in her and she was a little tight. She is also upset about Evelyn's leaving for California next month. "She got your Christmas card and is writing you. She thinks the world of you, Clara. You do forgive me for writing that mean letter, don't you?"

"Yes, Nora. I do. I deserved every word."

"Oh, don't say that."

"It's true."

"Are you happy, Clara? I mean, with your life."

"Not very."

"Neither am I."

San Remo Apts.
1100 Central Park West
New York
24/12/37

Dear Clara,
Thanks for the card. I don't send them as a rule. A letter is better, if you will forgive my glib tongue. Glibness comes naturally to one who toils in radio and is rewarded for doing so with the goods of this world. As you know, I am about to abandon this gilded isle for another fantasyland on the other side of the continent. These days I am capering around my apartment (okay, I'm not exactly capering) singing the old Jolson song, "California Here I Come."

Why am I doing this, you may well ask. Well, I've decided it's time I made a change before I am too old and all this gin I pour down my throat completely addles my brain. I once looked up the word *addle*. Did you know (bet ya didn't) that it comes from Middle German for liquid manure? Speaking of which, I've decided I might as well try to make my fortune in the moving picture business. Hundreds of lesser talented folk are doing it, so why not me? It can't be any worse than radio. I fully expect to meet the same brand of crumb and creep I see every day here in the broadcasting studios and ad agencies. The only difference, so far as I can tell, is that the crumbs and creeps in the m.p.b. have more money and seem to have a better time. I'm also hoping, of course, that out in Hollywood I will find some poor little budding star from Broken Nose, Nebraska, who is looking for an older, wiser roommate to help her cope with the wickedness of the West. As Winchell the Windbag puts it, "I am told by reliable sources" that the place is crawling with such damsels.

As you have no doubt discerned, I have had a few Beefeaters, but what the hell, it's Christmas Eve and I'm all alone.

Anyway, it was nice of you to wish me well as I head out next month to the land of orange juice and hopeless dreams. There is a great deal about New York that I am going to miss, including the friendship of your sister. I know that I am also going to miss the old city itself. When you come right down to it, there just ain't no other place like it on earth. But maybe I can get used to all that sunshine and stucco. Now, dear Clara, I am about to disgrace myself by polishing off the biggest martini ever made on this side of the park and tottering off to my innocent bed. Once I'm in California, I'll send you my address, so please stay in touch.

Best always, Evelyn

P.S. Here I have been nattering away about myself without inquiring about you. Nora mentioned something about your clinging to the wreckage of an affair and trying to stay afloat. That is, by the way, my tattered imagery, not your sister's. You can tell that I will have enough clichés in my valise to survive in Hollywood. Anyway, I hope that your heart hasn't been completely broken, and that the rat is now in his cauldron of hot oil, the ladle in the hand of his wife who is stirring vigorously. Au revoir for now.

1938

Saturday, January 1, 1938

Awakened in the night by the wind and this morning I looked out upon a blizzard. The elements in disarray. That line makes no cognitive sense, but I like the sound of the eight syllables, and so I spoke the words aloud several times. Will I be like this in twenty years? An elderly woman standing by the bedroom window in her housecoat talking to the weather. At least the furnace is well stoked and I am warm enough. Spent most of the day reading one of Nora's Christmas presents, a novel by A. J. Cronin called *The Citadel.* Not nearly sweaty enough for my depraved tastes these days.

In the afternoon, I bundled up and went for a walk; only a few children in the streets with their new sleds. The wind really was too difficult to cope with, and at the end of the village, I turned back. I was thinking of that night a year ago when I walked out into a storm like this and nearly allowed myself to perish.

By evening the wind had settled down and the cold had deepened. Here was the very breath of winter. A great deal of work at the furnace door, yet I could still feel the house cooling as the night wore on. Lay awake for the longest time thinking of Frank and wondering if I shall ever meet another man like him. Where would I? Felt a little melancholy on this bitter night.

135 East 33rd Street
New York
January 9, 1938

Dear Clara,
Why on earth did you have your phone taken out? It doesn't make sense in this day and age to be without a telephone. A party line in a place like Whitfield is a nuisance, but why didn't you get a private one? Honestly, Clara, you're still living in the last century. How am I supposed to get in touch with you in an emergency? I know, phone the Brydens! What about this Frank? Is he out of your bloodstream yet? I sure hope so. Les and I are still dating, but things seem to be cooling off. Maybe we just see too much of one another. We're across the microphone all day and then we meet a couple of nights through the week and sometimes on a Sunday. I'm still getting phone calls from his wife, but I'm used to them now, and sometimes, believe it or not, we even manage to have a sensible conversation. At least until she starts bawling. Oh well! Such is life for wicked women like me!

Evelyn is now working with our new writer, Margery Holt, though Margery has lots of experience. She's worked on "Pepper Young's Family" and "Big Sister," so she knows the ropes. I don't think she'll be as good as Evy, but you never know. We're having a going-away party for Evy on the twenty-fifth. Too bad you couldn't be down here for that. Speaking of being down here, I don't suppose I could persuade you to visit me for Easter, could I? Once Evy leaves, I'm going to be awfully lonesome and it would be nice to see you. We could watch the Easter Parade on Fifth Avenue. It's quite the event down here. Could you at least think about it? Damn it, Clara, I'm going to miss talking to you on Sunday nights. For my sake, at least, you could have kept the phone. Well, I guess we'll just have to keep in touch the old-fashioned way. So write me a letter, why don't ya?

Love, Nora

Whitfield, Ontario
January 16, 1938

Dear Nora,

I had the telephone taken out because it was a damn nuisance and a waste of money. It rang all day and half the night and it was never for me. A private line would have been a pointless extravagance; aside from your weekly call, I didn't get two rings a month. So would I not be just throwing money away? Most people in the village live without a telephone, so why can't I? Let's hear no more about telephones, for my house is blessed with quiet once again.

Am I over Frank yet? you ask. I don't know. I only think of him maybe ten or twelve times a day. How do you get over the presence of another in your life? The general maxim is to keep busy. Lose yourself in activity. Perhaps I should join the Missionary Society and write letters to orphans in Africa and China. Have Ida Atkins and her cronies over for tea once a month. Unmarried women do make a kind of life for themselves in villages like ours. Take Marion, for example. She seems perfectly content with her radio shows and society meetings, her shopping trips down to Toronto and her choir practices on Thursday nights; the glorious splurge of Sunday morning. In a way I envy her, but I know too that I can't be like her. Yet I am not strong enough or talented enough to go off to a strange city like you and earn my living. By nature I am reclusive. So I will have to wait for time to do its customary work. Time takes away our days, of course, unravels the threads of our lifespan. But it comforts too, and sooner or later, the lovelorn one gets out of bed and boils an egg. Starts dusting the figurines on the mantel. Ventures out to the moving pictures and even smiles at the antics of the fat fellow and his skinny chum.

It's been cold up here and I seem to spend a good part of each evening shoveling coal into the maw of the monster. My fuel bill this year will be horrendous. And it's only January! Well, in another couple of weeks I shall look for the returning light; watch it slowly spread into the hours of early evening, reminding me that spring is out there somewhere.

Easter in New York? I'll have to think about that, Nora. Say hello to Evelyn for me and tell her that I hope things work out in Hollywood. Hollywood! Imagine knowing someone who will be working in Hollywood. Take care of yourself.

Clara

Sunday, February 20

Yesterday a Mr. Dalton from Linden came by to ask if I wanted my piano tuned. I seldom play it anymore, but decided to have the work done anyway. Mr. Dalton was thin with a pale, homely face. Probably not yet forty. He folded his suit coat across a chair and rolled up his sleeves and set to work, laying out his tiny hammers and brushes on a mat which he spread across the rug. There was something altogether unprepossessing about him, and perhaps it comes from working alone all day in church basements and in the parlors of houses like mine. It felt peculiar to have a man in the house with his sleeves rolled up, even this lackluster fellow tapping away at the piano strings.

After an hour or so, I brought him a cup of tea and watched him pause from his labors to drink, grasping the cup with his long fingers. I tried to picture him moving those fingers over a woman's body in the dark of night. Thought it unlikely and asked him if he were married. He offered a slow smile and seemed to brighten. "Oh my, yes. Married now ten years. We have three kiddies." So he had caressed his wife with those hands. How strange to imagine others as sexual beings with their clothes off, and all this at five o'clock on a Saturday afternoon! After he left, I worked on a poem all evening called *Cow in a China Shop*. All about sexual desire and the havoc it can create. It was ribald, brazen and indecent. Threw the various drafts into the stove this morning.

4880 Barton Street
Hollywood, California
20/2/38

Hi there,
Well, here I am in the land God gave to orange growers and movie dreamers. I thought I'd drop you a line and give you my address. I've been here a couple of weeks now, and I'm settled in at Louis B. Mayer's sweatshop. They've put me to work fixing up a comedy about three young women in a college sorority and their troubles with boys. Mating-game stuff. You can imagine what it's like. They also want me to develop a series along the lines of Andy Hardy. I don't suppose you're an aficionada of such fare, but it's a series about small-town life and is wildly popular thanks to that brat Rooney whom audiences seem to find adorable. Beats me why, but there it is, and so they'd like a female version of the same with this character, Nancy Brown, who is cute and mischievous and gets into all kinds of silly trouble in small-town U.S.A. Well, that's why I'm out here, I guess. To concoct some amusing falsehoods for the Saturday matinee crowd.

I have found an apartment and it's in Hollywood, but the studio is in Culver City, so I'm going to have to buy a car. Everybody out here drives. You feel like the village idiot if you are caught walking. Los Angeles is a strange, somewhat goofy place, geographically speaking, especially if you are used to New York. To start with, you have all these towns, Hollywood, Glendale, Pasadena, etc. It doesn't really matter because it's all just one main street about twenty-five miles long. No skyscrapers. Gawd, I never thought I would miss big buildings, but I do. Here you can see lots of blue sky all the time, plus traffic lights, automobiles, palm trees, orange drink stands, studios and movie theaters by the dozens. Most of the swells live up in the hills between Hollywood and Los Angeles. Galley slaves like yours truly are confined to more mundane surroundings. The people out here are tanned and full of orange juice. A pale fat old New Yorker like me seems out of place among these bronzed creatures. Even the old folks with their brown ropy arms and legs look good. Maybe this is the place Ponce de León was looking for after all.

The people at the studio are okay, but they expect you to put in a full week, Monday to Friday from ten until six and a half day Saturday. If they don't hear your typewriter chattering away, one of the story editors is apt to poke his head through the doorway to see if you're malingering. A girl has hardly time to light a smoke. You have to understand that I am working on what are called B pictures. These appear as half of a double bill at your local Bijou on Saturdays. The big wheels are working in another part of the lot. It ain't very democratic. At the cafeteria (ominously called the commissary) the people are seated according to rank. It reminds me of boarding school where the head girl sat with her best friends and the rest of us made do with our places "below the salt." Sometimes you can catch a glimpse of the stars picking daintily at their chicken salad. Saw Norma Shearer the other day, so there.

There's a gentle fellow in the cubicle next to mine named Fred Anderson. Fred has written a mystery novel or two and came out here from Iowa a couple of years ago. Now and then he drops in to see how I'm getting on. I think he keeps a flask of vodka in his desk, though that is strictly verboten on the orders of Mr. M. My boss, Ed Barnes, warned me on the first day about the perils of John Barleycorn and the problem it can be with galley slaves. He asked me if I indulged, to which I replied with a simper, "Only socially, of course." His smirk suggested disbelief.

Anyway, this will take some getting used to. I already miss the old city with its curbside slush and its noise and its pale, abrupt denizens.

But the check every Friday looks mighty fine. We line up for it in front of a cashier's cage, just like factory hands. Another way of telling us, I guess, not to get too big for our britches. After all, we're just scriptwriters. How are you anyway? Broken heart all mended? I hope so. Stay in touch.

Love, Evelyn

Whitfield, Ontario
Thursday, March 3, 1938

Dear Evelyn,
How good it was to get your letter on a snowy, cold Canadian day! Your description of California with its palm trees and orange drink stands was just what I needed in this stark world of black and white and wind and snow. How I long for some color, for fresh green leaves and flowers! The past two weeks have just been terrible with one storm after another. But your letter has completely shattered my illusions of the writing life in Hollywood. Cubicles? Cashier's cages? I was picturing you in a grand office, leaning back in your leather chair, smoking your Camels and drinking coffee, as you dreamed up impossible stories for the screen, surrounded by eager stenographers who were taking shorthand and then rushing off to type your every word. So, it's not like that at all? What a shame!

It's kind of you to inquire after my broken heart. I have spent the winter recovering and I wish I could say I am over it, because life would be less confusing and complicated and I believe simplicity is at the heart of contentment. I can't prove that, of course, but I believe it to be true. To tell you the truth, however, I'm not sure that I am completely cured.

Nora and I have not been in touch for a while, and I'm feeling a little guilty about not writing to her. I had my telephone taken out; I was on a party line and it was such a nuisance that I could no longer endure it.

I believe this has so annoyed Nora that she is punishing me by not writing. She was used to phoning me every Sunday night. Of course, I am a quaint, stubborn soul who doesn't like to give in.

Have you been reading anything interesting lately or do you have the time? Last month I got Virginia Woolf's *A Room of One's Own* from the library in a nearby town and I enjoyed it so much that I took out two of her novels, *Mrs. Dalloway* and *To the Lighthouse*. Both are beautifully written, but I found their tone a little astringent. It's the only word I can think of at the moment. Perhaps I am still under the spell of James M. Cain. I can't think of two writers who are so apart in temperament and sensibility and yet both are strong and clear.

I apologize for the disjointed quality of this letter, but my thoughts seem astray these days. I am waiting for something, spring probably. I keep reminding myself that I must try to enjoy each day as it comes along, but I haven't been able to do as much enjoying as I would like to this winter. I hope all works well for you out there and do write again soon.

Clara

Sunday, March 13

All week the radio has been carrying news of Hitler's soldiers in Austria. There seems to be a general edginess in the air. Is another war possible? It's all so depressing and today I felt a sense of panic over everything: the radio news, the endless winter, this corrosive loneliness that eats at the hours of my days and nights. Perhaps this is what Catholics call despair. In the midst of it all, I sat down an hour ago and wrote Frank. I think the moment I dropped the letter through the slot I regretted it, but it's done. He may reply and I may see him again. Isn't that what I really want? If I had not written, everything would remain as it is. Now at least I may hope. And does hope not assail despair?

Saturday, March 19

Elation! Sheer as the smell of earth in March. This joy surging through me as I walked up Church Street from the post office with letters from Frank and Nora. A day of sunlight and pale sky and icicles melting. And so my neighbors saw me smiling for a change.

"Good morning. Yes. How are you?"

"Yes, isn't this weather wonderful? About time too."

Beneath this benign sky the snowbanks are hollowing and crumbling, and there is water on the roads and a fullness in my heart. I will read Nora's letter first and then his.

135 East 33rd Street
New York
March 13, 1938

Dear Clara,

I haven't heard from you in ages. How are you anyway? At least I have an excuse. I've been in the hospital. A couple of weeks ago I got so sick I honestly thought I'd die. I had such a temperature and felt so weak that I could barely make it to the studio. I managed somehow to get through the show and then Les took me to the hospital where they found out I had acute appendicitis. How about that? They operated right away and afterward the doctor said that it was a good thing because if I had left it any longer, I might not be around to tell the tale. Apparently thousands of people still die every year from appendixes that burst. Brother, it sure makes you think about how close you can come! I had been feeling lousy for weeks, but I just put it down to flu or something. Well, from now on I'm taking better care of myself. I now have a doctor and I'm going for a physical examination next week.

I was in the hospital for five days so Margery had to do some fancy footwork with the script. What she did in fact was simple but brilliant in my opinion. Alice too has an attack of appendicitis, only hers is much more serious. In fact, she is now at "death's door" and has this ever created a fuss with our listeners!!! Everyone is praying for my recovery and, of course, we are getting bushels of letters and phone calls. But the real me feels like a million.

How about you? How are things in old Whitfield? I can't imagine you're coming down here for Easter, or I would have heard from you by now, right? Oh well, maybe another year. I've had a couple of letters from Evelyn. She doesn't sound all that happy to me. I don't think California is everything she thought it might be. But I guess you have to take your chances when you make a move like that. Things between Les and me are just the same. Some days I feel like we're just an old married couple. Especially on Wednesday nights and Sunday afternoons. Funny how routine kind of breaks in on romance, isn't it? Well, I hope everything is okay with you in that department. How about dropping me a line?

Love, Nora

345 King Street
Toronto
March 16, 1938

Dear Clara,
What a nice surprise to hear from you! I thought you were finished with me, though, of course, I always hoped this wasn't true. I have missed you too, believe me, and isn't it wonderful to learn that you have been missed? So many people we meet in this life could walk out the door and we would never care, would we? Not for a second. And then there are special people. Like you, for instance. Oh, I thought you had given up on me, Clara, and here I have been thinking about you all these weeks, but I was afraid to get in touch with you because you sounded so angry with me in your last letter. Well, I am happy to hear from you now.

I have been "alone" all winter and have "buried myself" in work here at the office. Things are much the same at home though Theresa has moved out and now has a place of her own. She has a job at Simpson's but also wanted to get on with her novel writing. I can't believe anything will come of it. She is just too flighty to stick with anything for very long. She has these sudden enthusiasms and then they just fizzle to nothing. Edith and I are both worried about her but there is little we can do. After all, she is twenty-one. It's certainly time she settled down to something, but just what, I can't imagine. Michael seldom comes home. He's a strange young man and seems to have drifted away from us somehow. I worry about his drinking. Kathleen will soon be finishing her novitiate and will have to decide whether or not she wants to become a nun. She is coming home for Easter. Patrick thinks of little else these days but the Maple Leaf hockey team. I have taken him to some of their matches on Saturday nights, though I am not much interested in the game, but he gets such happiness from going that I look forward to it.

I would like to see you again and wonder if perhaps we couldn't meet for lunch some Saturday. I tried to reach you by telephone, but you have been disconnected. You never liked the telephone much, did you? I suppose we'll just have to keep in touch by writing. I was so happy to get your letter, Clara. Please write again.

Love, Frank

Sunday, March 20

Last night I wrote Frank asking him if he would meet me at Uxbridge station next Saturday. The car is still laid up for the winter, so it will have to be the train for now. I tried not to sound too eager, but I wanted him to know that I have missed him these past months. I loved writing the letter. It was raining and I was sitting at my bedroom desk, the white page before me in its circle of yellow light, all rain and darkness on the other side of the window. I told him all this and said I wished he were with me. Not too eager? What a foolish woman I am and yet I don't care. Let fall what may!

Marion came by on her way home from church. The minister's wife was again not at the service and this is attracting attention. She has now missed the last three Sundays and apparently seldom ventures out of the house. Marion thinks there is trouble in the marriage. She wanted me sober and thoughtful, listening to this news of Helen Jackson, but I fear I was playful. Marion settled herself into a chair, adjusting the heavy shoe to ease her leg. Those beautiful tragic eyes beneath the dark bangs. I thought what a shame she will never be touched by a man. She was pouting a little at my flippant mood.

"What's got into you, Clara? You're awfully gay this morning."

I made some reference to the drafts of pagan air I was inhaling. It was all nonsense and understandably met with a puzzled frown, a sigh. More adjusting of her leg for comfort.

"Darn old boot!"

She wants me to go to Toronto with her on the seventh of next month to hear Marian Anderson at Eaton Auditorium. Some of the ladies are organizing the trip. Wrote Nora this afternoon.

Whitfield, Ontario
Sunday, March 20, 1938

Dear Nora,

A thousand apologies for not being in touch sooner, but I have been in the "slough of despond" for the past several weeks, just dragging myself through the days. Alas, alas, poor lady! Anyway, the clouds seem to be lifting (metaphorically at least); it happens to be showery today, and I'm feeling less beleagured.

I was sorry to hear about your appendicitis. Like you, I had no idea it was still considered a serious medical condition. You must take better care of yourself in that big wicked city. I wrote Evelyn a note a while back and wished her well. I think she will be all right though she sounded lonesome in her last letter to me. Spring seems to have arrived up here and it is surely welcome. I feel almost giddy from the soft mild air.

Marion Webb dropped by today and asked me to go down to Toronto with her next month to hear Marian Anderson. It will probably do me the world of good to get out of the village, though I don't relish traveling with Ida Atkins and her gang. The big news in the village these days is the mysterious absence of the minister's wife at Sunday service. No one seems to know what ails her; she stays indoors all day and is seldom seen. I used to see her now and again walking with her husband but not lately. Living with that man cannot be easy; one would think that she would like to get out of the house once in a while. But how do we know how things are for the poor woman? She is really a very kind little soul and I feel sorry for her. Do you remember how concerned she was about me after my little talk to the ladies? I did make a fool of myself, but she didn't seem to judge me. It's just too bad if that Christian tyrant she is living with is causing her nerves to go.

I have been "attacking the keyboard" this afternoon. I had the piano tuned a couple of weeks ago. The job was done by a strange fellow from Linden—poor old Mr. Marsh has gone to his reward. Since then I have felt like playing again. So there you have the image. The woman plays her piano on a Sunday afternoon while the rain streaks the windows and Arensky's soft notes fill the air. Such is my life. But I am not unhappy. Do take care of yourself, Nora.

Clara

P.S. I am so sorry I missed your birthday. Many belated happy returns!

345 King Street
Toronto, Ontario
March 23, 1938

Dearest Clara,

Just a note that I am anxious to get into the early mail so you will get it by Friday. By all means, let us get together, though I'm afraid it can't be this weekend. Can we make it a week later, the second of next month? I will look for you at the station at the usual time. I loved your letter. Yes, I would have enjoyed being with you on that night in your room. You made it sound so perfect. You can't imagine how much I am looking forward to seeing you again.

Love, Frank

Sunday, April 3

How quickly a day passes and is transformed into memory! Yesterday was wintry again with gray skies and snow showers. Looking out the window of the train, I felt a bit overwhelmed at the thought of seeing Frank again. It came over me suddenly, and for a few moments I considered staying on the train and going on to Toronto. A powerful impulse and it seized me just as we approached Uxbridge station. Of course, I did no such thing and Frank was waiting in his car. His hair was freshly cut and his hat looked not quite right on him, though I liked the look all the same.

I had bought a new dress, a green thing I'll never wear again. It didn't suit me at all and I can't imagine now why I ever thought it would. Still he told me I looked nice. We were both nervous; there was a terrible clumsiness between us. I think it would have been better if he had just kissed me there in the car. Instead we drove on in silence to a hotel for dinner. There was a wedding reception and the dining room was nearly full, but they found a table for us in a corner away from the others.

The wedding guests were farm people in the middle of their meal.

They all looked famished and had fallen upon their roast beef dinners with ferocious appetite. The entire room was filled with the clatter of cutlery scraping plates. Hardly anyone was speaking as the waitresses set down platters of meat and vegetables; the room seemed to be overflowing with flesh and food. The bride and groom, a homely couple, sat at the center of a long table and they too were bent across their meal.

I wanted to remind Frank that it was a year since we'd met, but I decided against it. Men don't take much notice of such things and I didn't want to appear sentimental. Instead, I picked at my dinner and looked across at the bride and groom, wondering about their wedding night and how it would be for them. They both looked shy and ill at ease as they chewed their roast beef. Yet a year from now the bride will probably be a young mother, accustomed to the jug-eared fellow in the dark suit beside her.

After a while Frank began to talk about how things were changing in his business. It was odd. He had never talked much about this before, perhaps he had to say something; we both seemed tongue-tied. So he mentioned how he and his brothers are going to move into the oil business. Coal heating, he said, will soon be a thing of the past. I told him I would welcome anything that would relieve me from the slavery of winter nights in my cellar. He laughed at that and took my hand and squeezed it under the table. All this talk about coal and oil was only concealing our urgent nervousness with one another. What we both wanted were not words from the workaday world, but a forgetting in the flesh. At least that is what I thought and felt sitting in that ugly dining room at twelve-thirty yesterday afternoon. Did it show? I wonder. It must have, for neither of us was interested in our dinners and then Frank said, "I have an idea." He pressed my hand again. "Why don't I see if we can check into this place for an hour or two? We can be together again."

"Won't they want to see our luggage?" I asked.

"I'll tell them it's in the car and I'll get it later. They won't mind."

I watched him walk past the wedding guests, a small neat man in a gray suit. There is an authority surrounding Frank. The farm people glanced up at his passing, but they would not meet his eyes and quickly looked away. A few minutes later he was back and leaning across the table. "It's all right," he said. "We can go on up."

It crossed my mind that he had arranged all this earlier, but if he had, I didn't care. I was happy enough to get out of that dining room and climb the stairs to the first landing, my face burning as I passed a maid with an armful of linen. I was staring at the soiled carpeting, at the cigarette burns and the old invisible footprints of salesmen and adulteresses.

In the room all was abandonment. We undressed at once. All that fuss of removing our clothes. We didn't even pull down the coverlet on the bed. He kissed me all over, and when he entered me, I had a kind of convulsion within. Yes, it was all there, this sexual pleasure, though now I must reckon with remorse, for we were careless. I let myself go and he had put nothing on. We were in such a state. A few moments ago I looked up Sonnet 129.

Th' expense of spirit in a waste of shame
Is lust in action

Has anyone said it better?

We cannot meet next weekend because it is Easter and his family will be home. They attend the eleven o'clock service at St. Michael's Cathedral. He told me this as we sat in his car waiting for the train. Listening to him talk about attending Mass with his family made me feel like some kind of spiritual outcast, a veritable heathen.

Friday, April 9

Helen Jackson has disappeared. Some claim that she got on the Toronto train yesterday morning; others say she was seen walking along the highway west of the village. I learned all this as we drove down to Toronto last night to hear Marian Anderson. I was squeezed into the backseat of Bert Macfarlane's sedan next to Marion and her mother. In the front, the Macfarlanes and Ida Atkins. A great deal of clucking over this news; the secret pleasure we take at another's plight. I thought of Mother and how the village must have talked on that long-ago summer when she disappeared.

This gloom vanished listening to Anderson, a plain-looking Negress in a blue dress. When she sang "I Know That My Redeemer Liveth," there was scarcely a breath in the auditorium. There was not one of us who didn't feel chastened, humbled, enriched by this woman's remarkable voice.

Sunday, April 10

Yesterday a heavy wet snowfall that coated everything. Many roads are still blocked with cars half-buried by the sides of highways all over the province. Infuriating at this time of year and last night, watching it all come down, I decided to go to Toronto. I wanted to catch a glimpse of Frank and his family. A harebrained idea, but still irresistible at eight o'clock this morning. So I was among only a half-dozen passengers on this Easter Sunday, passing through a white world under gray skies, the snow still clinging to the village signs as we approached their stations. Men and boys were shoveling walks and driveways. The city streets were slushy and twice my winter coat was splattered by passing cars. I was wearing a kerchief for concealment, though I knew I would be careful not to let him see me. The bells of the big downtown churches, St. James's, St. Michael's, the Metropolitan, were pealing and the streets were filled with worshipers. Easter is surely the happiest of feast days for Christians, and walking up Bond Street I remembered the stirring of my own heart on this of all days.

I stood near the hospital, and from there I could see the people entering the wide doorways of the cathedral. About ten minutes before the hour, I saw Frank and his family. Now across the street from me were the people he had talked about. His wife Edith is taller than Frank and dark-haired beneath the new spring hat. A handsome woman who had once perhaps been very close to beautiful, but now the Irish good looks have turned a little haggard. She walked behind Frank, holding on to the arm of one of her daughters, a blond stout girl whom I took to be the nun-in-training. Frank walked ahead of them in his overcoat, white scarf and homburg, pipe in mouth; the man who had undressed me in a hotel room only a week ago. Beside him was his youngest son Patrick. The last two were the oldest of his children: a sullen-looking young man, fair like his father, and the dark-haired Theresa. I could see the mother's intensity in her oldest daughter's face, and I could picture this young woman filling a page with accusatory words, her fingers typing furiously. Judgmental, recriminatory, a fanatic heart; it was all there in the angry, pretty face.

I watched them disappear through the church doorways, Frank standing aside at the last to let them enter, knocking out the pipe ash on his heel and removing his hat. Then I lost sight of him among the other dark-coated figures.

Wednesday, April 13

Something has happened between Frank and me. I felt it in his words and voice today. After school I drove over to Linden. It was exhilarating to be in the car again, out on the country roads with the windows down and the smell of the dark wet fields rushing at me. I was so happy driving over there and I wanted to hear his voice; I wanted him to plan another Saturday for us. But when I phoned his office from the booth near the public library, he didn't sound himself; our conversation seemed strained and distant. I could have been exchanging words with a stranger. I asked him when we could meet again.

"Not this weekend," he said. "It's impossible." He even sounded a little put out by my suggestion. It was as if I were suddenly interfering in his life. I asked him if I was calling at a bad time and he said, "Not particularly."

There followed a terrible silence as I stood there in the booth watching people carry their books into the library.

"When can we meet then?" I asked.

"Can you come into the city on the twenty-third?"

"Not to that awful hotel, Frank," I said. "I am so uncomfortable in that place."

More terrible silence and then he said, "Maybe we should talk about all this. I can't go traipsing around the countryside every Saturday."

Traipsing around the countryside! Is this how he sees his time with me now? That word *traipsing*. I felt bewildered by the sound of it.

"I could come into Toronto on the twenty-third. Maybe we could just have lunch or a cup of tea together. I want to see you, Frank."

"Yes. Well, I'll meet your train at Union Station on the twenty-third. We can have a sandwich somewhere."

"Frank," I asked. "What's the matter?"

"Nothing's the matter. Why?"

"You don't sound yourself," I said. "You sound irritated with me. As if I'm intruding."

"No. You're not intruding. I'm just not having a very good time of it. Trouble at home. The usual thing."

I told him I was sorry about that and so we said goodbye. Yet now I wonder if it is trouble at home that made him sound the way he did or is it something else? Perhaps I have arrived at the day that awaits women like me; the day when things stop, because there is no other place for them to go. I feel ill about all this. That foolish, foolish moment of abandonment.

Friday, April 15

Mrs. Bryden just told me that they have found Helen Jackson. Apparently she was wandering the streets of Buffalo, New York. She has been taken to the asylum in Whitby for observation. Letter from Nora.

135 East 33rd Street
New York
April 7, 1938

Dear Clara,

Sorry not to have answered your letter sooner. You'll never guess what I'll be doing next weekend. I'm going to take an airplane ride!!! It's a birthday present from Les.

I was too sick back in March to care about presents, and so Les held off until this week when he surprised me with dinner at the Rainbow Room. The real McCoy with steak and champagne, and at the end of it all, he put an envelope on the table. Inside were two tickets to Chicago. He has some business there a week from next Saturday and wants me to go along with him. It sounds so exciting and I'm really looking forward to it. I think when I'm there I'll give Jack and Doris Halpern a call. Do you remember the Halperns and how good they were to me? It was Jack, of course, who helped me get my start in radio here in New York. It should be fun. Les has reservations at the Palmer House, which I am told is very swanky indeed.

This Sunday I am going to watch the Easter Parade with a couple of gals from the show. I've got my new Easter bonnet, how about you? Before that we're going to the Easter service at St. Thomas's right on Fifth Avenue. We've done this for the last couple of years, so it's becoming a kind of tradition, I guess. Then we watch the parade and have breakfast together with champagne and everything. If you had come down, you could have joined us. I love going to church on Easter Sunday. I think I enjoy it even more than Christmas. Do you remember how Father would always have new shoes and dresses for us when we were eight or nine years old? If Easter was early and there was still snow on the ground, we had to wear galoshes, and we'd take them off on the church porch so we could show everybody our new shoes at Sunday school. But if the sidewalks were dry, he'd let us wear our new shoes outside and for a while your feet always felt so light. It was as though you were walking on air. Do you ever think about things like that, Clara? Gee, I do. Before I go to sleep at night I think about times like that. About growing up in Whitfield with you and Father. And I'm only thirty-three! What will I be reminiscing about in twenty years? I'll sound like some old woman nattering on about "the good old days."

Well, I better go. I have to wash my hair and do my nails. Tourists come through the studio now and stare at us while we're doing the show. You look up from your script and there is a whole wall of strangers gawking at you from behind the glass. So we have to be as spiffy as we can make ourselves. Tomorrow is Friday and that's always a big day for visitors to the studio. So I am going to dazzle them with this new red dress I bought at Bonwit's the other day. It's a pretty nifty little number and I don't look half bad in it, if I do say so. I'll let you know how my airplane ride turns out. Oh, way up in the sky like that. I hope I don't get sick. Take care, sister.

Love, Nora

Monday, April 18

A letter from his daughter. In a way I expected something like this; I don't know why, I just did. Yet how could she know about us? He told me she was no longer living at home. Does she follow him on Saturdays? Does she follow him every day? I am at an utter loss, but I feel defiled by it all, and perhaps I deserve to be.

Toronto, Ontario
April 14

Dear Miss Callan,
I am disappointed to learn that you are seeing my father again. I thought you had come to your senses last fall, but apparently not. I certainly expected better from you. After all, Miss Callan, you are not some little shopgirl working at Eaton's. You are a schoolteacher and you should know better. I wonder if you realize that you are sharing him with another woman. She lives here in the city and he sees her through the week. He takes her to a cheap hotel room for sex. You probably don't believe me, do you? Well, I can prove it's true and I will. I am going to write this woman and tell her about you and my father. I expect you will hear from her one of these days. I don't know why women like you can't behave decently and leave married men like my father alone.

Yours sincerely, Theresa Quinlan

Friday, April 22

Marion came by this evening and perhaps it was good that she did, for all week I have been stewing over Theresa Quinlan's letter and my meeting with her father tomorrow. I am afraid he is going to end this. It was in his voice when I called him last week. He might as well have said, "Oh, it's you, is it? What can I do for you?"

I should have written him a letter. I always feel more comfortable with words in a letter. Tomorrow I will be tongue-tied. He will tell me that it's over and I will go to pieces quietly in the station cafeteria with its streaked tables and dirty cups. A waitress will stop wiping a counter and stare pityingly at me. Marion brought me out of all this for a while with village news, her head shaking in wonder at the follies and misfortunes of her fellow creatures. Yesterday she was down to the asylum in Whitby with her mother and Ida Atkins to visit Helen Jackson.

"What a place that is, Clara!" said my wide-eyed Marion. "The language some of those women use! It's terrible." She then told me about a girl who follows Helen around and says "shocking, dirty things to her." A revelation for Marion and her mother and Ida Atkins, I suppose.

I thought of Helen Jackson, a gentle soul in that world, and said "the poor woman" and I meant it. She cannot be mad, but merely distracted, overwhelmed by everything, unable any longer to deal with daily life. Anyone can reach such a point. Perhaps Mother felt the same way and perhaps one afternoon I will too. I think I came very near it when I returned from Italy.

Told Marion I would drive down one Sunday and see Helen Jackson.

"I think she would like that, Clara," Marion said. "She asked about you. She really likes you. She said you were the most honest person in the village, though I don't really know what she meant by that. It seems to me we're pretty honest decent people around here."

Marion was leaning forward with her elbows on the kitchen table, cooling her tea as she has always done by blowing short bursts of breath across her cup. It's a homely and endearing habit that I have watched since we were children in her mother's kitchen, drinking cocoa. Marion never asks me personal questions. It's odd in a way. I am sure she has heard all the stories, all the gossip about the man in Toronto, my precarious nerves and peculiarities. Yet she has never once come close to serious inquiry. The truth is that neither of us is comfortable with the kind of conversational intimacy that I am sure some women enjoy: the secrets of the bedroom, the sorrows and joys of love. Is it politeness, diffidence, fear of exposing our innermost longings? Neither of us has the map for such a journey into the heart. Marion wants everything between us to remain as it once was when I was her only friend. And yet, we weren't friends in sharing feelings. We never came close to doing so; there was always an emotional distance between us.

No one else would play with Marion because of her foot. I see her always on the edge of the circle, watching the other girls, waiting for them to tire of their games. Trying to catch up to me as I walked home. Following me about the house and getting in the way. I envied the mantle of shining clean hair which clung to her shapely head like a dark helmet. Her lovely eyes. Even sometimes her boot. I imagined what it would be like not to have to do things because you were crippled. I would scold her for being a nuisance and then promise to play with her another day. But we never shared secrets. Something within us held them back. So I could never reveal what's important to me. Despite the romance stories and the radio plays she loves, Marion would only be embarrassed by accounts of genuine happiness or heartbreak: I could never speak to her of summer nights when Frank and I lay waiting for the breeze from the screened windows to cool our bodies. I could never talk to her of last winter's loneliness. It would make us both uncomfortable. Marion's only nod to feeling is the frown that crosses her face as she leans into the cloth-covered mouth of the radio and listens to one of her heroines unburden herself.

Saturday, April 23

On the train this morning I remembered that it was Shakespeare's birthday. So thank you for the poetry, Will. I may need it in the months ahead, every syllable. He never showed up. He just wasn't there when I walked down the passageway toward all those people who were standing behind the rope awaiting friends and lovers. On the loudspeaker they were announcing the arrival of a train from Montreal and so the waiting area was crowded. I looked among all those faces for him. How awkward not to have the one you expected there to greet you with a hug, a kiss, a word, a handshake! In a matter of minutes you are reduced to puzzled anger, forced against the wall to watch the others moving away. I had bought a new hat in Linden Ladies' Wear, which the saleslady had said was "very becoming." I could see its jaunty absurdity in my reflection in the glass-paneled poster for train travel through the Rockies. "Becoming." It looked ridiculous and I felt like shouting, "Liar, liar, ten feet higher!"

Then everyone was gone and I followed too. One can't stand by a railway poster all day staring at an ugly hat. Through the main concourse and out onto Front Street, windy and cool on this spring morning. Walking briskly along as though at the end of my stride lay purpose and destination. In every store window I saw myself in that hat. How I longed to hurl it into the gutter and see it crushed beneath car wheels! Ten years ago I might have gone into one of the churches to pray for guidance. Today, I went to the movies and watched Clark Gable in *Saratoga*. I went to Loew's. Was I hoping I might see him with another woman? I don't know. I don't know what I thought sitting there looking up at the actor's huge smiling face. All that teeth and hair and everlasting glamour. All I know now is this: it is over and I think I am in trouble.

Tuesday, April 26

Letters today from Nora and a Florence Keefe. One of his women. What am I supposed to make of all this?

65 Edmund Avenue
Toronto, Ontario
Friday, April 22

Dear Miss Callan,

I hope you will pardon a stranger for intruding into your personal life, but your name was given to me by a young woman named Theresa Quinlan. She happens to be the daughter of a man I am seeing. I don't quite know how to approach this without sounding distasteful. There seems no other way except to be perfectly honest with you. In the circumstances, I am sure that you will appreciate candor. I have been told that you are a schoolteacher, and so I feel I am writing to someone who can understand and appreciate the situation.

Let me begin by saying that for the past several months I have been seeing a married man named Frank Quinlan. I am not particularly proud of my behavior, but I believe I am old enough to appreciate that these things happen. I emigrated to Canada from England ten years ago and I'm afraid that, for the most part, it has been a lonely ten years. By profession, I am a librarian, and in the course of my duties I do not meet many "eligible" men. I am now thirty-eight years old and had more or less resigned myself to living alone. Then last September I met Frank Quinlan and my life has changed.

You are probably now asking yourself, What has all this to do with me? Well, Miss Callan, last week I received a telephone call at the library from a woman who identified herself as Frank's daughter. She told me that I was making a serious mistake by seeing her father. At first, of course, I didn't believe her, but she seemed to know a great deal about Frank and me. It was an unnerving experience listening to her, I can assure you. She then went on to say that I was only one of several women her father had been seeing. I was doubtful about that, but then she told me that she could prove it by giving me the name and address of someone who was "sharing" her father with me. At first it sounded so spitefully outlandish that I could not bring myself to believe her. Then she gave me your name and address, and I was forced to ask myself how she could know about you if there wasn't at least some shred of truth to her story. Of course, I have asked Frank about all this and he completely denies it. He told me that Theresa lives in a fanciful world; that in fact she is writing a novel and often has difficulty separating fact from fiction. I understand that she has had some problems with her nerves and has had some treatment for this. Frank made it sound as if his daughter had made all this up. I didn't mention to him, by the way, that Theresa had given me your name because he was angry and I didn't want to upset him farther.

So now, Miss Callan, I am afraid I must ask you if you are presently seeing Frank. I have to assume that at some point you must have been involved with him. How else would Theresa know about you? But is it all over? At the moment I am at sixes and sevens. Can I prevail upon you to write and tell me the truth? I do understand how upsetting this kind of letter must be to you and I do apologize, but I just have to know.

Yours truly, Florence Keefe

135 East 33rd Street
New York
April 19, 1938

Dear Clara,
Got back last night from my "birthday weekend" in Chicago. What a time we had! At first I was scared in the airplane, but after a while you get used to being up there thousands of feet above the ground. Except for a little aching in your ears when you're taking off or landing, it's just like sitting in a bus only you're traveling at over two hundred miles an hour. Imagine!!! We were in Chicago in less than four hours. Of course, it would have taken all day on the train. We visited with some people in the agency (Les had business with them) and they said they use the airplane all the time now to travel to New York or Los Angeles. It just saves so much time. And the girls on board are so nice. They wear these smart uniforms and serve coffee and sandwiches. Linen napkins. It's very classy.

I was treated royally by the people at the agency. Everybody listens to our show and envies our ratings. I didn't get to see the Halperns, though I phoned and talked to Jack. He told me how proud he is of me. I just wish we'd had time to see one another, but our schedule was tight. On Saturday night friends of Les's had tickets for the hockey match between Chicago and Toronto for the championship. Of course, being a good Canadian, I was rooting for the Maple Leafs, but

Chicago won the cup. Afterward we went dancing at a supper club and didn't get back to the hotel until after three. Tired? You bet. But all in all, a wonderful weekend.

Back to earth now and I have to catch up on my sleep (it's only nine o'clock but I'm on my way to bed), so I'll say so long for now. Had a letter today from Evelyn by the way. Very funny about Hollywood. Sounds like her old self again, so I guess she is finally settling in out there. Take care and drop me a line when you get the chance.

Love, Nora

Saturday, April 30

I wrote this today, but I did not mail it. What would be the point? He is no longer interested in me or what I have to say.

Whitfield, Ontario
April 30, 1938

Dear Frank,

Your neurasthenic daughter recently wrote to scold me for seeing you again. How does she know about all your "arrangements"? I wonder. But perhaps I don't really want to know the answer to that question. It may be just too sordid for words. She is right, however, about one thing. I made a terrible mistake in seeing you again, and now I only hope that I do not regret it for the rest of my life. Your daughter also mentioned another woman (how do you find all the time and energy for this, Frank?), and she apparently phoned this Miss Keefe who, in turn, wrote me a heartrending account of her involvement with you. It seems that this dates back to last September; that would have been just about the time you were saying how much you loved me in some dismal hotel room. Is it any wonder your wife drinks and your children despise you? The dapper little Catholic coal merchant with his homburg and pipe and his women.

Well, I behaved stupidly in becoming involved with you in the first place, and certainly I should never have got in touch with you again a month ago. You must find the foolish antics of women like Florence Keefe and me amusing. But what bothers me even more is that I thought I was in love with a man who turns out to be a coward. Yes, you are a coward, Frank. If you didn't want to see me anymore, you should have met me at the train station last Saturday and told me so. Instead, I went down to Toronto and you didn't bother to show up. That was so cowardly and wrong. I don't know if your Catholic God will forgive you for all this, but I know I never will.

Clara

Sunday, May 1

Wrote Florence Keefe and told her she was welcome to him.

Monday, May 2

Lay awake much of last night regretting the vicious tone of my letter to that woman. I needn't have mentioned being in that hotel room with him a month ago. And the phrase "women like you and me." Unnecessary and hurtful when, after all, Florence Keefe is hardly to blame for any of this. However, what's done is done.

Tuesday, May 3 (12:10 p.m.)

At ten-thirty this morning I was standing on the steps by the girls' entrance waiting to call the children in from recess. As I rang the handbell and watched them scatter from their skipping games and softball, it came to me that I must be pregnant again. It is too soon to be certain, but I feel I am, and on this spring morning at that hour, I felt myself on the verge of change. Yes, there in the ordinary moments of today ("Thank you, Wilfrid. Put the ball and bat in the cloakroom please!"), I thought of transformation within the darkness of our bodies, when the cancer spreads or a human life begins. Thought of a poem to be called *Eventful Change Occurs Unseen*. But will I ever write it?

(8:00 p.m.)

Listening to the radio. Hitler is visiting Mussolini in Rome. Two years ago, I was dreaming of my visit to that great city. Now I can picture all those men in their uniforms, the crowds lining the stone streets to watch them pass, the German and Italian flags and banners hanging from windows. It's all so dispiriting. I should write Nora about my pregnancy, but I can't yet bring myself to tell her. I know she will have a fit when she hears about this. Sat down instead and wrote Evelyn Dowling.

Whitfield, Ontario
May 3, 1938

Dear Evelyn,
After reading this letter, you may well wonder what kind of woman I am. On the other hand, perhaps I am writing to you precisely because you are not the type to pass judgment on the sinful and careless of this world. I haven't written Nora, but I'm sure that when she hears she'll have a proper fit, especially after what happened three years ago.

Yes, I am pregnant again, or at least I am fairly certain that I am. It's a complicated story and has nothing to do with what happened three years ago. That also is a complicated story and perhaps one day I will work up enough nerve to tell you about that too. At the moment, however, I am in "the family way" and, of course, I am not sure what to do about it. There are only so many things one can do about it, and at the moment none of them seems particularly satisfactory.

Do you have any suggestions? I was thinking of how you came to my rescue three years ago in New York. I am not even sure that I want to go through that again, but is it still a possibility? Please forgive me for bothering you about this; I do feel rather foolish writing, but I'm not yet ready to tell Nora. Perhaps it is mortal shame, I don't know. I have always been the one who does the scolding and the finger pointing in our family and here I am again in this state. Well, I am trying not to give in to self-pity, for it's all my fault for being so careless and stupid. I hope at least that things are going well with you out there in those mythical regions.

Sincerely, Clara

Monday, May 9

Thirty-six days now and no sign of "the maid's little helper." And my breasts are beginning to tingle! I'm pregnant all right. As sure as leaves are green and life uncertain! Now what?

Letter from Florence Keefe, poor deluded soul. Her sentiments on love in general and Frank Quinlan in particular cry out for spirited correction, but let it rest, let it rest.

Toronto, Ontario
May 4, 1938

Dear Miss Callan,

Thank you for taking the trouble to reply. Your bitterness is quite evident and perhaps understandable. I don't pretend to have all the answers, but I do know that Frank has had a very difficult time of it, and what he needs, in my view, is a forgiving heart. He needs someone who is prepared to accept him as he is. Frank lives in a houseful of people who have turned against him, thanks to that hateful, alcoholic wife of his. Is it any wonder the poor man seeks affection elsewhere? I don't care about the other women in his life. I think that if you love a man, you should be prepared to accept everything about him, including his flaws. That is what love is all about, Miss Callan.

Yours truly, F. Keefe

4880 Barton Street
Hollywood, California
10/4/38

Dear Clara,

Yours of the third to hand (as my father used to quaintly put it), and all I can say is that I'm still a little stupefied. You lead some kind of life in that Canadian village. As a matter of fact, you make the characters on "Chestnut Street" seem a little dull in their various entanglements. Please don't get me wrong. All levity aside, I am very concerned and grateful that you got in touch. So now the question is, What's to be done? The first thing you should do, and pronto (a word you hear a lot out here these days), is tell Nora. What's a sister for if not to be there when you need her? So pick up the phone and call her, Clara. When she hears about this, she will run around her apartment for half an hour and then she will sit down and try to figure out how to help you. That's what happened three years ago when I went over to see her after she called about "your condition," as she coyly put it. Well, that was then, and depending on how you look at these things, we were fortunate to secure the services of Doc Holliday. As I told you then, he came highly recommended to me by people who encounter this problem from time to time. But I must tell you not to get your hopes up for the Doc, because the last I heard he was in jail.

I suppose I could make some phone calls to friends and see if anyone else is available, but as you can imagine, you take a terrible risk with some of these people. You have to be absolutely sure that they know what they are doing. I could try if you like, but I feel a little uneasy because I am so far away from things now. And anyway, are you sure that you want to go that route? Is keeping the child a possibility at all? Would the good citizens of Whitfield, Ontario, tolerate a schoolteacher who has a child out of wedlock?

You might also consider going away. Could you arrange a leave of absence and go to Toronto and have the child? Then give it up for adoption? I understand that the Salvation Army is very good about this kind of thing. They look after you in the final weeks and then find a good home for the baby. This happened to a girl I knew a few years ago. She put herself in their hands and things worked out very well. I really don't know what else to suggest, Clara. If it's a question of money, I'd be only too glad to help. But tell Nora. She'll want to know, and you owe it to yourself to tell her. Please stay in touch. I'll be thinking of you.

Love, Evelyn

P.S. If you really do want another abortion, I'll phone friends in New York and see what I can do, but I'm not too hopeful.

Tuesday, May 17

Sick this morning. Vomited copiously, as one ancient writer put it. Pepys? Boswell? De Quincey? Coleridge? Walked through the hours of this day as if in a dream. Milton in his office listening to the radio. Italy and France are close to war and he thinks Britain will be dragged in and us with them. He follows every turn of the screw over there and seems very excited by the possibility of war.

11:30 p.m.

When all is said and done, I have only three choices.

1. See Milton within the next few days and ask for a year off. Bad nerves and so on. He'll be flustered by the suggestion, but he might

go along to the board and plead my case. I will probably fool no one with this gambit. Go to Toronto or Hamilton or Timbuktu and talk to the Salvation Army. Find a place to live and some temporary work. What? Have the child and give it up for adoption. Return to the smirks and gossip and carry on with the rest of my life. Would the board rehire me? Surely they would have to if there were no proof of moral turpitude? What about the house? It would have to stand empty for a year; I couldn't bear the thought of someone else living in it, though the money would be useful.

2. Throw myself on Nora's mercy and see if she can arrange something in New York. Get it over with as soon as possible.
3. Declare my condition to this small world. It won't matter whom I tell because it will soon be widespread news. A match to dry grass, etc. I will almost certainly lose my job, and how then will I support myself? With Father's bonds, I probably have enough for a year or maybe two if I am very careful. Could move away, I suppose, but where to? Hate the thought of giving up my home, the house I love, my refuge . . . I will be vilified by many. There will perhaps be a few sympathetic voices: Joe Morrow, the Brydens, Marion (once she overcomes her astonishment), poor Helen Jackson, Milton(?).

Whitfield, Ontario
May 17, 1938

Dear Nora,
Please secure yourself in a chair and try not to scream as you read this. In plain words, I am pregnant again. Damn it and damn it again. I didn't mean for this to happen, but it has. I was foolish and careless and now I have to face the music. Don't we always? I'm not sure what to do about it. I should have written you before this, but I am so ashamed of my stupidity that I have simply spent the time stewing. Sorry to bear such news. As the saying goes, I am at a loss.

Clara

Saturday, May 21

Awakened before five o'clock and by six I was walking along the railway tracks. A fresh morning and sunlight low across the fields. A red-winged blackbird swaying on last year's cattail in a gully. It was nearly three years ago today and so I stood in the spot where it happened. Or where I think it happened. It could have been a few feet either way. Who can be absolutely certain in a field of grass? Where are you now, Charlie? Still careening through life with your wide-mouthed monkey grin, your hard, soiled hands and jokes? Still wreaking havoc on the lives of others? A man who deals in sorrow. Charlie, the griefmonger!

When I got home I thought of driving over to Linden to phone Nora. She would be home today, and she will not yet have received my letter. But I couldn't summon the heart to do it. "Why what a coward am I/ Who calls me fool," etc., etc.

Sunday, May 22

Marion and I went down to the asylum to visit Helen Jackson. Marion was abashed by the sight of the human wreckage around us; the frog woman especially fascinated and repelled her. "Golly, look at her" and so on. Helen Jackson was sitting on a bench under a tree reading a novel by Taylor Caldwell. She seemed distracted. Remarks came out of nowhere and were unconnected to anything. She said her husband would have visited today, but he must keep Saturdays free to prepare his sermons. The pale abstracted beauty of her face. The small hands clasping the book in her lap. A young woman appeared and stood leaning against a tree with her arms across her chest watching us. Cropped brown hair and startlingly angry eyes, a feral-looking creature on sturdy farm girl's legs. "That's Freda," Helen whispered. "Don't look her way." After a while, however, the girl approached and stood a few feet from us. Marion didn't know what to make of her and looked off instead at an old woman who was reciting the cardinal numbers over and over. Then the young woman said the most extraordinary thing; I have never heard anything like it in my life. And she said it to me. She said, "I'd like to suck your ___ forever and ever. Amen."

Helen looked up. "Now, Freda, please don't talk that way. These are friends of mine and they've come for a visit. They don't want to hear such things."

But the girl said it again, still looking at me before abruptly turning and walking away. It was very frightening and I wondered how anyone could be expected to recover her wits in such a place. On the way home, I let Marion talk. I scarcely listened, my ears still burning from that girl's venomous tongue.

Good news at last on the radio. France and Italy have come to some agreement and so it now looks as if there won't be war in Europe. Tomorrow is a holiday, thank goodness.

Saturday, May 28 (10:00 a.m.)

A harrowing sleepless night, but at four o'clock this morning I decided that I am going to keep the child. It was not yet daybreak but I could hear the robins. So I am going through with this. I am not going to have another New York experience. Fell asleep finally and didn't awaken until an hour ago.

(3:00 p.m.)

A special delivery letter from Nora who seems furious with me for being pregnant and without a telephone. Will write her tomorrow. All the urgency about what to do has now vanished. Time will take care of events. Feel much calmer, but good Lord, the difficulties ahead!

135 East 33rd Street
New York
May 25, 1938

Dear Clara,

By now you must surely realize how absolutely crazy it is for you not to have a telephone. We could have been dealing with this by now instead of fooling around with letters. I had thought of phoning the Brydens tonight, but I guess you don't want to talk about this in front of them. Well, at least you have a car now, so here is what I want you to do. I want you to drive over to Linden and *phone* me. Call after seven!!! I'm here every night reading over the script for the next day's show, so for heaven's sake, get in touch with me as soon as you get this. Then maybe we can deal with things in a sensible way. You know how important time is in these situations. How far along are you anyway? Is this the same guy as three years ago? If it is, the bastard ought to be locked up and castrated. If I'm talking about the man you love, Clara, I'm sorry, but I'm just very upset. I got your letter on top of a bad day. We have a new girl on the program and she's a perfect little bitch. And Les and I are now in the middle of something that started on the weekend. Christ, I wish I were married and just had three or four kids to worry about. Then I get a letter from my sister telling me that she's pregnant for the second time in three years. Really, Clara, don't you know anything about douching? Can this man of your dreams not afford rubbers? They may not be perfect but at least they are something. How could you be so careless after what we went through three years ago? To be honest, I don't know what to do at the moment. I phoned Evelyn, but she was still at the studio and they don't allow personal calls there. Maybe she can put us in touch with that "doctor" we had before. I need time to think about all this, Clara. Phone as soon as you get this letter. After seven! I'll be waiting.

Love, Nora

P.S. We'll work something out, I promise.

Whitfield, Ontario
Sunday, May 29, 1938

Dear Nora,

Received your letter yesterday and regret adding to your woes with my news. You're right to scold me for my carelessness, but this is not like the first time. Three years ago—I hope you are ready for this—I was raped. You are the only person who knows this.

Walking along the railway tracks, one Saturday afternoon that spring, I met two men (one of them simpleminded). These men had done some yardwork for me the day before, but it was sheer chance that they came upon me down by the tracks. I imagine that they were looking for a freight train to catch. In any case, they raped me (or one of them did, the other couldn't manage it, thank heaven). So that was that. You can understand now why I couldn't think of keeping a child from such an encounter.

This pregnancy is altogether different. It comes from "a moment of carelessness," true enough, but the man and I had been seeing each other for the better part of a year. It's the same man I wrote to you about last fall. I stopped seeing him for several months and then . . . well, obviously I saw him again, didn't I? And with obvious consequences. So now I have to deal with this and I will. I have thought of little else over the past month, and I wrote to you in a moment of panic when I seemed to be at my wit's end. I am over that now and in fact I feel quite calm. I have decided to keep this child, Nora.

Yes, yes, I can hear you. In many ways it is foolish and willful. I will almost certainly lose my job and whatever reputation I have ("Well, I know she's always been a bit odd, but this is perfectly scandalous," etc.). I thought of moving away, but where would I go? Anyway, I haven't the heart to leave. This is where I live and this is where I must raise this child. It will be difficult, and in years to come the child will have to put up with some ugly gossip. Still I feel that this is the best course. I intend to go through with it, Nora, so you may save your breath to cool your porridge, as Father used to say. And in case you're wondering, I am not interested in involving the man in any of this. He will never know. So there now. You have heard me out. Please try not to be too disappointed in me.

Clara

Monday, May 30 (6:10 a.m.)

Things That Must Be Done and Soon

1. See a doctor in Linden. There are, I think, four. Which one will be the least censorious? Perhaps ask Mrs. Bryden? Tell her the truth?
2. Talk to Milton this week. Hard to say how he will take this "remarkable" news. He will have to tell the board and they will be suitably outraged that one of their teachers, etc., etc.
3. See Bert Moore about Father's bonds. How much are they worth if redeemed, etc.
4. Work out a budget for the next twelve months. How much will I need to get by on? Must be frugal, but comfortable.

Friday, June 3

Confession is such a relief. The radio detectives are right when they are "grilling" their hoodlums under the spotlight. "Come on now, Spike, you'll feel a lot better if you spill the beans." And so this afternoon, I "spilled the beans" and in a way I do feel better. Trepidation, because I have now declared my condition but I feel better all the same.

Milton was in his office in shirtsleeves and braces. There were large sweat stains under his arms. I could smell the heat of the day on him. He never removes his suit coat until the children have left. Milton at fifty years of age behind his desk and I remember him as a nervous young man in the front room talking to Father. The summer of 1913. I was ten years old and I had come in when Nora said we had a visitor. I remember standing in the hallway listening to the murmur of voices from the front room. I was hoping that the new teacher would be tall and handsome, but Milton even then was stout and uncommonly plain and already married to his Agnes. Over the years, we have never said much to one another that didn't have to do with the school. We have always talked about this pupil or that pupil, and in fact we don't know one another all that well. In a way, I am still Ed Callan's daughter to him.

Milton was reading yesterday's *Herald* and looked up when I appeared in the doorway. He was too polite to ask what I wanted and so I began.

"Milton," I said, "I have some news which may startle you."

He took off his glasses to polish them with his handkerchief. I have seen him do that a thousand times while he gathers his thoughts. "Now don't tell me, Clara, that you're going to leave after all these years. You're not going to go off and get married on me, are you? I've heard there's a fellow in your life these days. Down in Toronto, is he?" He settled the glasses back into place.

"It's not quite like that, Milton," I said.

"Is that so? I'd hate to lose you, Clara. We get along pretty well, don't we? All these years together. I think highly of you as a teacher. I hope you realize that."

"I'm pregnant, Milton," I said. "I'm going to have a child, probably next January."

Milton looked down at the *Herald*, his neck reddening. "Well, well, well. Now that is something, isn't it?"

"I realize how awkward this is for you and I'm sorry, but you have to know sooner or later."

"Of course I do, of course I do. You bet I do." The poor man couldn't meet my eyes and continued to stare down at his newspaper. "My goodness, pregnant! And are you getting married then, Clara?" He looked up at me.

"No," I replied. "That's out of the question. The father of the child is already married."

Poor Milton. The glasses plucked off again. "Well, well, that is something now, isn't it?"

"Yes, it is and it must be dealt with."

"Of course it must. You're absolutely right. Goodness gracious, Clara, pregnant!"

He was about to say something else, but stopped. Then after a moment he said, "It's going to be hard on you. In the village, I mean."

"I suppose it will be, but I think I can manage that."

"Of course you can manage it. I know you can."

"I don't suppose there is much chance of my staying on once this is known."

Milton looked so glum that I wanted to tell him not to worry about it. Then he said, "Well, if it were up to me, you could certainly count on it, Clara. But the board? I foresee a problem there."

"I do too," I said. "Actually, I'm not counting on it. I just wanted you to know about this. You are the first person in the village to know."

Milton seemed touched and gave me a weak smile. "Well, thank you, Clara, for telling me. I wouldn't have expected anything but the straight goods from you. I'll speak on your behalf. I'll do my best for you."

There was nothing more to say, and after an awkward moment of silence we shook hands. I still don't know why.

Saturday, June 4 (9:30 a.m.)

I have just told Mrs. Bryden. I called her in from the garden where she was weeding her lettuce patch. We sat at the kitchen table and she cried a little. "Oh, Clara!" I asked her about a doctor. They go to a man over in Linden named Murdoch, but she thinks someone younger and less set in his ways might be better for me. There is a Dr. Miller who has just started a practice with Murdoch and she is going to make an appointment for me next week.

To Linden this afternoon to see the doctor. I had an appointment with Miller, but just as I arrived he was hurrying out the door with his raincoat and black bag. Miller is younger than I am and handsome enough to be in the movies. He will make many a female heart flutter. But he was quickly on his way, and I watched through the window as he climbed into his car. The nurse told me that he was off to a farm east of the town to deliver a baby that wasn't expected until next week. Oddly enough I was the only patient in the waiting room on this dark thundery afternoon. Then the nurse said, "If you'd like, I can ask Dr. Murdoch to look at you. You've come all the way in from Whitfield."

Just then Murdoch came out of his office, a tall, spare and severe-looking Scot. About sixty. Wiry eyebrows. An old man used to getting his way and impatient with the folly of this world. It was all there in his face. Father saw him once years ago, but didn't like his manner. He and the nurse began to talk about a patient who was coming in at five o'clock and then she began to whisper, and I knew she was referring to me, for Murdoch kept looking across the room. Finally he said, "I can see you today if you like. Miller is probably going to be out there for a while. You've come in from Whitfield?"

"Yes," I said.

"Come along then."

And so I got Murdoch instead of Miller, which will be fine; I don't think he is as difficult as he would like people to believe. He asked me how old I was and when I told him I would be thirty-five in another two weeks, the wiry eyebrows were raised and he said, "And this is your first, Mrs. Callan?"

"Yes," I said, and just then we heard an enormous clap of thunder and the lights dimmed. A warning from the heavens about mendacity? I had to set Murdoch straight.

"It's Miss Callan," I said.

The long stern face regarded me not unkindly, I thought. "I see."

We could hear the downpour. Gusts of wind were pushing the rain against the windows. It had also been raining that night in New York three years ago when the other "doctor" had stood over me preparing to scrape away the life within. Now I felt Murdoch's large finger in me. "Sometimes," he said, "having the first one at your age can be a problem, but you seem healthy enough, so I wouldn't worry."

When he finished he said, "I'll tell Miller that I've looked at you and you can make an appointment with the nurse to see him next month."

"If you don't mind," I said, "I'd like to come back and see you."

He was rinsing his hands at a basin. "As you wish. About this time next month. Try not to do too much in this heat. You're not married then? Do you work at something?"

"I teach school."

He came back toward me, drying his hands. "Well that will soon be over for the summer, won't it? Just put your feet up and take it easy. We'll get you through this."

135 East 33rd Street
New York
June 4, 1938

Dear Clara,
I'm so sorry for my last letter which must have struck you as awfully hurtful and cruel. I just feel terrible about it. Why in heaven's name didn't you tell me about those men three years ago? They might have been caught if you had told someone, though I suppose your name would have been dragged through the mud and everything. Still it seems so wrong they got off scot-free after doing something like that. Oh, Clara, what a thing to go through all by yourself!!!

As you say in your letter, this is very different. I'd ask you to come down and stay with me, but it just gets so hot here in the summer and you'd probably be uncomfortable. How are you feeling anyway? Isn't it funny how I am the one who always wanted to have a baby and here you are, about to be a mother. I guess it's my lot in life to be an aunt. Is there anything I can do for you at the moment? Do you need anything? I'll try to get up to see you this summer, probably in late August. Sorry again about my last letter. If only I'd had some idea. I just can't imagine how you lived through all that on your own.

Love, Nora

Sunday, June 12

Miss Callan's condition is now known to all and sundry. Whose tongue wagged? Mrs. Bryden's? Milton's? Who knows and what does it matter? Sooner or later it had to happen. In a way it's a relief; people can now get their fill of staring and talking. In the fullness of time they will turn to other things. Marion came by after church brimming with questions, though at first she was too wary and shy to ask outright. She sat in the rocker on the veranda in her Sunday dress and white gloves, the big hymnal in her lap. I tormented her a little.

"You look ready to explode, Marion. Have you been hearing things? What's the news on the church steps this morning?"

"Oh, Clara, is it true?"

"Why yes," I said. "It's true. I'm going to have a child. Probably late December or early January."

The look on Marion's face. That such things should come to pass! "Clara, what are you going to do?"

"Why I'm going to get on with my life, Marion. What else can I do?"

A few moments to consider that weighty resolution. Then, "Golly, Clara, a baby. Imagine!"

We both sat looking out at Church Street on this early summer day at noontide. Imagining.

Monday, June 13

My pupils do not seem particularly intrigued by my predicament. They were as usual bent across their scribblers and readers. Perhaps they have not been told yet. In the hallway, a few (from the entrance class) cast sidelong glances my way.

4880 Barton Street
Hollywood, California
5/6/38

Dear Clara,

Nora phoned last night with her news. So you are going to keep the child! What a brave soul you are! It won't be easy, of course, but you do have folks in your corner. Your sister, for one. She was so excited when she told me. I feel the same way, and I insist on being called Aunt Evelyn. I think it suits me now that I am beginning to take on a rather ample matronly look. I waddle around out here, a pale old thing among all these tanned sybarites. Anyway, I hope you are looking after yourself so you can deliver a big healthy baby that Nora and I can take turns spoiling.

Life out here takes some getting used to, but it's not so bad. I bought a car the other day from a shifty-looking character. I hope he didn't skin me. It's a secondhand Chrysler convertible. Cream-colored. Very sporty. I have to report that it's a pleasure to get into this thing in the morning and drive to the studio. I now feel like a true Californian, off my feet and moving on four wheels. On Sundays I drive over to Santa Monica or down to Ocean Park with Fred who tells me stories of the stars and their peculiar sexual alliances and preferences. Oh, if only the great public knew! As galley slaves, Fred and I spend a lot of time together, and we've become great pals. He is a funny bitter fellow, a natural storyteller who, like me, has a weakness for the bottle. I find myself in the unnatural role of playing mother hen to him, warning him about the excesses of drink and so on. Still it doesn't stop him from bringing along a bottle of vodka on our Sunday excursions.

My Nancy Brown stuff is now about ready to go. Mr. M. seemed to like the first script, and they are hoping that it will be as successful as the Hardy series. They are now looking for the girl to play Nancy. They want someone like Deanna Durbin, but she had a fight sometime back with the studio and apparently hates MGM. We're looking for someone cute and sexy, but not too sexy. The young American girl. I suggested this kid Garland who is in the latest Hardy.

Anyway, that's what I'm doing. Toiling and spinning out here in the Yarn Factory (another of Fred's locutions). Keep in touch and eat plenty of vegetables or whatever it is mothers-to-be are supposed to eat.

Love, Evelyn

Friday, June 24

It's been so hot and dry for the past few weeks that everything is parched. Summer has just officially begun, but already the gardens are burned up and the lawns are as brown as August. Today was the last day of school and the children gave me an illustrated New Testament. Did one of their parents have a hand in the selection of this gift? Hoping perhaps to reclaim me from my apostasy or, at the very least, provide me with a measure of moral instruction.

As the children said goodbye, the girls gave me shy, interested looks. They now know that I am going to have a child next winter, and in their own secret, little ways they are fascinated by the mystery of it all. One day they too hope to have babies, but not, of course, until after the white gown and the procession up the aisle on that distant, magical day. The boys don't know what to make of me and so it was just "Goodbye, Miss Callan," and they were running into the afternoon and all the afternoons of the summer that lie before them. From the open window in my classroom, I could hear their shouts and laughter.

As I was leafing through the Testament with its timorous-looking Christ standing by a door and beckoning to the reader, "Seek and ye shall find. Knock and it shall be opened unto you," Milton came into the room. The weather had got to him and his face was enflamed and glistening from prickly heat. He looked ill at ease and out of sorts. "Whew! You could have used a fan in here, Clara. I should have got you one." Walking across the room he stood by the open window, jingling the change in his pants and looking out at the bare dry schoolyard and the empty ball diamond. "How are you feeling anyway?" he asked.

"Actually, I'm feeling fine, Milton," I said. I was waiting for him to tell me what I already knew but he was having a difficult time. Finally, however, he got it out.

"Well, the board had a meeting last night over in Linden. Of course I spoke up for you, Clara. I did my best. I told them you had been a teacher in this school for sixteen years and your father was here before you." Milton shook his big plain head as though the perversity of his fellow humans was beyond his comprehension. "Those fellows can be so set in their ways. That Jack Morrison. I tell you, Clara, he's a corker. That man hasn't got an ounce of pity in him."

I didn't bother telling Milton that I want no one's pity, least of all some lawyer's in Linden. I told him instead that I understood how he had done his best for me and I appreciated that, but I couldn't see how the board had much choice. How would it look to have an unmarried woman with a child teaching in one of their schools? There would be a litany of complaints from parents. They had to get rid of me.

"I hope we can remain friends, Clara."

"Of course we can, Milton."

"If there's anything I can do."

I shook the warm moist hand and got him talking about Sparrow Lake. This time next week he will be at his cottage, and Clara Callan's embarrassing condition will only be an uncomfortable memory that will recede with each passing day.

After he left I packed up my things and took them out to the car: two boxes of books and papers, my window plants. I left the large brown teapot in the little kitchen. Father bought it years ago, but I have no use for it. I said goodbye to Jimmy Burke who was sweeping the halls and closed the door that I have entered nearly every day of my life for the past thirty years. I was holding Father's hand the first time; a warm September day. The year was 1909 and I was six years old.

Monday, June 27

Relief at last from this heat wave. Rain all weekend and now it is clear and fresh with a strong wind scattering fragments of cloud southward. A wonderful freshness in the air. The gardens and lawns have revived. Helen Jackson is back home. On Saturday morning I watched her husband help her from the car and into the house. I would visit her, but I dislike that man so much that I am afraid of running into him. Letter today from Nora.

135 East 33rd Street
New York
June 20, 1938

Dear Clara,
How are things with you? Is the heat wave up there too? New York is murder right now. It has been over ninety every day for the past week. The only place you can escape is the movies. Sometimes I go out right after supper and catch the first show. Even with the fans, my apartment is almost unbearable.

Well, we sure aren't having much luck with men, are we? Yesterday Les took me to Romanoff's for lunch. I thought something was up because it's a pretty fancy place and he doesn't usually splurge like that. And it turned out to be one of those lunches that remind you of that Cole Porter song "It Was Just One of Those Things." Of course, I knew it was coming sooner or later, but I didn't expect him to be leaving town. It turns out he's accepted a new job as staff announcer at a Chicago station. That's probably why we went to Chicago a couple of months ago though Lover Boy didn't tell me at the time. Anyway, he's leaving at the end of July and he's hoping that he and Miriam can start all over in a new place. Well, good luck to her is all I can say. I don't think it will be long before he finds himself a new dolly out there. Anyway, that's it and I guess I'm not really so heartbroken. I had been kind of expecting something like this for the past little while. The truth is we haven't been hitting it off on all cylinders since about Christmas, so maybe it's for the best.

I wouldn't have minded so much. It was a great lunch and Romanoff's is air-cooled. I could have stayed in there all afternoon. But here's the thing. After lunch we're standing out on Forty-second Street in this godawful heat and Mr. Wonderful suggested we go back to my place just once more "for old times' sake." The guy tells me we're washed up, and then he wants to go to bed with me one more time. What a nerve! I told him to go home and park it in his wife where it belongs anyway. I wish he were leaving for Chicago tomorrow because I'm going to have to stare at him across the microphone for the next six weeks. Oh well! I'll live through it, but really, Clara, why can't either of us find a decent guy who isn't already spoken for?

I've talked the producer into writing me out of the show for a few days, and so I can come up to see you this summer. How about Labor Day weekend? Can you drop me a line and confirm? I hope you've seen a doctor by now. Have you told anyone? I can just imagine the tongues wagging around Whitfield by now. It must be awful just walking down the street and knowing all those eyes are on you. But, I'm proud of you and I mean it. Did you know that right now your baby is approximately two inches long? I found this out in a book I'm sending you for your birthday (Happy Birthday, by the way). It's called *The Complete New Mother's Guide to a Healthy Baby* and it has all kinds of information on what to eat and what to expect over the next few months. It's fascinating what happens to your body when you're having a baby. I really had no idea.

You may think this is nonsense, Clara, but in a way I envy you. Let me know how you are getting along, okay?

Love, Nora

Whitfield, Ontario
Friday, July 1, 1938

Dear Nora,

Thanks for the book, which arrived yesterday. It must have cost a fortune to mail this tome, but I appreciate the thought. As you said, it has all kinds of information that I didn't know I needed to have. Rest assured that I am taking care of myself. I really don't feel that different yet, though I'm beginning to grow "quite the little bosom." I tend to get a bit tired so I sleep in later. Now, at first light, I just roll over and doze for another hour or so. I feel entitled to indulge myself like this. I've never paid much attention to my body. I've always regarded it as something that gets me around, but now I suppose I'm thinking of this child too, and so I am more conscious of being a living "body." I have a good appetite and that morning nausea seems to be over, thank goodness. Yes, I do have a doctor, and I am going to see him again in a couple of weeks. Murdoch is an elderly Scot and seems to have that nationality's dour and stern manner. But I like him. He's a no-nonsense fellow. I was supposed to see this new man (handsome as a movie star), but he happened to be out on the day I went, and so I had to make do with Murdoch. But as I said, he's fine. I'll stick with him.

Now that the heat wave has passed, I am enjoying the summer. It must have been awful last month down in New York; it was bad enough up here; the gardens and lawns were in ruins and are only now beginning to recover after some good rains.

I have gone back to the piano. I got away from it for a while. Spent too much time listening to that pernicious radio of yours. It does seduce us in our idle hours. But now I am thinking that I may teach this child to play the piano. I doubt whether I'll be able to afford lessons. Perhaps playing the piano is no longer as important in a youngster's life as it used to be. When we were young, so many girls wanted to play. Still it is an accomplishment. If I have a boy, I still think I will teach him. He will probably play jazz music instead of Schubert, but that will be all right too. When I am an old woman, he can bring in his friends for a night of jazz music while I sit in the corner. He will have to have some qualities or gifts to attract friends. If he takes after me, I can't imagine that he will be athletic. But perhaps he will inherit some of his Aunt Nora's athleticism. Do you remember how you used to play softball and hockey with the boys when you were eleven or twelve? And how I used to sneer at you for this! Now I believe that I secretly envied you, for I was so clumsy as a child. I still am for that matter.

I am sorry to hear that you and your friend have parted ways but perhaps it's for the best. We've both been down that road and so we both know what's at the end of it. There comes a day when it's all over. It's a story that has to end badly, isn't it? Men must return to their wives, Nora; it is the way of the world. And we must—let me turn that into a humble little couplet:

Men must return to their wives,
and we must get on with our lives.

A little lame, I admit, but it might be a useful reminder if we were to dress it up through handicraft: hand-stitched on fabric, and nicely framed to hang upon the kitchen wall next to the dairy calendar.

It's Dominion Day and there is hardly a soul to be seen in the village. Many have gone over to Linden for the parade this afternoon. The Premier will be there, I am told. Others have gone to their cottages for the weekend. Marion and her parents left for Sparrow Lake yesterday and I already miss her. It's so odd because she was getting on my nerves. Since she's learned of "my condition," she's been over nearly every day fussing about me and asking whether she can do anything.

Of course she means well, but at times I felt I was quite prepared to take her by the throat and kill her for her kindness. Yet now, knowing that I won't see her for six weeks, I miss her. What an impossible person I am! Well, in any case, you mustn't worry about me, Nora. I intend to take good care of myself. Thanks again for the book.

Clara

P.S. I will look forward to seeing you on Labor Day weekend.

Thursday, July 14

A visit to Murdoch who weighed and measured, and poked and prodded. The peculiar medicinal smell of him and the immaculate part in his gray hair as he bent across me. What an odd way for a man to make his living! Feeling the privates of a virtual stranger and peering into unlikely orifices! All in a day's work, of course, and thank goodness for those who are prepared to spend their working hours doing such things. I appear to be in good health. Murdoch, stern of mien (as old-fashioned authors used to describe such types) is a man of few words, but at the end of his examination he did lay a hand on my shoulder and said not unkindly, "Now, Miss, you are going to be just fine." His words made me feel like a young girl. Briefly.

At the library I took out *The Scarlet Letter*. I tried to read this when I was fifteen or sixteen, but it defeated me. Perhaps now Hawthorne's genius will shine through all the verbiage. Twenty years ago I found him a terrible old windbag. Now that I can truly identify with poor Hester however . . .

Saturday, July 16

A bad day. Two letters, one confirming the consequences of my moral turpitude, and the other, a rancid denunciation of my character. Written in pencil, badly spelled and, of course, anonymous.

Dear Miss Uppity,

Well it looks like youve been foundout doesn't it. Maybe this will teach you not to give yourselff such airs in this village. There are plenty of us around who are just as good as you and arent to snooty to say hello on the street. Just because your father was principle of the school and your sister is a bigshot on the radio in New York dont mean your so hot. There are plenty of people in Whitfield who think you have no business near there children. There are places for the likes of you down in the city so why dont you just get on your high horse and skeddadle down there where you belong. Im speaking for lots of folks in this village. You always thought yourselff so high and mightyt didn't you. Well it turns out your just baggage.

Morrison, Evans and Ross
Barristers and Solicitors
29 King Street
Linden, Ontario

July 14, 1938

Miss C. Callan
48 Church Street
Whitfield, Ontario

Dear Miss Callan:

At a meeting of the Board of Trustees for Whitfield Township Schools on Wednesday evening, July 13, it was decided not to renew your contract for the coming school year. As Chairman, it is my duty to inform you that your services will no longer be required as a classroom teacher at the Continuation School in Whitfield. Your salary will, of course, be paid until the end of August. On behalf of the Board, I thank you for services rendered over the past several years.

Yours truly,
John H. Morrison

Whitfield, Ontario
Monday, July 18, 1938

Dear Evelyn,

Forgive a dilatory correspondent. It must be six weeks since I received your last letter and I have no excuse for not writing before this other than laziness. These days I am quite idle, rising late and frittering away the hours playing the piano and reading poison pen letters. Actually I have only received one, though one is enough, thank you very much. I am thinking of framing it and placing it over the mantel in the dining room. I think it would make an interesting conversation starter with dinner guests. If I ever had any dinner guests!

I have been to the doctor, a surly old Scot in the nearby town of Linden. I drive over there once a month and he pokes and prods me; apparently I am as healthy as any of the young mares he sees in the course of his daily rounds. This is a farming community, Evelyn, and we are apt to use rustic imagery. Curiously enough, I am happy. Or to be more precise, as happy as someone with my temperament can be. Some mornings I awaken and for a few seconds forget what has happened. Life will just go on as it has in the past; then, of course, I say to myself, Well, it won't because I am pregnant and in a few months I will have a child to look after and live with. Then I begin to feel a bit overwhelmed by it all and this might last a minute or two. I lie there feeling stupidly sorry for myself, perplexed and anxious about everything that lies ahead. My life is certainly veering in a new direction. How will that work itself out? I don't know yet. How could I? Yet it is exciting and makes me almost happy. I suppose I am like someone who is embarking on a mysterious adventure and feels fearful yet exhilarated. I'm afraid I haven't described my state of mind very well, but it's the best I can do on this summer afternoon with only the cicadas and the rattle of a neighbor's lawn mower to disturb the drowsy peace.

Your Hollywood sounds fascinating. Can you tell me more about it? Do you see any famous movie stars? If you have a few moments in your glamorous life, I would love to hear from you.

Clara

Saturday, July 23

What thoughts course through my mind and at unlikely hours! At seven o'clock this morning I was cleaning the windows in Father's room, watching the sunlight pour across the backyard onto the Brydens' garden. Mr. Bryden was hoeing his potato hills. In an old suit coat and with a straw hat on his head, he was whistling "Yours Is My Heart Alone." An elderly man in his garden on a summer morning and I thought of his words about Mother; about how all the young men in the village had envied Father when he married her. Father used to say that after they were married they sometimes went dancing with the Brydens at the Orange Hall in Linden.

I like to imagine them returning from such evenings, pausing to say good night down there in the driveway, then entering these houses. Two young couples climbing the stairs to their bedrooms, the scent of lilacs through a screen and moonlight spilling across the bedroom floors. Hanging up suit coats and dresses in closets, unfastening braces and straps and pulling on nightclothes. Climbing into bed. It must have been something like that. The elderly man now hoeing his garden and whistling was once young; he must have been caught up on some long-ago summer night in all the erotic commotion, the tangled, frantic embraces of love. Naked. Splayed and thrusting. What thoughts for a mother-to-be who is washing windows at seven o'clock in the morning!

4880 Barton Street
Hollywood, California
26/7/38

Dear Clara,

Glamorous life! You bet! In my cell at Mr. Mayer's workshop. As I may have said before, I am a well-paid slave out here among the comely lasses and handsome lads and men with hairy brown arms in short-sleeve shirts who smoke cigars. The reek of cigar smoke out here is as dense as the mimosa in the evening. Well, it now looks as if this damn serial that I have concocted is going to go into production in the fall. Mr. M. seems to like my portrait of ideal family life, and so we'll be inflicting this on the public in another few months. We are still looking for the ideal girl to play our pert Miss Brown. The Garland kid would be ideal, but she is not available. They want her for the lead in a picture based on Frank Baum's *The Wonderful Wizard of Oz*, which they are hoping to shoot in September.

You want a glimpse of my "glamorous world"? Sometimes they allow us to unchain ourselves and go to the bathroom. Or stand by a window and stretch the muscles of an aching back. So the other morning I witnessed two scenes which will give you some idea of the contrasts in my world. I saw both through the bars of my garret window.

Scene One

Ten o'clock in the a.m. and a certain Mr. Big's Cadillac drives into the lot. Several flunkies get out and then Mr. Big emerges, all five feet two of him in a cream-colored suit, two-toned shoes, cigar, of course. Then from the side of our building comes this young woman, a delicious-looking blonde (she works on the third floor as a stenographer or typist), and approaches Mr. Big. She is obviously upset and there is a flurry of something going on. Flunkies move in and surround her. Hustle her into the big car which drives away while little Mr. Big adjusts his necktie and disappears below me. Now what do you imagine has happened? So, not a good day for the pretty typist.

Scene Two

An hour later on this morning of sunshine and orange juice, and who is crossing the lot under my window but Rooney and Garland, our mythical American kids. He is making her laugh with some of his antics. He is a brash little guy, but he can sure make the girls laugh. So there you have it! Heartache and success and all within footsteps of one another. As Fred keeps reminding me in that sensible Midwestern tone of his, the currency out here isn't money, it's dreams. Wonderful fantastic dreams of seeing your name in lights and being worshiped in darkened theaters across the country by millions of adoring fans. I find this perfectly acceptable, by the way, because I am a tough old broad and illusions and fakery don't bother me in the least. It's what we're all about. Working all those years in radio taught me that. And when I stand in front of the cashier's cage on Fridays and receive my check, I feel that I am not only being handsomely rewarded, but I am also doing my bit to keep my fellow citizens permanently inoculated against the ugly realities of life (and death). It is possible therefore to see myself as someone who is performing a kind of civic duty.

I must also tell you a little about my social life which up to this point had been somewhat sparse. Now, however, it shows signs of promise. Fred, who I discovered to my delight is another incorrigible invert, has taken me to a couple of parties and I met an interesting woman the other night. Now, my dear, I don't like to drop names, but she happens to be Aldous Huxley's wife. Do you know Huxley's books at all? *Antic Hay*, *Point Counter Point*, *Brave New World*? He is a Britisher who is out here for the money. As are we all, of course. His wife Maria is European, French or maybe Belgian, though she has an English accent. Anyway, she was very nice to me and, as it turns out, we happen to share similar tastes. She has promised to introduce me to some friends, and so at last I may actually have some fun out here. After all, that's one of the reasons I emigrated to this benighted state.

I'm glad to learn that you are coping so well with your "situation." By all means, frame and hang that letter by your mantel. Then invite your fellow citizens in to see what kind of homespun neighborliness exists in hamlets like yours.

Your sister phones once a week to give me all the news from New York. As I'm sure you know by now, she has broken up with Les Cunningham who is going off to Chicago. I think that's for the best. I wish Nora could find a decent feller and settle into family life. It's what she really wants. The problem is she has lousy taste in men. Well, I should talk? I have lousy taste in women. Maybe our luck will change. Maybe everybody's luck will change! Let's hope.

Love and luck, Evelyn

135 East 33rd Street
New York
Sunday, July 31, 1938

Dear Clara,

I have some wonderful news and it couldn't have come at a better time. Last Thursday we had a going-away party for Les, and I know it's over between us, but I couldn't help being a little blue about things and so I had a let-down there in the studio. Had to go into the ladies' for a damn good cry and then was so horrified by how I looked that I left early. I went home and was moping around the apartment when I got this phone call from Harry Benton, a producer at CBS. They are planning a new dramatic series for the fall called "American Playhouse on the Air." They are going to dramatize "classic" American novels. Full network on Sunday nights. Benton said he liked the sound of my voice and would I be interested in reading for the part of Aunt Polly in their first production of *Huckleberry Finn*. Would I?

It's just what the doctor ordered. Not only to take my mind off Les, but also for my career. I love "Chestnut Street," but it does get a little tedious day after day and this would make an exciting change. And who knows, it could lead to other things! Of course, I have to clear all this with the agency, but I don't think there will be a problem. Sometimes they are fussy about people on their shows taking on other roles, but this will be an evening program and a different audience. I think I can persuade them to give me a chance. Wish me luck, okay?

Marjorie has written me out of "Chestnut Street" for a few days, and so I'll be able to come up and see you on Labor Day weekend. I'm leaving on Thursday evening's train. Don't bother driving into the city to pick me up. It will be so busy with the Ex on. I'll catch the afternoon train to Whitfield. I hope you are taking good care of yourself.

Love, Nora

Wednesday, August 10

Turmoil in Murdoch's waiting room this afternoon just as I was leaving. Three men and a boy, country people in overalls and work shirts, had come into the room. The boy was clutching a blood-soaked towel, his eyes dulled with pain. He was helped to a chair by one of the men who looked like an older brother. The oldest (father? grandfather?) was apologetic for all the fuss and inconvenience. Shrugging at Murdoch. "He lost his hand. We were sawin' firewood."

Murdoch was already reddening with rage. "Why didn't you take him to the hospital, you damn fool? Where's the hand?"

The man shrugged again. "There's no use to it now, is there?" His face and neck were as brown as leather, a tough sinewy old man inside the baggy overalls.

"Get him into my office, for God's sake!" said Murdoch and the other two helped the boy through the doorway. I thought of Frost's poem about the youngster who lost a hand on a sawing machine.

In the library I saw Ella Myles holding an armful of books. So at least she was still reading. She had obviously heard the news about me and tried not to stare, but I could see it was difficult by the wary look she gave me. When I approached her, we talked only briefly; she asked me no questions but merely answered my inquiries about her. I was disappointed to see that all her books were romance novels. A sullen prettiness lingers in Ella's face, but she has coarsened since I last saw her; there's a pale slatternly look to her now. She told me she candles eggs at the creamery and boards with a family in Linden. She still sees the Kray boy and they are planning to marry next spring. As far as I could tell, she has at least managed to stay "unpregnant."

Sunday, August 21

Marion has returned from her summer at the cottage and today she came by. Filled with questions about my state. Almost childlike in her curiosity. What does it feel like to have a baby inside me? Do I think it will be a boy or a girl? Have I thought of any names? If it's a boy, Marion would favor the name Lionel. Lionel? After she left I listened to the news. Trouble stirring again in Europe with Hitler now claiming that part of Czechoslovakia's western frontier belongs to Germany. The man seems to have Europe in some kind of trance.

Wednesday, August 31

This afternoon I met the new teacher, Miss Bodnar, who comes from somewhere north of Linden. She is just out of Normal School and the board probably hired her for a pittance. No more than nineteen or twenty, with a fresh, attractive face and a head of blond curls. She managed to conceal whatever scorn or pity she may have felt and said the usual things one expects in these circumstances. "I've heard so many good things about you, Miss Callan. Everyone I've talked to has told me what a good teacher you were." Milton's jowly face was mottled with embarrassment. It's a burden to cause such distress in others. Miss Bodnar is a winsome little creature and the children will like her, though some of the rougher boys may take advantage.

Tuesday, September 6

A warm September morning and I am sitting on the veranda with this notebook in my lap. I can hear the cries of the children in the schoolyard at recess. Two hours ago I drove Nora to the train station and now the house is quiet again. Nora was up before me this morning, sitting at the dresser, preparing her face for the hours ahead. She has changed in small but important ways. She never used to fuss about time; she was nearly always late for everything. Now she is a model of precision; the radio business has taught her to be punctual. She wears an expensive-looking wristwatch and has a little alarm clock to awaken her. She looked smart this morning as she came out of the house in her navy blue suit and white gloves, a string of pearls encircling her throat. She has managed to stay pretty into her thirties, though it seems to take a great deal of work; she carries such a store of lotions and creams with her when she travels.

She arrived on Friday laden with gifts for the baby: clothes, toys, another book on child-rearing. Nora's generous spirit has always puzzled me; she must have inherited it from our mother because Father was always close with money and so am I. Yesterday after a cocktail Nora finally summoned the nerve to ask me about F. "Now Clara, you really must tell me. Will there be no help from the father with any of this? Did he just leave you in the lurch, or doesn't he even know about it?"

"He doesn't know," I said.

This required another drink and Nora busied herself with its making. "It's so like you," she said, pouring a measure of gin into her glass. "I can just see you walking away from him. Too proud to ask for help. Brother, I would have let him know in a hurry."

"It has nothing to do with pride," I said, but I wonder now if that is true.

We were sitting in the front room and I had put on a recording of Rubinstein playing the G-flat Impromptu. The window was open to the late summer afternoon. Nora asked me if I still loved him.

"I don't know," I said. I was thinking of Saturday afternoons in that motor court by the lake. The cry of the gulls beyond the open window. The slippery heat of our bodies and the pale skin beneath F.'s ribs. Had I loved him outside that bed? I couldn't say for certain. Perhaps at one time I thought I did. Now I am not so sure. Our time together? There wasn't much of it beyond half-eaten dinners in hotel dining rooms and brief afternoons behind venetian blinds. It was all calculating and devious on both our parts.

"You're thinking of him right now, aren't you?" said Nora.

"Yes," I said. "I suppose I am."

"I'll bet you still love him."

"I don't know much about love, Nora," I said. "Certainly I knew from the beginning that none of it could lead anywhere. A married man and a Catholic? Still I carried on, didn't I? When you ignore reality and carry on as if the world will never end, well, perhaps that's one definition of love. I sometimes wonder if it was like that for the woman in Rome. I know I envied the look on her face that day. I think I wanted to look as she did, at least once before I got old."

"What on earth are you talking about?" Nora asked. "What woman in Rome?"

"Don't you remember? She was a guide in Keats's house. Tall and plain, even homely, but she had this handsome lover. We watched them go off together on his bicycle one afternoon and she looked so happy. How I envied her! It was the day Lewis got into trouble with the police."

Nora shook her head. "The things you notice, Clara! I don't remember any homely woman on a bicycle with a man." She seemed irritated with my peculiarities, and so we sat without talking for a few moments, listening to Schubert. After a while, I got up to turn over the recording. Nora was not, however, ready to leave things alone and so she asked me how it had all ended. Had there been a quarrel? A scene?

"No," I said. "Neither of us is the quarreling type. A scene would have been embarrassing to both of us. There was another woman."

"What a heel!" said Nora, emptying her glass. "Lewis was like that. There were always other women. Right from the start. But if I had got pregnant, he would have known about it and fast. He would have helped too. We talked about all that, and so we were always pretty careful. You have to have some ground rules if you are going to have a love affair, Clara."

I sensed that Nora wanted to give me a good scolding for my careless ways, perhaps to pay me back for all the high-handed lectures I had inflicted upon her when we were girls and quarreling in our bedroom. I always seemed to have the upper hand then. Now I couldn't help myself; I wanted to tell her about those grainy photographs in the hotel room.

"You would never have guessed it to look at him," I said, "but there was another side to Frank. He showed me some pictures once." Nora looked at me sharply. She was a little tight by then.

"What kind of pictures?"

"Pictures of two women and a man," I said. "They were doing things to him. Sex things. I suppose he meant it as a stimulant. As a . . ."

I couldn't think of the word then, though it comes easily enough to me now. *Aphrodisiac.* I went on to say that the pictures had only made me feel a bit sordid. In a way, I wanted to explore all this with her. Was I being prudish to feel shame as I did? Was a woman supposed to be excited by pictures like that? I wanted to know such things.

"Lewis was like that," Nora said. "He took me to a sex show once.

It was in the middle of the night up in Harlem. Colored people were actually copulating. A man carried a woman across the stage on his thing. She hung onto him with her legs around his waist and had a climax right there in front of us. Or she faked it. I think she faked it. How could you have something like that in front of a roomful of strangers?" Nora still seemed bemused by this episode in her life and suddenly I began to laugh.

"What's so funny?" she asked.

"I was just thinking," I said, "of what you told me and how strange it is to be saying such things in this house. Have such words ever been uttered within these walls? If Father could hear us now!"

Nora too began to laugh. "Good Lord! What would the poor man think of us?"

I was trying to arrange it all in my mind: the light glancing off the leaves beyond the window; the Negro man and woman clinging to each other on a stage in Harlem; the fingers of Rubinstein on the keyboard in the recording studio; the sunlight on the rear fender of my little blue Chevrolet in the driveway. For a moment, I was captured by this bounty of images, offered up to my senses on an ordinary Monday afternoon. And I was grateful for them all. Ahead lay money worries and the averted eyes of my neighbors, my own dreadful uncertainty. Yet at that moment yesterday I was entirely happy.

Whitfield, Ontario
Saturday, September 10, 1938

Dear Evelyn,

It is cool and showery in my part of the world, a perfect afternoon for writing a letter, though I can't pretend to bear eventful tidings. I am leading a life of exemplary idleness these days, reading and nodding off as I read, my body ripening like the swelling gourd (image provided by Keats whose *Ode to Autumn* I have just been reading). My life is indeed languorous. Like an old woman I doze in my rocking chair, or stand by the stove eating tapioca from the pot. Most afternoons I manage to bestir myself, and walk the plank to buy my bread and butter under the stares of the townsfolk. Perhaps I exaggerate a little; by now most people are used to seeing me "in my condition" and only the truly morbid gawk.

Have you read anything interesting lately? At the beginning of the summer, I intended to study any number of worthy books. I even made a list though I have since lost it. I think I remember writing down such titles as *The Brothers Karamazov* and the *Iliad* and some of Shakespeare's lesser-known plays like *Titus Andronicus* and *A Winter's Tale*. Alas for good intentions! After each visit to the library in the nearby town of Linden, I came away with lighter fare, though some of it was nourishing: Rilke's *Journey to My Other Self* fascinated me (I don't know how it found its way into Linden Public Library). For moral instruction, I read *The Scarlet Letter*, but the book I loved most was Turgenev's *A Sportsman's Sketches*. It's odd in a way, for it seems to be a man's book: a rich idle landowner walks about the Russian countryside with his dogs, hunting wild fowl and talking to the peasants a hundred years ago, but Turgenev's style is so wonderfully lyrical in these stories. Also read John Steinbeck's novel about the two tramps looking for farm work in California. It reminded me of some of the traveling men we see around here from time to time, though you don't see as many now as you did three or four years ago. I also tried another book by Virginia Woolf, but couldn't finish it, and something called *The Return to Religion* by Henry C. Link. Very popular according to the librarian, but I thought it mostly nonsense and wishful thinking.

Nora was here for a visit over the Labor Day weekend and we had a good session on why married men who seduce women should all be ground to powder. After all, we are only weak vessels, etc., etc. Well, something like that at least; feeling sorry for ourselves is what it amounted to, but delicious just the same. As you probably know, Nora has the part of Aunt Polly in a radio play of *Huckleberry Finn*. She's very excited about this and I'm happy for her. It's something different and it could be very good for her radio career. And how, by the way, are you getting on in your constant effort to mislead us all about the Arcadian innocence of American family life?

Clara

P.S. Do you think war is likely? The news on the radio these days is terrible, at least up here. I'm afraid if Britain decides to stand up to Hitler, Canada will be dragged in just like the last time. What about the United States?

Sunday, September 11

A strange occurrence today. Marion was visiting after church; we had been sitting on the veranda, but then it began to rain and we came into the house. I was closing the door when I noticed a dark green car (or was it black?) moving slowly along Church Street. It looked like Frank's Pontiac, and the driver was wearing a hat. Because of the screen door and the rain I couldn't be certain and yet for a brief moment, standing there by the front door, I felt a wild surge of excitement. He had come up from the city to see me again but had forgotten which house was mine. That was understandable; after all, he had driven me home only once and that was over a year ago in the middle of the night. He would ask at the garage and then turn around and come back. When he knocked on the door and saw me, he would . . . Well, what would he do or say? My imagination faltered at that point, and Marion was calling me to the front room. For perhaps a half hour I waited tensely, but it had to be someone else. Poor Marion stoutly endured my distracted air and brooding silence.

Château Elysée
Room 210
5930 Franklin Avenue
Hollywood, California
19/9/38

Dear Clara,
As you can see I have moved again. A vacancy came up in this very nice apartment hotel with its very fancy name, and Fred (who also lives here with a pal) put me on to it. The place is filled with writing types from the east and so I feel right at home.

Yes, things look bad in Europe right now and I wouldn't be at all surprised if there was another war. Germany seems to be spoiling for a fight. There are a number of Germans out here now, mostly Jewish, who fled for their lives. They have no doubt that Hitler means business when it comes to running Europe and kicking out all the Jews. As for the rest of the populace out here (at least in my funny business), you'd never know that Herr Hitler and Signor Mussolini even exist. Out here people are more concerned with what's going to happen to two big pictures that are due for production. They are just about to start *The Wizard of Oz* and we also await the imminent screen birth of that American classic, *Gone With the Wind*, which Selznick is producing here at MGM. Right now they are looking for the ideal Scarlett and that's all anyone is talking about these days. Who will it be? Katharine Hepburn? Bette Davis? Jean Arthur? Paulette Goddard? Bella Lugosi? All this of course is taking place across the lot. Those of us who toil on the B pictures for jolly old L.B.M. only get to observe from afar these earthshaking events.

Your reading is certainly more impressive than anything I could muster. As soon as I am released from my cell, I crawl home to munch my nuts and berries. I do go out on a Saturday evening, however, and I have met a little friend through the kind offices of M. Huxley. There is quite a lively scene out here for folks like me. I apologize for this brief note, but I did want you to know that I am thinking of you.

Please take care of yourself and the little one. I am looking forward to being called Auntie Evelyn. I think it has a very nice ring to it.

Love and kisses, Evelyn

Saturday, October 1

Marion and I took the train down to the city today. I no longer feel exactly comfortable driving any distance so down we went on the train, two old maids, and one beginning to look like a rather wicked, old party. One snippy clerk at Simpson's was staring or glaring at my unringed hand as I fingered the maternity aprons. Marion, my protector, shouldered her way through the crowded stores with the sturdy cripple's lifelong claim to space, as we searched for something to cover my swelling self. All those sibilants! Where did they come from?

I bought the city papers to read on the train home. All were filled with news of Chamberlain's visit to Hitler. It now looks as if there will be no war and they are shouting hosannas to Chamberlain on the streets of London. Certainly today I noticed a cheerfulness or sense of relief on many faces in Toronto. Perhaps it will all work out, but one has to feel sorry for the people of Czechoslovakia. The Germans got what they wanted without firing a shot.

135 East 33rd Street
New York
October 2, 1938

Dear Clara,
I hope all is well. Aren't you glad this business in Europe is over? This past week has been just so depressing. I thought for certain there was going to be a war between Germany and England. Of course, down here everybody is so blasé. What is all the fuss about seems to be the attitude. It does annoy me sometimes how Americans seem to think that if it isn't happening in their own backyard, it isn't worth worrying

about. I had an awful quarrel with a fellow from the agency about this on Friday after work. Several of us went out for a drink after the show, and we got talking about all this. And this fellow says, "Where is Czechoslovakia and who cares anyway?" I just got so cross with what he said because it sums up their whole attitude about these things. To be honest, I didn't know where Czechoslovakia was either two weeks ago, but at least I took the trouble to find out. So I told him and then we got into this big fight about it. Maybe I got a little carried away, but I was so mad. Anyway, I'm glad Mr. Chamberlain worked things out. I think he deserves a medal for it.

I've been busy with the show of course and also with "American Playhouse." In fact, I just got back from an afternoon rehearsal. We go on the air next Sunday at eight so tune in, okay? I've seen the network schedule and you can pick it up on one of the Toronto stations, CFRB, I think, but you should check the listings. How are you feeling anyway? Are you all right for money? I don't want you worrying about money at a time like this. I know how proud you are, Clara, but just don't get too proud with me. We're all alone in this world, you know, and we have to look after one another. Write soon!!!

Love, Nora

P.S. Had an amusing letter from Evelyn the other day. She seems to have found some friends who share her "habits." A lot of grumbling about phony people out there, but she seems to be enjoying herself. She also mentioned how much she likes hearing from you.

Whitfield, Ontario
October 10, 1938

Dear Nora,

I listened to your program last evening. Congratulations! You sounded very good. You ought to do more of this kind of thing. Of course, fitting *Huckleberry Finn* into a one-hour radio program is slightly ridiculous, but the show did manage to convey the spirit of Twain's novel. So congratulations again. Marion came by and we sat there, drinking tea and eating Marion's oatmeal cookies (which I am becoming too fond of).

Yes, I too am glad that the Czechoslovakian business is over. I'm not convinced, however, that we have seen the last of the trouble in Europe. This Hitler is awfully ambitious and he seems ruthless, even perhaps a little mad. A dangerous combination. And the German people are behind him. I don't think they have ever really forgiven us for beating them in the war and they want revenge. So in my heart I fear there will be war with them one day. Perhaps not this year, perhaps not next year, but it will come, I think, and nearly everyone will eventually find their way into it except perhaps your Americans. They will probably just make money from it by supplying guns and bombs to both sides.

As for me, I am well according to Murdoch; in fact, I am feeling somewhat exhilarated by all this, and as you know, being exhilarated is not my normal state. I don't quite know why I feel as I do. I should be worried sick about what lies ahead. The stares and glares I get from some people should upset me, but they don't anymore. I am just fine, thank you. The child is beginning to kick at the door and Murdoch thinks I will probably have a boy. Apparently males are more boisterous in the womb. Well, of course, I don't care one way or the other as long as the child is sound. So I am growing fat and lazy, Nora, and I don't mind a bit. From the veranda I can hear the cries of the children in the schoolyard; a few weeks ago I missed all that, but now I am content enough to sit and wait for this to happen. Perhaps I'll seek out other men and have more babies. A houseful of children, like the old woman who lived in a shoe. I could rent them out as help, or run a boardinghouse with all these strapping sons and handsome daughters to help me. I am fine for money at the moment, but thank you for asking.

Clara

Wednesday, October 19

Today the coalmen came over from Linden and poured six tons into the cellar. I suppose I'll always think of F. on the day the coalmen arrive. Perhaps if he knew my state, he might have arranged for a lifetime supply to be delivered each October. Little enough, all things considered.

I had been worrying about how to keep the furnace going over the winter, but today the problem vanished. After supper, Mr. Bryden appeared at the back door with Joe Morrow.

"You're not to worry about any of this, Clara. Joe is going to look after the furnace for you. He'll come in every morning and evening and make sure it's well stoked."

Joe was shyly peering in at me from the doorway. They wouldn't come into the kitchen. I offered to pay, of course, but the notion seemed to outrage them both.

"Not on your life," said Mr. Bryden.

"I ain't takin' no money from you, Clara," Joe said.

I told them I could manage for perhaps another month and then their offer would be gladly and thankfully accepted. Oh for a God to believe in, so I could have said, "God bless you both!"

Monday, October 31

A visit from Murdoch this afternoon. We talked about whether I should have the child here or in Linden Hospital. Because of my age and the fact that it's my first, he wants me in the hospital. He warned me to pay attention to the weather too.

"The child could come any time after Christmas and you know what the weather can be like then, so make sure whoever brings you pays attention to the forecast. We don't want you to have this baby out on some concession road in a snowbank."

Having my baby in a snowbank! What a cheery old fellow he is!

Tonight the children came by for their treats and many of them said how much they missed me.

"Miss Bodnar is nice but . . ." Even if they weren't telling the truth, it was good to hear.

135 East 33rd Street
New York
November 2, 1938

Dear Clara,

Sorry I haven't answered your last letter before this, but we have had such a time over the past couple of weeks. Vivian Rhodes (I think you met her once at Evelyn's—she plays Effie and is married to a professor at Columbia University) lost her brother in a car accident and Margery had to change the script to give Vivian time to get away for the funeral. The whole thing shook us all up because Vivian was awfully close to her brother. Not only that, but right now Effie is in the middle of things; she has fallen in love with an ex-convict who has this job at Henderson's Hardware and now he's been accused of stealing money. So Margery had to do some fancy writing to get Effie off the show for a few days. But that's the radio business.

Speaking of radio, did you by any chance hear the "Mercury Theater" program on Monday night? What a sensation it has caused down here!!! It's just been the talk of the town all week. Some people actually believed that Martians had landed somewhere out in New Jersey and apparently one man had a heart attack over this. People were out on the streets in a panic and I guess the CBS switchboard was jammed with calls. I have to say it really was a clever show, all put together like a regular newscast. The whole thing was written and produced by a young man. Only twenty-one! It just shows you how powerful radio can be.

It was good to hear you sounding so cheerful in your letter. You'll be receiving a crib and some baby stuff one of these days. I had fun in

Macy's on Saturday buying these things, telling the clerks how I'm soon going to be an aunt. I think they got a kick out of me. Anyway, they promised delivery within two weeks, so I hope it arrives with nothing broken. Maybe you could let me know about that because they guaranteed safe delivery.

Love, Nora

P.S. Guess whose mug was in the *Herald Trib* on Saturday? None other than our dear old pal Lewis Mills!!! There he was with his new bride (number three). She is half his age, a graduate from some fancy women's college. Brother!!! I'll bet she'll be tired of him and his tantrums in six weeks.

Monday, November 14

A mild rainy day and at the post office there was an enormous box awaiting me. I had to ask Joe to bring it home in his truck and this afternoon he assembled the crib for me. What would I do without this patient, unassuming man who lives with his sister and brother-in-law and never seems to have much of a life beyond working at tasks that others can't or won't do: spading gardens, liming outhouses, assembling cribs.

We decided to put it in one corner of my bedroom and so I sat watching Joe work: fitting the various pieces together in his unhurried manner, whistling under his breath, the large hands marvelously capable with a screwdriver. He must be over sixty now, though he seems to look much the same as he did thirty years ago when I was a girl, and he came by each fall to put on the storm windows. Father wouldn't climb a ladder, and so Joe carried the big heavy windows aloft and fitted them into their frames. He still does this for me. In the watery light from the window I sat on the bed watching Joe work and thinking of my unborn child and the world awaiting him. Or her. On Saturday I read a long piece in the *Globe and Mail* about Nazi thugs destroying Jewish property in German cities. They seem to be on a rampage and the authorities are doing nothing about it. Last week a young Jew in Paris assassinated the secretary of the German Embassy and this has enraged the Nazis. Or given them an excuse to be enraged. What is it about the Jews that provokes such hatred among Germans? Nora says New York is run by Jews, and because they are clever and successful, others are jealous. We talked about this once, but I said that the Italians and the Irish also seem to run New York and they are not vilified in the same way. Strange thoughts for a gray wet afternoon here in the quiet of my home, far away from such things. I went over to the Brydens' this evening and phoned Nora to thank her for the crib.

Monday, December 5

After Joe finished with the furnace this evening, I sat in the front room listening to a concert from New York. Dvořák's *Serenade for Strings*. It is a still, cold night and the signal was wonderfully clear. For an hour I sat transported. I could not read; I could scarcely think of anything except for the enormous fact that this music was traveling through all that dark air to reach me. When the music was over, I awakened as from a dream.

Château Elysée
Room 210
5930 Franklin Avenue
Hollywood, California
11/12/38

Dear Clara,

They burned down Atlanta, Georgia, last night and it was some bonfire. Yes, I saw it with my own eyes right on the back lot of MGM. Through the fog the sky was pale yellow and all these figures were running about. Fred and I watched the eerie scene together. I'm sure that all of Los Angeles thought that MGM itself was going up in flames, and there are plenty around who probably think that's not such a bad idea. The Great Fire of London had nothing on this, believe me. What was it all in aid of? you might ask. The fire was no accident, of course. It was set so the cameras could roll for a crucial scene in the filming of *Gong Mit de Vind*, as it's called by a fellow who recently arrived from Hitler's Germany. Anyway, it was quite the sight.

I actually believe that I toil in a kind of madhouse: burning buildings, lunch in the commissary with cowboys and Indians and ballet dancers; for a while I was beginning to wonder whether the old gin bottle was finally playing havoc with my gray cells because I was starting to see "little people." I thought, Here at last are the delirium tremens I've been dreading all these years. It turns out, however, that "the little people" are only Singer Midgets brought in to play the Munchkin people in *The Wizard of Oz*. And what odd, mischievous little gaffers they are! You're apt to see them sleeping it off in a wastebasket or cupboard. They are awful boozers and they can't seem to keep their hands to themselves. More than one script girl has complained of a pinched backside. So they are proving to be quite a headache for their keepers. I am grateful to learn however that the DT's are still down the road a bit.

I saw the great L. B. Mayer the other day. I was summoned to his grandiose quarters and naturally approached in fear and trembling, convinced I had transgressed in some manner with my Nancy Brown series. But no, the great man thinks the scripts are fine and in fact went out of his way to congratulate me on writing that "reinforces the small-town values of American family life." He said he could see no reason why the series shouldn't be as popular as Andy Hardy, God bless the old coot. I might have told him, but didn't of course, that when it comes to reinforcing "the small-town values of American family life," I am the logical scribe. I have no family and have never lived in a small town. I also smoke and drink to excess and like to bed comely young women. Who better to write about American family life?

But enough about my sordid self! How are you? You must be getting very close to delivery time. I am, of course, crossing all fingers and toes that everything will go well.

Best always, Evelyn

P.S. I am enclosing a book that I think you might like. Maria Huxley told me about this woman and what a fine writer she is. I agree. Hope you enjoy it!

Christmas Day (9:45 p.m.)

A year ago today I was eating goose with greasy fingers and reading about lust and murder in California. How simple it all was then! Just don't see him again and wait for time to salve the injured heart. But that was then and this is now, and now is very different. Now I move around my house with a cautious tread, especially on the stairs, holding firmly to the banister as I descend. The cumbersomeness of it all! How I long to be light again and walk unhampered with my legs together! Emily D. never went through this, damn it. And yet I am happy enough and this has been a good day. Marion came by with her gifts: a blouse and skirt for when I am again able to wear such things; and for the baby, a book of nursery rhymes and a silver-plated spoon. I gave her the new Taylor Caldwell novel. She cooked a small chicken and after dinner I played the piano, though with some difficulty, for I could barely reach the keys. I was, I suppose, a comical sight, but Marion sang the old carols with feeling in her clear alto voice. The Brydens dropped in to listen. How good these three people have been to me over the past few weeks!

An hour ago, with the help of Marion and Mrs. B., I waddled across to the Brydens' and phoned Nora. Told her the baby is active and seems eager to get out and play a part in this tarnished old comedy.

Nora was relieved to learn that Marion is going to stay with me now for the next few days. The four of us decided a few hours ago, because I think the baby is very close. I will feel better with Marion here, even though her fussing gets on my nerves. I must try to be more patient with her.

Tuesday, December 27 (8:35 p.m.)

I have a daughter, Elizabeth Ann. She was born at ten minutes to six this morning. Yesterday afternoon, I felt the first pains. I had been reading a book slowly, for it is one of those books that you don't want to end. Evelyn Dowling sent it to me a couple of weeks ago and it is called *Out of Africa*. The author is a Danish woman who emigrated to Kenya twenty-five years ago and became the owner of a coffee plantation. I could not have chosen a more diverting book for a winter afternoon in Ontario. So I was among the lions and zebras with the vultures circling "in the pale burning air" when the contractions began. Marion went at once to the Brydens' and phoned the doctor who said he would drive over after supper. This was a great relief to me, since I did not have to bother going to Linden to a hospital full of strangers. My child would be born in the same house as I was thirty-five years ago.

Murdoch arrived about nine o'clock. He is such a grumpy old blister, but he helped me through the next nine hours, and I shall not easily forget his gruff kindness and sure hands. At the final moments, the sight of the child emerging from between my legs was too much for poor Marion's delicate sensibilities and she retreated to the spare room. Mrs. Bryden, childless herself but game, stayed to the end and was in tears. So perhaps was I when Murdoch placed the dark-haired little girl upon my breast.

And it is over and now I have a child and my life is changed forever. Elizabeth Ann Callan. It will be Liz, I think, rather than Beth, with Elizabeth Ann reserved for frowning moments. I have pulled up my knees to steady this page; the child is sleeping and I can hear Marion clumping around downstairs and Joe rattling the grates as he stokes the furnace. He is too shy to venture near this female world, and is happy enough to keep us warm on this clear winter night.

I want so badly to help you realize, Elizabeth Ann, how difficult and puzzling and full of wonder it all is: someday I will tell you how I learned to watch the shifting light of autumn days or smelled the earth through snow in March; how one winter morning God vanished from my life and how one summer evening I sat in a Ferris wheel, looking down at a man who had hurt me badly; I will tell you how I once traveled to Rome and saw all the soldiers in that city of dead poets; I will tell you how I met your father outside a movie house in Toronto, and how you came to be. Perhaps that is where I will begin. On a winter afternoon when we turn the lights on early, or perhaps a summer day of leaves and sky, I will begin by conjugating the elemental verb. I am. You are. It is.

AFTERWORD

My mother never did tell me any of those things. Perhaps on some "winter afternoon" or "summer day of leaves and sky" she wanted to, but something in her nature held her back. She was a difficult woman, secretive and self-possessed. It was her way, of course, but she had her reasons too. Having a child out of wedlock in an Ontario village in 1938 was more than enough to set her apart from the community. I grew up fatherless amid whispers surrounding my conception. By the time I was a schoolgirl, the people of Whitfield had grown used to the idea of Mother raising me by herself, and we were accepted in a polite and distant manner; a few perhaps even admired my mother's grit. Yet at the end of schoolyard arguments with other girls, I was always left defenseless and ultimately defeated by their taunts. "Where's your mother's boyfriend?" and "Where's your father?" Or the one question that seemed freighted with a kind of elemental truth that had perhaps been passed around family tables over the years to become a part of village folklore. "Where's the man your mother knew down in

Toronto?" In that childhood question, I heard something dark and unclean, and it inevitably reduced me to tears.

I asked my mother about all this, of course, and one day she told me that my father was dead, and I was to stop asking questions about him. I was nine, I think. Mother had just come in from her job in a law office in Linden, a town about twelve miles from our village. I could smell the smoke from the lawyers' cigarettes on her clothes, and her fingers were still grimy from the carbon paper she used when typing their letters and contracts. It was the only work she could get after the school board dismissed her, and it took three years, and a labor shortage during the war, before she got the job. On that raw November day when she suddenly and remarkably told me that my father was dead, she was still wearing her coat as she stood by the stove opening a can of tomato soup, frowning as she stirred it into the pot. "He was killed in a hunting accident before you were born, Elizabeth," she said. "Now, please. No more questions about him."

For the next few days I pictured a man in a hunting cap and checkered flannel shirt stalking deer through autumn woods. Then he was tragically killed before he could marry my mother! How had that happened, I wondered? And how would she have met him? Was this the man she *knew* down in Toronto? Yet the more I thought of it, the more I sensed that it was all wrong, a lie. How could my mother be attracted to a man who hunted animals? She was a lover of nature, of poetry and music; it all seemed unlikely, another of her stories to keep me quiet, contrived out of the fatigue of a long day. On her drive home along the township roads she had probably heard the gunshots of hunters in the woods. Years later I asked her why she had told me that outlandish story and she replied simply, "Oh, I don't know, Liz. You were pestering me, I suppose, and I was tired."

A child will look where she must, and growing up I turned from my mother with her Saturday armfuls of library books and her phonograph records of Rubinstein playing Chopin and Schubert to admire her sister, my Aunt Nora. How I wished she were my mother, for

Aunt Nora was a glamorous presence in my life, a radio actress who lived in New York. Unlike my mother, Aunt Nora was blond and pretty; she lived in the most sophisticated city in the world, and on the rare occasions when she would visit us for a few days in the summer, she always looked so smart in her New York clothes that I dreamed of running away with her. When she visited us, people stopped her on the street or came shyly to the door to seek an autograph. During those few summer days, I was no longer a child fathered by some man my mother *knew* down in Toronto, but a part of a richer, more important world. One Christmas when I was twelve, Aunt Nora sent us tickets, and we took the train to New York and stayed in her apartment on East Thirty-third Street. We went to the studio in Rockefeller Center, and Mother and I stood with other tourists behind enormous plate-glass windows, looking down at Aunt Nora and her fellow actors as they held their scripts and read into the microphones, while men in shirtsleeves and vests opened and closed doors or played recordings of automobiles in motion. From loudspeakers above our heads, we could hear the broadcast going across the country and even up to Canada where our neighbors were listening.

Mother's judgment of all this was predictably harsh though I never heard her express her views to Aunt Nora. She wasn't jealous of her sister's success; I am sure that she wished her well, but she was scornful of programs like "The House on Chestnut Street." To her they were only foolish diversions for housewives. She went out to work each day and had no time for such nonsense. I, however, was enthralled. "The House on Chestnut Street" came on in the middle of the afternoon when I was in school, and often I willed myself to be sick, so I could stay at home and listen. Usually Mother would have none of that; my being at home meant asking our neighbor, Mrs. Bryden, to look in on me from time to time, and Mother disliked bothering people. Now and then, though, I was genuinely ill, and on those afternoons I would come down from my bed to the front room and, wrapped in a blanket, wait impatiently for the program's signature theme, Elgar's *Salut D'Amour*, and then the announcer's voice inviting me "once again to take a walk past these stately trees and white picket fences to 'The House on Chestnut Street' where today we find Alice and Effie in the kitchen talking to Aunt Mary and Uncle Jim. Yesterday we learned that Alice . . ." To hear my aunt's voice coming through the cloth-covered face of that Stromberg-Carlson radio was magical.

Then, in the year following our Christmas visit to New York, the program was abruptly canceled. I could not believe it and neither, I suppose, could millions of others. It took a letter from Aunt Nora to explain the circumstances. I remember Mother standing by the dining-room table reading that letter and saying to me, "It seems they think your aunt is a Communist." She paused for a moment to stare out the window; she might have been talking to herself. "I haven't the faintest idea why. I can't believe Nora knows the first thing about Communism." But this was 1951, the McCarthy era, when zealots, convinced that Communism was threatening American democracy, sought out suspects in public life, particularly those in the entertainment industry. People in film, television and radio were hounded from jobs; careers were ruined and livelihoods lost. Many innocent people were swept up in the net and Mother was certainly right about Aunt Nora. She had no interest whatsoever in politics; her marginal involvement with a group of New York actors in the 1930s, however, was enough to blacklist her.

That same year Aunt Nora surprised us even further with a telegram announcing her marriage. She was then in her middle forties. It was one of the few times that I have seen my mother express surprise at life's strange and various turnings. She had to sit down to read it, and from her puzzled expression the telegram could easily have been in Sanskrit or Urdu. Later Aunt Nora sent us pictures of her husband, my Uncle Arthur. He was then in his fifties, but seemed years younger even with his curly gray hair. I thought he looked like Jeff Chandler, a handsome movie actor of the time. Not only was

Uncle Arthur good-looking, but he was also a rich and successful advertising executive who promptly whisked Aunt Nora off to California to live. It was like a final episode from "The House on Chestnut Street" or "The Right to Happiness," or any one of a dozen afternoon radio shows: the middle-aged woman endures and prevails and finally marries the prince who carries her off to the golden land.

My aunt's charmed life seemed to widen the gap between my mother and me; I often compared their fates; my chance-taking aunt who had uprooted herself to seek her fortune in another land, and my mother, the stay-at-home, stuck in a drab Ontario village. It was an unfair comparison, of course, but what teenage girl is ever fair in her assessment of a mother? On weekday mornings we climbed into her twenty-year-old Chevrolet coupe, and drove along the township roads to Linden, often enclosed in a week-old brooding silence that had been provoked by some argument. I was mortified at being seen in that old car. Mother would drop me off in front of the high school on her way to work, and one day I overheard a boy I was half in love with say to friends, "I wonder when Liz's old lady is going to get rid of that jalopy?" I never spoke to the boy again.

During the next several years I was away at university, and I seldom returned to Whitfield. Once or twice a month I talked to Mother on the telephone that she finally though reluctantly had installed. After graduation, I taught elementary school before returning to university for postgraduate studies of the American poet Edna St. Vincent Millay and a career in university teaching. I spent the summer of our country's centenary in Los Angeles living with Aunt Nora and Uncle Arthur, and reading the poet's letters in the UCLA library. There I met the rich young radical who would follow me to Canada and become my husband. The marriage was a mistake, but we were too engrossed in the temper of the times to notice: the civil rights movement, the Vietnam War, the protests and demonstrations absorbed us totally. I now believe that we scarcely knew one another in the three years we lived together.

In that inflammable summer of 1968, my mother died suddenly of a heart attack. We could not locate my aunt and uncle, who were on vacation in Hawaii. Only a few people attended the funeral, and after we buried her next to her mother and father and brother in the little cemetery beyond the village, we returned to the house where I was born and raised. We were served tea and sandwiches by Mother's oldest friend, Miss Webb, who could not help casting shy glances at my husband with his shoulder-length hair, his tinted glasses, his workboots worn to a funeral. Even country people knew better than that. Miss Webb wore an orthopedic shoe, and the sound of it on the floorboards stirred memories of her Sunday afternoon visits with Mother. On that warm and windy August evening, my young husband and I watched the news on the little black-and-white television that Mother had bought only a year or two before she died. The Chicago police were clubbing citizens in the street. We watched as the demonstrators and passersby were forced against the plate-glass window of the Hilton Haymarket Lounge. We saw the window shatter amid the screaming. Anarchy can be a tonic for the young, and we watched with the kind of gloomy excitement that often accompanies the possibility of change.

I also remember thinking how peculiar it felt to be witnessing all that brutality in the quiet of my mother's house, surrounded by the density and heft of another age with its heavy dark furniture, its yellowing lampshades and patterned wallpaper. That "low dishonest decade," as Auden called it, was as much the subject of this book as was my mother's quiet yet turbulent life during the four years in which she recorded what happened to her. As far as I have been able to determine, she never wrote anything else in a journal after my birth.

Aunt Nora's letters were in a trunk in my mother's bedroom, but I never saw them; I was far too anxious to get away from that cramped village where I had seldom been happy. A month after the funeral, however, I returned to Whitfield with Aunt Nora and Uncle Arthur, who had come from California to visit Mother's grave. We spent the weekend going through her things and arranging for the sale of the house. Years later Aunt Nora told me that she found the letters, but decided not to show them to me at the time. I think she wanted to spare my feelings, shelter me from the raw details of what my mother endured. Rape. Abortion. Adultery. Such subjects were not so easily and openly discussed by women of my aunt's generation. She did promise, however, that one day I would know what really happened, but only after she was gone.

Aunt Nora outlived my mother by over thirty years and died in a nursing home in Los Angeles last January at the age of ninety-four. Her final years were clouded by senility, and she talked only of things that had mattered a long time ago: the sunlight on her father's pocket watch, the taste of licorice, the whistle of a steam engine. When we went up to L.A. to sort through her belongings, we found all the letters exchanged between the two sisters, as well as those from my mother to the exuberantly cynical Evelyn Dowling whom I would had loved to have as an aunt. Unfortunately I never got to know Evelyn, for she was killed in an automobile accident in the hills of Hollywood a year after I was born.

For all her help and encouragement in the assembling of these letters, I would like to express thanks to my dearest friend and partner of the last twenty years, Moira Svensson.

Elizabeth A. Callan
Saltspring Island
British Columbia
December 2000